## PRAISE FOR SUGAR JAMISON'S *DANGEROUS CURVES AHEAD*

"A funny, sexy, and touching debut—just delightful!"
—Susan Donovan, *New York Times* bestselling author

"Fresh, fun, and insanely sexy. Jamison juggles snark, sensitivity, and to-die-for chivalry with dazzling success. *Dangerous Curves* is candy for the soul."
—Beth Ciotta, award-winning author

## ALSO BY SUGAR JAMISON

*Dangerous Curves Ahead*

# *Thrown for a Curve*

SUGAR JAMISON

St. Martin's Paperbacks

This is a work of fiction. All of the characters, organizations, and events portrayed in this novel are either products of the author's imagination or are used fictitiously.

THROWN FOR A CURVE



For information address St. Martin's Press, 175 Fifth Avenue, New York, NY 10010.

ISBN: 978-1-250-03298-0

Printed in the United States of America

St. Martin's Paperbacks edition / March 2014

St. Martin's Paperbacks are published by St. Martin's Press, 175 Fifth Avenue, New York, NY 10010.

10 9 8 7 6 5 4 3 2 1

To Jane
For whipping us into shape when we need it.

# CHAPTER 1

*I feel pretty . . .*

"Almost finished." A heavy blast of breath-stealing hair spray hit Charlotte Rudy just above her crown.

*That's thirty-two times.* She had counted every last spray as she sat cross-legged on the floor between her grandmother's substantial thighs.

*Thirty-two sprays and fifty-five minutes.*

She didn't have to look in the mirror to know that long gone was her mass of unruly waves. Armed with a comb and a can of chemicals, her grandmother had turned her once soft hair into a golden steel helmet.

*Tornado-proof hair,* she thought wryly as she patted the hard sticky mass. It felt a little like crystallized cotton candy. She wanted to eat cotton candy, not look like it.

"Move your hand, Cherri!" her grandmother scolded in her still-thick Ukrainian accent as she smacked it. "I'm not done yet."

Cherri moved her stinging hand just before another cool

blast of hair-freezing chemicals hit her square in the face. "Good grief, Baba!" she choked, the air in her lungs now replaced with spray. "Are you sure that stuff is legal?"

"Legal?" Her grandmother frowned at the can of industrial-sized of Hold Her Forever. "Of course it's legal." She sprayed Cherri once more. "I'm not sure why they stopped making it in 1986."

"Baba! It probably causes cancer." She confiscated the can and made a mental note to throw it out as soon as her grandmother wasn't looking.

"Oh, stop freaking up. I've used this ever since I came to America in 1957 and I'm still healthy as an ox."

Cherri shook her head. Fifty-plus years and her grandmother's grasp on the English language was still lacking. "The saying is freaking out, Baba. Not freaking up."

Baba shrugged. "Freaking out, freaking up. Whatever. You young people think everything causes cancer. In my country nobody has cancer. We die from hard work and old age. This hair spray does nothing but make one look beautiful."

Cherri touched the sticky mass atop her head once more, positive that *beautiful* was the wrong word to describe how she looked. But she nodded at her grandmother's statement. She knew that there was no use arguing with Baba. She couldn't win. Besides, her time left with the old woman was limited, and she wanted to make the best of it.

That's why she'd agreed to let her aging, half-blind, slightly unstable grandmother give her a makeover tonight.

"And don't think about throwing it out, either," Baba warned. "Because I bought two cases when I found out they were going to stop making it."

*Wily old broad.* Baba was three steps away from being featured on an episode of *Hoarders*. "I would never think to throw out your things," she lied sweetly. Cherri was going to have to start making trips to the dump again.

"Good girl." Baba patted her cheek. "Now go look at

yourself. You'll be the most stunning girl at your birthday party."

Cherri stood, hearing the rustle of the taffeta as she walked toward the full-length mirror. She didn't want to look at herself. When her grandmother had presented her with the homemade dress earlier that day, she'd gritted her teeth and plastered a smile on her face.

*Taffeta and crinoline and gold. Oh my!*

"Open your eyes, dumb-dumb." Baba poked her in the behind with her cane, which she only used when it suited her. "Who looks at themselves with closed eyes? You look ridiculous!"

"I'm just savoring the moment, Baba."

Cherri forced her lids open, taking in the whole spectacular picture she presented.

She flinched. *Holy frickin' crap on a cracker!* Ridiculous was an understatement. She was covered in bows. On her shoulders. At her bust. On her hips.

*I can't leave the house like this. I look like a six-foot-tall Christmas present.*

It was as if every 1980s prom dress and every horrible bridesmaid dress ever created banded together and threw up on her. Puffy sleeves and ruffles complemented the bows. The gold of the dress turned her skin a sickly green color. Even her feet hadn't escaped the horror. Her normally big stompers looked enormous in golden pumps, dyed to match her one-of-a-kind dress. And her hair . . . It was logic defying and oh-so-high.

She was a walking hot mess.

*Come and get it, fellas.*

"Well?" Cherri met her grandmother's hopeful eyes in the mirror.

"I love it!"

"You do?" Baba smiled brightly, her green eyes twinkling with pleasure.

"Of course I do." She bent to kiss her grandmother's, soft wrinkled cheek. White lies were fine. Right? Okay, so maybe this was a big fat whopper of a lie, but how could she tell the woman who'd raised her, who went without so that she could have, that she didn't like the thing she'd spent so many hours creating? She couldn't. "Thank you for doing this for me."

"It was nothing." Baba, not one for mushy emotions, briefly squeezed Cherri before clapping her hands twice. "Now get out of here. It's time for you to rip the carpet at your party."

"It's cut the rug, Baba," Cherri reminded her gently. "But I will."

"You'll be back before midnight?"

She was twenty-two, but her grandmother still didn't want her out late. And after the past few months Cherri made it a point to stick close to home. "I'll tuck you in and read you a bedtime story when I come back."

"Don't be fresh." She swatted Cherri. "You know only fast girls stay out late."

"Yes, Baba."

"And the only things open past eleven o'clock are legs and liquor stores."

"Baba!"

"It's true." She kissed both her cheeks and shoved her toward the door. "And call me if you get bitchfaced and can't drive home."

"That's shitfaced, Baba. And you don't have to worry. I won't drink tonight."

The prospect of her seventy-five-year-old grandmother driving at night caused Cherri to shudder as she navigated the icy driveway to get to her beat-up Dodge truck. She had to squish the huge dress to her sides in order to get in—and once she did, the cold seat touching her bare legs was a shock to her system. It was a chilly fourteen degrees that night, and as the harsh wind swirled around the vehicle she wondered why her grandparents had decided to settle in the Adirondacks instead of Miami.

*Oh well.*

She disregarded the thought as she stuck the key in the ignition and sent a silent prayer to her guardian angel.

"Come on, old girl," she crooned at the truck. "You can do it. Mommy loves you so very very much."

The old thing didn't start half the time; it had a tendency to stall, and the heat didn't work. But it was good for short distances. And it had belonged to her grandfather. Getting rid of it was not an option.

Mercifully the car roared to life, sending a blast of icy air into Cherri's face. She shivered. Car trouble would have been the perfect excuse to not go to the birthday party that her best friends and bosses Ellis and Mike had decided to throw for her.

"It's your I'm-an-official-ass-kicking-adult party," Ellis said when she had first mentioned it and Cherri shot it down. "Let me do this for you, honey. You deserve it."

Cherri agreed, even though the thought of being the center of attention made her stomach knot. She wasn't the type of girl who made a big fuss about things. She was perfectly content to stay in the background. Which was no easy feat, considering she was pushing six feet tall, had an unruly mass of dark blond hair, and resembled an eastern European giant. But still she tried.

It had been only her and her grandparents up until Papa died seven years ago. Even then birthdays were small affairs with just a cake and special meal. Never a big fuss. She didn't know who her father was. Her mother wasn't a fixture in her life and had stopped coming around regularly when Cherri turned eight.

Natasha didn't often sneak into her mind, but on days like this, on birthdays and holidays, she wondered why her mother never bothered to stick around. Why she'd left a baby with an elderly couple struggling to make ends meet.

"Have Yourself a Merry Little Christmas" poured from the radio, and Cherri realized that her thoughts had turned depressing. She shook herself out of them. It was probably a good thing she was going to a party. For a few hours she could forget about the fact that despite her master's degree she was still working in a dress shop, the student loans would keep her broke until menopause, and the roof was about to cave in on them. Or that Baba . . .

She shook her head hard. Tonight was her party and even though she looked liked the Jolly Gold Giant she was determined to enjoy herself.

*Be happy, damn it! It's your birthday. Christmas is coming.*

She pulled out of the driveway.

*Things will get better,* she promised herself. They had to.

She arrived at Ellis's door an hour before the festivities were due to begin, her coat tightly wrapped around her to protect her from the frigid wind that hadn't let up for days. She rang the bell and waited only a few seconds before Ellis's husband, Mike, opened the door.

He froze, mouth agape, his hand suspended in midair. "What the hell happened to you, kid?"

"What?" She made her expression blank, as if she didn't know what he was referring to.

"Your hair." He reached out and touched it, seemingly unable to help himself. "It's horrible."

"Mikey!" his wife snapped from behind him. "What are you saying to her?"

"I—I . . ." He glanced at his wife and then back to Cherri, who was having a hard time keeping a straight face. She wasn't offended by Mike's statement. She realized that she put the *B* in *bouffant*. "Come look at her, babe."

Ellis peeked around her husband's shoulder. "Oh, Cherri." She shook her head. "Oh, sweetheart. Oh no! Who did this to you?"

"What? Don't you like it?" In that moment Cherri was glad she'd braved the cold to come here. Ellis was the most fashionable person she knew, and being a boutique owner and designer she always had the best clothes. "I think it goes well with the dress." She slid the coat off her arms in a dramatic fashion and strutted into their living room like she was on a catwalk.

Mike, unable to contain himself, burst into laughter. Ellis, as if in pain, bit her knuckle. "Who did this to you?" she asked again.

"My grandmother." Cherri put her hands on her hips and attempted her best model pose, sending Mike into hysterics.

"Does she hate you?"

"No. She worked very hard on this dress. She thinks I look bee-yoo-ti-ful."

"Do another turn on the catwalk," Mike choked. She had never seen the tough former cop giggle like a schoolgirl, and it lifted her spirits to be the cause of his glee. She raised her head high and sashayed farther into their small house, stopping only to pose dramatically.

She heard slow clapping when she stopped, but it didn't come from Ellis or her laughing husband. She turned to see Colin O'Connell, Mike's women-loving, Irish-accent-having best friend gazing at her.

He wasn't in hysterics like Mike, but Cherri had definitely amused him. One side of his mouth curled into a lazy smile, and his soft brown eyes seemed to follow suit, crinkling at the corners.

She had known this man for over a year. The moment she'd laid eyes on him, she'd known he wasn't a man made for mere mortal women. In fact, he was so far out of her league that for once in her life she forgot to be uneasy around him. But tonight his unabashed male beauty affected her, and for a split second she wished that she were small, and thin, and graceful. But she wasn't any of those things. She was Cherri, built like a lumberjack, taller than most men, and very far from just plain average. So she ordered her cheeks to stop burning and turned to face him, posing as seductively as her six feet and big behind could manage.

"Hey, sailor," she purred, mocking her grandmother's thick Ukrainian accent. "You like what you see?"

Colin's slow smile bloomed into a full one, and for the tiniest moment Cherri was breathless. He raised his glass to her in a toast. "Aw, love. I think you just made my year."

# CHAPTER 2

*Girls, girls, girls . . .*

A high-pitched giggle assaulted Colin O'Connell's ears as he stood in his best friends' home. Earsplitting, headache-causing, girlie laughter. He gritted his teeth, unsure that he would be able to take much more of that sound.

*Ya, ha ha ha. Ya, ha ha ha.*

It was like an ice pick going through his brain. He took a long slow sip of the Irish whiskey that some beautiful soul had purchased just for him, hoping it would dull the intensity of that noise. It didn't. And he found himself checking his watch again. Nine fifty-seven. He wondered how much longer he would have to stay before he could get the hell out of there.

*Ya, ha ha ha. Ya, ha ha ha.*

He winced again, thinking the girl who produced the laugh must be part banshee.

A party was in full swing around him, and despite decorations, people in goofy holiday sweaters, and nonalcoholic eggnog, Colin didn't find himself in a festive mood. He should never have come. There were children here. Not small ones, but the kind who were old enough to vote yet too young to buy Guinness. And even though his hell-raising, drunken-stupor nights had diminished in the last few years, this event was not his type of party. Yet he was here because Ellis had asked him to come. And Colin had a hard time turning down the woman who made his best friend so damn happy.

He scanned the room for his friends, finding them sitting in a corner, arms wrapped around each other, engaged in deep conversation as if no one else existed. It made his stomach churn uncomfortably and caused a funny, empty feeling to form in his chest. He looked away.

More loud giggles punctured his eardrums. This time he turned to the source. There were four girls, all wearing too much makeup and tiny, ass-baring dresses, huddled together. He connected eyes with the tallest one, a brunette. She was a beauty. Tight body, high firm breasts, long legs, and eyes that screamed, *Fuck me.* Too young. He immediately dismissed the thought of getting to know her better. But she was staring at him with blatant interest. Not one to be intentionally rude, he nodded at her.

*Ya, ha ha ha.* She beamed at him, turned to her friends, and they all commenced the schoolgirl laughter.

He shuddered and turned away from the girl. She was the giggler. He hated gigglers. He hated girls, too, for that matter. Girls were inexperienced. Silly. They didn't know what they wanted out of life, or where they were going.

Girls were fine when he was just a lad, but now that Colin was a man he wanted a woman. But there seemed to be girls everywhere he went. That was the problem with living in a big college town. Colin thought Durant, New York, was the perfect place to settle after he graduated from its university. Plenty of bars. Lots of work. And girls.

Twelve years later his successful restoration business was

the only thing keeping him here. And looking at all those pretty young girls in their short, sparkly dresses made him feel old. But maybe being old wasn't such a bad thing. He liked old things. Old stories. Old people. It was probably why he'd opened Stone Barley Restorations. Every day he took antiques and breathed new life into them. It was hard, meticulous work, but his reputation was growing and he was getting clients from all over the country. Sticking with the old was going well for him. Maybe he should try dating older women. Anything worth having had a little extra age to it.

It might be time to start dating again. It had been two years since Serena knocked him on his ass. It was time he got up. Then again . . . Serena was driven, focused, and far from a girl. She was trouble, too. Maybe he'd give up on women period and join the priesthood. It would make his gran happy.

"Hey, Grinchy." At the sound of those words he looked up to see Cherri Rudy, the birthday girl, approaching him.

He hated to admit it but he was here because of her, too. Normally he wouldn't be caught dead at a twenty-two-year-old's birthday party, but there was something about the girl with the odd name that made him get off his ass and come here tonight. Because of her little fashion show alone, he wouldn't regret coming. The way she sashayed into the house in that horrible dress made him laugh. She was undeniably goofy, but there was also a bit of natural sensuality that floated around her. The poor kid had no idea what she was working with. When she grew up a little more she would break hearts.

He watched her make the short trip across the room. It was if magic had transformed her. Long gone was the hideous gold tarp, and the hairstyle that could hold up in a hurricane. She looked altogether different in a slinky green dress that hugged her body and made her eyes turn the color of emeralds. Her hair was back to its normal tumble of loose golden waves. She wasn't pretty by any stretch of the word.

She was taller than most women, her shoulders broader, her weight heavier, but there was something about her that kept his eyes riveted to her as she walked toward him.

"You look like you've been sucking on sour lemons for the past hour," she said as she stopped in front of him.

He grinned. "I was thinking about how ugly your shoes are."

She looked down at her golden feet and then back up at him and gave him a soft smile, showing off a pair of identical dimples. "They're something, aren't they? I don't think they'd be so awful if my feet weren't the size of small boats. I wonder if I could use them as Jet Skis? Maybe I could glide across the water on my bare feet."

Her smile did something to her face, lighting it up, making her appear so innocent. Something made him want to step closer. "I'd join you. I'm working with size fifteens myself."

"Ah." She looked down at his feet, and then her eyes made a slow trek up his body before settling on his face. A knot formed in his stomach. "You know what they say about men with big feet?"

"What?" He waited for a dirty joke to pop out of her mouth. Under all that nice-girl exterior he knew there was a bit of naughtiness inside Cherri Rudy. He was surprised to find he was anxious to see it come out.

"Horrible dancers." She carefully watched his face. "They step all over your feet." She placed her hand over her heart and feigned shock. "You didn't think I was going to say something else, did you?"

For a moment Colin was distracted by the placement of her hand, which lay very near her creamy exposed cleavage. "No." He forced his eyes upward. Then took a step back for good measure.

He had no business looking at Cherri like that or wanting to get to know her naughty side. She was a girl. Unworldly.

Immature. Young. It didn't matter that her curvy figure, intelligent eyes, and mature air told his hormones something different. Twenty-two was twenty-two. Plus Mike and Ellis treated her like she was their kid sister. To him she was strictly off-limits.

He glanced at his watch. It was time to get the hell out of Dodge.

"You don't have to stay for my benefit," she said softly, making him feel like the lowest piece of shit. "I'm surprised you lasted this long."

"I don't want to leave, love. I was just checking the time."

"Liar," she said without heat. "I've been watching you all night. You've checked your watch twelve times."

"You were watching me?" He grinned at her again. "All night?" He placed his hand on her bare shoulder and immediately regretted it. *Didn't you just talk to yourself about being appropriate? Ass.* Her silky skin was cool under his rough palm, and it caused him to wonder if it would feel the same under his lips.

"Yeah, well, it's hard not to notice the giant sulking Irishman alone in the corner."

"I wasn't sulking."

She folded her arms under her breasts, pushing them up into his eye line. "You weren't mingling."

*Steady, old man,* he warned himself. *Keep your eyes in your skull. She has no idea that doing that makes you want to jump out of your skin.* "Neither were you, if you had time to ogle me all night."

"I hate parties," she admitted. "I didn't want to come to this one."

"But this is your party, with your friends. You're supposed to be enjoying yourself."

"I know." She gazed at the floor and then gave him a sad smile. "Just because it's my party doesn't mean I stop being a social misfit. Ellis was so sweet to throw it, but those girls"—she gestured absently behind her—"are not my friends."

"They're not?"

"Of course not. Skinny bitch goddesses don't hang out with the enormous artsy kid. But they were in my education classes for the past four years so Ellis thinks we're friends." She frowned. "I sound like a whiny brat. I'm glad Ellis loves me enough to throw me this party. Let's change the subject."

"Not yet." She wasn't enormous. She spoke about herself like she was queen of the Amazons. She wasn't anywhere near that. He gave her soft shoulder a squeeze. There was an insecurity, a slight sadness that hung over her. It made him uncomfortable. "I'm glad you said those girls aren't your friends."

"You are?" Her emerald eyes widened.

"Yes, the laugh on that tall brunette sounds like a choking hyena, for fuck's sake. I had to stop myself from stuffing a cork into her mouth."

"You mean you don't find Bridgette's laugh intoxicating?"

"No, but I do think a man needs to be intoxicated to tolerate it."

She laughed—not a giggle, but a rich sound that came from her belly and twisted his in knots. "Damn, I lost a bet with myself. I thought she might be someone you'd like to—What do you Irish people say? Shag?"

"Shag her?" He shook his head. "Not my type." There was only one girl in the room he could imagine tumbling with in bed and it wasn't the brunette with the big mouth.

That was a dangerous thought.

He took a step away from her. "Listen, love, I really am beat. Would you be mad at me if I took off?"

"Well, that depends." She crossed her arms under her breasts again, causing them to plump nicely. "Did you bring me a present?"

"Of course I did."

She flashed her dimples at him. "Then you are free to go. But first let me hug you good-bye."

"No," he said abruptly. He had hugged her once before. He knew what she felt like. He knew her warmth would linger with him all night.

"No?" Her face fell slightly, and he realized what a colossal asshole he was being.

"I don't think I can. The vision of you in that other dress is still haunting me."

She gave him an exaggerated frown. "You're supposed to say that I was breathtakingly beautiful in the other dress."

"I can't, love. It soured my stomach."

"Ass." She threw her arms around him and kissed both his cheeks. "Thank you for coming, Colin. I'm glad you did."

He shut his eyes for a moment, savoring how her lush body felt pressed against him as she lingered. For those few seconds that empty feeling in his chest evaporated as his hands came up to settle on her soft waist. "You're welcome."

He opened his eyes before she let go. Mike's gaze clashed with his. His best friend shook his head slowly, his message so clear that it didn't need to be spoken.

*She's not for you.*

He knew that. She was off-limits with a fucking capital *O*. So he stepped back, giving Cherri's hand one last squeeze before he left the house.

Cherri pulled her scarf more tightly around her neck as she headed down her third deserted block. Durant was a beautiful eclectic little town, even in winter, with its snow-covered, tree-lined streets filled with colorful houses and funky buildings. If she had a more poetic soul, she might say the town resembled a modern Christmas card. But she wasn't feeling very poetic that day. She wasn't able to bask in the beauty that was her hometown. She was too freaking annoyed. And it was too freaking cold. Only two degrees. There were no people around. Hell, even the squirrels had hightailed it someplace else, and yet she was roaming the streets in search of the world's naughtiest dog.

"Rufus," she called sweetly for the forty-seventh time since she had left her house, even though she was feeling slightly murderous. "Come back, sweetie pie. I'll give you a cookie."

She had plenty of them. Her pockets were bulging with treats. Dog biscuits on one side and the expensive strawberry-preserved human cookies in the other.

*Bring both,* Baba had said. *See which one he likes better. Or maybe I should fry you a steak to take to him.*

All of this for a dog. Baba's dog. Who had escaped the house.

Again.

For the third time that very cold week.

Sometimes she wanted to say the hell with it and let the dog wander home on his own. And he *would* come home on his own, too. Rufus was that smart. Some mornings she would go out to get the newspaper only to find him sitting on the front step waiting to be let in.

And he always looked up at her as if to say, *Yeah I got out. What are you going to do about it?*

She was pretty sure he was visiting Mrs. Walton's German shepherd, Sharona. But she didn't want to think about Rufus's doggy booty calls at the moment. She only hoped she didn't get a call one day asking her to pick up her share of the puppies.

*Rufus, you are the father!*

But she couldn't let Rufus wander home on his own today. She couldn't risk anything happening to him. He was Baba's love. A huge eighty-pound husky–Lab mix who shed everywhere, stole food from her plate, and pooped way way too much.

"Look on the bright side," she muttered to herself. "You can walk off all that damn cake you ate at your party last night. Or maybe your fat will just freeze off. Rufus!"

She stopped at the corner deciding which route she should take. To the left was the park with the huge lake Rufus often liked to visit. He loved being surrounded by kids, by people who would bask in his great dogly beauty. But to the right was the little Mexican café with the garbage that Rufus so loved to dig through. She hoped to God that Rufus hadn't gone there again. The owner threatened to send him to the pound if she found him digging in the garbage one more time. And as much as Cherri would love to be relieved of the responsibility of walking, feeding, and cleaning up after the pain-in-the-ass dog, she couldn't because Baba loved him. Loved him from the moment they'd found him abandoned in the Dumpster near their house.

Despite his super-naughtiness Rufus was a good guard dog and kept Baba company when Cherri worked all day. She needed him to keep her company now. She had to be at work in twenty minutes. She had to find the damn dog soon.

She decided to head toward the Mexican restaurant. There wouldn't be many kids at the park. It was too cold, and Rufus probably knew that. "Rufus," she crooned. "Rufus. If you come here right now I promise I won't toss you into the nearest river. Come on, boy, where are you?"

"Need any help?"

Cherri whipped around to see Dr. Sean Brightworth, oldest son from Durant's richest family and Rufus's vet, standing in the doorway of a small blue house.

*Crap.*

Her cheeks burned, the embarrassed warmth actually welcome on the frigid day. There was something about the handsome vet that made her nervous, but she couldn't put her finger on it. It could be that he seemed to know that they sometimes fed Rufus fried chicken for dinner instead of his dog food. Or it could have been the way he looked at Cherri. Like he was trying to see inside her. Whatever it was, it made her kind of jumpy. "Um, no. Nope I don't need any help." Even to her own ears she sounded stupid.

"Really?" He raised one of his dark brows at her, looking at her again, knowing she was a big fat liar liar, pants on fire. "You sure? I thought I heard you calling Rufus."

"I wasn't," she lied again, worried that her nose was going to start growing. Rufus had a reputation around town. The police, fire department, and every person who lived within five blocks of her had a tale about her dog.

And none of them were good.

She didn't want her vet to be a witness to her bad pet-owning skills, too. He might report her or something. "I said doofus. Yeah, that's right. Doofus. I was scolding myself for forgetting to call the oil guy yesterday. We're nearly out of the stuff." She shivered for effect. "And it's going to be a cold one tonight."

"Oh?" He stepped out of the house, his eyes traveling down her body, just taking her in.

Okay. That was something that he had never done before. Her cheeks burned just a little bit more.

"I have plenty of heat here. If you want, you could spend a few hours here this afternoon. Maybe I could make you some dinner?"

She looked at Dr. Brightworth for a moment. Tall, handsome, rich, forty-two-year-old Dr. Brightworth.

*Is he giving me the look? Is he inviting me for . . . Did he just ask me for a date?*

*Girl, shut your mouth!*

"Oh!" she finally said when her mouth caught up to her brain. "What a kind offer, but I've got to be at work soon."

"Okay, Cherri. But the offer still stands if you need some warmth this evening. You can even bring your grandmother."

"Thanks," she said slowly, now utterly confused. "I'll think about it."

She waited until he stepped back inside his house before she took off down the street again. She was relieved to be out of his company.

That had been weird. Of course he hadn't asked her on a date. He'd said she could bring her grandmother, and if anybody could suck the romance out of a situation it would be Baba.

It might have been nice if he had asked her out. Just for her ego, though.

She wasn't asked out very often. Hell, she wasn't asked out ever. Her beauty seemed to be lost on guys her own age.

"Guys your age are stupid," Ellis always told her. "You need a man."

Ellis was right but now wasn't the time to lament over the nonexistent state of her love life. She needed to focus on finding her dog.

A loud crashing noise ahead made her jump, and when she looked up she saw a trash can rolling on the ground. "Rufus!"

He popped out from behind a parked car and looked at her.

"Come here right now!"

*No,* he seemed to say. He stepped on the sidewalk and slowly walked away from her up the block.

"Rufus," she warned. He looked back at her for a moment but just kept walking. "You little shit." She went after him, knowing that if he decided to take off there was nothing she could do about it. "I'll skin you alive and make a dog fur coat out of you. I'll feed you to the gators at the aquarium. I'll only feed you brussels sprouts for the next two weeks."

"Oye, love. That last one there was a bit harsh."

She turned around to find Colin walking out of a little blue house on the corner. She hadn't expected to see him so soon after her party. She didn't want to see him today.

She didn't need another witness to her crazy.

She quickly surveyed him in his black motorcycle jacket and gray beanie hat and gloves. He was the only person on the planet who could manage to look hot and bundled up at the same time. She felt rather like a pink marshmallow in her winter coat. "What are you doing here?" she blurted rather accusingly.

"Well, hello to you, too, darlin'. I was delivering a piece for a client, if you don't mind. But I think I should be the one asking you why you're threatening that poor dog."

"Poor dog, my ass! He bolted out the door when I went to get the mail and forced me to chase him all over Durant in the freezing cold when I have to be at work in ten minutes and the big jerk has the nerve to walk away from me when I find him. I feed him and bathe him and walk him and he treats me like shit!" she said, feeling very disgruntled.

"Calm down, love." He walked closer to her and placed his warm gloved hand on her shoulder. "I'll fetch him for you."

"What makes you think you can get him? He won't come to me, and he knows me."

Colin put two fingers between his lips and let out a loud whistle. "Rufus, my lad. Come."

And then to Cherri's surprise the big stupid dog came running toward them. Toward her. Before she could even warn him to stop he jumped on her, knocking her to the ground. And to add insult to injury he saturated her face with gross wet doggy kisses.

"Oh look, lass. He loves you to pieces."

She looked up at Colin. All six feet three inches of him were shaking with laughter. Colin always seemed to be laughing at her. Of course he was always laughing at her. She was a six-foot-tall walking misfit. As she looked up at him, she could see that the mirth had lit up his face and traveled to his eyes. They damn near sparkled.

He really was extra-gorgeous when he laughed. But it still didn't stop her from being totally ticked off at him. "You're an ass, you know. A big stupid ass. Rufus, get off me!"

"I am an ass." He grabbed Rufus's collar and pulled him off. "I'd rather be an ass than lying on mine in this freezing weather. What's the matter with you, girl? Can't you stay on your feet?"

She frowned at him as she took his hand and allowed him to help her up. Just yesterday she'd wished she could be small and beautiful and graceful for him. It was a stupid thought. Colin would never see her as the put-together charming woman she wanted to be. She would always be just Cherri, the youngest one of their gang, and a walking accident waiting to happen. The one everybody treated like a little sister. It was probably for the best anyway. Colin was the last guy she should have a thing for. She saw who he dated. She knew his past. He was an eight-cylinder man when she was a two-speed kind of girl.

"Don't move, dog," he ordered Rufus, then took Cherri by the shoulders. "You all right, love? You took a pretty hard tumble. I shouldn't have laughed, but you looked kind of cute on the ground with the dog lapping at your face."

"Oh, shove it."

He grinned at her again, slipped his gloves off before cupping her cheeks in his large hands and looking into her eyes.

*Damn.*

Now she knew why her crush on him seemed to never melt away. He was dreamy.

"What a mouth." His eyes passed over her lips for a moment. "You don't even thank me for getting back your mutt."

"Bite me."

"Tell me where." That smile was still in those soft brown eyes, and it mirrored the one on his lips. And she looked at him for a moment thinking she might like to get bitten wherever he wanted to bite her.

*What a horny thought!*

She knew he was a flirt. She knew sweet words flowed from his mouth like water from a faucet. She knew he was full of shit, but there was something about him that made her all tingly.

"I shouldn't speak to you like that," he said, sobering.

"Why?" she said, feeling disappointment sneak in.

"Mike . . ." He shook his head. "Never mind. Your cheeks are so cold, love." He ran his still-warm hands over them, reminding her that she had long ago lost feeling in most of her body parts. "I'll give you a ride home in my truck. It should still be pretty warm. I was inside for only a few minutes."

She would go anywhere with him as long as he kept his warm hands on her cold body, but his comment about Mike made her remember where she was supposed to be. "Shit. I have to go to work." She stepped away.

"When?"

"Like right now." She looked at Rufus, who was sitting quietly like the good boy he wasn't. "Double shit. I have to take him home first."

"How about I take you to work first and then take him home."

"You don't have to do that."

"I want to. It's the least I can do for laughing my head off at you."

He was sweet. There was something about him that was sweet. She had a feeling that not everybody saw it; that he tried to keep it hidden from the world.

"Okay then." She nodded. "I accept your offer."

Somehow Colin managed to get her to St. Lucy Street in

record time. Rufus—who was usually a nut job in the car—sat quietly in the back, his tail wagging happily. It was as if Colin was some kind of dog whisperer. He was a woman whisperer, too. If she had a tail, looking at him would cause it to wag.

"Thank you for this, Col. If there's anything I can do to repay you . . ."

"Go to work, lass. We're friends. You don't need to repay me."

Friends? That wasn't what they were exactly. With Ellis and Belinda and Mike there was a different kind of closeness, like they were a family with whom she could share anything. But not Colin. He didn't exactly inspire brotherly feelings in her. No, the feelings that rushed through her when she looked at him were not familial at all.

"Why are you looking at me like that, love?" He gently brushed the hair back from her face, causing that tingly feeling to rise up inside her. "Has snot froze to my face?"

It occurred to her in that moment that there wasn't much she knew about the man she kind of lusted over. It also occurred to her that she wanted to get to know him a little better. "Do you like homemade chocolate chip cookies?"

"Does a bear shit in the woods?"

"I'll make you some." She turned around to Rufus, whose eyes were adoringly set on Colin. "Good-bye, mutt. You're lucky you're not getting turned into doggy stew tonight." She hopped out of the car and looked up at Colin. "Thank you, Col. I appreciate this more than you know."

"It's nothing, love. Need me to come 'round later and pick you up?"

She was surprised by his offer and tempted to take him up on it, just so she could spend a little more time in his presence. "No thanks, but could you could check to see if Baba is okay? I worry about her being alone sometimes."

"Of course. I'll ring you later with an update."

"Thanks." She smiled at him once more before she headed into Size Me Up.

She loved walking into Size Me Up. Not only was the store beautiful with its colorful walls and art deco furniture, it was her second home, a place where special-sized girls like her could find great clothes and good advice when they needed it. She had been with the place since the doors had opened, and in that time she'd watched Ellis transform from a struggling shop owner to a designer with flourishing business, from a happily single girl to an in-love married woman. Belinda had changed, too, in subtle ways. They all had. She felt as if she'd grown up here. But she was going to have to leave this place soon, and it scared the crap out of her.

She'd gone to school to be an art teacher. She loved to paint. She loved to take a blank canvas and turn it into something amazing. She had a master's degree in fine arts and had spent the past five years studying the greats. She needed to find a job in her field soon.

"Hey, kid." Mike greeted her with a ruffle to her hair. "Was that Colin who dropped you off?"

"Yeah." She smoothed her hair back into place after Mike's brotherly greeting. "He helped me capture my naughty dog."

Mike looked at her for a long moment with narrowed eyes. "Did you call him or was Rufus near his house? Is your car okay? Is that why he drove you? Why didn't you call me to help you? You know we're here for you, right?"

Her head spun at his influx of questions.

Mike was protective by nature. As a former cop it was something he couldn't seem to let go of. For Ellis he was the perfect chivalric husband, risking his future by quitting his job and buying this building for her. But Mike wasn't Cherri's husband, and as much as she appreciated his concern, she was an adult and she didn't need him to be so overprotective. "You know, I often wonder why you left the force. If you miss interrogating people so much I'm sure Durant PD will let you come in and help out a few days a week. You can think of it as community service."

"Whoa." He stepped back, putting his hands in the air in surrender. "Turning twenty-two has made you sassy. I was just checking in. You're like my baby sister. It's my job."

"I'm sorry," she apologized with a sigh. "I spent the last hour chasing after a dog in the freezing cold. I'm cranky, and to answer your questions: My car is fine. I bumped into Colin on Acorn Hill. I know that you and Ellis are here for me, but I am perfectly capable of wrangling my bad dog myself. Thank you very much."

"I know," he said with an indulgent smile. "You're a big girl now."

He ruffled her hair again and walked away before she could say another word.

"Cherri Berry!" Belinda, co-owner of Size Me Up and Cherri's other best friend, came rushing out of nowhere. "I'm so happy to see you." She looped her arms around her and squeezed Cherri so hard she couldn't breathe. "I can't wait to tell you about my vacation. Guess how many hot men I slept with? None! My mother was there. That chick sure knows how to cramp a girl's style. But I want to hear about you first. How have you been this past couple of weeks? I can't believe I missed your birthday party. You have to tell me all about it. Were there any cute guys there? Did you get any good presents? How's Baba? Did you get called for any interviews? I know you only filled out applications for Durant but maybe you should look in the neighboring towns. I can help you fill out some more. I'm good at fudging applications. How do you think I got so many jobs?" She squeezed Cherri again. "We'll find you a job, you don't have to worry."

"Slow your roll, Belinda," Ellis said from behind her. "I know you've been gone for two weeks, but take a breath. Cherri just walked through the door and she's an adult, with responsibilities and her own life. She doesn't need you to help her fill out applications. She'll get a job when she gets a job; until then she can work here until she dies."

"Thank you, Ellis." She smiled gratefully at Ellis who always treated her like an adult, like her equal. She appreciated that.

"I know," Belinda said. "I'm too much. I realize you're an adult, but I watched you grow into a woman. It's hard for me to forget that you're not the same shy kid who walked in here two years ago unable to walk in a pair of high heels. Plus I just missed you. I never realized how much we text each other until I was overseas and couldn't speak to you every day."

"I missed you, too." She studied Belinda for a moment. Belinda had the kind of exotic beauty that a girl had to sell her soul to get. With honey-colored skin, dark red hair, and green eyes, she was a walking ethnic enigma with a pinup-girl body. People often wrote Belinda off as some sort of tart but she had a mind like a steel trap, and despite her sexpot looks she was one of the most maternal people Cherri knew. "There was nobody here with me to make fun of all Ellis and Mike's annoying newlywed kissy-face crap."

"Hey!" Ellis put her hands on her hips. "We're not annoying. I'm a lady, after all. I do try to sneak off when I make out with my husband."

"They're gross." Belinda rolled her eyes. "When I walked into the storeroom Mike had his hands all over her ass. Married folks shouldn't work together. It's just not right."

"I know!" Cherri agreed. "He's got his own office next door, but he's always in hers. It's like they're conjoined at the lips."

"Oh, so it's two against one again? You bitches are just jealous that I found me a sexy man who likes to buy me shoes and can't get enough of me."

"You're right," Belinda said, "we are. In fact we kind of hate you."

"Damn right," Cherri nodded with a grin. "I'm glad the three of us are back together."

"Yes." Ellis placed a hand on both of their shoulders. "All is right with the world once again."

Cherri couldn't have agreed more. Being with her best friends seemed to make everything better.

# CHAPTER 3

*Nice guys finish last . . .*

Colin's phone went off just as he was walking back to his truck from Mama's Bake Shop. He had a box of warm apple fritters and two large cups of coffee in his hands, and at first he was going to ignore the call. He didn't feel like talking much at the moment. He was freezing his bollocks off, and he still had to drop off a dog and spend an indeterminate amount of time with a little old lady when he had a shitload of work to complete at his shop. He should have walked the other way when he saw Cherri Rudy coming down the street, but something made him stop and stare at her. It could have been her puffy Pepto pink coat that attracted his eye—or her long golden hair blowing in the wind that made him stop. He didn't know what the reason was, he just knew he couldn't walk away without speaking to her.

The phone finally went to voice mail as he stepped back into the warmth of his truck. Rufus greeted him happily with a nudge to the face, and for the first time Colin thought it might be nice to have a dog to come home to.

*Or anybody to come home to.*

That thought alarmed him. He liked his solitude. But it was time he got back into the game. It had been two years since his last relationship, a year since he finished his woman binge. It was time to put that shit behind him once and for all. Maybe a few dates would get him out of his funk and, more important, get his mind off Cherri.

His phone rang again, whoever it was not satisfied with leaving him be. He pulled his iPhone out of his pocket.

*Mike.*

"I see you removed your lips from your wife's long enough to speak to me. What can I do for you, lad?"

"Was that you I saw dropping off Cherri?"

"Yeah," he said slowly, knowing Mike was expecting an explanation. He knew Mike thought of Cherri as a kid, as his little sister. Mike was protective of all the women in his life. His father had left when he was just a kid. He was a lad left to take care of three sisters and a mother. Somehow that role never ended. So when it came to Cherri, a woman without a father or brother in her life to look after her, he tended to be an overbearing jackass. Just like a lot of big brothers. Maybe she was still a kid when they had first met, maybe she did need somebody to look out for her a bit, but Cherri Rudy was very much a woman right now. Mike didn't need to protect her from him.

"Why didn't you stop in?" he said instead of grilling him like Colin expected.

"I would have but I've got some things I need to get done."

"Oh." Mike was silent for a moment. They had been best friends since college, closer than brothers, but since Mike had met Ellis, since he had gotten married, they hadn't seen much of each other. They didn't talk like they used to. Most of his time was spent with his wife. But Colin didn't blame the man. He loved Ellis. She was the best damn thing that had ever happened to his friend. *It's just that . . . It's hard when your best mate gets married.*

"How's your mum? I haven't been getting my Sunday calls like I used to."

"I know. She barely calls me, either. Since she and my dad remarried they have been traveling all over the world together. They're on safari this week. It's always been her dream."

"I know." He smiled at the thought of Margie Edwards, sweet little flower shop owner, gallivanting around the world. "She sent me an email with some pictures in it."

"Could you understand it? My mother is the world's worst typist."

"But she looks damn happy."

"She does."

They went quiet for a moment.

"You want to come over and watch the Knicks play tomorrow night?" Colin asked. "My new fifty-inch came a few days ago."

"I can't tomorrow. We've got to have dinner with Ellis's folks. You should come with us. Dr. Greg is hysterical. It's always a good time."

Colin sighed inwardly. Mike even liked his bloody in-laws. Where had his friend gone? They used to raise hell together. Now he was happy going on family picnics.

"I'll leave you to your family time. Maybe next week?"

"Yeah, Next week. Definitely."

They disconnected and for some reason Colin doubted he would be spending time with his best mate soon.

A few minutes later he pulled up to Cherri's tiny house. He had been past her home a thousand times. Durant was a pretty big small town, but because of his job he had been in and out of many homes in her neighborhood. This was the first time he had been to hers.

It was a little white house with a white picket fence surrounding it. It was cute, probably built in the 1950s and not updated since. It had an old tumbledown look to it, and for a moment he was wondering how Cherri and her little old gran managed to keep up with all the repairs a house this age must need.

"Come on, old boy," he said to Rufus as he opened his door and grabbed his bakery purchases. "It's time to go home."

Rufus bounded from the car and ran full-speed to the front door only to find it wouldn't open. He looked back at Colin, then sat, his eyes begging to be let in. "I don't have a key. We're going to have to knock."

He whimpered, causing Colin to smile as he knocked. But there was no answer. He knocked again and waited, but no one came to the door. Rufus scratched, but there was still no response. Colin put his hand on the knob and turned, nervousness rising up inside him.

Cherri mentioned to him that she was worried about her gran being alone.

*Shit.*

The last thing he needed was to walk in and find the old lady in trouble.

"Baba?" He walked in calling to her. He didn't know her real name. He only had ever referred to her as Baba. "Where are you, darlin'?" He walked farther into the house, sending a silent prayer above that she was okay. "Baba?"

"Who are you? And what the hell are you doing in my house?" Baba wasn't the little old woman he had pictured. She was robust, tall, with sharp green eyes and silver hair that fell down her back. He just took her in for a moment. Bright pink housecoat, red slippers, and the biggest damn butcher's knife that he had ever seen.

*Bloody fucking hell.*

"What are you doing here?" She stepped forward, her huge knife slashing through the air. "Just because I'm old doesn't mean I can't kill you."

"Whoa. Whoa!" He stepped back. She was quick for a woman her age. "Relax, you nutter. I'm Cherri's friend. I'm just bringing your bloody dog back."

"Cherri?" She came at him with the knife again and backed him against the door. It was so close to his Adam's apple, he was afraid to swallow. "What did you do with my pixie? She was supposed to bring Rufus back. Did you hurt her?"

"I dropped her off at work. She asked me to bring the dog back and check on you so she wouldn't be late," he said in a rush. "Call her and check. My name is Colin O'Connell. I'm her friend." Rufus squeezed between them, rubbing his head against Colin's leg as if to vouch for him. "See, the dog likes me, and look." He held up the coffee and box of still-warm apple fritters. "I brought you treats. What kind of maniac brings you treats?"

Baba lowered the knife, but only a bit. "It could be a trick. You could have drugged those things so you could have your way with me." She turned her head to the side and studied him, reminding him very much of Cherri in that moment. "But you are cute so I might allow it. It's been a long time since I have gotten any friction."

"Friction?" He shook his head, not sure he understood her thick accent.

"You know friction. You men always go out looking for friction at the discos."

"You mean action?"

"Yes, yes." She took the pastries from him and walked away. "Friction. Action. It all means the same. I know who you are, Colin O'Connell. You have seen more panties than

Victoria's Secret. You know all about friction. You stay away from my Cherri or I'll cut off your acorns."

"You mean nuts?"

She looked back at him for a moment. "You don't want to find out. Come to the kitchen and talk to me. I'll put booze in the coffee. You'll like it. Maybe if you are nice I'll let you have your way with me."

He followed her, a little bewildered, a little amused. He might be crazy but he kind of liked the nutty old woman.

Cherri sat next to Belinda at Hot Lava Java. They were sharing a warm piece of apple cobbler while Cherri pored through job listings and Belinda checked out potential merchandise for Size Me Up from new designers. Hot Lava Java was the best place to work on their stuff in town. Especially since Cherri didn't have WiFi and Belinda never had fresh baked goods at her condo.

"Find anything good yet?" Belinda asked her as she shut her laptop.

"Nope. There are no openings for art teachers this time of year. But I guess I knew that when I opted to graduate a semester early. You find anything good on your end?"

She shrugged. "I found some great lightweight scarves that I want to bring in for spring, but I haven't found anything new on the plus-sized market that would work for Size Me Up. I wish I could inspire more people to start designing."

"Why don't you design, Belinda? I've never seen you look anything less than smoking. You know what looks good."

"I do." She nodded. "But I don't create. I'm a buyer. I'm a put-er together-er. I wouldn't even know where to begin. Now you, gorgeous girl, have something special going on. When is the last time you picked up a paintbrush?"

"Um . . ." She had to think for a moment. "When I painted that mural in your office."

"Cherri! You haven't painted in six months?"

She felt guilty about it, but with work and school and Baba she didn't have time to lose herself in painting. "I know. I know. I need to. I'm going to start again."

She just didn't know when.

Cherri left Belinda a few minutes later. She had been feeling a little worn down lately. The holiday rush had arrived, and Size Me Up had been busier than ever the past few days. Today was her day off, and as she walked to the snowy cold streets of her hometown she could think of no better way to spend the afternoon than in her grandmother's bedroom.

Baba had the only warm room in the house thanks to the lovely little space heater Cherri had purchased for her two years ago. A nap in a warm room sounded delicious right about now. She could fall asleep to the sounds of clicking knitting needles and *The Bold and the Beautiful* playing in the background.

"Baba? I'm home." She wandered through their cluttered living room expecting to hear the woman answer. She didn't. Not even Rufus greeted her as he usually did when she walked in. Something in her chest lurched, and she moved a little faster through the house. Baba's bedroom was closed and unlike most days it was quiet. No noise coming from the television that was usually turned up just a little too loud.

*She's probably taking a nap. Don't be an idiot. She's healthy as an ox.*

Now was one of those times she felt lonely, bone-achingly lonely and more than a little scared. She wished there was someone else here she could turn to. She wished that Baba wasn't her only family. She felt that way a lot lately.

"Baba?" She turned the knob and breath filled her lungs.

Baba was in her usual spot, her easy chair placed in front

of the television. But all was not well as Cherri had hoped. Her grandmother was in tears, her eyes unfocused. In her arms was a broken music box that she was cradling like a baby.

Rufus, whose head was in Baba's lap, turned to look at her, his big eyes full of worry. That was one of the things she loved about him.

He loved Baba.

"Baba?" She crouched in front of her. "What's wrong?"

"It's broken, Natasha! Can't you see that?" She pushed her away, letting the music box drop into her lap.

Rufus backed away, pressing himself to Cherri's side.

Tears welled in her eyes, but she took a deep breath and held them back. It wasn't the first time her grandmother had confused her for her mother. "It's okay. We can fix it."

She looked at the beat-up music box her grandfather and she had given to Baba a few weeks before he died. It was in three pieces now, the backing where the mechanical parts were held completely off.

"Do we have glue?" Baba asked. "Go! Go get it. You must fix it! It has to play again."

Cherri wasn't sure if she could do more than glue the pieces back together. It was a cheap box, found at a yard sale, and fixed up by an old man and a fifteen-year-old girl. It played the theme from *Love Story* and had no value besides sentimental.

"Natasha, you have to fix it!" Baba screamed at her. "Your baby and Joe gave it to me. Joe is gone now. You have to fix it."

"Baba." Cherri put her hands on the old woman's face. "Look at me. It's Cherri. Natasha's not here."

"Cherri?" Her blurry eyes focused. "Oh!" She cupped her cheeks and pressed three kisses to her forehead. "I'm sorry. You look so much like her." She dropped her hands from Cherri's face. "Look what happened. I dropped it. I like to play it once in a while when I'm missing Joe. But I-I-I dropped it and it smashed. It won't play. I need it to play."

"I don't know if we can fix it."

"But we have to try! Go find a screwdriver. I know there is glue somewhere."

She gently took the broken pieces from her grandmother and kissed her forehead. "I'm going to take it to get fixed. I'll call Mrs. Petrovich. You two have tea and relax and I'll be back in a few hours."

# CHAPTER 4

*Promises. Promises.*

"Slimy English bastard," Colin swore as he checked the newest email on his iPhone. His day was not going well. He'd banged his head on an armoire that morning, his coffeepot had died, and to top it all off he'd just lost a bidding war for a 1952 Schwinn Hornet pedal to his biggest rival, a Brit. In the restoration business, original parts made or broke the value of things. And losing that piece royally screwed up his plans to re-create the perfect bike. Too bad that was the only one up for grabs in the country.

There wasn't a damn thing he could do about it, either. So Colin sighed and placed an order for a pedal from another year. It wasn't exactly right but he had gotten the client's permission to perform the substitution. Colin wasn't a perfectionist except when it came to his work. He had nothing but it and his good name, and he did not like making mistakes.

His phone rang as he was submitting his order, the caller

ID indicating it was his father. He hadn't heard from the old bugger in months, which wasn't odd. Magnus O'Connell usually only called when he was in between girlfriends, he'd gotten himself into a jam he couldn't get himself out of, or he wanted something.

"Hiya, Pop." He braced himself for the conversation.

"Hello, son. Whaddya up to?"

Colin grimaced at the slightly slurred speech of his father. He must have gotten dumped. It was the only time he drank and when he did, he drank enough to fill the Hudson River.

"You know, your love of alcohol gives us Irish people a bad name. It's like you're a fucking walking stereotype. What are you going to do next, Pop? Start a brawl at a pub?"

"What are you talking about, lad?" Magnus sounded offended. "I'm not drunk. I haven't drunk anything all day."

"How much did you drink last night?" He placed the phone on speaker and began to tidy his work space.

"Ah, well that's a different story," he said sadly. "I'm heartbroken, devastated, boy. Joanne left me."

Colin nodded, knowing as much. His father could never keep a woman more than six months—not even Colin's mother, who just walked out on them with no explanation and never returned. All through his childhood woman after woman came into and out of his life. For years he thought one of them would stick around; that he would finally have a mother, a real family like everybody else. But after a few years Colin stopped wishing. There wasn't a point. As soon as he got close to one of them his father would screw up and she would leave. "What did you do this time?"

"Nothing! And why do you always assume it was my fault?"

"I dunno, Pop, maybe because the sky is blue."

Magnus gave a long miserable sigh. "She's says I've got a wandering eye. Wandering eye my bollocks! I'm a people person. I'm a social creature. I like to talk. Some of the people I talk to just happen to be women. I didn't cheat on her. I haven't cheated in years. I'm a reformed man."

He raised a brow. "Are you, Pop?"

"Well . . . semi-reformed. But I've been good to her. I moved to America for her!"

"I know." Even Colin had to admit that was a big deal for his father. He never thought Pop would leave County Cork, Ireland. The bugger had the biggest shit fit when Colin announced he was going to America for college. "How do you like California?"

"My boy! It's fantastic. The weather is beautiful. There's so much to see and do. Oh! The women here are—are . . . so spectacular looking. Big titties and bronzed skin and more long blond hair than in Sweden. I fall in love eleven times a day."

Colin cracked a smile at his father's enthusiastic description of the state. "Maybe that's why Joanne sacked you."

"I really liked Joanne. The only woman I've loved more was your mother."

Colin didn't have anything to stay to that. He didn't remember his mother. She was just like every other woman Magnus had met: temporary. But he did remember his father speaking of her, telling him how beautiful she was, how he wished he hadn't screwed things up with her. His father wasn't a bad man. Colin truly believed he didn't intentionally do things to end his relationships; he was just too charming for his own good. He was also immature. There was only a twenty-year age difference between father and son. Through his childhood Colin was often left wondering who was the parent and who was the child.

"Do you think I should go after her, lad?"

"Um, I don't know, Pop. If she can't accept you for who you are, then maybe you should move on."

"To a young blonde with big titties?"

"Pop," he groaned.

"What?" Magnus sighed again. "I'm missing my best mate, you know."

"Why don't you go back to Ireland for a little while and see Pete."

"Not Pete, you wanker. I was talking about you, boy. It's been a long time."

"Yes," Colin agreed. He hadn't seen his father in years. And the last time he had, Magnus had his lips connected with his girlfriend for most of the visit. There had never been a time when it was just the two of them. It might be nice to have his father stay with him for a while. "You should come out to this side of the country."

"We can hit the nightclubs in New York City. American women love the way I talk. I'd bet the two of us could have the whole city eating out of our hands. Whaddya say to that?"

"No."

"Oh come on, you haven't still got your panties twisted about Arabella?"

"You shagged my girlfriend, Pop." He rubbed the throb that formed in between his eyes. "I think my knickers will always be a little knotted."

"She was way too old for you. And that was fifteen years ago. I think I've been punished enough. You moved to America to make your point. Besides, I did you a favor. That girl was a slag."

"When are you coming here?" He changed the subject, not wanting to rehash old arguments.

"In a few months. I've got business to take care of here first."

"Okay." Colin didn't bother to ask what business. He really didn't want to know. "Let me know when to expect you."

"Will do. I'll talk to you soon."

They disconnected as Colin tried to stomp on the little

ball of disappointment that unfurled in his chest. It was stupid of him to expect his father to act like . . . a father. They never were much of a family. It would be foolish to think they could be one now.

"Colin?"

He looked up at the sound of a female voice calling his name. Cherri stood in the doorway of his shop, bundled up in a hat, her homemade scarf, and a puffy coat. His heart malfunctioned at the sight of her, performing some kind of stupid squeezing thumping thing.

Something was wrong. She had never stepped foot in his territory before.

"Cherri?"

He took two steps toward her before stopping. She held some sort of wooden box in her hands. It was in pieces, and judging by the look on her face she wasn't too far from falling to pieces herself.

*Don't cry. Don't cry. Don't cry,* his mind chanted. He wasn't sure he could take it today.

She looked unsure for a moment, taking a step backward. "Are you busy? I—I don't want to bother you if you are."

"Come here, love." He stayed frozen as he watched her come toward him. Even in a too-puffy coat that hid far too much of her body, she was lovely to look at as she crossed his shop.

"I can't pay you much," she said, handing the pieces of the broken box to him. "But do you think you might be able to make it play again?"

She looked so innocent, so heartbroken, as if somebody had stomped on her favorite toy. "You don't have to pay me anything, you daft girl." With his head he motioned toward the stool he kept at his workbench. "Sit. I'll take a look at it."

"Thank you." She smiled, flashing him those pretty dimples of hers. "Baba was so upset that she dropped it. I want to make it whole for her."

He had yet to examine the box or to focus on her words. He was too busy watching her strip out of her winter gear. Under it she wore a pink cardigan with a white tank top that was just low-cut enough that he could make out the tops of her buttermilk-colored breasts. A voice, probably his conscience, ordered his eyes upward.

*She's not what you need right now.*

His gaze traveled to her head and the ugly wool hat she wore on it. It was the last to go, and he stared as her rowdy mane of golden hair tumbled to her shoulders.

She really had no idea how beautiful she was. No clue. He had heard her say that she was built like a lumberjack but all he saw was a tall curvy goddess. Even with her cheeks red from the cold and her eyes glossy from the wind she was lovely. It made him forget that she was the last person he should be attracted to.

"What?" Her emerald-colored eyes widened and her cheeks darkened with embarrassment. "If you tell me I have snot on my face I'll die."

"No." He chuckled. "I was wondering if you walked here. You look a bit like a Cherri Popsicle."

*That I would like to lick.*

He mentally castigated himself for that one. He lost all common sense around her.

"I did walk here. But I walk everywhere and it's not because I own the world's shittiest car. Walking helps me keep my big bottom from spreading into a huge one."

*But I like fat-bottomed girls.*

Colin kept his mouth shut to make sure his inappropriate response didn't come out. An image of her very curvy behind shot into his mind and . . . *Knock it off!* He shook his head and finally looked at the box. "So you've brought me a music box." He studied it for a few moments. It was factory-made, mostly cheap wood. There was nothing spectacular about it except for the intricate pink roses painted on the lid. That alone made the box worth saving.

"Beautiful." He glanced up at Cherri. "You wouldn't happen to know who painted this? This is some of the best detail work I've ever seen."

She beamed at him, dimples flashing, skin glowing. He gulped. "I painted it."

"I don't believe you."

Her eyes lit. "Dorky art major. Remember? My painting skills make up for my lack of beauty and grace."

"You're very beautiful, Cherri," he said without thinking. "I don't think you realize how exquisite you are."

"Exquisite?" She laughed that deep throaty laugh of hers, and heat unfurled in his gut. "You must get a lot of ass."

"What?" Her statement knocked him off guard.

"Ass? Tail? Panties dropping? Any of those ring a bell? I'm saying that you must have a lot of women trying to have sex with you. Probably some men, too."

The blood rushed out of his brain as soon as the word *sex* formed on her lips.

*Shit.*

She was just twenty-two years old. And in the two years he had known her, he had never seen her date. He had never seen her with a guy. She was mature for her age but she had this innocence around her. And yet something about hearing those words come from her mouth made his remaining brain cells malfunction. She was the only woman he had a hard time keeping his cool around. He was more than just attracted to her and he wasn't sure why.

"For fuck's sake, Cherri, where the hell did that question come from?"

She waved a dismissing hand at him. "Oh, don't tell me you don't know. The brogue, the pretty words, not to mention the way you look, all make you deity-like with your sex appeal. You probably don't have to work hard to get women to drop their drawers."

No, he never did. Using his hands and getting women to fall into bed were the only things he excelled at. He was like his pop that way. It took running into an ex whose name he couldn't remember to show him that. So many women. So many empty *I love you*s. It never took away that empty feeling in his chest. He promised himself he wouldn't say those words again unless he meant it.

"But you don't have to use any of that charm on me. I won't fall for it. Well . . . Not too hard," he heard her say when he tuned back into the conversation.

It was the first time in as long as he could remember that he wasn't trying to be charming, but he didn't tell her that. Instead he pulled up a stool next to her and turned his attention back to the box. There was something about Cherri that always left him feeling like the world was slipping beneath his feet. It sucked. The sooner he fixed it, the sooner he could get her out the door. "Did you paint this recently?"

"No, I did that when I was fifteen. I'm better now."

"Bollocks," he mumbled, staring at the intricate brushstrokes. "I couldn't do this if you put a gun to my head. The shading alone puts me to tears. It makes my work look like rubbish."

"You're dramatic." Her cheeks burned with embarrassed pleasure. He liked the way she looked when her cheeks were pink. It made him want to put that expression on her face all the time.

"You're talented." He grabbed the bottom of her seat and spun her around, enjoying the surprised little yelp that escaped her mouth. "I changed my mind about fixing this for free. We'll barter. Can you grab that gray metal box and the step stool on the top shelf?" She stood and he realized how high the shelf was. "Let me help you. It's high up."

Her hand gently connected with his chest, stopping him from assisting her. "I don't need your stinking help," she said with a grin. "I'm six feet tall."

She proved her height by stretching her long curvy body upward. He watched the way her body moved, her sweater rising as she lifted her arms. He caught a glimpse of the creamy-looking skin just above the top of her jeans. He couldn't pull his eyes away if he wanted. His hand wanted to reach out and touch that skin, just to see if it felt as soft as it looked.

"I hated being this tall growing up," she said when she returned. "But now I can see its advantages. Plus I was the only girl in the whole ninth grade who was begged to play on the varsity basketball team."

"You played basketball?"

She snorted inelegantly, which he found kind of cute. "Are you crazy? I'm lucky if I can make it through the day without falling on my ass." She sat at the table, put her hand on her chin, and studied him. "Did you play any sports?"

"No, love. I wasn't always the man you see before you. I was skinny with bad spots and big feet. I wasn't athletic or talented or popular. I spent most of my formative years in my pop's shop alone learning how to fix things. I hadn't even kissed a girl till I was seventeen."

One of Cherri's brows went up. "I don't believe you."

"You should. I had a crazy growth spurt when I hit eighteen. That's when things started looking up for me. Women started noticing me."

"I bet you they noticed you all right. Tell me about losing your V card."

"My V card?"

"Your virginity," she said as if it were obvious. "I bet you have the kind of wonderful story that all teenage boys fantasize about. Was it an older sexy woman who showed the way in a tender, passionate lovemaking session? I bet she gave you lessons on how to please a woman. Cougars are good for that."

"No," he said flatly. "Just no."

"I know. It was twins! Big-breasted country lasses who let you have your way with them in a hayloft. Oh Colin," she moaned dramatically. "Yes, Colin. We both like that."

"Cherri!" he barked at her.

"Tell me." She grinned with that twinkle in her eye. "Tell me how it happened."

"It's none of your bloody business."

"Why won't you tell me?"

He didn't want to talk about sex with her because it caused him to think about sex with her and that was the last thing he needed to be thinking about right now. "Because I won't."

She lightly rested her hand on top of his. It was an innocent gesture but it shot heat right through the core of him. "Tell me how you lost yours and I'll tell you how I lost mine."

"I don't want to know!" He didn't want to think about her with another man, much less hear about it.

"Tell me."

"No."

"Please."

"I was in the back of an old Chevy Nova with a girl I went to school with. There were no twins or cougars or grand passion, just some fumbling, awkwardness, and a release on my side. Are you happy now?"

"I like my busty-twins-in-a-hayloft story better." She shrugged and then studied him for a moment. "I pegged you wrong. You were shy, weren't you?" she asked as if stumbling upon some great revelation.

"What makes you say that?"

"Because a small part of you still is. The way you hung in

the background at my party. The way you don't say much around people. You work alone. You live alone. Actually, maybe those are signs you are a serial killer. It's always the quiet ones."

"Smartass." He found himself grinning at her despite himself. He may have lusted after her body but he liked her. He liked the mischievous little smartass in her.

"I always thought you were this cool aloof guy, but you're a big ol' shy dork just like me." She grinned at him again, her eyes kind of twinkling. He looked away from her. Her comments were a little too close to home.

He shrugged. "I don't know. I try not to put myself in a box."

"Is it the same for boys?" she asked him, her eyes searching his face again. "Did you have those days, those moments when you felt self-conscious, like God had placed you in some alien's body? Did you ever have a time when you felt like everybody was staring at you and all you wanted to do was hide?"

"Don't we all, love? Isn't that what being a teenager is all about?"

She reached over, squeezing his hand. "We're all freaks, aren't we? Some of us just hide it better than others."

*Amen.*

He slipped his hand from beneath hers, realizing that the longer they touched the more he would want to touch her. And that was a bad thing, so he lifted the unfinished wooden stool he had picked up a few weeks ago to show her. "Let's talk about our bargain. I'll fix your music box if you'll paint this stool for me. I've got a designer who's on my back to start selling decorative items. I don't do decorative."

"But I've seen your work, Colin. You're amazing. You could if you wanted to."

Her compliment was very nice for his pride, but he shrugged it off. "I fix things. I don't do flowers and girlie shit and I hate detail work, but since you're here you can do it."

Cherri sat down and opened the box, studying the supplies inside. He noticed the way she nodded in approval of his paint supplies. He also noticed the slight glow of anticipation in her eyes as she looked at the stool. She loved to create.

She removed the sandpaper from the box to smooth out a rough spot in the wood. Her long-fingered hands worked smoothly and efficiently, as if she were an old pro. His respect for her went up a few notches.

"So you're telling me that you're going to take hours of my hard labor and sell it to somebody else?"

"Yup, and for lots of cash too." He nodded. "I'll give you credit as the artist of course."

"I smell an unfair trade coming on, but if you fix my grandmother's music box, I'll be more than happy to do this. I might even give you my firstborn."

He watched her smooth on the first coat of primer before returning his attention to the broken box. "It's a clean break, love. It shouldn't be hard to fix."

A worried look passed over her face. "It's not the box itself, but the song it plays. I can't bring it back to her unless it plays."

"What song is it?"

"Don't laugh." She wrinkled her nose. "But it's the theme from *Love Story*."

"Really?" He couldn't help but smile. His lovelorn father adored that song, singing it when he was deep into his cups after a breakup. "Where do I begin . . ." He sang the first verse, imitating Andy Williams, as bittersweet memories invaded him. He nearly forgot he wasn't alone in his shop. And despite another person's presence he still got that little charge when he sang and his voice bounced off the walls of the shop.

"Holy crap." Cherri rested her hand on her cheek while a mischievous little smile played on her lips as she watched him. "Tell me, do you sing to all your ladies in that beautiful tenor or are you trying to charm me out of my pants?"

He was never sure if her words were intentional or not. Either way, she was messing with his head. And he cursed himself for allowing it to be messed with.

He'd never sung to anybody before. Never. Singing was his dirty little secret. His personal pleasure. Something he did only when he was alone in his shop or in the shower. Not even Serena knew about his hobby, and she was the woman he'd planned to marry. "I don't usually burst out in song," he said, disgruntled. "My life isn't a bloody episode of *Glee*."

"Too bad," she sighed. "If you can't fix the music box maybe you could come over and sing that song to my grandmother once a week. I'm sure she'd like that just as much." She tilted her head to the side and studied him. "Especially if you did it in the nude. Baba told me that she wanted you to get fresh with her." She looked at him sideways, a little naughtiness in her eyes. "She said you have nice big hands, and nice big feet, and that you must have a nice big—"

"Cherri!"

"Hey, I'm just reporting what she said. And, boy did she say a lot. My seventy-five-year-old grandmother still has a sex drive. I don't know if I should applaud her or throw up a little."

"Applaud her, girl. She's madder than a bag of cats but there's something I like about her."

"There is." She smiled softly, and if he wasn't mistaken there was a hint of sadness in her eyes. He started to ask what was wrong, but he stopped himself. The more he talked to her, the more he wanted to know about her. He wasn't somebody she could get involved with.

He was thinking of settling down.

She needed to sow her wild oats.

His best mate disapproved.

It wasn't worth the trouble.

He returned his attention to the music box. They worked for a few minutes in comfortable silence while Colin dismantled the base. It looked as if it had been overwound. Not a difficult fix, with a little oil it would . . .

The beginning notes of the song twinkled out across the room and before he could register what was happening a soft mass of unruly blond hair had tackled him, peppering his face with dozens of happy kisses.

"You did it! Thank you. Thank you. Thank you." Colin sat there for a moment, oddly content to let her spread her warm affection all over him. But when her lips brushed his, and a jolt of pure need surged through him, he regained his senses.

"Enough." He held her at arm's length. "Stop kissing me." He swiped his hand over his mouth, trying to remove the warm tingle that she left behind.

"Jeeze, Colin." She looked hurt for a flash of a moment. "I realize I'm not your type, but you don't have to wipe your mouth like I have the frickin' plague." She took a slight step back and raised her nose haughtily. "I'll have you know the other guy I kissed this morning was happy to be kissing me."

*Mine,* he thought primally. The hairs on the back of his neck rose at her statement. "Who were you kissing this morning?"

"Nobody." She raised her eyebrows. "Why? Are you jealous?"

"No," he lied. "I think of you like my baby sister," he lied again, much bigger that time. "I just want to know who's been slobbering over you."

"You're just like Mike." Her eyes flashed with annoyance. He could feel her frustration and didn't like that he was the cause of it. "I'm a grown woman, baby sister or not. It's none of your business who I've been with."

He knew that. He knew she was capable of even more

than she gave herself credit for. He wished he could only see her as a girl. It would make life so much easier for him.

"Why are you looking at me like that? Say something."

He couldn't say what he wanted. He couldn't tell her what he really thought about her so instead he said, "Give me a few more minutes with the music box and then it'll be all patched up."

# CHAPTER 5

*Looking for love in all the wrong places . . .*

"Do you think I should sign up for one of those online dating sites?" Belinda asked Cherri as they dressed one of the mannequins.

"Do you want to?" Cherri asked neutrally. Belinda had been so anti-love since she had known her that the question surprised her. Belinda never talked much about her past, but Cherri knew that somewhere in Belinda's history some guy had stepped on her heart. And it was a shame: Belinda was a great catch.

She shrugged. "I don't know. I'm turning thirty. Ellis is married. All my college friends are married. I'm feeling a little left out. Plus I'm afraid that if I don't start using these eggs soon they'll dry up and I'll be a barren, loveless spinster. Maybe I'll go buy some sperm and have a kid on my own. Maybe I'll be like Josephine Baker or Angelina Jolie and adopt a bunch of kids."

Cherri blinked at her friend as her head spun with information. "Do you want to get married? Do you want to have kids? Seriously? You?"

"Who said anything about getting married?" Belinda asked defensively. "I'm talking about a baby or some well-behaved dogs like Oprah has. With really regal dog names like Maximilian and Wilhelmina. What's with the twenty questions? You're one of my besties. We talk about shit like this."

"No, we talk about the hot guys on *True Blood* and where to get panties that won't give you a wedgie and the best place to get a grilled cheese sandwich. We have never talked about you procreating. What's going on with you? A couple of weeks in Spain and you're talking about huge life changes?"

"I don't know." She sighed. "Being away from home puts things in perspective a little. It just got me thinking about stuff."

"If you want to do something that will make you happier, I'm all for it. The only thing that matters is that you're happy." She could see Belinda as a great mommy. She could see Belinda taking the world over, too. She just had to put her mind to it.

"I love you, kid." Belinda kissed her cheek. "I think we need to have a sleepover and talk. But let's not invite Ellis. Her newlywed bliss makes her too damn cheerful."

"She wouldn't leave Mike for an entire night anyway. Would you mind coming to my house? I don't want to leave Baba alone."

"Um, of course we're having it at your house. I've been craving Baba's cheesy potato balls for weeks. Plus that woman likes to drink. I appreciate that in a senior citizen."

The bell over the door rang, alerting them that a customer had arrived.

"You go." Belinda shooed her away. "I'll finish up here."

"I need a sexy dress that will put the zippity back in my husband's do da," the customer said by way of greeting. Judging by her thick New York City accent, she wasn't a local.

Cherri loved tourists. They tended to spend more, which upped her commission, which made tiny bits of her debt vanish.

"I think we can manage that. We just got a new shipment in." Cherri led the woman to the new arrivals. "We can knock his damn socks off, too, if you want."

After a few moments of browsing the woman turned to Cherri. "Okay, honey. I need your honest-to-God opinion. No bullshit, okay?"

"No bullshit." She smiled as she placed her hand over her heart. "Scout's honor. I'm Cherri by the way."

"Melina." She yanked a dress off the rack and held it in front of her. "Am I too old for this dress? Remember, no bullshit."

The dress was silk satin, baby doll pink, obscenely low cut, and very short. It also cost three hundred dollars and she could use the commission.

*If you can't say anything nice . . .*

*But you can't let this lady walk out in public in that.*

"Um . . . I find only women with dark skin can pull off baby doll pink. Maybe you should try a darker color." She pulled a less expensive long-sleeved shirred-side black dress off the next rack. "It may not look like much on the hanger, but trust me, with your figure jaws will hit the floor."

The customer raised a brow. "You didn't exactly answer my question, did you?"

*Busted.* "You really want honesty?

Melina nodded. "No bullshit."

"Okay. This kind of pink is for prom queens and princesses. Plus after you hit twenty you've got to pick either legs or boobs to show off—not both."

"I'm forty-nine. Which do you think I should pick?"

"I'd go for the legs. This dress paired with some kickass stilettos and you'll have men eating out of your hands."

The woman stared at her for a moment. "Are you single?"

"Oh . . . Um . . . I-I," she stuttered. *Lost for words* didn't begin to describe how she was feeling.

"Not me, honey!" Melina laughed. "I'm taken but I've got a twenty-four-year-old boy who would go gaga for you. You're tall, you're blond. You've got big knockers. He'd die."

"Phew! You're cute but you aren't my type."

"But you're the type of girl I would like for my son. You could have let me walk out of here with a dress that would have earned you some serious cash, but you chose to save me from making a total ass out of myself. Are you Jewish?" She waved her hand. "Bah! Never mind, you can always convert."

"Do you think you could do that, love?" Colin's voice drifted through the store, and the hairs on the back of her neck stood up. "Change faiths? I'm not sure I could. The most I've ever done for a female is change my sheets. That could be why I'm single."

"Hi." She turned slowly to face him, her stupid heart thumping. She definitely hadn't expected to see him today, on her turf, not after their last meeting in his shop. She'd thought about him all night after she left him, about how he thought of her like a baby sister, about how despite that she still had a thing for him. It was damn annoying. "Are you looking for Mike? He's not here right now. He's at the bank."

Colin's dark eyes studied her face, and heat crept up her neck. "What if I came here to see you?"

"I would call you a big fat liar. Unless you want me to help you pick out a new frock for a cocktail party, there is no reason you came to see me."

"Actually, love, I did come here just for you. I need your help finding shoes to go with my new handbag." He winked at her, a small smile playing on his lips. "But take care of this beautiful lady first. I'll be right here waiting."

Cherri turned away, trying like hell not to blush. She

hated when guys winked at her; it seemed so smarmy. But not when he did it. It looked . . . sexy when he did it.

"Holy shit! Forget about my son," the customer whispered as soon as Cherri turned back to her. "Hell, I'm going to forget about my husband. Please tell me you've seen that gorgeous man naked."

"We're just friends," she said, telling the truth. They would always be just friends.

"Oh, look at you! You're blushing," she said in a singsong voice. "Do you like him? He looks very likable."

She *was* blushing.

*Shit.* Her face was on fire. But why?

He came here. To see her? It was weird.

"Yeah, he's likable. I like him as much as every other woman in the world." She gave the lady a gentle push toward the dressing room. "Now get in there, you nosy thing."

"If you tell me everything I'll buy half the store. But I want to hear everything. Don't leave out a single detail."

Cherri dumped the dress she had picked out for Melina on top of her and shut the door. She raked her fingers through her hair, hoping that just this once she didn't look like she had stuck her finger in a socket.

*Calm down, dummy. It's just Colin. He doesn't care what your hair looks like.*

"Hey," she said. "What's up?"

"Hey," he responded. "The stool. You never finished it." He seemed as unsure of himself in that moment as she did. "I think your work is good. I need to see it completed."

"Oh." She hadn't expected him to say that, and for some reason she was a little disappointed hearing it. "I thought that the stool was just something you gave me to keep me out of your hair while you fixed Baba's music box. Giving me paint is like giving a kid a new toy." She had been all out of sorts since she'd left his shop that day. She had gone to him expecting him just to fix her grandmother's broken music box but what she got was different. She got a glimpse of who Colin really was. She had always thought of him like an expensive painting, beautiful and untouchable.

But now . . . Things had changed.

"Can you come by and finish it?"

"Yeah. Of course. I told you I would. We had a deal. If you bring it by the house, I can work on it after I leave here. Is that okay?"

"Yeah." He looked a little disappointed, and she wasn't sure why. "It's perfect. You forgot this at my shop." He took the scarf from his neck and wound it around hers. She hadn't noticed that he was wearing it when he came in and now she wished he hadn't. It smelled like him, like warm skin and spicy man.

"Thank you."

His hands lightly gripped the scarf, the heat of them seeping through the fabric and warming her chest. He was looking at her, studying her, and she felt self-conscious. That was new for her. When she'd first met him, she had thought him beautiful, a player and so far out of her league he might as well be in the stars; there was no reason to be or to feel anything less than her normal self. But today she couldn't meet his eyes. Today her feelings were jumbled, and again she wished she could be different. Smaller, graceful, beautiful. Maybe he would see her differently if she were.

She hated herself for thinking that way. For wishing she were different. If he couldn't appreciate her for who she was, then screw him!

She only wished he had the courage to say that, or raise her eyes to meet his. So she looked at the floor instead, then at his chin, and then past him through the shop window instead of looking him in the eye. "I wondered where I left this."

"Cherri . . . You aren't upset with me, for saying you were like my baby sister?"

"Of course not," she lied, because it did bother her. Of course it did.

"Then why won't you look at me?"

She attempted to drag her gaze back to him, but an older woman caught her attention. It was mid-December and bitterly cold and the woman wore only a sleeveless blue housedress, her long white hair flowing around her shoulders.

Cherri's heart lodged in her throat.

"Baba!" She was out the door, barely hearing Colin as he shouted her name.

"Baba?" She ran after her grandmother down the street. "Baba, stop!" She did, and when she turned around her eyes were glassy and unfocused. "Baba, it's me." Cherri touched her face, ran her hands down her icy arms, checking to see if she was okay.

"Cherri?" She blinked. "What are you doing here?"

"Baba, you're on St. Lucy Street without your coat. What are you doing here? Are you okay?"

Her eyes refocused and she looked around her, finally snapping out of her spell. "I—I was hot. I wanted to take a walk."

"A walk? But Baba, the house is so far away." Cherri paused, lost for words.

"Cherri, honey." She felt a touch on her shoulder and turned to see Colin and Belinda standing behind her. Their faces wore identical expressions of concern. "Let's get her inside," Belinda said.

They ushered her inside to Ellis's small office. Baba sat quietly with a blanket draped around her. Cherri's hands shook but she held on to her grandmother, kissing her frozen forehead. She couldn't stop the what-ifs from entering her mind, and the fear made her nauseous.

"Stop slobbering on me, pixie! I'm fine. You know my blood pressure medication makes me hot. Stop freaking up."

"It's freaking out, Baba! And don't tell me not to freak out. You were in the middle of town half dressed. What am I supposed to do?" She never got angry with Baba, but this time things were different.

"You're a good girl." Baba patted her cheek. "But take a chill aspirin."

"It's take a chill pill and I will not. I was worried about you!" How could she be so cavalier about this? Didn't she realize what could have happened? The last shred of Cherri's fragile patience snapped and she laid into her grandmother.

"You're speaking Russian?" Baba raised a graying brow. "Your grandfather only spoke it when he was angry with me, too. He must have been pissed off a lot judging by how well you speak it."

"That's because you're a stubborn old mule and somebody should have spanked you a long time ago."

Baba only grinned at her.

"Why are you smiling? You're not supposed to be smiling! I'm yelling at you."

"You speak Ukrainian flawlessly, too. Much better than your mother. I'm so proud of you."

She let out a frustrated growl and left the room. The storeroom was the closest and Cherri found herself there, with her hands braced on the counter to prevent her from trembling. She tried to breathe in but choked, her lungs and throat burning with frustration and paralyzing fear.

She couldn't leave Baba alone anymore. If she did, every moment would be filled with worry. But she had to go to work. They had bills to pay. The house was falling apart around them and Baba's Social Security check wasn't enough to support them. Cherri needed to do something. She needed help.

Hard arms wrapped around her waist just as she was about to sink into panic. Warm skin. Spicy male. Colin. Her mind shut off and her body took over. She turned into his embrace and leaned on him. She couldn't remember the last time she had somebody to lean on.

"I'm scared," she admitted aloud for the first time.

"You'd be a fool if you weren't, lass." He kissed her cheek, and she let her eyes drift shut as she rested her head on his shoulder. "Take her to the doctor. This happened to my gran and it was her medications. They don't always interact with each other well. It made her a bit off. Maybe that's your Baba's problem, too."

She hadn't taken Baba to the doctor yet. She should have months ago but she was afraid of what he might say. Part of her would rather live in denial than have to look the truth in the face.

His hands slid up her back and tangled into her loose hair. "Will you do that, love?"

She nodded. "Tomorrow."

"Look at me, lass."

For the first time that day she fully met his gaze. There was nothing but concern for her there, and she remembered why she considered him a friend in the first place. "It's going to be all right. You have to believe that."

"You have no way of knowing that, but thank you for trying."

He smiled softly, his lips brushing hers and lingering for a moment. It was the sweetest of kisses. It was one of those kisses that was too long and too short at the same time and it left her head even more muddled than before.

"Oh, excuse me!" They turned to see Ellis frozen in the doorway with the most curious expression on her face. "Uh, Cherri? Baba's calling you. Oh and Colin, Mike's back. He wants to know if you can help him next door."

"I'll be there in a second," she said, expecting Ellis to walk out the door, but she didn't. Cherri turned her attention back to Colin but felt Ellis's gaze on her back. "Thank you." She quickly hugged him. "I'll let you know what happens."

He kissed her cheek. "Call me if you need anything—a ride to the doctor, a lap dance, anything."

Her lips twitched at his stupid joke and she broke away feeling slightly calmer.

She followed Ellis out the door, but instead of heading directly back into her office Ellis stopped right outside. "Is there something going on with you and Colin?"

"No. Why?"

"Cherri, he kissed you."

Ah, the kiss. She didn't want to think about it too much. She didn't want to read into it. She still felt the warmth from his lips on hers. It was all she could do not to touch her mouth to seal the feeling in. "It was innocent." She believed that. Colin didn't see her that way. Colin was like that with every woman.

"Oh, I—" She shook her head.

"What?"

"It was just the way he was looking at . . . Never mind. See to your grandmother. Belinda is in there with her. I'm going to man the front of the store."

She left, and Cherri walked back into Ellis's office to see her grandmother braiding Belinda's hair. Fifteen minutes ago she had given her the scare of her life and now she was playing beauty parlor with Belinda. What the hell was she going to do with her?

"Red hair is beautiful, no?" Baba glanced at Cherri. "Back in the old country children with red hair were locked in the basement and thought to be evil."

Belinda looked frightened. "That's not true, is it?"

"No," Baba answered. "We were too poor to have basements. Where is my sexy Irish boy? I like looking at him."

"Baba!"

She was unconcerned by Cherri's scold. "You keep your legs closed around him. You hear?"

Her face flushed slightly. Could the old lady read her mind?

"He's the one who fixed your music box," she said in a lame attempt to change the subject.

"I know who he is, dumb-dumb. I didn't say I had to keep my legs closed around him."

Cherri slapped her hands over her ears. "I can't believe you just said that."

"I'm a widow. We can be friends with insurance."

"That's friends with benefits, Baba!"

Cherri smiled despite all the other emotions churning inside her. Baba had a way about her that Cherri couldn't stay mad at.

# CHAPTER 6

*Us against the world . . .*

*I shouldn't have kissed her,* Colin thought grimly as he made the short journey to see Mike. The kiss didn't mean anything, he reassured himself. It wasn't *supposed* to mean anything anyway. He had only meant to offer comfort to a scared girl. But things didn't work out that way. She made him feel things he wasn't used to.

"Hey," Mike greeted him as he entered. "Is Cherri okay? Elle said she was pretty shaken up."

"She was. She probably still is, but I think she'll be fine."

"That's good," he said, returning his attention to the blank wall he was studying. "I'm glad you stopped by. I need your help hanging these mirrors. I wasn't expecting to see you."

He wasn't expecting to see his oldest friend, either. He hadn't even expected to leave his shop that morning, but restlessness drove him out. And Cherri's sugar-scented scarf. He had stared at the scarf for two whole days. Its soft scent filled his workshop, overpowering the paint fumes and oil. It served as a constant reminder of her, distracting him from his duties. And like a fool he watched the door waiting for her to stop by and finish the stool he should have never offered her in the first place.

But she never came. He had hurt her feelings the other day. Lord knew he hadn't meant to.

It was just that she drove him batshit crazy and he wasn't used to that. With all the other women in his life he had been in control, or at least he thought he was.

*You should have stayed away today.*

He saw a new side of her when she was caring for her grandmother. It made him think: What would it feel like to have someone love him like that? It made him realize how alone he was. His father was busy with his women. He hadn't seen his half sister in a decade. He never knew his mother. He didn't have a family. He wasn't getting any younger. Maybe it was time for him to change.

*When did I become so fucking maudlin?*

"Hey, O'Connell! If I knew you were going to stand around like a goddamn bump on a log I would have gotten somebody else to help me."

"I was thinking," he said, pulling himself from his deep thoughts. "And maybe you should have." He snatched the tape measure from Mike and quickly measured the glass. "I think you're taking advantage of my plethora of skills and my pleasing personality. Your cheap arse should hire somebody like every other bloke in this town."

"Why should I?" Mike bent down to make a pencil mark on the wall. "I moved back to Durant so I could exploit your labor."

"And here I thought it was because you wanted to be near me. I was beginning to think you fancied me."

"Nah, I like my men with tighter asses."

Colin grinned at that parting shot as they hoisted the

heavy mirror on the wall and secured it in place. It was easy to work with Mike. The two of them had been flat mates in college and caused so much trouble that they should have been kicked out. But they made it through, and somehow over the four years Mike had become his family, taking him home for holidays and long summer breaks. Mike's mother and three sisters gave him a glimpse of what a real family could be like. It made him think it was possible for him to have one.

"You think you want kids, Edwards?"

Mike paused and looked at him thoughtfully. "Yeah. I didn't think so before. Ellis and I agreed we weren't going to but lately . . . I don't know. I've been having this urge to see my wife pregnant, and I see the way she looks at babies. I think she might want to have some, too."

"You going to talk to her about it?"

He nodded. "But not for a few months. We need to open the bridal salon before we think about having a baby."

Colin chuckled. His best friend the former badass detective had quit his job to spend his days working in a dress shop.

"What the hell are you laughing at?"

"You. If somebody told me that you would have traded in your gun for a handbag I would have called them a liar."

Mike shrugged. "I fell in love. Didn't expect that to happen, either, but since I did, nothing else seems to matter to me but her happiness."

Colin had never thought Mike was capable of that kind of love—the change-who-you-are kind of love—but apparently he was. He gave up his life to make a woman happy and in return he found happiness that Colin had never seen before. While thoughts of starting a life and a family filled his mind, he wasn't sure he could ever have what his friends had.

Once upon a time he thought he was in love. He thought

he would be married by now, but Serena had shattered that dream when she betrayed him. When he found out about her deception it knocked him on his ass. But when he was finished licking his wounds he realized that he'd never loved her the way Mike loved his wife. He wasn't willing to change his life for her. He wasn't sure there was a woman out there he was prepared to do that for.

"Aww, lad." He smirked, pulling himself away from his thoughts again. "You should trade in your bollocks right now. I think you're becoming a woman."

He shrugged. "Who cares? Have you seen my wife? Who's been warming up your sheets lately?"

"Nobody," he said with a grimace.

"What the hell happened to you?" Mike said teasingly. "Ever since I've known you, you haven't gone more than two weeks between women. You must be losing your touch."

"Fuck you," he said without heat. His friend had a point. He was the guy who always had a woman, a girlfriend, somebody to fill his nights. But when he hit thirty he realized he was turning into his father. His didn't want to be Magnus. He didn't want to be over fifty and still chasing tail. "I've just become more selective now that I'm mature."

"Mature? Don't you mean old?"

"We're the same age for fuck's sake!"

"Yeah, but I've been married for a year and you're still scratching your ass."

"You're a cocky arsehole when you're getting laid," he said, but part of him envied his friend. Maybe it was time he got serious about settling down.

At thirty-three degrees it was the warmest day of the week.

"Take Rufus for a long walk, pixie. He's been inside for too long. That's why he tries to escape." She scratched behind Rufus's ears. "You've been sad, yes? You are upset with Cherri because she has been taking you on those shitty five-minute walks. She doesn't mean to make you miserable, but she is an American. Americans cannot take the cold like Ukrainians. We have much thicker blood. She wouldn't last five minutes in my homeland."

Cherri looked at her grandmother as she insulted her and shook her head. Baba was right. She had been taking Rufus on short walks and it had nothing to do with the cold. She didn't like leaving Baba alone in the house since she'd found her walking past Size Me Up. And for the past week a rotating cast of Baba's friends had been taking turns staying with her when Cherri had to work.

"Come with me. We can go to the park with the big lake in it. You like it there. The doctor said it would be good for you to get some exercise."

"Bah." She waved her hand. "I'm not going to the park, it's too cold. Walk the dog."

Cherri shut her eyes for a moment, trying to pull strength from somewhere. Baba had been fine since her doctor adjusted her medication. No traces of forgetfulness, no disorientation. In fact, she had been sharper than ever, but Cherri still didn't want to go.

"Please, Baba." She opened her eyes. "I'll buy you a cupcake when we're finished walking."

"Buy me a cupcake anyway. A chocolate one. I'm fine, pixie, stop being such a worry mole."

"Worrywart, Baba. Worrywart."

"Whatever. Judge Judy is on." Baba turned on her television and turned away. The conversation was over. Cherri had to go walk the dog.

If she had to walk the dog, she was glad she lived in such a good place to do it. Durant was dubbed a walker's paradise. It was a college town nestled in the middle of a mountain range, populated by a mixture of former hippies, New York City transplants, and people who could trace their history back to the first settlers. And because all of those people cohabited, it made for a pretty cool-looking town. Historic buildings were mixed with colorful modern ones on the tree-lined streets. Coffee shops, independent bookstores, and funky art galleries were mixed in with little mom-and-pop shops.

And as she came upon the big open space that was Elder Park she knew she couldn't leave this place. For weeks she had been looking for jobs as an art teacher. Yesterday evening she finally found one. It was nearly an hour away. But the pay was great and they wanted her to come in for an interview as soon as possible. One of her former professors' husbands was the principal. The job was hers if she wanted it.

But it was an hour away. Not close enough to get to Baba if she needed to. Too far away from Durant to ask Baba to move with her.

Plus she really didn't know if she wanted to be an art teacher. She liked kids. She loved art, but she wasn't sure that's what she wanted to do with the rest of her life.

*You're just scared.*

The money would come in handy. She loved Ellis and Belinda. She loved Size Me Up, but she needed benefits and sick days and a salary. And . . .

"Is that my favorite escaping dog?" She looked up at the sound of Colin's voice. Rufus did, too, and bounded toward him, nearly pulling her arm out of its socket as he did.

She let go of his leash as he leapt up to put his paws on Colin's chest.

"Hold on, boy." He gave Rufus a rough pat before he gently pushed the dog away. "You almost yanked her arm clear off." He approached her, placing his bare hand on her cheek. "You okay, love? I thought you were going to topple over for a minute there."

"I hate him," she said without heat.

Rufus whimpered, clearly hurt by her words.

"She don't hate you, boy. You've just got to calm down a bit. She's a lady. You've got to have a soft touch with her. Trust me, if you do she'll be eating out of your hand."

"I can just see you saying that to your son. But I'm afraid that's not true. For most women it takes more than just a soft touch to make us melt. We're all not that easy."

"No?" He stroked his thumb over her cheek. He leaned in and placed a very soft kiss on her other cheek.

She shivered and not from the cold. Her eyes almost drifted shut and she was tempted to lean into this warmth, into his kiss, but she didn't. It would give him too much satisfaction. So she forced her eyes up to his. "Maybe the women you date are, but not all of us are. Some of us have standards."

"Maybe that's why we are just friends and not lovers." He stroked his thumb over her cheek again. "You're way too smart for me."

She blinked at him, confused by his words, by his actions, by the way he looked at her as if they were more than they were.

She thought back to the kiss he gave her. It was innocent. She kept telling herself that, because if it wasn't an innocent kiss . . .

She didn't like that that he made her feel confused, that he made her feel uneasy. This was not their relationship. They were friends. Kind of. Sort of. They were supposed to be comfortable around each other. She was a social disaster with nearly everybody else. She refused to be that way with him. So she did the only thing she could think to do. She teased him.

"Why is it okay for men to go around doing everything with a pulse, but it's not okay for women to do that? Can you enlighten me? Is it like a secret male gene that we don't know about that gives you the undeniable urge to stick your poles in every honeypot that's open."

She had gotten to him. The slight smile he had melted off his face. "For fuck's sake, girl. Why are you going on about that?"

"It's just not fair. Women have urges, too. And needs. We see hot guys on the street and think *Hey, I might like a piece of that.* Why isn't it okay for me to go up to a guy in a bar and take him home?"

"Because he could be a bloody murderer, that's why!"

"And I can't be? It's unfair. Men get to have all the fun. They get to have all the sex and be all the serial killers. And you know what? Women line up to marry those suckers while they're in prison. Why don't you see men lined up at women's prisons? Huh? Nobody ever thinks about that."

Colin shook his head, looking more chagrined than she had ever seen him, and then he pulled her close, placed his lips on her forehead and gave her a kiss. "Sometimes I find you damn adorable, Cherri Rudy, and sometimes you drive me so fucking nuts I think about dunking you in that lake over there."

"Really?" She looked up at him, rather pleased with herself. "Not the lake part, but the adorable part? I'm six feet tall. I don't think anybody has ever used that word to describe me. Not even when I was a baby. You know I was born with size-nine feet? I bet you I'm in the record books somewhere."

"Shh." Colin slid his hands up to her shoulders. "Just be quiet, beauty. You'll drive a man batty."

He called her beauty. He probably called all women that, but it didn't stop the rush of pleasure that traveled through her. He was looking at her again, studying her face, drinking her in almost, and right then she would have paid a million dollars to see into his mind, to get a tiny glimpse of what he was thinking. She would also pay a small fortune to close the little gap between them and press his lips to hers. They looked warm on this cold day—in fact, right now they looked the way a warm blanket felt.

"I finished the stool," she blurted, trying to snap herself from those thoughts. They were dangerous. "I can drop it off."

He looked taken aback by the rapid subject change but nodded absently. "I'll swing by later to get it. How are you, love? You look beat. How's your gran? I forgot to ask."

"Baba?" It took a few moments for his words to sink in. "She's been her normal pain-in-the-ass self."

"That's good," he said softly. "You love her very much."

She nodded. "She's my world. My mother left when I was a kid, so it was just me and my grandparents, and then when Papa died it was just me and her."

"Where's your father?"

She shrugged. "Don't know him. Baba says he went to the university, but she never told me anything else. I don't think my mother told her much more than that. But we do know Natasha had a thing for football players. It makes sense considering my linebacker build."

"You're built like a woman, love. Trust me. You don't look anything like a football player."

"I wasn't fishing for compliments," she said seriously. She'd rather he not give them. It only confused her more. They were silent for a long moment. "You know all about me. But I know very little about you. Tell me about your family."

His expression grew guarded, and for a moment she thought she had touched on a raw nerve. "There's not much to tell. I never knew my mum. I get along with my pop but we never see each other and my sister only calls me once a year on my birthday."

"You've got a sister?" Her eyes widened at the news. "I never knew that about you."

"Well, not many people know. I haven't seen the little thing since she was a kid. Her mum lived with us for a year." He shrugged. "I liked Mary. I thought she would have stuck around, but my father was too much of a womanizer for her. So she left and married some English chap. They live in London now. The last time I saw Rebecca was when I stayed with them the summer before I came to America."

"Do you miss her?" It was none of her business and yet she had to know. Colin was always a mystery to her, so far away and yet so close. Learning about him made him real to her.

"As much as a man can miss his near-stranger half sister. It would have been nice if she had stayed near. I'm sure she's a good lass but I feel like it's my duty as a big brother to scare the bloody hell out of any man who comes near her."

"How old is she?" Cherri asked.

"She'll be twenty-one in June."

"Oh, so we're close in age." That explained a lot.

"You are."

"Is that why you treat me like a kid?"

"I don't treat you like a kid all the time," he said gruffly. "I know all too well how grown you are."

"Oh." She didn't know what to say to that so she changed the subject. "Do you have plans for Christmas Eve?"

"Mike and Ellis invited me over for dinner but I'd rather chew off my leg than sit through dinner with those two again."

"But Mike's your best friend," she said, surprised at his answer.

"Yeah, but when he's with Ellis he ceases to be an individual person. They tend to morph together into a creature with one mouth and four arms."

Cherri threw her head back and laughed. "Oh my God, you're right! They're all over each other."

"It's a bit sickening," he said absently. She had such a rich laugh, it changed her whole face. Her eyes sparkled. Her cheeks grew pink. It made her pretty, and for a moment he was so caught up in listening to her, in trying to ignore the stirring that had been going on in his groin since he'd first walked up to her, that he almost didn't hear Rufus whimpering beside him.

"What is it, boy?" he said as Rufus rubbed his head against his thigh. The dog was a reminder that he was getting too close to her. He must be in a sorry state. He found her chatter adorable, the innocence in her eyes refreshing, the way she got under his skin alarming and charming.

The only way he could describe it was like he was going through life seeing everything in gray; and then she came along, and she was like brilliant blasts of vivid color.

*Look at you, you wanker. You've turned into a bloody poet.*

He pulled his eyes off her and stepped away, hoping to clear his nose of her sweet, soft scent. "You feeling neglected, old man?"

"I'm supposed to be walking him," she said, looking down at her charge.

He always knew she had a lot on her plate, but he'd never realized how much she actually did. And alone, too. She had no one to lean on. Most twenty-two-year-olds had their parents to guide them, but Cherri didn't. She had her grandmother, but Cherri did more for the old woman than the old woman did for her.

She didn't need to be taken care of, but he wished that she had somebody to do so. "I don't think he needs to be walked. I think he needs a good run around." He picked up a nearby stick and gave it a mighty throw. Rufus took off after it, his leash flying in the wind. "Let me get that off him before he chokes himself. We'll play a nice game of catch. I'll make him good and tired so he'll be a calm boy tonight."

"You don't have to do that, Colin," she said softly.

"I do." He gave her arm a squeeze. He needed to get away from her just for a few moments, to clear his head and think of all the reasons that he shouldn't want her.

*She's lovable.*

*She needs to be loved.*

He wasn't the man for the job.

"I don't mind. I like the bugger." He trotted off after the dog who was sitting about twenty feet away with the stick in his mouth, just staring at Colin. "I thought the point of playing fetch was that you're supposed to bring it back?" Colin said to the dog when he reached him. He removed the leash, but when he went to reach for the stick Rufus turned his head so that he couldn't get it.

"Give it here, mutt." Rufus got up, took four steps away from Colin, and sat, looking up at him expectantly for his next move. "Oh, so we're playing that game." Colin took a step forward. Rufus took a step forward. Colin lunged. Rufus darted. "I want that stick, dog." Colin ran full-speed at him and Rufus took off like a shot, running halfway across the park. He knew that there was no way he could catch the dog, but he ran after him anyway. It was a long time since he had played with a dog. It was a long time since he'd had fun like this. When he was a lad he used to chase after his granddad's dog, Lucky, until they were both panting and exhausted. That's what Rufus needed, a child to play with, to chase after.

Suddenly the dog stopped, dropped the stick, and growled, but not at Colin, at something behind him. Colin turned around to see what the matter was.

He nearly growled, too. There was a man with Cherri.

"That is one fast dog."

Cherri looked away from Colin and Rufus and smiled at Dr. Brightworth as he walked toward her. "I know. It's kind of surprising with all the heavy food Baba feeds him. The other day I caught her giving him éclairs." Her cheeks burned. "I shouldn't have told you that. You of all people! Oh yes, Mr. Veterinarian, we feed our dog chocolate and fried foods, but you already knew that. You're probably going to call the ASPCA as soon as you leave here."

"Relax." He took a step closer, touched her shoulder, and looked into her eyes. "Everybody needs a little sweet something sometimes."

She blushed again. She knew his words were innocent, but the way he said them—well, they didn't sound so innocent. "You'll give me a pass this time," she said, taking a step to the side so she could watch Colin and Rufus play, "but I know how this works. You'll scold me for not feeding him that fancy dog food that your staff keeps trying to push on me at every visit."

"It's good-quality food. I feed my own dog that stuff, but let's not talk about work."

She glanced at him. "What would you like to talk about?"

"Colin O'Connell."

She gave him her full attention. "You know him?"

"Yes. He's done work for my family for years. My mother cried when she saw the restoration he did on her great-grandfather's writing desk. He's actually the reason I'm in the park today. I wanted to get his opinion on restoring the fountain at the north entrance."

"I don't think Colin does that kind of work."

"Maybe not, but he knows the best people who can. I want his contacts. I also want to know if you're dating him."

"Colin?" She nearly snorted. "No. We're definitely not dating."

"Are you seeing anybody else?"

For a moment she didn't answer him, she was so taken aback by his question. "No. I—I. No, I'm not seeing anybody."

"It's a shame. You're very beautiful. I would have thought you would be snatched up by now."

"I thought so, too," she said with a shake of her head. "But then again it's kind of hard to snatch a six-foot-tall girl. Don't you think?"

"I could snatch you up. All six feet of you." He smiled at her. "What would you say if I asked you out?"

*Holy crap.*

He was interested in her. She never thought of Sean Brightworth as a man. Only as Rufus's doctor. The man who treated his ear mites. But now as she stood in front of him she noticed how handsome he was with his all-American looks and subtle charm. He was a man a lot of women would kill to go out with, but he was asking her.

And it freaked her out. "I would say that would be weird. You're my vet. It would be . . . awkward."

"Only if it didn't work out. But you could always take him to Dr. Richards if that happened. I've heard good things about him. Come out with me."

Barking prevented her from answering. Rufus was at her side a moment later and then he sat in front of her, right between her and Dr. Brightworth. Then he growled.

"Rufus," she scolded. "It's Dr. Brightworth. You know him."

"He might still be a little upset with me from the last visit. I had to give him three shots. Dogs don't forget that."

"Nope." Colin walked up, stepping in between them, too, resting his large hand on Rufus's head. "Dogs don't forget anybody who's a threat to them."

"I'm not a threat to him. I only help him."

"Well, if you jabbed three needles in me I wouldn't be fond of you, either. I can't blame the lad. You're with his owner. He's just trying to protect her."

"I don't need protecting." Cherri stepped out from behind

Colin's big shoulders. "*He's* being ridiculous." She shot Colin a look.

"Listen, Cherri. I've got to go," Dr. Brightworth said. "I hope to speak to you soon."

He walked away, leaving Cherri with two growling jackasses. "What the hell was that?"

Colin said nothing to her. He just bent down and kissed Rufus's head. "You're a good lad. Always protect her. Always."

"Colin."

He walked away from her, Rufus immediately following. "I'm going to take you home so I can pick up my stool, but first we are going to stop and get your gran some sweets."

She followed him silently, but only because she couldn't gather the billion thoughts that were spinning around in her head.

Maybe she had misinterpreted what just happened. Maybe she misread him, but she was pretty damn sure he had just acted like a macho jackass and chased Dr. Brightworth away.

But why?

He made it clear he only saw as a sister.

She stared at him the entire ride to the bakery. He was stonily silent and with each passing moment she was getting more and more pissed.

"Colin." She broke the silence when he stopped at the bakery. "What the hell is going on?"

"I'm bringing your gran some sweets. In my country you bring a person a gift when you go 'round to visit them." His words were clipped. His face unreadable. He was pissed off.

But what right did he have to be?

He just looked at her for a long second and walked away.

She sat in the car fuming. And when he came back he

didn't even acknowledge her, just turned to Rufus, her traitorous dog, and gave him a large dog biscuit.

"What the hell just happened?"

"I'm giving him a biscuit. He's a good lad. He protects you. That's his job."

He put the key in the ignition. When she opened her mouth to speak again he turned the radio on loud enough that she would have to shout to be heard above the music.

Something inside of her snapped and she reached down to his thigh to pinch him as hard as she could. He simultaneously yelped and growled.

"What the fuck did you do that for?"

This time it was she who didn't answer. She just changed the station, turned the radio up louder, and sat back in her seat.

The rest of the two-minute car ride to Cherri's house was spent in silence. He was being a wanker, he knew it, but he just couldn't help it. He knew Sean Brightworth. At forty-two years old he was eight years older than Colin, and even though they never went to school together Colin knew Sean well. They frequented the same parties while Colin was at Durant University. Sean had no business being there even then. He was the guy who never wanted to grow up, the guy who never seemed to want to leave college. Colin never liked him. He couldn't put his finger on it, but something about Sean just wasn't genuine. Or maybe it was the fact that he'd never lost his taste for coeds. He just knew he didn't want the man around Cherri.

He pulled up to her house and stepped out of the truck, Rufus at his heels.

"If you can't be bothered to speak to me, then you shouldn't bother coming into my house," Cherri said from behind him.

"Trust me, I'm not here to see you. I want to say hello to your gran and then I'm out of here." He walked ahead of her and opened the front door. "Don't you bloody women ever lock the damn door? Somebody is going to ransack the place one day."

"Baba said locks don't keep people out, but her knife does."

He thought back to his first meeting with the old woman. The nutter had a point. "Baba, lass. Where are you?"

Baba appeared at the end of the short hallway that led to the bedrooms. "My boyfriend is here." She smiled at him. Even at seventy-five he could see the earthy beauty in her. Cherri was lucky to have such genes. "What's in the box?"

"Red velvet whoopie pies."

Baba groaned. "Bring them here."

"Baba, you shouldn't eat those. You already had a Danish this morning. The doctor said only one sweet a day."

Baba cocked one of her gray brows at Cherri, staring her down. "You were supposed to bring me a cupcake. You just don't want to let me have fun with my boyfriend. Leave us alone."

"Fine. You want to eat them, go ahead. I don't care! You're impossible. He's a jackass. You deserve each other."

She stomped away. For a moment Baba and Colin grinned at each other. "She's quite cute when she's mad," he said to Baba.

"Yes, come talk to me."

They closed themselves in her bedroom. He hadn't planned it but somehow he had gotten in the habit of visiting Baba. He liked her. He liked to talk to her. Mike's mother had been there for him, but after a serious health scare and years of caring for everybody else she was taking time for herself. He couldn't begrudge her that. Still, he missed her. Baba provided him the something motherly that he was missing in his life.

"She's mad at you," she said once she settled into her chair.

"Why do you assume she's mad at me?"

"You are a man, no? What's going on with you and my pixie? Have you seen her panties?"

"What? No. Of course not."

"Of course not? What is wrong with Cherri? She is beautiful. You should be lucky to see her panties."

"Baba!"

"Go. Make her un-mad and leave me alone with my red velvet."

"Maybe I shouldn't. You never told me your doctor said one sweet a day."

This time Baba cocked her brow at him. He got up. He knew better than to argue with the old woman.

Cherri was in the kitchen. Her back was turned, but Rufus was by her side, just sitting there watching her. Cherri claimed that Rufus belonged to Baba, but he was her boy. She fed him and walked him and took care of him. He might have been a pain in the ass but he was her pain in the ass.

"What the hell happened in the park this afternoon?" she asked without turning around. "If I didn't know any better I would think you were trying to chase Dr. Brightworth away from me."

"It wasn't clear that I was doing so?"

At that comment she turned around.

"What? Why?"

He wondered if he should tell her what he knew about Sean. The stories he had heard over the years. The things he had seen. Sean Brightworth wasn't a bad guy, but he was a guy who liked to party as hard as he worked. He was way too much for Cherri.

"I've known him for years. He's just not somebody you should be getting involved with."

"He's a good man and a good vet. Who the hell said I was getting involved with him? We were just talking."

Just talking? No it was more than that. He stood too close to her. He touched her. He was so focused on Cherri that he didn't notice Colin approaching. He almost couldn't blame the man. Cherri had that kind of effect on him, too. "What were you talking about? Even fifty feet away I could tell he just wasn't being social. What did he say to you?"

"It's none of your business."

The way she said it. The way she crossed her arms across her chest. He knew. "He asked you out, didn't he?"

"So what if he did?"

"So what? He's twenty years older than you."

"Just because you think I'm a child doesn't mean the rest of the world does."

"This is not about that."

"But it is! You just made it a point to mention how much older he is than me."

"He is twenty years older than you. It's just a fact. He's never been married. He's never had a serious relationship. There's a reason for that."

"Really? He sounds just like you."

That hit a nerve. He may have had his share of women but he never mistreated them. Sean was going to discard Cherri like a used tissue. "All he wants to do is fuck you and forget you."

"Excuse me?" She rounded on him, jabbing her finger into his chest. "You are not my father or my brother. Hell, sometimes I wonder if we are even friends. I do not need you or Mike or anybody else interfering with my life. I can see who I want. So what if he just wants to fuck me. Maybe I want that. Maybe that's just what I need."

"Don't say that." He couldn't see his sweet Cherri with Sean. It made his stomach churn.

"Don't tell me what to do. I know exactly what I'm getting myself into."

"Do you?" He grabbed her by the waist, his control snapping. Her soft body slammed against his and for a moment she struggled but he held firm. "Have you ever had a boyfriend?

Not some green lad, but a real man?" He slid his hands up the back of her shirt, and she stopped moving. Her eyes widened. Her face went flush. It was as if his hands had developed a mind of their own. They brought her closer. They wanted him to smell her scent, and feel her skin, and have every inch of her long beautiful body against his. "Do you know what it's like to be with man?" he whispered roughly in her ear. "To have one on top of you? Inside of you? Can you handle it, lass? Would you even know what to do?"

"Stop it." Tears flashed in her eyes. "You're being cruel."

"Cruel?" The word was like a bucket of ice water to his face. "Oh no, love."

"You know I don't get asked out. You know how hard it was for me to grow up being this tall, looking like this. And when somebody does asks me out, when somebody does finally like me, you try to take it away. You try to make me feel ashamed of the way I am."

"No, Cherri." He palmed the back of her neck in his hand and kissed her cheeks. "No. No." He smothered kisses across her forehead, down the bridge of her nose. "That's not what I meant." He should tell her the truth. He should tell her that she made his damn heart beat faster. That he thought about her more often than he should. That seeing her with another man, knowing that somebody out there wanted what he did, was too much for him. But he didn't say that. Because he couldn't. In a way she was right. For a year after Serena, and his entire adult life before her, it had been woman after woman. Party after party. He had lived his life. He had had his freedom. But she was just starting out. She didn't need the likes of him or Sean Brightworth in her life. "You're so beautiful, love. Why can't you see that? Why don't you know I would never try to hurt you like that?"

"You should go," she said softly.

"No. Not yet. Not until I convince you that I would never hurt you so." He pushed his fingers deep into her hair, and she rested her head on his shoulder. "I can't leave here until you've forgiven me."

"Pixie?" Colin turned slightly at the sound of Baba's voice but he didn't let go of her. And when he locked eyes with the old woman he knew she knew how he felt. "Are you still angry?"

"Yes. Colin is going to take us to a very expensive dinner one of these days to make up for it. When's the last time you had a good steak?"

"Get your coats," he said. Cherri had it right. There wasn't anything he wouldn't do to make it up to her. "I know a great little place about an hour away. We can have an early supper."

# CHAPTER 7

*The trouble with love is . . .*

The house phone rang as soon as Cherri got home two days later. The sound barely registered. The phone was always for Baba, who had a surprisingly active social life. Cherri grinned as she shed her coat, hat, gloves, and scarf.

*My grandmother has more friends than I do.*

She blew into her icy hands in a vain attempt to bring feeling back to them. It was still bitterly cold, and the walk home from work had been brutal. She'd thought about taking the car this morning when she'd heard it was going to be four degrees but decided against it. The old girl was on her last legs and she didn't want to risk her breaking down in the middle of the road. She kept telling herself the walk was good for her.

"Cherri," Baba yelled from the back of the house. "The phone is for you."

For a split second she thought about not answering her grandmother. The old woman couldn't hear her television but she knew exactly when Cherri stepped foot through the door. She just wanted to warm up and relax for a few minutes. She hadn't slept much last night and the store had been extremely busy that day, leaving Cherri barely enough time for a break. There were a lot of men there, rushing to find last-minute Christmas presents for their wives. Hopefully her check would be nice and fat next week so she could pay the taxes on the house, which were a few months overdue.

It was why she had taken yesterday morning off from work to go on that interview for the teaching position. The school was beautiful. The staff was kind and welcoming. Plus they told her she could have a hand in planning the curriculum. The job was hers. All she had to do was accept.

It was a dream job.

But she wasn't sure if she wanted it. It wasn't just the commute. It wasn't just that she didn't want to be so far away from Baba. She really didn't know what she wanted to do with the rest of her life.

Colin had it right. He owned his own business and he made things beautiful again. He had his own schedule. He was his own boss. She envied him. Why couldn't she have it like that?

"Pixie! I'm calling you."

"Coming," Cherri responded, holding back a sigh. When she finally made her way to the phone her grandmother was tapping her foot, annoyed as if Cherri made her wait three years instead of thirty seconds. "I'll take it in the other room."

"Don't be on the phone too long. You need to help me finish cooking."

She nodded and walked into the living room, realizing she'd forgotten to ask who called. "Hello?"

"Hello, Cherri. It's Sean."

"Oh," was all she said. She was surprised to hear from

him after Colin chased him away in the park. "Hi. You're calling me at home?"

He was silent for a long moment. "I'm sorry. Maybe I overstepped. I just wanted to talk to you. You never did officially turn me down. I thought I'd call and get my heart broken."

"I'm sorry. I don't know what to say to you."

Colin had gotten to her. She kept thinking back to two days ago in her kitchen. She played the scene over and over in her head, but she couldn't make sense of what transpired between them. She should hate him. She should be mad at him, but she knew he wasn't trying to hurt her. He was trying to protect her, even if that was the last thing she wanted.

She also wondered if maybe he was right about Sean. That maybe he only wanted to sleep with her. But when she thought about it, the idea was ridiculous. Even though Cherri was freakishly tall and the opposite of petite, she knew she wasn't ugly. Some days she even felt quite pretty but it seemed that it would take more than a passing prettiness to attract a man like Sean. He had to be interested in her as a person. The fact that he'd called again made her sure of that.

"Say you'll go out with me."

"You treated my dog's anal gland infection. Somehow it just doesn't seem right."

"If you go out with me I'll treat the next infection for free," he laughed. "Come on, Cherri. I like you. I just want to get to know you. But . . . I realize that I'm probably coming on a little strong. I'll back off. If you want to go out with me, call me. I promise to show you a good time."

"Okay, Sean. I will."

"Cherri! Come help me."

"My grandmother's calling me. I've got to go."

"Good-bye, Cherri."

"Good-bye, Sean." She disconnected. "Coming, Baba."

She got up, stretching out her sore muscles, and made her

way to the kitchen wondering how her grandmother could have so much energy after the hard night they'd had last night. Baba's memory had been fine since the change in medication but last night she was anxious, terrified that somebody was trying to break into the house. That wasn't like the woman she had grown up with, who once punched a man in the face for mistreating his dog. She wouldn't calm down even after Cherri had checked all the doors and windows twice. Eventually she settled but only after Cherri climbed into bed with her. It reminded her of the times when she was a little girl, after her mother had gone for good, when the nighttime was terrifying. Baba used to climb in bed with her and soothe her until she fell asleep. Things were the same now, just reversed. The only difference was Baba hadn't slept at all last night. She was quiet, but the vise-like grip she kept on Cherri's hand caused that tight little ball of worry in Cherri's belly to return. It was the news, she tried to tell herself to explain away Baba's behavior. There had been break-ins a few towns over. That had to be it. From now on she was going to have to monitor what Baba watched before she went to bed. Cherri didn't think her body could handle many more nights like the last.

And she knew she couldn't take that job.

Colin shifted on his couch in a fit of restlessness. *It's a Wonderful Life* was playing. Again. Every time he turned on the television it seemed to be on. Or *A Christmas Carol.* Or *Miracle on 34th Street.* Or *Elf.* Even those damn *Peanuts* kids were on constantly. Every movie, every television show, every damn commercial had the same message: *If you don't have a family then your life is meaningless.* No wonder people got depressed around the holidays. He was pretty sure it was a conspiracy created by the drug companies to boost their sales of antidepressants.

"You're madder than a sack of cats," he mumbled to

himself as he reached for the remote. There had to be something else on. Ah, *Pawn Stars.* He tried to pay attention to the guy who clearly had no idea that the Civil War–era knife he was trying to sell was a fake, but his thoughts drifted.

Christmas was never his favorite holiday, even as a kid. There was no Santa Claus for him, no funny little cartoons. It wasn't as commercialized in Ireland as it was in America. Most people gathered together as families, went to midnight mass, had a big meal, and exchanged a few small presents. His experience was a little different. If Magnus had a woman at the time, he would drag Colin to her house to dine with her family. If he didn't, they'd go to Molly's, the only place open in their town, and afterward spend the evening the way they spent every evening: fixing other people's things. It was the way Magnus supported them. Unlike most people, Christmas didn't mean much to Colin. It was just another day.

"Colin!" A voice called his name, starling him from his memories. "It's cold out here."

Who the hell was bothering him on Christmas Eve? He got to his feet and opened the door to find a heavyset older woman whose hair was covered in a scarf and hands were full of aluminum-foil-wrapped pans.

"Let us in, Irish," she said in her thick accent and pushed past him. "I'm freezing my breasts off out here."

"Baba, it's freezing my ass off. Not breasts," Cherri called after the old lady.

"Are you telling me what is freezing on my body? Come look at them and you will see!" She then said something in a language he didn't understand and disappeared farther into the house.

"Hi," Cherri said softly, her face a pretty shade of embarrassed pink. "She wants to know where your kitchen is. Oh, and we're here for Christmas."

Seeing her here caused a funny warm feeling to spread through his belly. He thought she was still angry with him over Sean. But she was here. The corners of his mouth tugged upward. "Are you?" He wanted to throw his head back and shout with laughter. She looked so adorable wrapped up in countless layers, but he didn't laugh because she looked so . . . unsure of herself.

"Is it okay that we're here? You said you weren't doing anything that day in the park and I . . . we wanted to feed you."

She was sweet, and the urge to kiss the uncertainty off her lips overwhelmed him. Instead he squeezed her arm and invited her in.

Sometimes when she thought of Colin she imagined what kind of place he lived in. For some reason she had pictured black leather couches and sleek modern furniture. A bachelor pad. But she should have known better just by seeing his work. What she stepped into was beautiful. Big. Old. Victorian, with hardwood floors so shiny she was afraid to walk on them. This was more than a house for him. It was a home.

His fingers brushed hers, and she was alerted to the fact that she was gawking.

"Let me take that from you, love."

Her cheeks burned. *Crap.* She was nervous. She'd argued with herself all day before she decided to walk over. Maybe they shouldn't have come—well, barged in—but she hadn't asked him beforehand because she didn't want to give him the chance to say no. The thought of him spending the holidays alone made her feel . . . hollow. Not sorry for him, but understanding. She only had Baba, and she hoped that she was never faced with spending Christmas alone.

"It's board games, homemade chocolate chip cookies, and good vodka," she said as he lifted the heavy box with ease.

"Good vodka?" He gave her a lazy smile that did more to her than she would like to admit, then headed in the same direction Baba had taken off in.

"Yes, it's Russian vodka. My grandfather's favorite. You can tell it's good because the label isn't in English."

"Tell me something, love." He glanced back at her. "What the hell are you anyway?"

She grinned, having been asked that question a lot. "I'm Ukrainian."

He looked confused. "But you speak Russian?"

"It's okay, honey. Most people can't find Ukraine on a map but we border Russia so our cultures overlap. And yes, I speak three languages fluently. My papa refused to speak to me in English till I picked up Russian."

"That's a bit fucked up." He led her into his dining room, which was enormous for a single man. Again Cherri's eyes drank in everything about the room. Nothing was new, or cookie-cutter, or had seen the inside of a store in the last thirty years. It was him.

"I was a pretty quick study," she said absently unable to stop herself from studying everything.

He set the box down on his table.

"This is amazing," she breathed. It was a French door turned into a dining room table. But that alone didn't make it special. In between panes of glass were black-and-white photos, serving as a time line into his past. There were a few of Colin and Mike back in their college days, with drinks in their hands and naughty-boy grins on their faces; one captured him as a boy sitting on his father's lap. There were places he had been, people he had met, and friends who had made an impact on him over the years. But the photo that caused her breath to catch was of her. She was barefoot, on the beach in a little sundress, a sprig of baby's breath tangled in her hair, smiling at something the camera didn't capture.

*Shiitake mushrooms.*

Her heart slowed as she looked up at him. He had a picture of her? She warranted a spot on the table? "This was taken at Mike and Ellis's wedding."

He nodded once. "Your real name isn't Cherri. Is it? It's a bit odd for a girl."

"Charlotte." He was changing the subject! "You made this? You put all these pictures in here?"

"No. It came like that. Got it off eBay. How did you get that name?"

"Soap opera." She faced him, hands on her hips, unwilling to let the subject go. "My mother liked it. Why am I on here?"

He stepped closer. Damn, he was tall, and apparently not easily cowed. "I like the name Charlotte and you're on there because it's a good picture and I needed something to fill that space."

"Oh." That shut her up. It was a logical explanation. There was no need to read anymore into it. Right? "It's a beautiful table. When I get rich I want you to make me one."

"You don't need to be rich, Charlotte. You can use this as your down payment." He turned away for a moment, pulling an envelope off the hutch in the corner and handing it to her.

*Holy rotten metal, Batman!*

His grin grew wider, and she had the urge to pinch him. "It's for the stool."

"The stool?" She frowned. "You're not supposed to pay me. You fixed Baba's music box."

"Lass, when I asked you to paint that stool I expected a ladybug or a monkey." He set his hands on her shoulders. "You painted an Impressionist-style ballerina. It was brilliant. You deserve this."

"But it was a total rip-off of Renoir's *The Dancer.* I just made it prettier and pinker."

"What you did was make it valuable. That decorator I told you about stopped by this morning. She bought it on the spot for her own house, and she wants you to paint an ottoman for her next."

"What?"

"You heard me. The check is a bribe to get you to work with me."

"Work with you?"

"Yeah. Apparently rich people want to piss away their money on shit they don't need. We could be the supplier of that shit, love."

Before she'd even thought about what he was proposing she wanted to say yes.

*Paint for money? Sign me up.*

But her mind caught up with her heart and she thought for a moment. "You want me to leave Ellis and work for you?" Ellis was her friend and a great boss, but painting was her passion.

"I'm not saying that. We could work around your schedule or you could cut back on your hours there, but seriously, Cherri. That dress shop is Ellis's dream. It's not yours and you're too talented to spend your life working in somebody else's store."

When she opened her mouth to speak, he continued. "You need to paint. It's what you were born to do and if I haven't convinced you yet, you could make more working with me than for her."

His argument sounded really good, almost too good to be true. It had been a long time since she had been able to paint, and when she'd dipped the brush in that creamy pink color, calm had fallen over her. Painting was the only thing that made her truly happy. "You said I would be working with you. Don't you mean for you?"

"No. With me. We'd be partners in this. I can't do this without you. Plus I've got a bum hand. I could use some help around the shop."

She took his bandaged hand between hers and studied it. "What happened?"

"I burned it on the blowtorch. It was stupid. I've been distracted lately."

That made the two of them. "Your bandage is dirty."

"Is it?" he said absently. She could feel his gaze on her face, and for some reason she couldn't force her eyes to connect with his. "I was working in the shop earlier."

"You have to keep it clean, Colin," she scolded. "This is not a little-kid boo-boo. There is no kissing it to make it better."

"It depends on where you kiss me, love." At his flirtatious words, her eyes flew up and locked with his. "Sorry, lass. I shouldn't have said that." He pulled his hand away from hers.

Mortification swept over her. She turned away, sure that her face was molten-lava red. "I should find Baba." She unloaded the box she had brought with her, arranging each item meticulously so that she wouldn't have to look at his handsome face.

"You should answer my question. Are you going to work with me?"

She nodded, even though the thought of spending more time alone with him frightened her. It was a good opportunity. If she passed on this chance she might never get another one. "When do you want me to start?"

"As soon as you can."

"Hey, Irish." Baba shuffled into the dining room. "How are you hanging?"

"What?" He looked startled by her question.

"How's it hanging, she means." Cherri couldn't contain her laughter.

"Oh, I'm fine. How are you feeling?" He wrapped a long arm around her shoulder. "I hope you're not giving Cherri a hard time?"

"Ha! I take good care of her. She would waste away without me." She turned and sniffed Colin. "What are you wearing, Irish? Old Spice? I like it. You smell like a man." She gave his stomach a couple of hard pats. "I like this, too. I could grate cheese on this."

"Baba," Cherri warned before the old woman got too frisky.

"Hush." Baba leveled her with a gaze. "I am old. I'll do what I want." She patted his abs again. "Like a rock! You stay away from this man, pixie. He's not for you."

"Am I for you, love?" Colin kissed Baba's soft, chubby cheek. "You know, I was thinking about starting things up with an older woman. You want to give it a go?"

"Gag!" Cherri shook her head. "Can you two stop this freaky flirting thing? It's turning my stomach."

"Fine," Baba sighed. "It's time to eat. My pixie was worried about you, Irish. She was right. You are too skinny. I made pork roast and three types of potatoes for you. Irish people like potatoes, no?"

"We love 'em. Come ladies, let's eat."

# CHAPTER 8

*Sweet dreams are made of this . . .*

Colin glanced at the clock over the mantel of his fireplace as he stretched out on his couch. It was getting late—nearly ten PM—and he was having a hard time keeping himself from yawning. The Rudy ladies were very entertaining. Ten years ago if somebody would have told him that he was going to have more fun with a senior citizen than he'd ever had at a bar, he would have called them a liar. But Baba was entertaining and so was Cherri. He watched the two playfully go at it all night, his head bouncing like a tennis ball as they went back and forth. They played board games, sipped vodka, and laughed. He was glad that he didn't have to spend the night alone.

"She's out cold," Cherri announced as she reemerged from the back of the house. "I probably shouldn't have let her drink all those shots." They were still in his house. Normally Colin wasn't one to entertain but this time the invasion didn't bother him. He'd purchased the big house because he loved the possibility of it, but he'd never anticipated how empty it would feel.

"She's seventy-five and it's Christmas. Let her have her fun."

"I think she had too much fun." She plopped on the couch beside him, kicking off her shoes in the process. "She's passed out in your guest room wearing only her slip."

"Oh?"

"I was going to wake her up so we could go, but I'm going to let her be for a little while. She hasn't been sleeping well."

"And neither have you." He reached over and brushed the hair out her face. It was late and she was tired, but he'd known when she'd walked in that she wasn't herself.

She yawned widely. "I'm fine." He didn't want to accuse her of lying but she clearly was. Some of the sparkle had gone out of her big green eyes, and he was surprised to find that he missed it. "Are you sure it's okay that we came over? I just planned to feed you, not take up your whole night."

"Don't worry. I'll kick you out before my date comes."

A tiny smile crossed her lips. "Don't let Baba see her. I think you may have a catfight on your hands. Trust me, that old woman is scrappy. I've got the bruises to prove it." She relaxed against the back of the couch, her eyes drifting shut. "Talk to me. So I don't fall asleep. Okay?"

"Okay," he said, but for once he was lost for words. Her curvy body was pressed against him, and just like every other time when he'd felt her against him his brain wasn't functioning correctly. *She's your friend,* he kept reminding himself, *just like all the others.* Except he was having a hard time thinking of another woman he called friend. It was probably because he'd never had one before, and there was a reason for that. Men and women could never really be friends.

Sex always got in the way. He was going to have to try

extra-hard to distance himself from Cherri. Insanity had prompted him to offer her a job, but logically it made sense for both of them. He needed help around the shop and a simple way to expand his business. She needed to use her God-given talents to earn a living.

"Dinner was good," he finally said as her head landed gently on his shoulder. "I can't remember the last time I had a home-cooked meal. Thanks for thinking of me, love."

"I think about you a lot, Colin," she yawned, and before he could respond to her jarring statement she was out cold.

She slept soundly on his shoulder and Colin was content to let her rest her head there all night, but he was getting a crick in his neck from the position. He should wake her up, bundle her and her grandmother into his car, and take them home, but he didn't want to. He didn't want his house to go back to feeling empty so soon. So instead of listening to his brain he responded to his body and pulled her down on the couch so that her soft body lay on top of him.

"What are you doing?" She couldn't even open her eyes to ask the question. "Maybe it's time for us to go home. I left Rufus with the neighbors. They said they would keep him, but I don't want to impose."

"It's after midnight. I don't think they'll take kindly to you knocking at their door now. Go back to sleep. He's a tough lad. He'll survive the night without you." He yanked the blanket that he kept on the couch over them. "You're staying here tonight."

Usually by this time of the night Cherri woke up in a near-Popsicle state, but tonight she found herself deliciously warm. She snuggled closer to her hard bed, trying to absorb more heat into her aching body. Tomorrow was Christmas and for once she had no place to be. Maybe she could steal a few extra hours of sleep and rest up before she had to be back at the store the day after.

Something brushed her lower back and she startled but she refused to open her eyes, afraid of what she might see. If it was a mouse she was going to scream. They'd had this problem two years ago but this time she refused to set sticky traps all over the house. She was getting a cat no matter what Baba said. Whatever it was brushed her back again, but this time it touched her skin beneath her sweater. Warm, firm, and heavy. The mysterious object felt more like a hand than a creepy little mouse.

She opened her eyes and finally recalled where she was. Colin gave her a sleepy smile, those little lines around his eyes crinkling, seeming to smile at her, too. "Hi," she said sheepishly. "You don't have to be polite. You can tell me that I'm squishing you." She tried to get off him but his long arms closed around her like a clamp and she was stuck.

*There's no better place to be stuck than to a hard-bodied, spicy-smelling man.*

"You aren't." He loosened his grip slightly. "I'm comfortable. Now go back to sleep."

If only she could. She felt him everywhere; the tingles she tried so hard to ignore were affecting every part of her body, especially her brain. "There's something hard poking my thigh," she said in a feeble attempt to put some space between them. "Can't you feel that? I think it's the remote."

"Cherri, don't—"

She reached between them and instead of touching hard plastic she felt a different kind of hardness. She trailed the length of it, unable to process what it was, or what she was doing for a moment.

Colin's breath hissed out of him. "For fuck's sake, stop it."

"Oh." Her eyes connected with his. "Oh!" But for some reason she couldn't pull her hand away. She touched him again through his pants, causing him to grow even harder beneath her touch. "It's . . . big."

His expression was somewhere in between horrified and

turned on, and it made her smile. She didn't want to stop touching him. This could all be a dream, and she didn't want to wake up to find she had chickened out. "Tell me, Colin. How did this happen?"

"Knock it off, lass. This isn't funny."

"It's a little funny." She laughed as she stroked his impressive length once more.

"Enough," he growled, and before she knew it she was on her back, her arms pinned above her head. "You want to know how this happened? You're a soft warm woman who smells good and I'd have to be dead ten fucking years not to be affected."

He was pressed between her legs and she felt him *there* and suddenly every tingly feeling in her body had traveled lower and she wanted to feel more of him. All of him, without clothing, but she knew his conscience would never let him get that far. She would just have to settle for a kiss.

He knew what she was planning even before her lips touched his. "Don't do this, lass," he begged her. He was a man after all. He only had so much self-control, and Cherri was beautiful. She did things to his brain and stirred his blood and he wanted her more than he had wanted anybody in as long as he could remember.

He held his body rigid as her soft lips brushed his. If he didn't respond, if he didn't kiss her back, he might have a chance in hell. A very small chance. She tasted like chocolate and vodka. Sweet and intoxicating. Her kiss was gentle, her mouth wet, her tongue exploring. A team of wild horses couldn't force him to drag his mouth away from hers, and so he surrendered. He closed his eyes and let her do what she wanted.

This kiss was different from any other. He had always been the aggressor; the kisser. The one who went after what he wanted but being kissed by her was different. It rocked his world, made him think there was more to sex and love and intimacy than he thought he knew.

"Colin?" She broke the kiss, but he had a hard time opening his eyes. Maybe if he kept them closed he wouldn't have to face the fact that he was kissing the last woman on the planet that he should. "Look at me."

He obeyed her order, wishing he hadn't. Her skin was dewy, her lips pink and kiss-swollen. Her eyes were wide and filled with a need that he wanted so bad to fulfill. "I'm only so strong, lass. Please don't do this to me."

"Kiss me back."

He groaned. "Don't ask me to do that, love."

"Please," she whispered. "Just this once."

*You have no future with this girl.*

*She's not a girl. She's more of a woman than you deserve.*

*You know this is wrong.*

*But it feels right and she did ask very nicely.*

He'd lost the argument with himself and lowered his lips to hers.

"Pixie?" Baba's voice bounced off the walls. It was like a bucket of ice water, a bucket of sorely needed ice-cold water to cool the heat between them. "Where are you? What are you doing?"

"Nothing," she called back. "Colin and I were . . . talking. He said we could stay the night."

"It's after two. I don't leave the house after seven. Of course we're staying but you need to come to bed right now."

"I'm coming." She gave him an impish smile as he lifted up so she could roll from beneath him. "Good night, Colin."

He wanted to tell her that she didn't have to sleep in the same room with her grandmother. His house was huge. There were three other bedrooms she could spend the night in. But his brain knew better. If he knew she was alone in a bed he might not be able to stop himself from crawling in beside her.

•

The temperature gauge on the outside of the store read minus four degrees. That could explain why they'd barely had a customer today. Cherri and Belinda sat side by side in the comfy armchairs Ellis kept in front of the dressing rooms. There was nothing else to do. They both had been at the store for hours. They put out all the remaining stock. They cleaned every surface. They even tried on all the new shoes that had been delivered. Belinda had tried to send her home twice but Cherri refused to go. Baba was playing cards at a neighbor's house and Cherri would rather sit in a cozy warm store with her best friend than alone in an old cold house.

"How is she, Cherri Berry?" Belinda asked, breaking a long comfortable silence.

"Who? Baba?"

"Who else?"

"She's been fine. Still a big pain in my rump."

"I'm a bad best friend. I can't believe I couldn't figure out that that's what has been bothering you. I also can't believe you didn't bother to tell me."

Cherri looked at Belinda, who on the outside looked as glamorous and flawless as ever—but Cherri knew her best friend well enough to see that she was hurt by Cherri's silence.

"I was hoping there was nothing to tell. She's going to be seventy-six soon. I thought it was normal for her memory to slip. I thought it was normal for her to confuse me with my mother. Plus you were away. I didn't want to ruin your vacation by telling you I was scared shitless about my grandmother."

"I would have come home for that, Cherri. All you had to do was call. I would have helped you."

"I know you would have, and that's why I didn't." She

sighed. "I'm not a baby, Belinda, and while I love that you love me enough to rush home to help me, I can take care of myself."

Belinda shook her head. "You are probably one of the most mature twenty-two-year-olds I have ever known but you don't have to do everything by yourself. That's what you have friends for. To lean on." She reached over and gave Cherri's ponytail a hard tug. "Don't ever keep anything like that from me again." She sat up in her chair. "I feel like there's a lot of stuff you haven't been telling me lately."

She should have known she could never really keep anything from Belinda, who was far more perceptive than anybody ever gave her credit for. She always wanted to fix things for everybody. She was always there to comfort.

"I got offered a job," she said. "Well, two jobs actually."

Belinda's mouth dropped open. "I'm going to cry. I knew this day was coming. I'm happy for you but I'm going to miss the hell out of you."

"No you won't. It's a great offer but I don't think I can take it. It's an hour away."

Belinda nodded understandingly. "You can't move from Durant, and you can't be that far away from Baba during the day."

"Yeah. My dilemma."

"I can help," Belinda said, her eyes narrowing the way they did whenever she was brainstorming. "I know they have day care for senior citizens down at the community center. We could sign her up and you can put me and Ellis and Mike down as her emergency contacts. That way if something happens we can get to her right away."

"I couldn't ask you to do that."

"You didn't ask. I volunteered us. We're a family. We help even if some of us don't think to ask for it."

"I know," she said, guilt sneaking up on her. "I'm trying to sort through things in my head. For five years I was so set on becoming an art teacher and now that the time is finally here, I'm not sure that that's what I want to do with my life."

"No? That surprises me. I thought I was the one who could never decide who I wanted to be when I grew up. Sometimes I still try to figure it out. It's okay not to know how you want to spend the rest of your life. It's okay to feel a little lost sometimes."

"You seem to have it all together, Belinda," she said, surprised by the wistful note in Belinda's voice. "I thought you were doing what you wanted to."

"For now." She nodded. "I love working with Ellis and Mike. I love owning a part of this business, but this shop is really Ellis's dream. It's something she talked about since she was a little girl and this is the place she is going to be for the rest of her life. It's going to be her legacy."

"And you feel like you want to leave your own mark on the world."

"Exactly. I just don't know what that mark is." She shook her head. "We were talking about you, though. You said you got two job offers. Tell me about the other one."

"Colin asked me to work for him."

"Ah, Colin." A smile curled Belinda's lips. "So he offered you a job, huh? I hope it's a job servicing all his sexual needs. I'd take that job. Hell, I'd push you in front of a bus just to steal it from you."

A tiny beat of jealousy stirred in Cherri's chest. "Do you have a thing for Colin?"

"Yeah, in the same way I have a thing for Channing Tatum, or that hot guy from *True Blood.* You know I like my men in expensive suits. Colin's too rugged for me. I don't like him like you do."

"I—"

Belinda raised one of her flawless brows at her. "If you lie to me, I'll pinch you."

"Sometimes I want to climb him like a tree," she admitted aloud for the first time.

"So climb him. Ride him. Spank him. Pull his hair. I'm sure he won't mind. Judging by the way he looks at you, I'm thinking he might like it very much."

Cherri frowned as she remembered back to Christmas Eve. Colin let her kiss him. Kiss him when he claimed she was a child. Kiss him when he claimed Dr. Brightworth was too old for her. Kiss him even though he treated her like there was nothing between them but friendship. She shouldn't have kissed Colin. He had heartbreak written all over him. But when she was with him she felt like there was something between them, something she didn't feel with anybody else. Sometimes she thought he might feel it, too.

Except that he thought she was too young. He was just like all her other friends that way.

"I think Colin is looking for a woman a little more his speed."

"He hasn't been looking for a woman at all. At least not lately," Belinda pointed out. "A man like Colin O'Connell doesn't stay single unless there is a reason."

"Maybe he's gay."

Belinda snorted. "And maybe I'm a size four."

"He wants me to paint furniture for him. I already did a piece for him. A tiny little stepstool earned me three hundred dollars."

"That's good money, Cherri."

Money she felt guilty for taking. Painting didn't feel like work to her. If felt like joy. "He showed me the next piece he wants me to do. He's going to charge a thousand dollars for it."

"You get to paint, make big bucks, and stare at Mr. O'Connell all day. I don't blame you for wanting to leave."

"I don't want to leave!" The thought of doing so jolted her. "I could paint after work or before work. Colin said he would work around my schedule."

"No." Belinda shook her head. "You work too hard. Trust me, I'm not kicking you out. If you want to sleep here I would let you, but it's okay to cut back on your time here. You're not just an employee, you're my bestie. You'll always be that no matter how many hours you put in. Besides, if you're not working here all the time we could have more time for fun stuff. You've got to try this thing with Colin for a little while. You should be painting, Cherri. That's your legacy."

"I don't want to leave you guys hanging."

"You won't. Ellis and I knew we were going to lose you eventually." She sighed. "You're too talented to just be a salesgirl. I've gotten a dozen applications from women who want to be a part of Size Me Up. I think it's time we hired some new girls. With the bridal salon opening in a few months, we were going to have to do it anyway. You let us know how many days you want to work and we'll make it happen."

"I feel like crying." They had taken her in off the street when she'd walked in looking for a job. They had given her friendship and support and now they were giving her freedom so she could do what made her happy. They were better to her than she deserved.

"Me too, but all you're doing is cutting back your schedule. When I was your age I picked up and moved to San Francisco. As long as you don't do that I think we can manage to keep it together."

"What did you do in San Francisco? You never talk about it much."

"I got a degree in fashion marketing there. It was the fourth college I had been to, and my third major. Then I had a paid internship there with a decorating firm for a year. Then I worked in a few high-end boutiques and then I fell in love with the wrong man, got my heart stomped on, and came running back here." She shrugged. There was a little sadness in her voice that Cherri couldn't help but notice.

"We were too different. He was a little older and his family was from money. It would have never worked out for us anyway." Belinda looked down at her fingernails, a heaviness settling over her. Cherri was dying to know the details of her friend's great love, but she knew she couldn't ask. Now was not the time.

"Speaking of older men with money, Sean Brightworth asked me out."

"Really?" Belinda wrinkled her nose. "You're young and gorgeous. I'm not surprised a man like him would want to get in your pants."

"You don't think he just wants to get to know me better?"

"Oh Cherri, a man's only goal in life is to get in a woman's pants. If they get to know you in the process, that's a bonus. I'm not saying you shouldn't go out with him. If you want to then by all means do so. Just know what you're getting yourself into."

"Colin says he's too old for me."

"How old is he?"

"Forty-two."

"Oh," Belinda said and then looked away. "I wonder if we are going to get any customers today."

"You changed the subject. Do you think he's too old for me?"

She shrugged. "I want to believe that age is just a number. I know how mature you are, but I wish I knew why some men don't date women their own age. Don't get me wrong, Cherri, you're tall, blond, and gorgeous, but there are so many smart, vibrant, sexy women in their thirties and forties that I can see Sean with. Women he might have more in common with. Twenty years is a big gap, but if you want to see him then far be it from me to discourage you."

"Colin discouraged me. In fact, he and Rufus chased him away in the park a few days ago. He's getting more and more like Mike."

"You're wrong there. He's not like Mike at all. Mike has got the macho serve-and-protect thing going on. Colin likes you. He's got a soft spot for you, honey. I can see it every time he looks at you."

"You're wrong. We're just friends."

"There is no just friends with a guy like Colin. I don't know him as well as Mike and Ellis, but I can tell there's a lot more to him than he lets on. The man has probably gone through ten headboards, he's got so many notches in them, but there's something about him that's hard not to be drawn to. If you want my advice I would say if you're looking for an older man, Colin O'Connell is the kind of man you should go after."

# CHAPTER 9

*Kiss the girl . . .*

Ten forty-five New Year's Eve, and Colin couldn't keep his eyes off the door. He was supposed to be in the middle of playing some game that Ellis had purchased for the occasion, but his mind was elsewhere.

"What the hell is your problem?" Mike complained. "The girls are kicking our asses."

"I know. I'm playing like shit."

Mike looked at him, concern touching his face. "What's up? You're usually kind of an obnoxious dick when we play games. And frankly I like that guy on my team better than you."

"Blow it out your ass, Edwards. I've got a bit of a headache," he lied.

But the truth was he was missing Cherri and not because she wasn't with them, but because he had a feeling deep in his gut that something was wrong. She was supposed to have been there nearly two hours ago but had called to say she was going to be late. What baffled him was that nobody seemed to be concerned. Belinda and Ellis were supposed to be her best friends. Didn't they wonder what was taking her so long? Or was it just him? Had he turned into some kind of crazy mother hen? He needed to get out more. He needed to stay away from Cherri.

Belinda doing a victory dance distracted him from his thoughts for a moment. He needed to shake off the feeling and get his head back in the game.

Eleven o'clock. And the uneasy feeling stuck with him like a tick on a hound dog. "You have any aspirin, lad?" he asked Mike when sitting there pretending to enjoy himself was too much.

"Kitchen," Mike said, studying him. "In the cabinet next to the sink."

He excused himself, but instead of reaching for the medicine he reached for his cell phone and only hesitated a moment before he dialed Cherri's number. It rang and rang and rang and his stomach grew tighter and tighter with each second that passed.

And then she picked up. "Colin?"

Relief coursed through him. "Are you okay, love?"

"Yeah." She sounded tired. "*I'm* fine." The way she said it . . . He knew there was more to her story.

"Where are you, lass?" He would go to her if he had to, just to make sure she was as fine as she said she was.

"Right here." She walked in the kitchen, slipping her phone in the pocket of her jeans.

He stared at her for a moment. She wore the white sweater and boots that traveled up her legs, stopped just below her knees, and made her ass look spectacular. With her hair in those wild loose waves, there could be no mistaking her for a girl. He was faced with a fully grown woman. A woman who had more on her plate than she let on.

"Come here," he ordered. Her eyes were dull, her skin was slightly pale, and his worry returned with a force.

She had barely reached him before he grabbed her, pulled her into his arms, and squeezed her tightly against him. "What's wrong, Colin?"

"I was going to ask you the same thing."

"Oh." She frowned in confusion. "You were worried?"

He nodded stiffly.

"About me?"

"No, about the pandas in China. For fuck's sake, lass. Who the hell did you think I was worried about?"

She smiled at him, her dimples appearing, causing her to look adorably beautiful, if such a thing was possible. "Thank you." She rested her head against his chest, still smiling.

"What happened, Charlotte?" He rubbed his hand down her back, feeling her relax under his touch.

"Baba didn't want me to come out tonight."

"Why not?"

"I don't know. She started crying when I was getting ready to leave. I didn't know what to do. Nobody ever tells you that the woman you thought was invincible won't always be that way."

"But that's life and sometimes it's complete shit."

"I know. I called our neighbor because I didn't know what to do. She forced me out of the house, telling me that it wasn't a young girl's job to take care of an old lady. But it is my job and I feel awful for leaving her." She was quiet for a long moment. "I don't think I can stay long tonight."

"You should have called me. I would have come over." He knew that he should be keeping his distance from her, but being near her was better than wondering and worrying about her all night.

"I didn't think of that." She gave him a small smile. "I'm sure she would have cheered up if you'd showed her your abs."

"All women cheer up when they see my abs, love. It's impossible not to."

Her eyes twinkled but only for the briefest of moments. "She talked about my mother. She said she misses her."

"What happened to her?"

"I don't know. I think they had a fight. She walked out and never came back."

"Sounds a lot like my mum. Aren't we a sad pair of motherless children?"

"We are." She sighed, her eyes drifting shut. "We should head back to the living room." She made no effort to move, and neither did he.

"We should."

He wasn't sure who moved first but soon they were kissing, slowly, lightly, not with passion but with an emotion that made him too uncomfortable to name. It was just like he'd felt on Christmas Eve when he'd kissed her. It was a feeling he didn't want to go.

"I needed that," she said when he broke the kiss.

"Mmm." He tangled his fingers in her curls and kissed her forehead. His brain kept telling him not to, but his body couldn't stop itself from doing so. "I might have to start charging you for those."

"Then I might have to go bankrupt."

They smiled at each other before he let her go. It was Cherri who noticed they weren't alone. She stepped away from him, her cheeks going pink. Mike and Ellis stood in the doorway. Ellis's face was unreadable, but Mike's wasn't. He knew his friend too well. He was going to hear about this later.

She only stayed half an hour before rushing home, not even staying to see the New Year come in. But what surprised him more than that was that she didn't tell the rest of their small party the truth about her grandmother. Instead she made some vague excuse about the old woman not feeling well.

There was more that she wasn't telling even him. Something more serious than a weepy old lady. He wanted to ask her point-blank but it was none of his business. Cherri's problems were not his own.

The party seemed to be coming to an end. The ball had dropped. Kisses had been shared. Mike sat quietly beside him on the couch mindlessly staring at some horrible boy band performing in Times Square. Ellis was busy clearing up the small mess they made. Belinda had gone, and Colin found himself itching to get out of there, too. What happened to him? To them? On New Year's Eves past he and Mike used to stay out all night, dance on tables, and drink till they couldn't remember. They had grown up when he wasn't paying attention. In his twenties he led such an exciting, busy life. He wondered why he didn't miss it more.

"You shouldn't mess with Cherri."

Colin turned to look at Mike. He was expecting this conversation. Instantly his defenses went up. It was on the tip of his tongue to tell him to mind his fucking business, but he couldn't say that.

*Don't speak. Just listen. Mike's your mate.*

"Don't you have anything to say to that?"

"I'm not messing with her."

"You were kissing her." He was. He couldn't deny it and he wouldn't defend it, so he chose to say nothing. "She's twenty-two, Col. You know that. You know you shouldn't be messing around with a kid."

"She's not a damn kid." She was younger than them by twelve years. She still had a bit of innocence floating around her. But Mike was wrong. She wasn't a baby. She wasn't like most of the twenty-two-year-olds they met living in a college town. Colin sure as hell wasn't messing with Cherri. If anybody was messing around, it was Cherri who was messing with him. She crept into his thoughts more often than any one woman should. "She's a good lass. She's more of an adult than you and I were at that age, and she certainly isn't stupid."

"Yeah, but she's just starting out her life and she needs to date guys her own age. You've had this thing for her for a year now and I don't get it. If it's sex you want, you can get that anywhere. Why Cherri?"

Yes, why Cherri. He had asked himself that a million times.

"Why Ellis?"

Mike blinked at him. "You aren't comparing what I have with my wife to what you have with Cherri. If you look me in the eye and tell me you are in love with that girl, that you want to spend the rest of your life with her, then I'll back off."

Colin said nothing. Love? He wasn't exactly sure what that felt like anymore.

If he had a choice he wouldn't have picked her to be preoccupied with. He would have chosen somebody who was experienced and focused and knew how to please him in bed, not a girl who kissed him like she was kissing a man for the first time. Or who laughed at silly things or would rather spend the night in with her grandmother than out on the town. But for perhaps the first time it wasn't about sex. "When did you get so fucking sanctimonious? Did marriage do that to you, lad? You can get your panties out of that knot now. I'm not sleeping with Cherri. I don't plan to sleep with Cherri. We kissed. It's New Year's Eve. It's no big deal."

"Not to you, but she's the type that bruises easily. I know you, Colin. After Serena you were with a different woman every week. There were so many of them I couldn't keep them straight. You can't do that to Cherri. She's not just a stranger. She's our friend. You have to be careful with her."

He knew that. He probably knew that more than anyone else. "You're one to talk. Before Ellis you were just like me. You dated her sister, for fuck's sake. How can you sit there and warn me away when just a couple of years ago you were no better yourself?"

Out of the corner of his eye he saw Ellis enter the room. He was done for the night. He didn't want to hear her warn him away, too.

"You can quit lecturing me. I've got it. You think your best friend would set out to hurt her." He stood up. "Look, I have to get going." He walked to Ellis and kissed her cheek. "Thanks for having me over, lass."

"I'll walk you to the door." She linked arms with him and waited till they were out of earshot before she spoke again. "I don't feel the same way Mike does."

Surprised by her words, he stopped walking and stared at her. "What?"

"If you love her, then you have my blessing. She needs to be loved, Colin. She doesn't have too many people in her life who can do that for her. But if you can't love her, then stay away. I'd hate to have to castrate you for hurting one of my best friends." She gave him a little naughty smile. "You can ignore Mike. He can be an overbearing jackass sometimes, but his heart is in the right place. Cherri doesn't have a father or brother to look after her. He assigned himself the role."

"Nobody bloody asked him to." He chuckled. "You don't have to worry about Cherri, Elle. I'll do right by her." He wished her good night and walked out wondering if he knew what the right thing was.

# CHAPTER 10

*Moving on . . .*

Grocery shopping was one of the things that Colin hated most. It was akin to having his toenails ripped out one by one. The only reason he did it was because he had to eat. He liked eating, too, but going to the store, picking through hundreds of items, and then standing in line to pay for them sucked. Cooking for one also sucked, and so he lived on hot dogs, hamburgers, and frozen food. Anything so he didn't have to pull out a pot or a pan and actually cook.

"Instant mashed potatoes? Who thought this up, for fuck's sake? It's bloody disgusting."

"You Irish and your potatoes," a woman said. He looked over to see Coral Jenkins beside him. She was a former customer of his; he hadn't seen her since he'd delivered the antique soda fountain to her house. "They actually aren't so bad. You should try the garlic cheddar ones." She placed a box in her basket. "It beats making them from scratch."

She smiled at him and out of habit he grinned back at her.

Coral was an attractive woman, blond, very well put together, and from what he understood recently divorced. When they'd worked together two years ago he didn't pay much attention to her looks. Married women were a big no in his book, but now he had the chance to study her.

She was a little older than him, very tight little body, and had a pair of pretty gray eyes that seemed to have seen a lot. She was the kind of woman he should be dating.

"I think they would revoke my Irish pass if I ever ate a potato that came from a box. It's blasphemy."

She laughed. It was a pleasant sound—not one to stir his blood, but not one to grate on his nerves, either. "We couldn't allow that to happen, now, could we? How have you been, Colin? I wish I could say that the soda fountain looked great in my house but it went with my ex. I might have to find something else for you to restore just so I can have you in my house again."

That was an invitation if he ever heard one. He could ask her out. No. He *should* ask her out. He needed to get himself out there again. It was time for him to think about settling down, and a certain six-foot-tall blonde was distracting him from that. If he dated, if he sowed the few remaining oats he had left this year, he could be ready for the domesticated lifestyle.

"You like Thai food?"

"You like women in little black dresses?" she countered.

He smiled. He didn't know why he'd waited so long to date again after Serena. Dating was like riding a bike, and he was getting back on again.

A pair of lips brushed Cherri's forehead and her eyes popped open. She smiled softly at Colin, her cheeks burning with embarrassment. She had fallen asleep in his workshop, a paintbrush dangling from her fingertips.

"I'm sorry." She put the brush down and tried to wipe the sleepiness from her eyes. "Feel free to dock my pay."

He ignored her comment and pulled up a stool beside her. "You look like shit, love. What happened?"

"Only you can tell a woman she looks like shit and get away with it." She gave him a half smile. "I think it must be the brogue. That almost sounded like a compliment."

He frowned. "Don't avoid the question. Talk to me."

She almost refused, not wanting to unburden herself on him. She had been working with him a little over a week now and they barely said more than a few words to each other. They had kissed New Year's Eve. Kissed again. And then silence, like he was avoiding her. She didn't want to believe that he was purposely avoiding her, but she didn't know what else to think.

Did he regret their kiss? Probably. She knew she wasn't the type of woman he wanted. She wanted to believe they were friends, that they could work together comfortably—but she couldn't. Because after Christmas Eve when he'd held her so close on that couch that she wanted to be inside him, after New Year's Eve when he been so concerned for her that she could see the worry etched on his face, she knew she could no longer think of him as just a friend. Even though she wanted to. There was something different about him, about the way she felt about him. And it wasn't anything near like what she felt for any of her other friends.

If she got any closer to him. If she let herself fall, her heart would pay for it, and she couldn't afford that now. Especially when she had so much on her plate. "The water heater," she yawned, unable to suppress it. "It sprang a leak. Actually it was more like a waterfall. We knew it was on its last legs but I was hoping it would hold out till spring but it didn't. So I spent half of last night trying to stop it and today will spend all of my savings to replace it."

"You should have called me." He gave her that stern, don't-you-know-anything look.

"For what reason? There was nothing you could have done."

"I could have lent you my dry vac and dehumidifier. Plus I could have gotten you a deal on a water heater and installed it for you."

"Oh." It never would have occurred to her that he could be helpful in that situation. She had been so used to doing things on her own that involving somebody else rarely occurred to her.

"You feel dumb now, don't you, lass?"

"Yes, but only a little."

"Ring whoever you called to install the water heater and cancel. I'll have everything done by the time you take your evening bath."

"I feel bad asking you to do this. I'll always feel like I owe you."

He gave her his lazy smile, the corners of his eyes crinkling. "I think I like that idea just fine, lass. A bit of gratitude from a woman is never a bad thing for a man."

"Ass," she said, but his slightly naughty words hit her right in her core.

"Don't be daft." He squeezed her shoulder, the pressure from his warm hand causing her to relax. She hadn't realized she was tense until he touched her. "You know you don't owe me anything. We're mates, aren't we? I do things for you. You do things for me. "

*Mates.*

She nearly smiled at the word.

"What could I do for you, Colin?" She looked at him, her eyes passing over his body, the need to tease him overwhelming in that moment. She didn't want him to forget that she was a woman. She didn't want him to think that he could easily tuck her into that friend category when it suited him.

Not after what they had shared. One day he was kissing her, the next few days he was barely speaking to her. It wasn't fair. She may not be the type of woman he wanted, but she didn't want him to pretend like there wasn't something there. "I'm good at a lot of things." She looked at his lips, and then slowly took in each part of his body, trying to get a reaction out of him. "Some things I need a little more practice with." She placed her hand over his, lightly, just enough to make contact. The cords in his neck tightened, and his Adam's apple bobbed. His face went totally blank. She liked to make him uncomfortable, because that's how he made her feel. Uncomfortable and confused.

"What do you think, Col? Can I practice on you?"

"Cherri! Enough."

"What?" she tried to say innocently, but she couldn't manage to keep the smile away. "I could cook for you. I was only talking about cooking. I could use the practice."

"You were talking about being a huge pain in my ass," he grumbled.

She felt better. She had gotten to him. "I'm serious about cooking for you, though. You can come over and play cards with me and Baba again. You know she's still pissed that you beat her."

"I know." He grinned. "She told me she knew mobsters who would break my legs for cheating. Batty old broad."

"Do you have plans tomorrow night? I think she would like to see you."

"I do have plans actually." An uncomfortable look passed over his face. He left his seat beside her and went back to the spot he was working at when she came in. "I have a date."

"A date?" Her stomach lurched. This is why she couldn't get any closer to him. She liked him more and more and he . . . He was dating other women.

She knew it was none of her business, that she had no

right to inquire, but—"Do you mind if I ask you who you have a date with?"

"Coral Jenkins." He didn't look at her as he said it. "She used to be a client."

"Oh. I know her," she said, trying not to sound deflated. Coral looked like Grace Kelly. She was classy and graceful and lovely. All the things Cherri wished she could be. "She's very nice," she told him and hated to realize that she was telling the truth. "She's an associate professor in the art history department at Durant U. I think you two should have a lot in common."

"Maybe." He shrugged, seeming uncomfortable with the conversation. "You can cook for me the next night though. I'm in love with those little potato balls you and your gran make."

"Okay." She left her seat and headed toward his office. "I'll ask her to make them for you. I'm going to call the water heater guy."

She closed the door behind her and stood against it for a moment.

*So this is what jealousy feels like.*

*You're not jealous, you idiot. You're hurt and you have no reason to feel this way.*

She told herself to snap out of it. She had to. There were other things on her plate. Baba's health, the broken water heater. She didn't have time to lick her wounds over a crush she shouldn't have in the first place.

*Knock it off, dumb-dumb.*

She pulled out her cell phone, intending to call the man about the water heater, but another man's name popped up on her screen, distracting her. A text message from Sean. Sean who didn't give up very easily. Sean who actually seemed to want to be with her.

*How's your day going?*

"Shitty," she said to the screen, but seeing the simple

message lifted her spirits slightly and before she had a chance to think about what she was doing she dialed Sean's number.

"Cherri! I'm so glad you called."

He sounded happy to hear from her, which made her feel better about the decision she had just come to. "Ask me out again. I promise I'll give you a different answer this time."

# CHAPTER 11

*Welcome to the lonely hearts club . . .*

"Do you want to come in for a little while?" Coral asked him. "Maybe have another glass of wine. And if that's not enticing enough, I've got whiskey."

Colin looked down at his date as they stood at her front door. Coral was one of those women who had everything a man like him thought he wanted. She was independent. She was beautiful. She had her own money, and she was willing to go to bed with him. He knew if he stepped foot inside her house, his night wouldn't end with a drink.

The invitation in her eyes was clear, and they did have a good time together. She was easy to talk to. She had seen the world and they had a lot in common. And he knew if he went to bed with her she wasn't expecting more than that. Being newly divorced, she wasn't eager to start a serious relationship. It was a win–win situation. The man he was ten years ago wouldn't still be standing on her bloody porch. He would have been in her bed ten minutes ago. But the man he was now could take things slower. Unlike with Serena, he was under no illusion that he would fall in love with Coral. He would see how things went with her. They might be able to build something.

*Who are you kidding, lad?*

He stepped closer, placed his hands around her trim waist, and pulled her into him. They didn't line up the way he expected. The way he and Cherri . . . He shook that thought clear from his mind. Coral was much shorter than he was. Her thin body didn't mold to his like a damp glove. They were a bit off, yet he kissed her anyway, trying to ignore the funny little niggle in the back of his mind.

He hadn't been with a woman in a long time. After he broke up with Serena he went on a binge, sleeping with woman after woman. He became disgusted with himself after a while. It was madness. It was as if he had something to prove. He learned quickly that sex didn't fix the nagging empty feeling in his chest—and it certainly didn't do anything to get back at Serena. So for a year he went without sex, without companionship, going through the motions, hoping one day he would snap out of it. It was only now that he could admit that women made him wary. But then his best friend fell in love right in front of him, and it made Colin see that they all weren't like Serena and made him even more determined not to go through life without living it.

Coral's mouth was warm and welcoming. She tasted a little like the chocolate cake they had shared. He should have found her delicious. He should be thinking about their kiss, but nothing felt right. He pressed a little harder, opening his mouth wider over hers, in the hope that in a few more moments something might burn between them.

*Stop.*

He listened to his brain . . . or maybe it was his heart that directed him to do so. Carefully he watched Coral's face. He didn't want to hurt her feelings. She was a nice woman. It wasn't her fault he was mad.

"Wow." She smiled and reached for the doorknob behind her. He knew what was going to happen if he followed her inside.

"Wait." He grasped her wrist. "I can't come in tonight. It's only our first date. What kind of man do you think I am?"

She seemed surprised for a moment but then smiled brightly at him. "It looks like I've finally met a gentleman. My mother wasn't lying when she told me they existed. I guess I'll have to see you again."

They said their good nights and Colin returned to his house wondering why he hadn't felt the slightest bit of arousal when he was kissing that beautiful woman. The thoughts plagued him all night, so much so that when he went into his shop the next morning his eyes were blurry from lack of sleep.

"You look . . . surprisingly awful," Cherri said, standing by a rocking horse he was restoring. She frowned at him and then walked over, placing her cool hand against his cheek. "Are you getting sick?"

He leaned into her hand and shut his eyes for a moment, her touch now familiar and strangely comforting. "No. I just didn't get much sleep last night."

"Oh." She dropped her hand and quickly stepped away from him.

He knew that she was aware of his date last night and was almost positive she'd just gotten the wrong idea. He was about to reach out and grab her, prepared to clarify his statement, but he stopped himself. Cherri was just his friend. He didn't owe her an explanation and wasn't sure why he felt the almost panicky need to give her one. The truth was, he might end up in bed with Coral or another woman. He was supposed to be getting back out there. He didn't want to be his father, over fifty and still picking up women.

"You can go back to bed if you want," she started. "I'll handle things around here for a few hours. I can finish the rocking horse now that you've fixed the crack on the side. The delivery man dropped off the piece for the cash register you've been waiting on. He said to tell you hi. Oh, and a Mr. Naples called for a quote on a cuckoo clock he bought from a yard sale. I told him to bring it in for you to look at. He said he could be here by two. So you have plenty of time to go recuperate."

She was speaking a mile a minute and her cheeks were fiery red. Poor lass. "I slept alone last night, love."

"You did?" Her eyes went wide and she froze for a moment. "Why did you tell me that?" Without waiting for his answer she turned away from him, grabbing a piece of sandpaper before returning to the rocking horse. "Well, it's none of my business anyway. You don't have to tell me anything, Colin. In fact, I don't want to know who you sleep with ever. I just say those things to get under your skin. I bet men talk about that kind of stuff with their guy friends. Do you and Mike talk about that kind of stuff? Well, I guess he wouldn't talk about his sex life with Ellis with you. That would just be weird and if he does tell you, please don't tell me because I don't want to know. Guy friends must talk about different stuff than we would or maybe they don't. We're friends, right?"

"Right," he said when she finished her confusing, flustered babble. "We're friends."

Friends.

*Just friends.*

It was bullshit and they both knew it. He knew why he couldn't take Coral to bed last night even though he tossed and turned all night trying to deny it.

He liked Cherri. All the serious adult conversation he had with Coral last night, all the shared interests they had, didn't hold a candle to how he felt when he was with Cherri.

He liked Cherri's bubbly innocent sweetness.

But he needed Coral's experience, maturity, and independence.

*Damn.*

He buried himself in his work that day, unable to face the uncomfortable thoughts bombarding him. It was nearly one o'clock when Cherri tapped him on the shoulder and waved a giant sandwich under his nose.

"I bought you lunch."

"You didn't have to do that, love." He didn't like the idea of her spending money on him.

"You brought my dog home and are sweet to my grandmother and you don't have to be. I think a sandwich is just a small token of my appreciation. So take a break for half an hour and eat your lunch."

"It's a big sandwich. Share it with me?"

She nodded and they ended up in his office. He tossed the sandwich on his desk and unwrapped it. "Aw, Charlotte. This is so beautiful it brings me to tears."

"It's an Italian combo from Roma's." She grinned at him. "You look like a man who enjoys his meat."

"Ha ha." He shook his head at her bad joke. "I think there may be some paper plates in the bottom of that cabinet."

He cut the sandwich in half and turned to her, but her head was still buried in the cabinet, her curvy behind sticking up. He hardened immediately. He took a step toward her but stopped when he realized the urge to pull that soft round behind into him was overwhelming. *Bloody fucking hell.* For the hundredth time he questioned his sanity for offering her a job. His body wanted her. His mind was a far different story. It wanted to tell her to get the hell away from him. She was dangerous to his well-being. But he couldn't just send her away. Despite his insane attraction to her, he needed her at the shop. She was good at what she did. Good for his business. He'd known for a long time that he needed help running things, but he'd balked at the idea of hiring another person.

His work was his pride and his life. He'd thought finding another person who could meet his exacting standards would be impossible. Somehow Cherri managed to, though. She did more than decorative pieces. She sanded, and cut and lifted and got dirty, and she did it all with a smile. But most important, and perhaps most troubling, she filled up that empty space in his chest when she was around. Getting out of bed was a little easier when he knew she would be in his shop.

"Col, when's the last time you cleaned out this cabinet? There's so much crap in here." He pulled his eyes away from her ass and sat on the couch, crossing his legs. It was better that she didn't know she had the power to arouse him without even touching him.

"It's been years, but if you want to tackle that job, love, I would be more than happy to let you do it."

"I'll do it tomorrow. Aha! I found them. They were stuck under this picture." She stood up, frame in one hand, plates in the other. But she didn't look at him. She was frowning at the broken picture frame in her hand.

"What is it, love?"

"Nothing." She shook her head. "Here." She handed him the frame and all at once memories of a time he'd rather forget came crashing down on him. A throbbing hand. A hole in the wall. Betrayal. "Who is she?"

He stared at the picture of Serena and him taken on their last vacation together. They both looked so happy with their tanned skin and big smiles. Colin had been happy then. He'd had no idea that the life he had been living with the woman he thought he loved was a lie. "She's nobody," he finally answered.

Cherri slid her warm body beside him on the couch, causing him to forget what they were talking about.

"Want me to beat her up for you? She looks little. I bet I could take her."

"She's not worth the fight."

"Let me be the judge of that." She took the photo from him and threw it in the trash can. "Tell me who she is, Colin."

"She was the woman I thought I would marry."

"What happened?"

"She cheated on me. I might have been able to forgive her for that, but she lied to me for a year and that's what did us in."

"Somebody actually cheated on you?" She shook her head. "But you're so freaking beautiful."

He was surprised to find himself smiling down at her. "That had little to do with it."

"You loved her." The way she said it he knew it wasn't a question. But he had asked himself that many times since they broke up. Did he really ever love her?

"I thought I did."

"What does it feel like?" She looked up at him with innocent eyes.

"What? Love?"

"Yeah, I never felt it before."

"I don't know. I look at Mike and Ellis and I don't think I ever really knew what it was."

"Well, what do you think it feels like?"

"I think it's uncomfortable. That your chest feels heavy with it, that love, real love is involuntary. Because no matter what you do or say you can't stop yourself from thinking about them, from wanting what's best for them, from putting their happiness and needs before your own."

She scrunched her face. "Sounds like it kind of sucks."

"Yeah. It more than sucks." He laughed. "But it can't be all bad if so many people are searching for it." He ruffled her hair. "I came in here to eat a sandwich and you've got me being philosophical instead."

"I'm talented that way." She grinned at him. And they stared at each other for one long, charged moment. He wanted to pull her mouth to his to taste her sweetness, to hold her to him until he could capture what it was that made Charlotte

Rudy so refreshing to him. In his adult life he had wanted to have sex with women. He wanted to satisfy his baser needs with them, but this was the first time he'd simply wanted to kiss a woman, to hold one close, to feel her softness, to just be with her.

*Damn it.*

He was losing it. He felt that pull again, that overwhelming need to have more of her, all of her. Why couldn't he feel this with Coral—or any other woman, for that matter?

*You're not right for her.*

He moved away from her. Getting up to sit at his desk. "I'm starving, love. Toss me a plate so we can get back to work."

She nodded, a little sadness crossing her face, and he knew that he had hurt her feelings. He hadn't meant to but he needed space from her. It was the only way he was going to keep his sanity.

Cherri ignored the pair of sharp green eyes on her back as she fussed over her appearance in the mirror.

*They're like frickin' laser beams.*

"Where are you going again, pixie?" Baba asked for the third time that hour.

The old woman was suspicious, and as much as Cherri hated to admit it she might have a reason to be. It wasn't every day Cherri went on a date with a wealthy veterinarian. Or any day for that matter. Okay, so she had never been on a date at all, but it was rude for her grandmother not to expect her to eventually. She had always wanted to go out with a guy. She'd always wanted to be one of those girls who never had a Friday night free. So much so that she prayed for some boy to sweep her off her feet.

*Dear God, Hook a girl up. Amen.*

But after three dateless homecomings she soon realized that boys were dumb and that God had better things to do than worry about her love life. It seemed her charms were lost on most men her age. Or any age, for that matter. But not tonight. She was determined to have a memorable first date with a guy who wasn't put off by her six-foot stature.

Baba had been watching her get ready for the past half hour, tsking intermediately and making Cherri feel guilty for declining her offer to help.

*She just wants you to be beautiful.*

*Do you want to go on your first date looking like the Ukrainian version of Bouffant Barbie?*

Cherri frowned at herself as she ruthlessly twisted a curl around her finger, but her slightly shaking hand slipped from the lock she was trying to tame. Frick! She hated that she was nervous. She hated more that her hair never behaved when she needed it to.

"I'm going to the Red Note Room," she replied to her grandmother's question and gave up trying to smooth her hair. She studied herself in the full-length mirror, running her hands over the simple but sexy black dress that she'd borrowed from Ellis. She wanted to look good tonight, but she was debating her choice in shoes. Ellis had given her patent-leather red stilettos but Cherri put on flats instead. She frowned at them. Flats were very unsexy. But if she wore heels she would tower over Sean.

"Why are you going to the Red Note Room?" Baba raised one of her wispy white brows, stopping the argument in Cherri's head. "You don't like jazz."

Apparently Baba had missed her calling. She could have been a master interrogator for the CIA. Forget enhanced interrogation methods. One look from Yuliana Rudy and even the hardest soldier would crack. Too bad her talents were wasted trying to figure out why Cherri was going on a date.

"I'm going because I have a date, Baba," she said gently. "Remember? I told you about this."

"You told me about this, but you talk so fast, maybe I don't understand. It is like there are marbles in your mouth."

This coming from a woman with an accent so thick, you needed a machete to cut through it.

"You have a date."

"Yes, Baba."

"With a man?"

"No, Baba, with a fish. Of course it's with a man!"

"Don't be fresh." Baba swatted her behind. "You could be a Lebanese. I'm a cool grandma. It would be okay with me."

"That's lesbian, Baba. And I am not one."

"So who are you going out with?"

"His name is Sean."

"And Sean is not Colin."

"No." Cherri frowned at her grandmother in confusion. "I'm not going out with Colin. We're just friends." He'd made that very clear the other day when he'd moved halfway across the room just to get away from her.

*I don't want you, freakishly tall girl,* was practically written on his forehead. And that was okay. She didn't want him, either. She just liked kissing him and touching him and talking to him . . .

She shook herself out of those thoughts to find Baba studying her from head to toe with pursed lips. "I think you should go out with Colin instead. You call him." She offered Cherri the cordless phone.

"It doesn't work that way," she sighed. "Sean asked me out, so it's Sean I will be going out with."

"I know how dates work, dumb-dumb," she sniffed. "But I'd rather you go out with Colin. I like him better."

"How could you like him better? You don't even know Sean."

"He's Rufus's doctor?"

"Yes."

Baba folded her arms under her substantial breasts and shook her head. "Then I don't like him."

Cherri took a deep breath. She wasn't going to lose her

patience tonight. She was already nervous enough as it was. She was a little uneasy leaving her grandmother home alone. That combined with the fact that she had no idea how to behave on a date was turning the butterflies in her belly into big stinging wasps. The last thing she needed tonight was Baba being difficult. "You told me that Colin wasn't right for me. Why do you want me to go out with him all of a sudden?"

She shrugged. "I say a lot of things. Colin is a good boy. He bought me apple fritters this morning."

"He did?" He hadn't said a word about it to her.

"Yes." She nodded. "He stopped by while you were at work and we had coffee and fritters. He stops by a lot. So if you are going to go out with all your boobies exposed, I'd rather it be with Colin."

She looked at her grandmother, wondering how many fritters it would take for her to stop bugging her.

*All the fritters in the world couldn't achieve that. It's her job to be a pain in your tuckus.*

"I'm sorry, but that's not going to happen tonight. I'm going out with Sean."

"Then wear a sweater."

Cherri wobbled into the Red Note Room that night. She had gone with the heels. Yes, they were sexy, but they were the highest pair she had ever worn and instead of feeling like Marilyn Monroe she felt like she had entered the land of the Lilliputians. Why hadn't she gone with her gut?

*Head up. Shoulders back. One foot in front of the other. Look sexy. You can do it.*

She suddenly felt like she was walking on stilts.

Sean spotted her and waved with a broad smile on his face.

*Head up. Shoulders back. One foot in front of the other. Look sexy. You can do it. Don't fall. Don't slump. Walk. Walk. Walk.*

He put the cloth napkin that was in his lap on the table and began to rise. *Oh, don't do that. Please don't stand up,* she silently begged him. Standing five inches above her date was not sexy. For some reason it was important that Sean saw her that way. She desperately wanted him to see her as a desirable woman. Not the huge dork she felt like. As she wove her way through the black-clothed tables, he stood to greet her. *Damn it!* Her nose met his hairline. That settled it. She was officially a giant.

He looked a little different than she was used to seeing him. Slick, in a navy-blue suit and black shirt that was unbuttoned to the middle of his chest, long darkish hairs curling over the edge.

"Hey, sweet thing. You look amazing." He pressed a kiss to her lips again. She stopped herself mid-cringe. Why she felt the urge to wipe his kiss from her mouth, she did not know.

"Hello, Sean." *Smile, damn it. You're on a date.*

He pulled out the chair next to him, inviting her to take a seat. From their semi-secluded table she could see the band beginning to set up for the night. For a few moments she took in the setting. She had never been to the Red Note before and she didn't know what to think about it, except that it was dark and it was . . . red. With candles on every table and lights so dim you could hardly see the person you were with. It seemed like a place that clandestine lovers would meet. She wasn't sure if it was right for a first date. At least not the first date she was hoping for. Being a low-key kind of girl, she was expecting dinner and a movie.

*Gosh, Cherri! You're not in high school. This is how grown-ups date.*

She wiped her damp palms on her dress and smiled at Sean. Awkward. She wished that just once she wasn't.

"You want a drink? I've already had a scotch and soda while I was waiting for you."

So that was the smell on his breath."Maybe a ginger ale. I'm not much of a drinker."

"Then maybe that's the reason you should drink even more."

She laughed at his joke but when the waitress came over and he ordered a rum and Coke for her she no longer found him funny. She corrected the order and tried to brush off her irritation as well as her budding sense of unease.

*Enjoy yourself, dumb-dumb. You wanted this, remember? You refuse to be one of those dating disasters.*

She tried to relax as they shared an order of calamari and talked about their lives. They had very little in common. Sean was from old money. Cherri was from no money. Their families were different, their childhoods, their experiences. She was afraid she was the dullest date in all of humanity. But Sean seemed to be having a good time. He kept touching her to prove it. His hands kept wandering to her shoulder, her elbow, her thigh, that broad smile of his never slipping from his face. She tried to chalk it up as normal date behavior but she wasn't sure she was comfortable with it.

"I think the show is starting," she said to him when the first notes from a piano drifted to her ears. She turned away from him and toward the stage, eager for the chance to put a few inches between them.

"I love jazz." He inched closer to her and wrapped his arm around her middle. She tensed but ordered herself to relax. So much for space. She was on a date. This is how men acted. Wasn't it? "This music is so sexy."

His hand brushed the bottom side of her breast—no, it was more like his fingertips brushed her nipple.

*It was an accident. Don't be a ninny.*

"Are you having a good time?" he asked in her ear.

She felt his hot, alcohol-scented breath on her skin. "Um, yeah."

"Good, because I like you, Cherri." His hand cupped her

breast and she froze. She looked around the half-empty room as bile rose in her throat. Nobody could see them. The club was dark, and everyone's eyes were either on the stage or the person they were with.

*That was not an accident.*

"Sean, please let go."

"Nobody can see us, baby. Relax." His groping intensified as he squeezed her nipple between his fingers. She jumped as slight pain and panic invaded her. "I can't wait to get you back to my place. I'm going to fuck your brains out. I've been waiting a long time to meet a girl your size. I know your body can take what I've got to give. I don't have to worry about hurting you."

"Sean . . ." She tried to pull away, but his hold on her was firm.

"We could have a lot of fun together. I can't wait to show you off to my friends. If you play your cards right you could end up with a ring on your finger." He sucked in a breath. "Innocent in public but a slut in the sack."

"Get off me, you slimy bastard." She elbowed him in the gut and stormed out, not bothering to look back.

Her eyes stung with tears as she got in her truck. She had wanted this date. She had wanted to prove to herself, to the world that she wasn't some stupid kid. But nothing had turned out the way it was supposed to.

*How could I be so stupid?*

Of course he didn't like her for her personality. He wanted her body. He wanted to use her. What was it about her that made him think he could? She reached for her keys, eager to be back in the safety of her bedroom, but when she put the keys in the ignition the damn thing wouldn't start.

"Fuck."

Colin glanced at the clock for the fourth time. He shouldn't keep looking at it.

*Get back in the game, lad.*

It was sad he had to give himself a pep talk when there was a beautiful woman kissing his neck. What the hell had happened to him? Before, all it took was a stiff breeze to make him hard, but tonight all the wind in the world wasn't doing it for him.

He had accepted Coral's offer when she invited him in this time. Why not? She was beautiful, smart, and willing. Bedding her shouldn't be a hardship. And yet it was. It was like going to the dentist, unpleasant but necessary. Maybe *unpleasant* wasn't the right word. She was doing all the things a woman did to a man to get him going. And she was good at it. On some level it did feel nice, but it wasn't right. All the spark and chemistry was missing, and no matter what Coral did or said he couldn't keep focused on the task at hand.

She unzipped his pants and slid her hand inside. "Maybe we should go to the bedroom. I think we might be more comfortable in there."

"I—" His phone rang, saving him from having to answer her and the embarrassment of not being hard yet. He reached for it and saw Cherri's name pop up on the screen.

*A sign from God.*

"Sorry, Coral. I need to take this."

He eased away from her and zipped up his pants. He felt guilty and not because of how things were going with Coral but because of the girl who was on the phone. "What's the matter, love?" He heard a choked sound, a sob, and his blood ran cold. "Charlotte. Talk to me. Where are you?"

"At the Red Note Room. Will you come and get me?"

"Don't hang up, love. Okay? I'll be right there." He was out of the house before he remembered that he hadn't spent the last few hours alone. Coral was at the door, her face twisted with disappointment. *I'm sorry,* he mouthed. And he was, because he knew he was probably never going to see her again.

He pulled up behind Cherri's beat-up truck a few minutes

later, leaping out of the car as soon as he threw it into park. Looking at her, a tight ball formed in his gut. Something had happened to his girl. Her light had gone out. The normally cheery Cherri had disappeared.

"Tell me what happened?" He ran his hands down her cold arms, checking to see if she was hurt. It was bitterly cold, and her car didn't have heat. He wanted to scold her for being out without much more on than a thin dress. But there must be a reason she opted for the freezing outdoors over the warm inside.

"My car is dead." She looked down at her shoes. "Can you take me home?"

"Of course." He ushered her around to the passenger side and helped her in, knowing there was much more to her story.

"Cherri!" A man called her name. "Wait." Sean Brightworth. The hard knot in Colin's gut had turned to ice.

"Please, Colin." She grabbed his hand. "Can we go now?"

"What did he do to you?" He turned to face the balding blowhard, his hands already clenched.

"Nothing. It was a misunderstanding. Please let's go."

"Cherri." Sean moved closer. "I'm sorry. I—I thought you . . ." He frowned at Colin. "Do you mind if I talk to my date?"

Something snapped in Colin, and he reached out and grabbed Sean by the throat. "She isn't your anything and if you come near her again I'll stomp you into the fucking ground."

"Colin, stop!" Cherri tugged on his arm. "I want to go home. Please take me home."

He looked back at her, tears spilling from her eyes. It was the only reason he released Sean, who fell against Cherri's truck gasping for air. "Okay, love. Let's go."

She didn't say anything the entire ride home. He waited for her to talk, wanting her to tell him what happened so he could make it better. But she was silent, and he looked at her so many times he almost drove off the road.

"Thank you," she said as he parked in her driveway. All the lights were off inside the house, giving it an eerie feeling, and she blindly groped for the door, in such a hurry to get away.

He grabbed her hand, stopping her from fleeing. Something inside told him not to let her go inside alone. "Wait."

She did, but she didn't look at him. "I'm fine, Colin. I'm sorry that I pulled you from your date. I forgot you had one. You can go back to her now."

When he'd walked out of Coral's door that night he'd known there was no going back. He was with who he needed to be with. "The date ended a long time ago, love. I'm going to walk you inside."

"Oh." She blinked at him, her eyes swimming with unshed tears. "You don't have to."

"I want to." He was out of the car before she could say any more, opening her door and following her inside the dark house.

Like a zombie she moved through the rooms, turning down the heat, locking the windows. Performing her nightly rituals as if nothing had happened, as if tears weren't threatening. Even then he had a hard time not noticing how she looked that night. Sexy black dress. Red shoes that made her legs look miles long. Not a pretty girl but a gorgeous woman. He stayed closed to her, unable to remove himself from her presence, more worried about her than he'd like to admit. That bastard had done something to her and he wanted to kill him and kick himself for allowing her to go out with him.

Only he hadn't known she was going out with him tonight. She'd never told him.

"Baba," she mumbled to herself. He followed her to the back bedroom, where they found the old woman peacefully sleeping. Cherri, just like a mother, tucked the blankets a little bit tighter around her and kissed her forehead before walking out.

*Say something.*

She knew he was there, and yet she didn't ask him to leave or try to reassure him she was fine. He needed to hear it from her. He needed to know that she was fine. Then maybe he could take himself away from this place.

Who was he kidding?

He followed her to her bedroom in the cold dank basement. He hated that this was the place she rested her head. It was no place for a girl like Cherri—any girl, for that matter. She had tried to make it cheerier. The walls were painted yellow, her beautiful artwork was displayed, but it didn't take away from the fact that the plaster was peeling or that the hum from the boiler was loud enough to keep even the deepest sleeper awake.

Kicking off her shoes, she climbed into her bed, not bothering to remove her dress. It was then she finally looked up at him. Looked into his eyes. "Colin, can you stay with me for a little while?"

He didn't answer, just slipped off his shoes and climbed in beside her. Their bodies were like magnets sticking to each other as soon as they met. "What happened, love? What did he do to you?"

"I feel so stupid." A tear slid from her eye. "I should have known he was just using me."

Colin tensed. "I need to know what he did to you, love."

She shook her head. "You'll just get mad."

"I'll probably go a bit ballistic and smash the wanker's face in. But you need to tell me so I can stop walking around feeling like I've got a lead ball in my belly."

"He only likes me because I'm a fat freak. He said my body could take what he had to give. He—he said he wanted to fuck my brains out."

It wasn't funny but a hysterical bubble of laughter rose in his chest. She was still so innocent. Despite what she thought about the world, Colin knew what men were like. The first time he saw Cherri himself, he'd thought about how much he would like to tumble her into bed. She was beautiful no matter what she thought about herself. He knew Sean Brightworth wouldn't be the last man to think those thoughts about her.

And maybe that's why he liked her. She had no idea how beautiful, how naturally sexy she was. Sweet bubbly Cherri, wrapped in a long curvy package. She made him lose his mind without even trying.

"Why are you laughing at me?" Fresh tears rolled down her face.

"I'm not, love. It's just that I'm not surprised he said that to you. You're not a fat freak. You're a beautiful lass and there will always be men who want to sleep with you. I did warn you, did I not?"

"Now is not the time to say I told you so. I'm just confused why he thought that I wanted to sleep with him on the first date. I thought he wanted to get to know me better."

"Jaysus, love. You're a sexy girl in a short dress. Of course he wants to get to know you better. It's just not in the way you're thinking." He ran his hand across her lower back. Her dress had ridden up, and he couldn't stop himself from stroking the softness of her creamy skin. "Men think with their dicks."

She gave him a watery laugh, and his chest grew looser. "That's not helping, you ass." She kissed his chin. "Thank you for coming to my rescue. I think I'm more upset about the car than anything. It was my grandfather's."

"Mmm." He slid his hand farther up her back as he pulled her closer. "Tell me about him."

Her body settled nicely against his, all their parts lining up. He grew aroused just holding her. She must have felt it but she said nothing, only wrapped both her arms around him as if they had been sleeping in each other's arms for lifetimes. "What can I say about my papa?" She grew thoughtful for a moment. "He looked like Rock Hudson and was one of those strong silent types. Baba used to go out of her way to get a rise of out him. She was the only one who could get to him. I think that's why he loved her so much. Her real name is Yuliana and he never referred to her as *your grandmother* or *my wife*. He called her *my Yuli*." She sighed. "Sometimes I would catch him staring at her like she was the most beautiful woman on the planet. And I used to think that's what real love is. I want that. I can't wait. But when Papa died . . . Baba . . . I don't know how to describe it. It was like half of her was missing. Like she's empty. I don't know if I want to love that much. That's why I don't want to get rid of the car, because when she gets in it she says she can still smell him and I can't bear the thought of getting rid of the thing that makes her feel connected to him."

Sweet girl. Saving that rusty death trap to make her gran happy. He kissed her forehead. Cherri had no idea that she had more capacity to love than anyone he had ever known. He could imagine it even though he didn't want to. He could imagine what it would feel like to be loved by her. The feeling would be overwhelmingly good. "It might still work. We can get it towed to a shop. I'm sure it's fixable."

"Last time I went they said I would need a new engine."

"Oh. Well, let's get you enrolled in some auto repair classes then."

She laughed. "I should have done that instead of wasting a hundred thousand dollars on an education degree."

She was lovely when she laughed. Seeing her upset made him realize that he needed to see her happy. Even if he was the one who had to make it possible. He opened his mouth to invite her and her grandmother to dinner with him tomorrow night but he got distracted by how heavenly she looked.

Her mouth was curved into a slight smile. Her hair was loose. Her eyes twinkled in the dim light.

"Mmm." He didn't realize he was kissing her until he heard a little moan escape her lips.

Cherri never realized how good a kiss could feel. Coherent thoughts ceased and for the first time in her life she let sensation rule. His mouth moving over hers, his hands touching her bare skin was so . . . sensual. This wasn't like their Christmas Eve kisses. No. Those were softer, sweeter, exploring. She was in charge of those and now that she wasn't, she realized she had no idea what it was really like to kiss and be kissed.

She wrapped her arms around him, unable to get close enough. His heat, his hard body, his tenderness—it was all like home to her. And she wanted to be home with no barriers between them. Reading her mind, he pulled her leg over his hip so that he could inch their bodies closer. His erection pressed between her legs, and she gasped as liquid warmth flooded her.

"I'm sorry, lass." He pulled away. "I shouldn't have kissed you like that."

Disappointment filled her for a moment, but she wouldn't let it rule her. There was need in his kiss. His body couldn't lie. He wanted her. As much as she wanted him.

Before fear could enter her she climbed off the bed and stood before him. "Lass," he started, but he stopped when she unzipped her dress and let it fall to her feet. If she had a camera she would have taken a picture to capture the expression on his face.

The way he looked at her . . . she forgot to feel self-conscious about her plump thighs or her belly that was less than flat. He looked at her like she was beautiful. It wasn't hard to slip her bra off her shoulders or let her panties drop to the floor. This was her one chance, her one night to have exactly what she wanted. She wanted him.

He growled deep in his throat and reached for her, but he stopped himself. "Damn it, Charlotte. What are you doing to me? I'm just a man."

"Colin." She knelt in front of him and placed her hands on his knees. "I'm just a woman. And I want to be with you tonight."

That got him. Groaning, he pulled her into his arms, holding her tightly against him. She could feel his struggle and she hated that he had to grapple with it so she took away his choice and set her lips to his.

"Aw, love." He gently lay her down on the bed, kissing her eyelids. For a horrible moment she thought he was going to walk out, but he only stepped away to pull his sweater over his head. His body was so beautiful. Lean where she was thick. Hard where she was soft. She watched as he revealed himself to her inch by inch.

"You've got a tattoo?"

"Yeah." He grinned at her, took his pants off, and then slid into bed beside her. "I swore I would never be one of those assholes who got a Celtic tattoo but Mike and I got shitfaced in college and I woke up with this cross on my chest."

She reached for his pec, tracing her fingers over the intricate cross as he pulled the blankets over them.

"It's bloody freezing in here."

"Hmm?" She got distracted fingering his perfect male nipple. "I'm not cold."

He leaned down and gifted her with a soft kiss. "I am and if I weren't as hard as a steel beam I would be mighty embarrassed."

"You would not." She reached between him and ran her hand down his length. "This thing is epic. Enormous. Tree trunk, really."

He threw his head back and laughed, exposing his Adam's apple to her. She kissed him there. His smell, combined with the rough texture of his slightly bearded skin, aroused her even more. "You feel so good, lass," he murmured. "So damn sweet."

He swept his hand down her side, veering off to cup her behind. And then his hands were everywhere, followed by his mouth. She had often dreamed of what it would feel like to be kissed all over. And now this beautiful man was doing so. She stretched her arms over her head, inviting him to touch her breasts. He did more than touch. He kissed, taking each one into his mouth and suckling. She wanted to smile from the sheer pleasure of it all but it felt too good. She couldn't lift her head or speak. The only thing she could do was surrender to emotion.

His fingertips brushed through the soft hair between her legs. She nearly jumped from the shock of it. Nobody had touched her there before. It felt . . . odd, but in a wonderful way. Yet her first reaction was to squeeze her legs together.

"Relax, love," Colin whispered. "I need to feel you." His fingers probed her, and he sucked in a breath. He played in her moisture, his fingertips lightly flitting over her painfully engorged nub. She arched into his hand, wanting, needing to feel more. "You're so beautiful, Cherri. Don't ever forget that."

His eyes devoured her for a moment before he moved to kiss her belly. He stayed there for a while, his tongue circling her navel, his teeth giving her tiny little nips that made her laugh and moan at the same time. It was when his mouth moved to the insides of her thighs that the smile drifted from her lips. She was so lost in feeling that it took a moment for her to realize he was kissing her in a place she hadn't thought would ever be kissed.

"Uh, Colin." She tugged on his hair as his tongue swept inside her. "Wha—mmm, are you . . ."

"Hush." He licked deeper.

She could only gasp after that. The power to form words left her, and soon she was moving to meet the strokes of his mouth.

*So this is what this feels like.*

It was heavenly and part of her wondered why she'd waited so long to do this. But she knew. It had to be right. She needed to be with someone she trusted.

"Colin?" She called his name and he stopped loving her for a moment, pressing dozens of little kisses to her thighs.

"Yes, love?"

"I'm a virgin."

He lifted his head and blinked at her. Then he swallowed and looked adorably horrified. "It's okay, lass." He swore violently under his breath. "We don't have to go any farther than this." He lay beside her and gathered her into his arms, his breathing heavy. "We can make each other feel good just like this."

"But I want to be with you." She twined her fingers through his hair and kissed him.

"You want to give yourself to me?" His expression turned very serious. "I know this feels good, but if you say yes there is no going back. There can be no regrets."

After hearing those words she fell a little in love with him. But only a very little. "I want to do this with you."

"No regrets," he said, and she wasn't sure if he was asking her or himself.

"None."

He looked skyward for a moment as if seeking divine intervention, but then he placed his body on top of hers and his lips on her mouth and she knew the time for talking had come to an end.

He moved slowly, burying his fingers deep in her hair. He kissed every inch of her face, the underside of her chin, her ears, the tip of her nose, as he rubbed his shaft against her. The need for him became so strong it was painful. It was urgent.

"Colin, now."

He lifted his lips from her skin. "Are you ready, love?"

She nodded.

"Wrap your legs around me." He helped guide her. "Good girl." Slowly he pushed into her, his gaze intent on her face. He was big and stretched her more than she thought was possible, but it wasn't like she'd expected. There was no pain. This was no first-time horror story. It was magic.

"Are you okay?" His face was taut. He stilled inside her and she knew it was taking everything inside him to hold back. "Did I hurt you?"

"No." She kissed his chin. "You don't have to hold back."

"Good." He pulled out slightly and pushed deep inside her. "You feel so amazingly good around me."

"Amazingly good?" She smiled. "I think I'm going to get that phrase tattooed on me."

"Mmm." He moaned. "If you can speak then I must not be doing my job." He bent his head to her breast and took her nipple into his mouth. His strokes changed from delicious and deliriously slow-paced to quick, toe-curling ones.

She lost all sense of herself after that. No thoughts entered or exited her brain. She was like a bundle of nerve endings. She only felt him inside her, on top of her. Warm skin and his spicy smell mixed with hers.

"Charlotte," he whispered into her ear over and over. She had to open her eyes to look at him. He was so beautiful. Pleasure was etched on his face. His eyes were closed. His mouth was slightly open.

She had to kiss him. She ran her tongue over the inside of his lips, and he shuddered.

"Sweet girl," he groaned. "You're going to be the death of me." He put his hand between them and rubbed her. She came apart immediately, and he seemed to lose all sense of control driving inside her harder and faster than before. But it was still so good and before she understood what was happening she came again, digging her nails in his wide back because the feeling was too much to stand.

He kissed her deeply, locking eyes with her before he spilled himself inside her. "Thank you," he whispered before he collapsed on top of her. "Thank you." He was heavy but she didn't mind because he was solid and safe and she wanted to savor every moment of the only night she would ever have with him. Eventually he rolled off her and she mourned the loss of his warmth, but he gathered her close, dropping kisses on her shoulders. "How are you?"

"Can't feel my legs, but otherwise very good."

He grinned at her and sat up. "Let me take care of you."

She watched him leave her bed and walk into her bathroom. She lay back smiling. Colin O'Connell had made love to her. Now she felt like a woman. And they were going to be adults about this. There would be no awkwardness. No strain to their working relationship or friendship. She was determined not to let this one night change things.

"You've got a bit of smoke coming out of your ears, lass." Colin walked back to her holding the bowl she used to wash her paintbrushes and a washcloth over his shoulder. "What are you thinking about?" He was naked as the day he was born. It was the first time she could see him. All of him. He was bigger than even she imagined. His skin there slightly darker than the rest of his body. He was quite beautiful. Better than any statue or movie star. *It* was quite beautiful, too, as it softly bounced while he walked toward her.

"My eyes are up here, Charlotte."

*Busted.* Her cheeks burned with embarrassment. "Sorry."

"Don't be sorry." He smiled softly at her and pressed a kiss to her forehead. "I've never been ogled before. It's not a bad feeling." He knelt in front of her on the bed and gently pushed her legs open.

He stared at her, and even though she had been naked for a long time it was the first time she'd felt exposed. "What are you doing?"

"Shh." He dipped the washcloth in the soapy water and

tenderly cleaned her. "I need to see for myself that I didn't hurt you."

"You didn't." She felt herself blush again. "You were . . ." She couldn't tell him how wonderful he was to her without giving herself away. "Fine. I barely felt a thing."

"Ouch, love." He grinned at her and bent to kiss her slightly aroused flesh. "You're no good for a man's ego." He kissed her twice more, causing her to want to repeat what they had just finished. She moved her hips, prompting him to do more than just kiss her.

"Sorry, darlin'." He rose up and gathered her in his arms. "I got carried away."

"Can't we do it again?"

"No. It's too soon. You're a bit swollen and I don't want to hurt you." He kissed her hair. "You might be sore in the morning."

"What if I promise I won't be?"

He laughed and then gave her the slowest, sweetest kiss of her life. "Stop trying to tempt me and go to sleep."

# CHAPTER 12

*What a difference a day makes . . .*

Colin awoke when he felt a rush of cold air hit his torso. He didn't open his eyes, blindly groping for his blanket. Instead of a fluffy down comforter, his hand met with naked skin and a pair of warm lips that traveled along his chest. "Cherri." How could he have forgotten where he was? How could he have forgotten the night that would change everything?

He'd taken her virginity and by doing so made himself the man she would always remember. He searched deep inside himself for regret or uneasiness or guilt . . . But he couldn't find any.

*She makes me feel good.*

And because he was the man who took her virginity, he knew he had done it right. That she wasn't hurt. That she had a good time. He would no longer have to worry about some other man mucking it up, making sex less than beautiful for her.

"Pull the blankets back up, lass, and come here."

"No." She flicked her tongue over his nipple. His cock rose to epic proportions.

*Go away,* he warned his erection. *It's too soon for her.* But his member wasn't listening and neither was the girl who was growing closer and closer to it. "What are you doing, darlin'? It's freezing. Come here."

"No. I'm going to warm you up." Her soft kisses grew hotter as they traveled to his lower stomach. Her hair tickled his skin, and it took everything inside him not to push her down on the bed and take her again.

*Steady, lad.*

"I don't like you sleeping down here." He looked around the room to distract himself from her warm wet mouth on his body. The basement hadn't gotten any better-looking in the time he had been there. It was still ugly, dank, and eerie. "I'm surprised you don't wake up with frostbite every morning. It's got to be under fifty degrees down here."

"Colin," she whined. "I'm trying to seduce you and you're complaining about being cold."

"You're trying to seduce me?" He laughed. It wasn't necessary. All she had to do was breathe and he would be ready to make love to her.

"What's with you laughing at me all the time?" She sat up pouting and crossed her arms beneath her breasts. His eyes traveled there. She was an innocent. She didn't have a clue how sexy she looked with her breasts all plumped up and on display. She reminded him of one of those nude paintings, made when women looked like real women instead of like sticks. "I want to make you feel good," she said softly.

He tugged her hand toward his mouth and kissed the back of her fingers. "You do that without even trying."

"Oh." She smiled at him, and that feeling he was loath to describe hit him in the chest like a bullet. "That was a very smooth line, and just for that I'm going to start a fire for you."

She quickly left the bed and scurried to the ancient wood-burning stove in the corner. He almost stopped her, fairly sure that the dilapidated-looking thing was unsafe, but he kept his mouth shut because the sight of her naked bottom bent over in front of it caused the blood to rush from his head.

"It should get warm in a few minutes." She scampered back to bed and rested her head on his thigh. "Now, where was I?" She cupped his tight sac in her hands and kissed him before gently sucking him into her mouth.

He gripped the sheets. "Stop it, lass." She ran her tongue up his shaft and he was about to lose it. He grabbed her wrist, pulling her away from his organ. "For fuck's sake! How did you learn how to do that?"

"I'm learning now. I've been thinking about it for a while, you know."

"Have you?"

"Yes." She nodded as she settled down on the pillow next to him. "I think I would like to be good at sex and I want you to show me how."

"Trust me, love. You don't need any tutoring. You're a natural." More than that, they were good together. When he slipped inside her it felt like he had been making love to her his entire life. It was oddly like coming home. "You should know that sex isn't going to be like this with everybody."

She scrunched her brow in thought. "It *was* nice, wasn't it? I thought it was just me, but you felt it, too." He nodded and she continued. "Do you think it's because we're friends, it feels different?"

"Yeah," he said, but he knew that what he felt for her was far different from friendship. They were more than friends. They always were, and now that he had her he wasn't sure if he could go back to life without her.

"I'm glad we're friends." She placed his hand between her legs and stroked herself with his fingers.

His mouth went dry as he touched her wetness. She really was going to be the death of him. She made it impossible for him to be considerate. "What are you doing to me now, Charlotte?"

Her eyes were closed, her mouth slightly open, and she panted as she quickened the pace of his fingers. "You started it earlier with your kissing. I've been uncomfortable ever since." She moaned deep in her throat. "I need you."

"You have me." He pulled her on top of him, lining her warm curves with him. *Shit.* She had gotten to him. He was never going to be the same after tonight.

She looked down at him, her expression a mix of lust and pure innocence. "Tell me what to do now."

"Whatever you want, love. This is your night."

"Help me." She looked down between them.

Reading her meaning, he lifted her hips and slid deep inside her warmth. She moaned and without further instruction she began to rock on him, back and forth, setting a tempo that drove him insane. "Touch me," she ordered, and he did. No part of her skin went untouched or unloved and before long they were so lost in love that the rest of the world faded away.

Cherri woke up early the next morning with Colin's warm hard body wrapped around her. Instead of feeling pleasure that she was in bed with a gorgeous man, she felt depressed. Now that her night was over, she was going to go back to her everyday reality.

*Bummer.*

She didn't regret it, though. It was the best night of her life.

"What's wrong?" He kissed her eyelids. "You look a bit sad."

"It's all over."

"What is?"

"This is. Us. We have to go back to being normal."

"I don't know about you, but I was never normal."

She smiled and held him close. "Thank you for last night. The ride home. The taking of my virginity. The multiple orgasms."

"Happy to help." He tilted her chin her and kissed her. He kept it light and sweet at first, but soon it changed. And she had no idea who deepened it, but soon her leg was thrown over his side and he was sliding in and out of her at a frantic pace. She couldn't control herself, meeting him stroke for stroke because she knew this was her very last time with him. From now on she would have to go through life knowing what it felt like to be with him but unable to have him again.

She cried out, an orgasm striking her when he drove so deeply inside her that she didn't know where she ended and he began. He followed soon after her, kissing sweetly, saying dozens of pretty love words she was too blissful to understand.

"Aw, lass. I'm sorry." He kissed her forehead half a dozen times. "I didn't mean to start that."

He went to pull out of her but she held him tight. "Please, not yet." She enjoyed the way he felt inside her.

"It feels good." He readjusted himself so that he could fill her a little more. "I could stay here—"

"There you are!" Baba came rushing down the stairs as fast as her old heavy body could take her, Rufus at her heels. "I knew you couldn't keep your promise."

"Baba?" Cherri sat up, covering herself with blankets, trying to ignore Rufus as he barked at Baba. "What are you talking about?"

"Your baby, Natasha! You said you would take care of her but you have been out running in the street, opening your legs for every bum you come across."

*Oh no,* Cherri thought. *Oh no. Oh no. Oh no.* There

hadn't been any memory lapses since they'd changed her medication. She'd hoped that was the end of it. "Baba?"

"Yes, her Baba had to take care of her last night because you don't care enough about her. Cherri cried for you for hours." She raised her hand, slapping Cherri so hard her head snapped back. Tears filled her eyes even before she felt the sting on her cheek.

"Whoa." Colin flew out of bed and grabbed Baba. "Don't you dare raise your hand to her."

"Get off me, you bum! Did she tell you she has a one-year-old baby upstairs? That my husband and I can barely make ends meet because we are taking care of her. Did she tell you she couldn't even be bothered to get that beautiful little girl a birthday present? You're a bad girl, Natasha. I don't know where we went wrong with you." Baba lunged for her again, but this time Colin had her firmly in his grasp.

Rufus jumped onto the bed and licked Cherri's face where it stung and she almost broke down. "Please, Colin." She patted her dog's head, unable to push him away. "Don't hurt her. She doesn't know what she's doing."

"No shit." He struggled to restrain the furious old woman against him. "How long has this been going on?"

He never got an answer to his question because as soon as he asked it Baba started to hyperventilate. Naked as the day he was born, he hauled her upstairs to her bedroom. He wanted to call an ambulance but Cherri begged him not to. He almost ignored her wishes, but when he saw the tears roll down her cheeks he let it be. She said Yuliana hated hospitals. She associated them with dying, with her husband. She would be miserable if she had to stay in one.

It took them hours to get Baba settled. He didn't know what happened to the feisty woman. Her skin was gray, her words incoherent. She was lost. His heart broke every time he looked at her. And if he had a hard time seeing her that way, Cherri must have found it nearly impossible.

She hadn't meant to hurt Cherri, but her handprint hadn't faded from her face yet and each time she glanced at her granddaughter she sobbed.

"I'm so sorry, Natasha." She shook her head. "No, that's not it." She searched her granddaughter's face. "You're Cherri, right? You're not a baby anymore. Natasha is gone."

"Yes, Baba."

"I don't understand why I don't understand." She got that faraway look in her eyes and then she drifted off to sleep, the dog by her side.

He urged Cherri to go clean up. She didn't want to go, but he promised he wouldn't leave the room until she came back. He watched Yuliana sleep for half an hour from the easy chair, thinking about how scary it would be if his memories deserted him.

"I think I can manage now, Colin. Thanks for staying." Cherri returned to the room freshly showered, her hair still wet, her face still swollen.

When he saw her, all their other problems, everything else faded away in that moment. He said nothing, only opened his arms to her and held her while she sobbed. "Shh, sweet girl." He smoothed kisses down her face. "You're going to make yourself sick."

For the first time in his adult life he felt like crying. Seeing her this way . . . it felt like his chest was caving in. He couldn't bear her being so unhappy. The need to fix things for her overwhelmed him. But he was afraid this was one problem he couldn't solve. How could he combat sickness?

Eventually her sobs subsided into quiet tears and he felt brave enough to ask, "How long, Charlotte? How long have you been living like this?"

"Months. It started when she forgot where she put things.

Then she forgot who people were—the mailman, the pharmacist. And then it was me. She was frantic one day when she thought she'd lost me. It took me ten minutes before I realized she thought I was my mother. But it only happened once in a while, so I let it go. Lately it's been happening more and more, though. She left the house that time and now she's scared of things that never used to bother her. I'm afraid to leave her alone, Colin. But what can I do? How can I take care of her if I don't make any money?"

She started to cry again, and his heart was so heavy for her it felt like it was about to drop out of his chest. He couldn't leave her like this. She needed somebody to take care of her. He was going to be the one who had to do it.

# CHAPTER 13

*Another day. Another dollar.*

"I do not need a babysitter!"

Cherri turned away from her grandmother and rested her head against the wall.

*Don't smash your head into the wall. You need your brain.*

Rufus seemed to read her mind and nuzzled her hand with his cold nose. He had been surprisingly well behaved lately. He must have known how hard things were, and for once Cherri had no complaints about him.

It was her grandmother who was driving her crazy. Why couldn't she just for once be a sweet old lady? She was the most stubborn person on the planet and she was losing her memories.

"Why do you have your face pressed into the wall? You look like a dumb-dumb."

"I love you, Baba," she said, more to remind herself than her grandmother. She wasn't ready to turn around yet.

A nurse had been sitting in their living room for the past twenty minutes waiting for Cherri to leave so she could start her job. It had gotten to the point where Cherri couldn't leave Baba alone anymore. She had called Ellis and Belinda the day before to let them know she needed more time before she went back to working at the store. Things had changed. Before she was worried about leaving Baba for long periods of time. Now she was worried about leaving her at all. Hiring a nurse was the right thing to do but she still felt guilty. Baba used to be so independent. But that didn't change the fact that their lives had changed.

Cherri handpicked Rena. The Trinidadian nurse was sweet enough to be likable but had enough steel in her spine not to take any crap from Baba.

And no matter what Baba said, she did need to be watched. It took her two days to recover from her last episode. Her memory going in and out. Her mood changing with the direction of the wind. Cherri had been so terrified for her. She had never seen Baba so bad. She was actually sick, and that caused Cherri to be terrified for herself. She didn't want to think about a world where Baba wasn't Baba. Where she wasn't strong and funny and always there.

But before she sank into complete panic, Colin pulled her out. He didn't let her get bogged down in her thoughts. He stayed with them for two days, helping her care for Baba, never saying much. But never letting her think she was alone. At first she didn't know how to handle his presence. She had always been on her own. Especially this last year, trying to hide this secret from the world. But he wouldn't let her be alone. He had been with her, a quiet force, invading their space and her solitude. And no matter how uncomfortable it was to let another person into her tiny circle, it was nice to have somebody there when she needed him.

"I love you, too, pixie. Now tell the babysitter to go home."

Cherri finally lifted her head off the wall and faced her

grandmother. She was sitting in her easy chair, her knitting needles clicking at a rapid pace as if they were arguing over taking out the garbage instead of her health."She's not a babysitter. She is a licensed practical nurse and she needs to be here when I'm not here."

"Bah! I do not have demented. That doctor doesn't know what he is talking about."

"It's called dementia, Baba, and I wasn't aware that you attended medical school. Tell me, when did you get your degree?"

Baba raised one of her wispy brows at her. "Don't be fresh. Ever since you turned twenty-two you've been sassy. I can still swat you."

"Well, I'll just have to live with that because I am not sending Rena away. You are going to have to behave yourself and deal with it. I have to go to work. I have to pay Colin back for filling the boiler and doing all the work that needed to be done around here in two days that needed to be done for the past five years."

"So go to work! I never said not to. Just take the babysitter. Now go." She shooed her with her wrinkled hand. "I want to watch the *Today* show in peace."

"Old woman," Colin barked from the doorway. Both Cherri and Baba jumped. "Are you giving the lass a hard time? She's late for work."

Seeing him standing there made her heart beat a little faster and not from the fright he'd just given them. She wasn't sure how it had happened, but over the course of the past week he had become part of their lives. He was . . . dependable. And she hadn't felt like she could depend on anybody since Papa had died. It was a very strange feeling.

"I'm sorry, Colin. I was just—"

He put his hand up to stop her. "Run along to the shop, love. I'll be there in a bit. I'm going to have a chat with your gran."

"But—"

He wrapped his arm around her waist and pressed his lips to her ear. "You haven't been out of this house in days. If you don't leave now I'm going to toss you over my shoulder and carry you out." She tried to focus on what he was saying but his lips pressed to her skin, his warm minty-smelling breath, turned her mind into mushy scrambled eggs. It had been exactly a week since she had given him her body and despite everything—the stress, the worry over her grandmother—she wanted to crawl back in bed with him. To kiss his neck and feel his naked skin pressed against hers.

She blushed to her roots. "Okay." She pulled away from his embrace and knelt in front of her grandmother. "I'm going to work, Baba. You call me if you need me. All right? And you mind your manners with Rena. I made you a sandwich for lunch, and don't think about looking for the chips because I threw them away. And no extra sweets today, either. I locked them up. The doctor said—"

"Pixie!"

"Cherri!" Both Colin and Baba yelled at her. "Go now, love. It will be okay."

"Fine." She kissed Baba's cheeks, patted Rufus's head, and left the room—but not before Colin reached out and gave her hand a reassuring squeeze.

"I saw Cherri leave." Rena came into the room wearing her heart-printed scrubs and a curious expression. "Did you finally stop giving the girl grief?"

"Bah." Baba waved her hand in dismissal. "I don't give her grief. I am an adult. I changed *her* diapers. I don't need a babysitter. That means you can go away now."

Colin watched as Rena put her hands on her hips and stared Baba down. He knew why Cherri had picked her. She was the right match for the feisty old lady. "Listen, old woman, you're lucky that you've got that sweet girl to worry about you. You don't know how many patients I've cared for who don't. You be good to her, because she's the bright spot in your life."

"I know that." Baba thumped her cane against the floor. "Now leave me alone with my boyfriend for a few minutes. If you hear noise coming from here, don't worry, I'm just showing him a good time."

She winked at Colin and he grinned back. Rena only shook her head, mumbling something about wildest dreams. When they were left alone Colin pulled a footstool in front of Baba's chair and held her chubby wrinkled hand in his. "You're a pain in the arse. You know that, don't you?"

"I'm very pleasant."

"You're as pleasant as a colonoscopy on Christmas morning." He sighed. "You've got to let up on the lass. She's worrying herself sick over you."

"I'm fine. So what if sometimes my memory ain't so good? I'm still very strong. My mother was sixty-two when she died. My grandmother was fifty-five."

"What's that got to do with the price of whiskey in Ireland? We are talking about Cherri. You're not a dumb lady. You know what you're going through and you know that that girl loves you more than anything on this planet. So you'd better knock off this stubborn bullshit because I'll not have you upsetting her."

Baba stared at him for a long moment. Her sharp green eyes reminded him too much of her granddaughter's. "You've got a big willy, Irish."

Colin froze, then blinked, then opened his mouth trying to form words. "What?"

"I saw you naked." Baba shrugged. "You've got a big willy."

"I-I-I . . ."

*Fuck. Shit. Bollocks.*

Baba tapped her chin. "They say I have this dementia and

I can't remember so good but I remember you naked in my bedroom. I just don't remember why you were naked in my bedroom."

"Well, darlin', I'm sad to hear that because that means you don't remember the good time we had here together."

Baba smiled at him and raised his hand to her lips. "She's a good girl. Take care of her. Or else I'll find somebody to kill you."

He wanted to reassure Baba but for some reason he couldn't find the words. Cherri was such a sweet fresh breath of air to him, one he would be happy to continue to breathe in, but— He felt crazy these past few days. He needed to take care of Cherri. His soul wouldn't let him rest until he did. His phone rang, tearing his mind from his unsettling thoughts. "O'Connell." He answered without looking at the caller ID.

"It's your pop, lad. What kind of shit greeting is that?"

"Hiya, Pop. How are you? "

"In heaven. Or some people might call it South Beach. Oh lad! You should see the women down here. They come in so many different colors. Brown ones with red bikinis. Chocolate ones with pink ones. Ivory ones in black. So many different flavors. A man could get a cavity trying to taste them all."

He couldn't help but smile at his father's exuberant description of women. "Enjoying single life, are you, Pop?"

"It's fun for a while but I miss having a woman. One sweet, soft-smelling lass who I can come home to and bed down with every night."

The hint of sadness in Magnus's voice was unmistakable. He was going on fifty-five, never married, and a failure at more relationships than Colin had teeth. He didn't want to be like his pop. Leaving middle age and still searching for somebody to love. "Call your ex . . . what's her face. Maybe she'll take you back."

"Yeah, and maybe pigshit smells like roses."

"I don't know what to tell you, Pop. Why don't you stop being an old bugger and bring your arse to New York for a while?"

"Who you calling an old bugger? I could still kick your arse if I wanted to. Besides, I can't get away just yet. I've got business to attend to here in Miami. It will be a little while before I can see you, lad."

"Of course," he mumbled. He wasn't sure why his father's absence still bugged him after all these years. He should be used to it by now. Magnus was a man who did things on his own time, even if that meant missing important events in Colin's life, like his college graduation or the opening of his business. He wasn't sure why he suddenly felt like he was six years old again, waiting for his father to come see him in the Christmas pageant. "I got to go, Pop. I was in the middle of something."

"That something is a woman, right? I knew it! My lad is just like his pop. Tell me, what's she like? Does she have big ones?"

He shook his head and turned to look at Yuliana. She had one eye on him and the other on her knitting needle. He winked at her. "Yes, she's a beautiful Ukrainian lass. Long light-colored hair and a smile that makes my heart race."

"Is she good in bed?"

Colin shook his head. There was no hope for the man. "Bye, Pop."

"Good-bye, lad."

Ellis, Belinda, and Cherri strolled across Durant's town green. It was unusually quiet for a weeknight. Durant University was still closed for winter break. All the college kids who usually hung out downtown were gone for another week or so. It was still brutally cold, but this was Cherri's favorite time of year to be in this part of town. It was peaceful here. She had memories of her papa taking her to the green in the dead of winter, buying her hot chocolate and telling her stories about the old country. It almost made her sad to be there at times, but Cherri needed to get out of the house for a little while, and she needed her best friends. She needed to tell them about the decision she had come to, but she couldn't force the words to come out of her mouth. Her stomach cramped just thinking about it, but she had to do it. She had to do it for her grandmother.

"You guys want to head over to Hot Lava Java for some mocha lattes and brownies? I could really use something warm right now," she said, breaking the long silence.

"No," Ellis said, pinning Cherri with a glare. "I want you to come out and tell us what you need to tell us."

Cherri shut her eyes, feeling the tears burn in the back of her throat. Never in a million years had she thought when she walked into Size Me Up that she would meet people who would change her life.

"I need to quit the store," she said in a rush. "I'm going to work for Colin a few days a week and stay with Baba the rest of the time. It's gotten bad. I don't know what else to do."

"How could you?" Ellis whispered.

"I'm sorry I have to leave so abruptly. I didn't mean to leave you in the lurch."

"It's not about the damn job, Cherri!" Ellis stopped walking and faced her. "This is about you not telling us what's going on with you. We could have helped you. We're your friends. Asking for help doesn't make you any less of a woman. It makes you human."

"I'm—I'm sorry." Tears stung her eyes. She didn't know why she kept everything to herself. It was probably because she was as stubborn as Baba. And maybe because she thought that needing help was a sign of weakness.

Belinda's arm came around her, offering her comfort as always. "Quit being a cranky bitch, Ellis. I know you're upset, but yelling at her isn't going to help things."

"I'm sorry, Cherri." Ellis looped her arms around her. "I just hate that it got so bad. I hate that you had to go through that alone."

The three of them stood huddled on the green for a few moments.

"I didn't have to go through it alone. Colin was with me."

Both Ellis and Belinda pulled back to look at her.

"We had sex."

"Oh, Cherri," Ellis breathed.

"It's about damn time," Belinda grinned. "Tell me it was as good as I think it was."

Cherri smiled back, glad that she had finally gotten that little bit of information off her chest. "It was better. He was gentle and sweet. It was perfect."

"If you're happy about this," Ellis said, "then I'm happy for you, but I have just one question."

"Yeah?"

"What the hell does this mean for you two now?"

Colin watched Cherri as she studied the chest she was painting. Some might call it a work of art, but he was more content studying the artist than the art. He had work to do and he knew that since she'd started working with him he'd stared at her more than he should. But the lass was so damned cute with a paintbrush clasped between her teeth and her brow furrowed in concentration.

She took her work seriously, and it showed in each brilliant piece she turned out. On his end asking her to join his business was the best business decision he'd ever made. But what was in it for her? Her last two pieces brought in thousands of dollars, and when he tried to give her all the profits she refused.

"We're partners," she said. "And nobody would care about buying anything made by me if it weren't for you."

She might have been right at first, but new customers were flocking to Stone Barley Restorations because Charlotte Rudy turned dreary pieces of furniture into colorful works of art. In a few months she could set out on her own and go into business for herself. When he brought up the idea to her, though, she simply shook her head, mumbled something about numbers, and went back to work.

She walked around the chest, studying it from a different angle. She had a smudge of green paint on her chin. Her work shirt was covered. Her hair was a mess, yet he found her sexier than any other woman on the planet. The younger him would have laughed at that thought. He used to like his women elegant and dressed to the nines in short skirts and high heels. He used to seek sophistication in a woman. Someone he thought could elevate him from his pigshit Irish background. What the hell did he know then? None of those women made him feel half as good as the girl before him.

*Stay back, Colin.* For weeks his conscience was serving as her bodyguard, warning him to keep his distance. He had, but it seemed that in the past few days the bodyguard was quickly losing strength.

He walked up behind her to admire her work but got distracted by her soft smell and the way her behind curved in her jeans.

"Do you think I went overboard with this one? Mrs. Rich said she wanted Alice in Wonderland, but I think it looks a little circusy."

"Is there a difference, love?" He slid his arm around her waist and pulled her soft backside into his front. She leaned against him.

*Shit.* She made it hard to stay away. It was almost as if she needed to be touched as much as he needed to touch her.

"Of course there's a difference, dummy." She sighed. "I just want it to be perfect. She came to us as a referral and we need more referrals like her. That's what's going to keep us going."

"Mmm-hmm." He lifted her hair and kissed the curve of her neck. He had promised himself he wasn't going to kiss her like this anymore but he couldn't help himself. They spent every day and most nights together. But instead of warming each other up in bed they spent it around the dinner table with Baba, playing card games, doing puzzles, or talking, things the doctor said were good for her brain.

Little did Colin know that those things were good for him, too. It gave him a glimpse into what family life was like.

Even when his father had women in the house, they never spent their time with him. Magnus never kicked him out or shooed him away but he didn't go out of his way to spend time with him, either. He really didn't have a family. More like three people living together.

*Stop whining about your childhood. You're Irish for fuck's sake. Grow a pair.*

"Mm," Cherri moaned as he continued his kisses down the seam of her neck. The more he kissed her, the better he felt. "Mm, Colin, that feels good. Mrs. Rich is submitting photos of her house to *Life Is Lovely* magazine. If they do a spread of her house that could be good for us. Think about how much business we could get."

"We're a bit busy now, love." He slid his hand beneath her shirt to curve his hand over her soft belly. *Us* and *we*. Hearing those words come from her mouth did something for him even though he knew he should back away.

They had already gone down this road once, and there could be consequences for it.

She hadn't said anything to him about that night. It had almost been a month. He had a right to know what was going on but was almost afraid to ask her. Too afraid he wouldn't like her answer.

*This is why you should be with women your own age. Less trouble.*

*Oh, will you get off that already.*

She came with baggage. A sick grandmother. A tumble-down house. Stuff he wasn't used to from other women. But none of that seemed to matter when he was with her.

*Find somebody else.*

"I know," she sighed. "You want to keep things small. I get it. This place is your baby. I wouldn't want that to change for you." She paused for a moment. "Colin?"

"Yes, love?"

"You're kissing me."

He nuzzled her neck. "It bloody took you long enough to notice."

"You're doing it on purpose?"

He spun her around so that he could frown at her. "What kind of daft question is that?"

She shrugged. "Maybe you shouldn't kiss me anymore."

"Why?"

"I—I—We slept together and it was nice—"

"Just nice?"

She gave him a wobbly grin. "You're a total stud and you know it, but maybe it was something that should just be a onetime thing. We're friends. We lead different lives."

"This is sounding like bullshit to me, love. What are you trying to say?"

"You might break my heart."

*Hell.*

He didn't want to. He couldn't see himself doing that because he couldn't see himself ever wanting to be away from her.

Those were dangerous thoughts. Those were forever thoughts.

*Walk away from this girl. Walk away. Walk away. Walk away. Fuck it. Run away.*

But he didn't. He knew the timing was bad. He knew that she was so worried about her grandmother—about everything that had been piled on her plate—that some of her bubbliness had evaporated, but even so he found her sweet and charming and adorable. Many might have crumbled under the circumstances, but she didn't. He almost felt like love for her grandmother alone kept her going. For once in his life he wanted to know what it was like to feel that kind of love. Charlotte could teach him what it was like to feel that kind of love.

He wasn't about to let her go.

He tilted her chin back and kissed her. And like always when he kissed her the rest of the world melted away and he was left with a warm sweet-smelling girl who felt right in his arms. He popped open the buttons on her ratty shirt, eager to get to her creamy skin.

*She's the last thing you need in your life right now.*

*But she's the only thing you want.*

He ignored the voices in his head and continued to pepper kisses all over her exposed skin. Right now thoughts had no place with him and Cherri. He just wanted to feel, so he kissed her neck. Her collarbone. The space between her breasts, and when he finally peeled the shirt off her body he froze. Her arm and the side of her breast were bruised. Little red nail marks angrily stood out against her white skin.

"What happened to you?"

"Nothing." She stepped away from him and pulled her shirt on.

"Cherri." He grabbed her arm, unable to accept that from her. "Don't lie to me. I need to know."

"I scared her. She was asleep—" She looked at the floor. "Please don't ask me anymore."

As much as he needed to know, as much as the need to protect her overwhelmed him, he didn't push her to answer. Instead he pulled her close and smoothed a kiss across her brow. "You'll tell me if it gets worse?" When she said nothing he forced her chin upward. "Love?"

She nodded and hugged him. "You know, I like it when you call me *love.* And yes, I'm changing the subject, and no I don't care that you want to talk about it." She looked up at him and smiled, revealing that dimple that always did him in. "In my mind I know we shouldn't be doing this, but do you think you could kiss me some more?"

There was still doubt there. Doubt about them. He felt it, too. But he wanted to be with her. Not just to sleep with her. He wanted her to be his. And he needed to tell her that. But he couldn't get the words out right then, because the need to be with her overrode all other thoughts.

"You're going to be the death of me, lass."

She cupped his face in her paint-splotched hands and stepped up to kiss his nose. "Do you think they'll name a disease for me after you go? I could be Rudy-itis. Or the Charlotte Rudy disease. Or Cherri Pox."

"Cherri Pox." He captured her bottom lip between his teeth. "I'll take some of that and gladly die from it."

"Mm." She slid her hands up the back of his shirt. His entire body came to life in an instant. "You taste good."

His mouth left hers and he trailed his lips across her skin. He kept his eyes open so that he could watch her expressions. That was the best part of making love to her: seeing how his touch made her feel. At the moment she was smiling and so lovely that the last of his common sense fled. *Aw, the hell with it.* There was no way he could let her go without having all of her. "What time do you have to be home tonight?"

"Six."

"Good." He gripped her wrist and pulled her toward the door. "Then we've got all day."

According to the clock on Colin's bedroom wall it was five oh two. She had to leave soon.

*Damn. Time flies when you're making love.*

She had to get back to Baba, to her real life, and leave her beautiful distraction behind. Spending all day in his bed wasn't in her original plans but she was damn glad her plans had changed. She needed him to help her take her mind off things. Last night had been a rough one.

But then that little niggle of doubt crept into her mind. He was becoming just one more complication in her already overcomplicated life. Where would he fit? What was really going on with them? How did he feel about her? Every time he looked at her she could feel herself slipping into love. But she knew that he didn't feel that way about her.

He felt sorry for her. And for Baba and for their situation. She couldn't help but wonder: If things were different, would he still be here now?

Colin stroked her damp hair out of her face, breaking her from her thoughts. "You smell like me, love. Well, you smell more like my soap."

"Mm." She shut her eyes, welcoming his touch. "It's my favorite smell," she told him, wishing she hadn't.

He pressed his lips against her cheek, and she could feel the lazy grin spread across his face. How could his ex have cheated on him? Even Cherri knew that relationships weren't all sunflowers and rainbows, but Colin was a good man. She knew he didn't love her and yet when he looked at her she felt like she was the only woman in the world. Imagine if he did love her. The feeling would be more than intense. Maybe that was the problem with his ex. Maybe being loved by a man like Colin O'Connell was more than she could take.

*Poor sap.*

"What are you thinking about, beauty?"

"Nothing. Everything." She opened her eyes to look up at his slightly bearded face. He looked so damn sexy with his rumpled hair. His hard body felt like a human heating pad on her weary body. "I have to go soon," she told him, but for once she didn't want to go home. Guilt flooded her at the ugly thought. Of course she wanted to go and spend time with Baba. She loved her.

"Do you?" he asked sleepily as he gathered her body close and stroked his hand down her bare back. "It can't be near six o'clock yet."

"It is. I have to get up in a few minutes."

"I suppose the day got a bit away from us." He kissed the shell of her ear. "Why don't we take your gran out for dinner tonight and then you both come back here for the night?"

She grinned up at him despite the uneasiness that settled in her chest. "You want to have a sleepover after all that sex with just had? I never realized that I was so good in bed. Not bad for a newbie, huh?"

"You're superb, love, but it's not that." He frowned at her. "Your house is shit, love. I don't like you staying there. Especially in the basement. Half the time I'm afraid it's going to topple on you during the night."

She would be lying if she said she hadn't thought the same thing a few times, but it kind of stung when somebody else pointed it out."My house is not shit, Colin. My papa built it forty years ago. With a little work it could be great."

He shook his head. "The foundation isn't sound. I had an inspector come in and look at it."

"What? When did you do that?"

She sat up, not noticing the sheet slip from her body.

He did, and God bless him he only looked at her chest for

a moment. "When I noticed the cracks in the Sheetrock two weeks ago."

"So you had a man come to my house to inspect it and you didn't tell me?"

"I told your grandmother." He paused for another distracted moment. "Technically I don't need your permission. It isn't really your house."

"Excuse me? I've paid the bills there for the last five years. I stayed behind, sleeping in a moldy basement, when everybody else I knew was going away to college. I put my life on hold. I've turned down semesters abroad and internships in the city so I could be there with my grandmother and you have the nerve to tell me that it's not my house? It is my house even though sometimes I wish I could have run away when I got the chance. It may be shit to you, but it's the only thing besides Baba that I'll ever have."

"Aw, love." He touched her shoulder. "That's not true but I'm sorry your life is not what you want it to be."

She realized how ungrateful she sounded. Her grandparents gave up their retirement to raise her and didn't complain once. "I didn't mean that." She shook her head. "My life is fine. I'm glad I didn't go away. It's just . . . It's just . . ." She couldn't find the right words. "I don't want to think about this anymore."

"Don't cry, Charlotte. Please, love. I didn't mean to make you upset."

*Damn it.* She hadn't noticed the tears until one hit her cheek. She was tired of crying. Tired of feeling sorry for herself. Her life was fine. Why didn't she feel that way? "Make love to me." She wrapped her body around him, needing the distraction that being with him would bring. His erection rose against her belly but he didn't act; instead he held her at arm's length and studied her face.

He shook his head. "You're upset."

"Yes, but you can make it better for me." She reached between them, stroking him until he was hard in her hand. "Please, Colin. Make it better for me. Don't tell me no."

His expression grew so intense that it frightened her a little, but she kept at him. Touching and kissing till his hard body relaxed and he had no other choice but to make love to her one more time.

# CHAPTER 14

*Once. Twice. Three times a lady.*

"I'm sorry I'm a little late," Cherri said to Rena as she walked into the kitchen. The nurse was putting away dishes, which was clearly not in her job description but Cherri was grateful for her help. She had taken a lot of the burden off Cherri's shoulders.

"It's my fault," Colin said, entering behind her. "I didn't mean to make her break curfew." He wrapped his arm around her waist and kissed below her ear. Surprised by his actions she turned to look at him, but his eyes were on Rena and his arm was still firmly around her. "I'll make sure she's early tomorrow."

Rena passed her light brown eyes over them and nodded. "I know why you were late. Can't say I blame you. If it were me with him I would have been a hell of a lot more than ten minutes late."

Cherri's face burned. Apparently it was quite obvious what they had been up to. It was also apparent that Colin had no intentions of hiding . . . whatever they were. "How's Baba?"

"Yes, how is the old woman? You think I could convince these two to stay at my house tonight?"

"Heard it was supposed to snow, did you? Don't want your woman freezing her pretty little behind off in the godforsaken basement? If she had any sense she would go with you. Now, as for Yuliana, she was a bit weepy this morning after you left. But she's been quiet most of the day. She went off to her room about half an hour ago and told me not to bother her. I checked on her just before you two walked in the door. She's sleeping in her chair, holding that old music box in her lap. "

"Maybe I should let her rest. She hasn't been sleeping well lately."

"No." Rena shook her head. "Wake her up. She needs to eat. She'll be cranky as a bear if she doesn't."

"Okay. Thank you, Rena. I hope you know that I appreciate you."

"No problem, sweetie. I'll straighten up in here before I go."

They left the kitchen, Colin's fingers linked with hers. She didn't want to think about what this could mean for them. Apparently there was no going back to the way things were.

"Where do you want to go for dinner tonight, love?"

"I don't care. Maybe we should let Baba decide since you want us to stay at your house. If she's happy she's more likely to agree."

"She'll agree," he said confidently. "Your gran and I are good mates."

"Is this where you come when you leave the shop in the morning?"

"Yeah, we eat sweets and watch Jerry Springer together. Your gran is quite bloodthirsty. I said I'd take her to a boxing match if she was a good lass for you."

Cherri stopped in front of Baba's door and looked up at

him. "Is this how you get girls to fall for you? You reel their grandmothers in first with sweets and trashy TV?"

He kissed her forehead. "I use whatever works."

"It's a shame you had to work so hard. I probably would have gone to bed with you if you had simply taken off your shirt."

"What about the days when I'm feeling a bit bloated?"

They laughed as they walked into Baba's room. The lamp was off. The only light visible was the one flickering from the TV. Baba was in her favorite place, her eyes peacefully shut, the music box Papa gave her cradled in her lap. She must have been missing him that day. She only held it like that when it got too much for her. Rufus lay at her feet, his head resting on her old pink slippers.

"Baba, it's time to get up now." Cherri approached her carefully. She didn't want to startle her. She didn't want a repeat of the night before. Colin, seeming to read her mind, placed his hand on her shoulder to stop her and switched on the light.

"Darlin', we've come to take you to dinner. Anyplace you want to go."

Normally Baba jumped at the chance to go out to eat, but this time she didn't stir. She didn't raise her head. Her eyes didn't flicker. Her mouth didn't move. Rufus looked up at her and whimpered.

In that moment the earth stopped moving for Cherri. The air whooshed out of her lungs. Her heart stopped beating. *Not yet.* She prayed to whatever god might be listening. *Please not yet.* But she knew. Even before she touched Baba she knew.

Her wrinkled hand was still warm when she pressed it against her cheek.

"I love you."

"Charlotte?" Colin placed his hand on her shoulder, but she barely felt its weight.

"She's gone." She was surprised at how strong her voice was. The day she had feared her entire life was finally here and her life as she knew it was over.

Cherri passed from guest to guest, thanking them for coming, the small sad smile never leaving her face. So many people had showed up for Baba's service. So many more than they had anticipated that they had to move the repast to Colin's house to accommodate everyone paying their respects. Colin stood against the wall watching Cherri float around the room. He was unable to take his eyes off her, afraid that if he did, something might happen. *How the hell does she do it?* he wondered. Comfort other people when the bottom of her world dropped out. She was hugging Mrs. Petrovich, her weeping next-door neighbor, at the moment. Colin could see the grief plainly on her face, and then there was Cherri, with almost no expression at all, rubbing her neighbor's back, offering her comfort as if it were the other woman's time of need instead of hers. The service had been sad but sweet, with no person unable to stop their tears. Even he cried and Colin never cried. But Cherri didn't.

She hadn't said one word during the service. She sat quietly beside him. Her two hands wrapped around his. It was as if she were an outsider looking in on someone else's tragedy. For him that was the saddest part. He knew that she felt the loss of her grandmother acutely. The woman had raised her, and he worried that Cherri's grief might be too big. That she might not know how to process it. It was as if someone had reached inside of her and turned her brightness off. That thing about her that made the world smile. He wanted to turn it back on, to fix it for her. He wanted to make it all right.

*You can't fix death, dumbass.*

But if he could he would.

"Cherri." Belinda grabbed hold of her hand before she

could greet another person and pulled her into the safety of the circle she and Mike and Ellis had created. "How are you feeling, honey?"

"I'm fine. Mr. and Mrs. Petrovich offered to take care of Rufus for a few days until I get everything sorted out. They have another dog Rufus can play with. There's no reason he should sit around an empty house all day." She looked away for a moment, and Colin thought she was about to cry. "Have you guys eaten yet? Somebody made a rum cake that looks yummy. Baba loved rum cake. I can bring you some. Wasn't Colin nice to let us do this here?"

"He was," Mike agreed and looked uncomfortably to the women he was with. "Cherri, why don't you stay with me and Ellis for a while? I don't think you should be alone at the house."

"Or stay with me," Belinda said pleadingly. "You might get sick of staying with the lovebirds." Her eyes filled with tears. "We could have a good time at my place."

"Thank you." Cherri shook her head and patted Belinda's shoulder. "But I'm fine."

She wasn't fine. Colin could see that standing ten feet away.

"Go to her," Rena said from beside him. He had all but forgotten about the nurse he was supposed to be having a conversation with. He was too busy watching his girl. "The old woman wanted you for her. Now go to her."

Baba had asked him to take care of her. All those times his brain had warned him to stay away from her and he didn't listen. He hadn't wanted to listen. As soon as he was near enough to touch her he pulled her into a hug and dusted kisses across the bridge of her nose. Her soft body tensed but relaxed a little when he stroked his hand down her back. "Did you eat anything, love?"

"I'm not hungry."

"I want you to eat anyway."

She nodded and burrowed closer to his body as if she was cold. Mike gawked at them, while Ellis and Belinda looked away. He didn't give a shit what they thought about Cherri and him. He smoothed his hand down her back, bringing her closer. He no longer cared about what the world thought. He was done with the internal battles. He wanted this girl to be his because she made him happy.

"I want you to stay here tonight."

"Okay." She reached up and gave him a comforting kiss on the lips, like he was the one in deep pain, as if it were his great loss. She was being too strong. "I have to get back to the kitchen."

"I'll go with you," Belinda said. She squeezed Colin's arm before she followed Cherri out.

Colin watched her go, telling himself he could take his eyes off her but unable to do so. "I'm worried about her," he admitted out loud for the first time. "She hasn't cried yet. The girl loses it during sappy commercials but she has yet to shed a single tear."

"Not even when you found Baba," Ellis asked. "You were with her, right?"

He finally looked at his friends. "I was with her." The back of his throat started to burn. "I think it hasn't hit her that her gran's not coming back. She didn't let go of Yuliana's hand until the paramedics came, talking to her the whole time, like Yuliana was going on a holiday. It bloody broke my heart."

"Col . . ." Ellis hugged him. "I know this is hard for you, too. I'm so sorry."

"What do I do?"

"I don't know," Ellis answered helplessly. "I think maybe you just need to give her a little time."

# CHAPTER 15

*Ch-ch-changes*

The house didn't feel the same. There was no sound of clicking knitting needles, no one to call her dumb-dumb. No one to take care of. That was the hardest part of losing Baba. They took care of each other. A lot of people saw their relationship as strange, and maybe it was. But family was important to them. Family was all they had. Now she had nothing. But guilt. While Baba was dying she was feeling ungrateful about the way her life turned out.

She lay on the sofa, curled up in one of the many afghans her grandmother had made, trying not to think about her but finding it impossible. The blanket smelled like potpourri and medicated powder. Like Baba. And so many memories washed over her, she was afraid she was going to drown.

In the back of her mind she'd known that this day was coming, but she hadn't expected it to come so soon. She wasn't ready to let Baba go. But Baba was ready. She missed

Papa, and it gave Cherri a small amount of comfort to think that they were together somewhere.

It made her think about her mother. Natasha. Where was she? Why hadn't she come to the funeral? Had she even heard her mother was dead? Would she care? It was foolish for Cherri to want to see her mother when she hadn't bothered to call or write or visit in twenty years, but she felt so utterly alone. So disconnected from everybody else, she thought it might be nice to know somebody who shared the same blood as her.

"Hello, love." Cherri sat up as Colin walked through the front door. He wouldn't leave her alone, visiting her every day since she left his house. Tonight was no different from any other. He came in carrying a bag of food that she had no intention of eating. Food wasn't fun anymore.

"Hey."

He placed the bag on the coffee table and sat next to her on the couch, gathering her in his arms. It felt good. He felt good, and if she could somehow create a coat that felt like and smelled like him she'd be rich. And maybe she wouldn't feel the constant heaviness that invaded her.

"How are you feeling today, beauty? And don't tell me fine. Tell me the truth."

"I feel the same as yesterday."

"Hmm." He kissed her hair. "Slightly worse than shitty?"

She nodded. "How did you know?"

"Because that's what I feel like when I see you like this."

He was so sweet sometimes. He was a good man. A man who shouldn't be wasting his time with her anymore. He should fall in love, get married, move on. That's what she wanted for him, to fall in love with a woman who loved him in return. But he was too busy messing around with her. Before he knew Baba was sick he did everything in his power to keep her at arm's length. And after . . . She knew he only made love to her because he felt sorry for her. It was the reason why he kept coming around, trying to take care of her. He didn't have to anymore. Surprisingly, Baba had a will, and she'd left Cherri with enough money to start over someplace else. She never told Cherri about the money, and instead of being happy about its presence now she felt angry. They had lived hand-to-mouth for years. Always just scraping by. They could have used it for so many things. They could have taken one last trip together. They could have fixed up the house. Baba's last days could have been spent in comfort rather than relative poverty.

She didn't want to dwell on it. There was nothing she could do to change it, and in the end she knew that her grandmother was only looking after her.

"Why do you keep coming over here?" she asked.

"Because I'm used to seeing you every day, lass, and if I don't it feels like something's missing."

"Oh." She cupped his face in her hands and softly kissed him. "You're full of shit but I like it."

He hauled her into his lap and gave her a real kiss this time. His hands tangled in her hair, his mouth was hot and demanding over hers. It was like he couldn't help himself, like he couldn't get enough of her. If she were an idiot she might think he was in love with her. But she wasn't and she knew that Colin O'Connell kissed every girl like this. And he was only kissing her because he felt sorry for her. And yes, he liked her, but that was all.

"I'm not full of shit. You feel different." He cupped her behind in his hands and squeezed.

"My bottom is shrinking. Do you like that?"

"Definitely not. I want you to start eating more." He shook his head. "Didn't I tell you that I only like my girls with big bottoms?"

"Did you?" she muttered. "That's something I thought I would've remembered." She shut her eyes and leaned against him, the heavy lonely feeling lifting. "Thank you for being with me through all this. You didn't have to, you know."

"You can't get rid of me." He kissed her again, sliding her hands beneath her sweater, tracing the curve of her spine with his fingertips. "Marry me, Cherri."

For a split second she felt delirious. Had the man she loved just asked her to marry him? It was impossible. "What?"

He looked unsure of himself for a moment, but then a determined look crossed his face. "I want you to marry me."

"What? Why?" She shook her head and climbed off him. "No, Colin. Just because I'm pregnant doesn't mean you have to marry me. People don't even do that anymore."

His head snapped back to look at her. He gripped her shoulders. "Are you pregnant, lass?"

She had just realized what she'd said. It was the thought she had buried in the back of her mind for weeks. But all along she knew. She just didn't want to face it. She didn't want to face the fact that her life wasn't going to be her own. There would be no freedom for her.

"I'm not sure. Maybe." Yes. She had felt the changes in her body, the tenderness in her breasts, even before Baba passed away. "I'm late but I've been stressed out."

"And not eating or sleeping or taking care of my child," he snapped, but his face cleared immediately. "I'm sorry, Charlotte. But why didn't you tell me sooner?"

"I don't know for sure, Colin. It could just be stress."

"We'll know tomorrow, because we are going to the doctor."

Cherri stared at Colin as they waited for the doctor to come back into the exam room. He had been so quiet all day, and she wondered what was going through his mind. She wondered if his thoughts mirrored hers. They couldn't have a baby. She just couldn't be pregnant. But they'd had unprotected sex. On more than one occasion. He probably assumed she was on birth control. Every female she knew her age was. But that had never crossed her mind; condoms had never crossed her mind. Maybe everybody was right about her. Maybe she was too naive to realize that she could have gotten pregnant from being with him.

There was still a chance she wasn't pregnant, though. Still a chance that stress and Baba's death had just taken a toll on her body. It was a slim chance but one she held on to. She couldn't be a mother. She didn't know how to raise a baby. She wasn't secure enough to be totally responsible for another person's life. And then there was Colin. Every time she looked at him she felt guilty. He hadn't planned on fatherhood. Her stupidity took away his choices. His freedom, too. He was going to be just as stuck as she was.

He should resent her because now no matter what, he was going to be saddled with her for the rest of their lives.

"I wish you would stop looking at me like that, Charlotte."

"I'm sorry," she blurted out. "I didn't do it on purpose, you know. I just never thought about getting pregnant."

"Hush." He placed his hand over her mouth. "Don't you dare apologize to me. We don't even know if you're pregnant yet, love, and if you are it isn't a tragedy. It's a gift. You know I'll love my child. You know I'll take care of you."

She did know that. She also knew that if he didn't feel sorry for her, if Baba hadn't died, he wouldn't feel this powerful need to take care of her.

"I don't want you to have to take care of me. I want to take care of myself."

The doctor walked in just as Colin parted his lips to speak.

"Congratulations, Cherri and Colin. You're going to be parents."

They walked out a few minutes later, neither of them surprised by the news.

Seven months. She had seven months to prepare to become a mother. How the hell was she going to manage that when some days she didn't want to get out of bed?

"Having a baby with me isn't the worst thing in the world," he said quietly when they were both seated in the car.

She looked over at him, surprised by the hurt in his voice. "I'm sorry, Colin." She pressed her lips to his face in apology. "If I had to pick a man to have a baby with it would be you, but you honestly can't tell me that having a baby right now is a good thing."

"We're bringing a life into the world, Cherri! A little piece of me and you. You should be grateful to have it. Especially now. Especially now that Baba is gone."

His words, the way he said them, made her heart seize. "I'm never going to have a life of my own."

She was going from taking care of an old lady to raising a baby.

"We'll make a life together, Cherri. Marry me."

She shook her head, panic starting to beat in her chest. "I—I . . ."

"You have to. Who's going to take care of you if you don't?" He shook his head. "That didn't come out right. I want to take care of you. I want you in my home. I want to raise our child the right way. I want to be married to you."

"I'm sorry, Colin, but no."

Colin didn't think that any man had ever fucked up a marriage proposal more than he had a few minutes ago. He was an arsehole. A world-class idiot. A jackass.

*Who's going to take care of you?*

He shuddered every time he thought about what he'd said to her. Women wanted to hear *I love you*s and sweet promises, not be reminded that they had few other choices. Watching his father woo women most of his life should have made him a pro with pretty words and proposals. He sounded no better than a green lad asking a girl for a first date. Colin O'Connell, the man who never heard no from a woman, couldn't even get a poor pregnant lass to marry him.

"Who the hell proposes to a woman ten minutes after she finds out she's pregnant," he scolded himself.

He definitely shouldn't have asked her to marry him today. She needed time to digest their news. Hell, he shouldn't have proposed yesterday, either, for that matter. The words just popped out of his mouth. *Marry me.* They came out involuntarily, and once he said them he couldn't take them back. More surprisingly, he didn't want to. She looked so sweet and sad and she felt damn good in his lap. Plus she was alone. He could take care of her. He could take her away from that shitbox little house and give her what she wanted. She really did need him.

Plus she wasn't anything like Serena. He could trust her. They were good friends and good together in bed and now they were going to have a baby. Marriage was the logical choice.

*Who the hell are you kidding, lad? She doesn't need you. You need her.*

*I don't need her or anybody,* he attempted to argue with himself. He had been on his own most of his life and he liked it that way. He might want her more than any other female in creation, but he certainly didn't need her.

*Lying wanker.*

He pulled into Mike's driveway. He hadn't seen much of Mike lately. Maybe a chat with his best mate would help him put things in perspective.

"What's up?" Mike said, inviting him inside. "I haven't seen you in a while. Do you want a beer?" Without waiting for him to answer he walked to the kitchen and handed him one anyway.

Colin twisted the cap off but didn't take a swig. His damn stomach was doing somersaults. There was no easy to say it. "Cherri's pregnant."

Mike froze, his bottle halfway to his lips. He said nothing for a long time. But his mouth smoothed into a straight line and his free hand clenched into a fist. "You moved fast."

Colin laughed off the comment, but the little hairs on the back of his neck rose. "How about a congratulations, mate? It's not every day I tell you I'm going to be a father."

"Are you proud of yourself?" Mike put his beer down and stepped closer to him. "You knocked up a twenty-two-year-old girl. You think I'm going to congratulate you on your latest conquest?"

Colin stiffened. "Conquest? What are you talking about?"

"Your need to fuck everything that isn't tied down. Your need to have every woman fall in love with you. You could have had anybody else in this town. But you were so damn focused on Cherri. Was she some kind of challenge for you, or did you think that sleeping with someone your little sister's age would be fun?"

"Watch it, Edwards. I did not go after her."

"You did. I saw you. Every time you were near her you couldn't keep your eyes off her. You think somebody as naive as Cherri had a chance?"

"I couldn't keep my eyes off her because she's beautiful. And Cherri may be young but she is not naive. We both went into this with open eyes."

"Really? Because it seems like you took advantage of a grieving girl."

"She wasn't grieving when we made this baby and you knew we were together before Baba's funeral. Why the hell are you being such an arsehole about it?"

"Because you ruined her life and yours because you couldn't keep your dick in your pants."

Before he realized what he was doing he had Mike pinned to the wall. "You're my best fucking mate. You think I would set out to ruin her life. I want to marry her. I want this baby. I was there for you when you fell in love with Ellis. I supported you. I thought you of all people would be happy for me. You know how much I've always wanted a family. But all you can do is sit there and be sanctimonious. You were just as bad as I was. Nobody is holding your past against you."

"What the hell is going on in here? Are you two fighting?" Ellis walked in, her heels rapidly clicking on the floor. She grabbed Colin's shoulder, causing him to release her husband. "What baby? Who do you want to marry?"

"Cherri."

"Oh." She blinked at him. "It's Cherri who's pregnant?"

He nodded. "We just found out today."

"Are you happy about this?"

He nodded again, unable to find the right words to explain how he felt.

Ellis searched his face for a moment. "Then I'm happy for you." She looked at her husband. "We are happy for you."

"You're okay with this?" Mike threw up his hands in frustration. "She's a kid!"

Ellis shook her head. "She's not and you—we all have to stop treating her like she is." She reached up and hugged Colin. "You do know that if you mistreat her I'll cut your balls off."

"I would expect no less from you."

"I'm glad you know that. So when's the wedding?"

"I don't know if there's going to be one. She turned me down twice already."

She shook her head. "Then keep asking her until she says yes."

# CHAPTER 16

*Celebrate me home . . .*

The heavy footsteps pounding on the floor above her should have woken Cherri from a deep sleep. But she'd never managed to fall asleep that night, so instead of being frightened of her intruder she sighed and turned over, waiting for him to make his appearance.

"I'm going to freeze my bollocks off," he cursed as he entered the basement.

She wasn't surprised to see Colin. But she was surprised he waited so long to make another appearance. It was the first night in two weeks that he hadn't come by for dinner, and she realized that she might have missed him.

"I can see my bloody breath. Bloody icebox basement."

Without saying a word to her he dropped the large duffel bag he had brought with him on the floor and bent in front of the wood-burning stove. She propped herself up on her elbow and watched him, his muscles bunching under his shirt as he worked to light a fire.

*So this man is going to be the father of my child.* She placed her hand on her belly and gave it a small rub and instead of thinking about her impending motherhood, or the fact that she only had seven months to prepare, she thought about how much it was going to hurt. She was six feet tall. Colin was six foot three and had the kind of large body that seemed to take up the entire room. They were going to have an enormous child. With long stilt-like legs, linebacker shoulders, and big water-ski-sized feet. *Ouch.*

He wiped his hands on his shirt, peeled it off and then his pants. Her breath caught and her eyes froze on his nearly nude body, especially on his tight behind that rounded nicely in the black boxer briefs he wore. And as he crawled into bed beside her, she focused on his face with his chiseled jaw and soft brown eyes. He was very easy to look at and the mental image of what their future children looked liked changed in her mind. Maybe they would have beautiful children with soft brown eyes, gorgeous faces, and big water-ski-sized feet.

"Come here and warm me up, love."

"Are you moving in?"

"Yup." He reached for her, gently removing her hand from her belly and placing his under her nightgown to hold the place where their baby grew. "I don't like you sleeping in this house alone, or away from me for that matter. So I figured I'd move in to make things easier."

"How is moving in here easier? Your house is next to the shop where we both work. Wouldn't it make sense for you to sleep closer to it?"

"Common sense tells me that it would be easier if both of us slept there but since when do I listen to common sense? So I'm here because I don't get much sleep if I'm up all night worrying about my stubborn girlfriend. And if I don't get any sleep then my work is shit. So it's better for me to be where my family is."

Her heart pounded in her chest at his words. "Your girlfriend? Your family?"

"Yeah." He glanced at the clock. "I should get going soon. They're probably wondering where I am."

"Ass," she muttered. He smiled at her, taking some of the heaviness off her chest. "I didn't know we were a couple."

"Why else do you think I'm putting up with you, love? You're a big pain in my arse and I'm really not that nice of a bloke."

"You're too nice and that's the problem. I really don't see why you're trying so hard to be with me. Tons of women would push me in front of a train for a chance to be with you. Who in their right mind would rather have a six-foot-tall, poor, grieving, pregnant girl?"

"A man who likes to feel her long legs wrapped around his waist." He pulled her closer and ran his hand down the back of her thigh. "A man who can take care of her. And as for the pregnant thing. You won't be pregnant forever. At least I bloody hope not."

She laughed for the first time since Baba passed away. It almost felt foreign to hear the sound come out of her, of but it also felt good. "No. This baby is coming out of me one way or another." She looked into his eyes. "I'm scared."

He kissed the tip of her nose, then under her eyes. "Of what, love? That we are going to have a two-foot-tall twenty-pound baby? You're from sturdy stock. You can take it."

"Colin! That's not funny."

"It is, a little."

She took his hand and placed it back on her belly. "What if I'm like my mother? What if I don't love our baby?"

"You will. You love him already."

"How can you be so sure? And why are you being so damn calm and reasonable about this?"

He shrugged. "I'm having a baby with my best friend."

He was so sweet and seemed so positive that things

would work out. Didn't a constant barrage of doubts flow through his head? Ever since the doctor had told her she was pregnant the thoughts hadn't stopped. While she never doubted Colin's devotion to his child, she wondered how long it might be before he realized that she wasn't who he wanted to spend the rest of his life with. The child would bind them forever, but the marriage would make it official. She had seen the women he had dated. All of them, especially his ex, the woman he wanted to marry, were beautiful and graceful and made her seem like an awkward giant in comparison.

Colin was kind to her and would probably treat her well but she wanted a husband who was madly in love with her, not one who was sacrificing his freedom to give her some security. She didn't want either of them to look back years from now and wish their lives were different. Then there was the freedom that she would never have. The life that would never be her own. She couldn't change that. She was just going to have to accept that she would have to put her dreams aside so that her child would be happy.

The need to speak to her grandmother hit her so hard in that moment that it took her breath away. She wondered what the old woman would think about her being pregnant. Cherri knew she liked Colin, but would she be happy with the news?

"Say something, love." He trailed soft kisses across her forehead. "You're thinking so hard it's causing my head to hurt."

"You aren't going to propose to me again, are you?"

He grinned at her. "I don't think my fragile heart could take it if you turned me down a third time."

"Your proposals sucked."

"They were a bit shit, weren't they?" He rubbed her belly. "But I'm not sorry I asked. If I hadn't we still might not know about Colin Junior."

She looked up at his face, but he wasn't looking at her.

Instead he stared at her belly, the lazy grin never leaving his face. "You really are excited about this baby, aren't you?"

"I am." He nodded and bent to press a slow kiss to her mouth.

"What if I decided I want to move to France and study painting for a year?"

"Then I would have to learn to speak French and live with the frogs." He kissed her again, a little longer this time.

And when he lifted his lips she asked, "What if I met a sexy Frenchman and fell madly in love?"

"Then I would kill him."

"What if I told you I never wanted to leave this house?"

"Then we would have to make a home here."

"What if I never want to get married?"

"Then we'll just have to live together forever in sin."

Holy crap, she loved him. If everything went to hell at least she could say she was madly in love with Colin O'Connell and she was going to have his baby. Her child deserved what she'd never had: a mother and a father, a normal childhood. And even though she was still so sad and unsure they were about to do the right thing, she said, "Okay, Colin. I'll marry you."

"Will you?" He buried his face in her neck, and she could feel him smiling against her skin. "But I didn't ask you."

"Colin!"

He rolled away from her, reaching out with his long arms to drag his duffel bag over to the bed. He pulled out a small velvet box and slipped a ring on her finger. "Belinda said I should get you something big. Ellis said I should get you something modern, but I like this one. Will you marry me, lass?"

She stared at the simple round-cut diamond set on a plain platinum band that suited her to a tee. "Yes."

He picked up her hand to admire it. "It's good for when you work. It won't be hard to get the paint out of the—"

She reached up and kissed him before he had the chance to finish his sentence. "Mmm. When are we getting married?"

He slid his hands up her torso and cupped her breasts in his hands. "Tomorrow, the next day." He kissed her deeply. "The day after that. I don't care. I just want to shag my wife as soon as possible."

"You're such a romantic." She wrapped her legs around him and brought him closer. "How about next week? It would give your father a chance to get here. We should at least be able to scrounge up one living family member between the two of us." As soon as she finished speaking, the weight of her words settled on her chest. Baba wouldn't be there to see her get married, or greet her great-grandchild.

"Aw, love." Colin stroked the hair out of her face. "We will have one family member there for sure." He touched her belly. "That's all we really need."

*Pixie,*

*I love the Irishman. For you, dumb-dumb, not for me. Even though I would still like to grate cheese on his belly, I can't. I've only loved one man in my life and that's your papa. I'm going to see him again soon. I'm glad because I've saved up a good ten years of busting his balls. We will have beautiful loud arguments in heaven. I hope they don't kick us out. Don't be sad, pixie. I am an old fat lady and my time has been coming for a while, but I pushed it back because I didn't want to leave you alone. But now you have Colin and he's a good boy, and he will take care of you and that baby you're carrying. Of course I know you're pregnant, dumb-dumb! I've been tracking your period since you got boobies. It's okay for me to leave you now because you'll have a family of your own and a man who loves you and you won't need me anymore. You haven't needed me for a long time, anyway. I was the one who needed you. I just wanted to tell you that you are such a good girl, and so beautiful, and the best thing I've ever done in my life. I'm sorry that things went so wrong with your mother. I blame myself, but if you ever see her again, tell her that I love her and thank her for giving me the chance to raise you. Give my great-grandbaby a hundred kisses for me,*

*Baba*

A sob tore from Cherri's throat as she finished reading the letter. She had come into Baba's room to look for her pearl earrings. Cherri wanted a piece of Baba with her on her wedding day. The wedding preparations had all gone by in a blur for her. Questions were asked. Decisions were made. She was there for it all but she had no idea what was going to happen. None of it seemed to matter.

Because it all felt wrong. No bride should wake up on her wedding day with this many doubts. Colin didn't deserve it. He deserved a woman he loved. He deserved an event that was carefully planned. He deserved to have his father there.

The wedding had been thrown together so fast that Colin couldn't get in contact with him. He shrugged it off as unsurprising coming from his father, but she knew that it hurt him. She knew that this was not the day he wanted for himself.

She wished she could talk to Baba about it. Once she woke up and walked into her room to talk to her before realizing that she was no longer there. It had been a shot to her heart, and now seeing this letter made her ache. Baba let go because she thought Cherri didn't need her anymore now that she had Colin. Well, that wasn't true. She needed her now more than ever.

She heard a knock on the door but couldn't pull herself

together enough to acknowledge it. "Love, I know it's bad luck for us to see each other beforehand but . . . Charlotte." He was across the room in moments. "What's wrong, darlin'? Why are you so upset?"

He gathered her close and kissed her wet face. She cried harder, the sobs causing her whole body to shake. "Please stop, love. You're going to get sick. Tell me you're crying because you miss your gran and not because you don't want to marry me. You know how much I want to be with you. We rub along well. I'll take good care of you. I know we can be happy and think about our baby, love. We need to give the little bugger a good home, where he feels loved. Just please stop crying."

Love. In all the reasons he'd just listed, he didn't say that he loved her, and maybe that's the one thing she needed to hear the most in that moment. For that alone she should back out of the wedding, but there was the baby growing inside her and she had to give him a good home. It was her only purpose now. Baba left because she thought this was the path Cherri's life was going to take. Baba wanted her to marry Colin. It didn't matter if he wasn't in love with her. It didn't matter if this life was the last thing she wanted.

She managed to nod even though her tears didn't stop flowing. Colin hugged her so tightly to him she lost her breath. "I miss her."

"I know you do, love. I'm so sorry she's not here today."

She said nothing, knowing he wouldn't be here today, either, if Baba were still alive. He was only marrying her out of pity. She should be grateful. It wasn't as if anyone else was knocking down her door to marry her, but a little hard ball of resentment formed in her belly. She tried to push it away, remembering that Colin was a good man and that even if he didn't love her, she loved him.

"Cherri!" Belinda and Ellis came through the door. "What's the matter, sweetheart?"

"I'm glad you're here," Colin said, relieved. "I feel wholly inadequate right now."

"It's okay, Col." Ellis patted his shoulder. "We'll take over from here."

He nodded but never took his eyes off Cherri. "I'll see you in a little while." He cupped her face in his hands, tilting her head back so that she looked into his eyes. "Won't I?" He kissed her wet droopy eyelids. "Say yes," he whispered.

"Yes, Colin."

He kissed her slowly, and even though she was still upset she felt it in her toes. "Let the girls take care of you. I'll see you in a little while. Right?"

She nodded.

He kissed her once more, for a very long time, as if his kiss could make everything better, and left the room.

"Wow," Belinda said. "Did it feel as good as it looked?"

She opened her eyes and blinked at Belinda.

"Don't ask her that!" Ellis scolded.

"Yes." She turned away and faced herself in the full-length mirror.

"Yes, your face does look like shit." Belinda patted her on the shoulder. "Come on, let's fix you up. If you want to talk about what's bothering you, we can."

"No. I'm fine." She shook her head.

"I was surprised," Belinda started. "I was surprised when you told me you were pregnant, but I'm happy for you," she said quietly. "He's a good guy."

Cherri nodded, her eyes going to Ellis. She needed to know what Ellis thought. She needed a little reassurance that what she was doing was right.

"You know I love Colin," she said. "You're both like family to us. I'm happy for you, too."

Fresh tears welled in her eyes. Her friends were supportive. They loved her. She was grateful for them, but it still didn't stop the doubts.

"Oh, honey." Belinda wrapped her arms around her, and then Ellis. "Please talk to us."

"I'm fine. I promise. I'm just a little hormonal." It was one of the biggest lies she had ever told, but the time for the truth was over. She was getting married.

Colin stood at the front of his living room alone. The justice of the peace was there, looking ahead, waiting for Cherri to make an entrance, but on his wedding day he stood alone. Mike was at Cherri's side today, walking her down the aisle. He'd always thought his best mate would be his best man, but that wasn't the case. He'd always thought his father would be there, but he couldn't be bothered to pick up his damn phone. He'd always thought he would have a happy smiling bride. But he was faced with a grieving, miserable woman.

This was not the wedding day he wanted for himself. He had waited for the doubts to come all week, as he watched the girls scramble around to make the wedding preparations, but they didn't. He thought they would come when Mike had pulled him aside to ask him if he was sure about marrying her. Even then they hadn't come. He wanted to marry Charlotte Rudy. He wanted her as his family. He could see a life spent with her.

And as if on cue she walked into the room on Mike's arm. Music started to play. She was beautiful in her wedding gown. The buttery soft skin on her arms and shoulders was exposed. Her long wild hair was loose and tamed in soft curls, and even though she thought she was far from graceful she kind of glided down the aisle toward him. His bride. He smiled at her but she didn't smile at him. Her eyes didn't even lock with his. She looked right through him.

*She doesn't want to do this.*

The thought had been going through his mind all week, but he ignored it. Marriage was the right thing to do. They had a baby coming. He wouldn't be like his parents. His child would be raised in a happy home.

*That's impossible if the wife is not happy.*

It was too late for doubts. Too late because the music stopped and she was standing beside him.

"How are you, love?" he whispered to her. He cupped her cheek unable to keep himself from touching her.

"I'm sorry," she said. Nausea rolled in his belly. His head spun. Only one thought rolled through his mind.

*Please don't do this to me.*

It wasn't for fear of embarrassment. It wouldn't be a shot to his pride. But one to his heart.

"Love." He took both her cheeks in his hand and kissed her forehead. There was nothing else to say. Words wouldn't come. It was probably a good thing. He knew he couldn't convince her to marry him if it was the wrong thing to do.

"I wish she was here."

It took a moment for the words to penetrate his ears. This was about Yuliana. She was still so sad about her passing.

His eyes shot to hers. His hands fell from her face. Maybe he should stop this. It wasn't the right time. It was all too soon.

"I'm ready," she said. She looked over to the justice of the peace. The choice was taken out of his hands. They were getting married.

# CHAPTER 17

*Family Values*

Colin watched his wife as she stared at the armoire she was supposed to be painting. They had been married three days and she hadn't smiled once. He knew she was missing her gran, that she hadn't properly mourned for the woman who raised her, but this . . . This Cherri wasn't his girl. She barely spoke or moved, going through the day as if she were a zombie.

That was his fault. He was supposed to protect her, take care of her, but he was selfish. He wanted to be married to her, to call her his wife. *Want* was probably the wrong word. *Need* was better. He felt like he needed her to marry him, to prove Mike wrong, to prove to himself that somebody actually wanted to spend the rest of her life with him. His friend's words still haunted him.

*You ruined her life.*

He hated to think that, but maybe he had. He had never once forgotten to use protection. It was safe sex or no sex—

but not with Cherri. He took her virginity and got her pregnant. Now she was stuck with him and a baby. He wondered if she would be like his mother, just pick up and leave one day.

*No.*

He shook his head as he watched her stare off into space. She wasn't like his mother. She wouldn't leave her baby. He trusted that about her. He wasn't like his father, either. They would be all right. They had to be.

*But she hasn't moved her stuff in yet.*

That thought kept playing in the back of his mind. She had lived in his house since the day after they got engaged, but she'd never moved her things in. Just her clothes. Not her painting supplies or artwork. Not the photographs of her friends and family. Nothing personal or important.

He had asked her if there were things that she wanted him to fetch from the home she'd shared with her grandmother. But she always told him she had what she needed. It was almost as if she wasn't planning to stay; wasn't willing to make this her home. And that bothered him. They were married now. They had a baby on the way. They needed to make a home together.

He walked over and ran his fingers through her thick hair, needing to feel some connection to her. She barely reacted to his touch, only looking up when he touched his lips to her forehead. "You feeling okay, my love?" He gently kissed her. "You look tired. Why don't you go upstairs and take a nap."

"Hmm?"

"Go upstairs and take a nap."

She nodded and got off the stool. There was no argument, no telling him she was fine. She just left the room. He thought about following her, thought about laying her down on the bed and sliding inside her until she was moaning and breathless. They hadn't made love as a married couple yet, and more than consummating their marriage, he wanted to make her feel something different from what she was feeling right now.

His cell phone went off, causing him to tear his eyes off the doorway his wife had just left through. He pulled it out of his pocket and glanced down at the screen. It was his father. Two weeks of unreturned calls and now he decided to ring.

*Where the hell were you?* "Hello, Pop." His father had not shown up too many times before. He was fed up with it.

"Hello, my lad! I see you were trying to get in touch with me. I was caught up in a bit of Latina fluff, if you know what I mean. I love South Beach. I think I found my new favorite kind of women. I like 'em hot-blooded and in teeny little string bikinis if you know what I mean." Magnus laughed his booming chuckle. "So how are you, son?"

"Married."

"Come again, lad? Did you just say you were married?"

"Yes. I've been trying to call you for two weeks to tell you I was getting married. I wanted you to come, but you were so deep in tits and ass you couldn't pick up your fucking phone."

"Oh, lad." He was silent for a long time. "I-I-I'm sorry. I didn't know. Why didn't you leave that in a message? I would have come for that. I've always wanted to see my boy get married."

"You're a selfish wanker, Pop. You shagged my first real girlfriend. You didn't come for my college graduation. You didn't come when I opened my shop, or when I won that award. And now you missed my wedding. I don't know why I'm surprised. You were always too busy with some slag to give a shit about what I was doing. I never come first for you."

"I'm sorry, lad. I would have shown up for you this time. I would have. "

"Whatever, Pop. Have a good life."

Cherri hadn't lifted the fork to her mouth more than once or twice during the entire dinner. Colin watched her as she sat beside him, pushing the food around her plate. He'd sent her upstairs early to nap but he knew she didn't sleep. He'd heard the theme song for *The Bold and the Beautiful* coming from the guest room.

"Do you want to talk about it, love?" He put down his fork, unable to stand the absolute silence a moment longer.

"What?" Her eyes focused on him. "Oh, no thank you."

She was being polite. Painfully so, treating him like he was a stranger and not her husband. He thought he married his friend, but three days in he hadn't seen one trace of the girl he knew.

"You know, Charlotte. You might never hear those words out of my mouth again. You should probably take me up on my offer."

"I'm fine," she said softly.

She wasn't and even though he knew the reason why, irritation still passed through him.

*Give her time, you wanker. Her gran just died.*

But as much as he reminded himself of that the little burn in his gut didn't go anywhere. He was her family now. In the back of his mind he knew he was still bothered by the conversation he'd had with his father. He needed to let it go. To let Cherri be for now. She would come around in her own time.

"Well, if you're not going to talk, how about you eat something? I can't have you wasting away. It's not good for the baby."

"I ate earlier. I'm really not hungry, Colin."

He sat back in his chair, folding his arms over his chest.

"If you want to starve yourself that's fine, but you've got my baby inside of you and I'm having a bit of a hard time sitting back and letting you do this to him."

She stiffened and looked him in the eye. "Why do you care?"

Something inside him snapped. "Because I'm your husband, damn it, that's why. We're having a baby in seven months and I refuse to let you hurt him because you're too sad to pick up a fucking fork."

He wanted to take the words back as soon as he said them but he didn't get the chance because she said, "I shouldn't have married you."

"What?" Her words were like a blow to the chest.

"I shouldn't have married you," she snapped. "You didn't marry me because you love me. You married me because you pity me. Poor pathetic Cherri. Dead grandmother. No family. No life. I'll marry her. But I don't need pity from you, Colin O'Connell. You didn't have to martyr yourself for my benefit. I can take care of myself." She put her hands on her belly. "This is my baby and I refuse to let you ruin my life because you think you have some kind of misguided claim on us." Her eyes filled with tears. Her voice broke. "She wrote me a letter, you know. She wrote me to tell me that she felt it was okay to die because I had you now. She died because she thought you loved me. She died because she thought you would take care of me. But nobody bothered to ask me what I wanted. And if I had the choice to live in that little shitty house with her or be stuck here with you, I would choose her every time."

"Cherri—" Despite, his bewilderedness, despite the harsh words she said, he reached for her when a sob tore from her chest, but she didn't let him comfort her or even come near enough to touch her, because she ran out of the room.

And not for the first time, he wondered if his lack of self-control had ruined her life.

* * *

It was almost like he was living by himself again. Three days and he hadn't seen many signs that his wife still lived there, but she did. He peeked into her bedroom at least once an hour. *Her bedroom.* She hadn't slept in the same room as him since their fight. Of all the images he'd had in his head of what married life would be like, he'd never thought it would be like this. Him walking on eggshells. Her so depressed that she barely left her room. He had no idea what to say to her, no clue how to make things better. He tried yelling at her. Reasoning with her. He called her friends, hoping they would have some kind of solution, but they were just as clueless as he. He even spoke to her doctor and slammed the phone into the wall when she couldn't give Colin an answer, either.

"She's hormonal," the woman said. "And depressed. You have to understand how she felt about her grandmother."

He did understand. He knew what it felt like to have nobody there for him, but it pissed him off that she didn't realize he was there for her. No. It pissed him off because she accused him of marrying her to martyr himself. God knows he hadn't married her for that reason. But when he asked himself why he had married her, he couldn't come up with an answer.

*She said yes, damn it.*

She could have said no. It would have been easier if she'd turned him down. She could have walked away a hundred times before the wedding. Even the day of the wedding. He would have preferred that. He would rather be alone than with somebody who hated him. But she'd gone through with it. They were married now. And unless she walked out the door, he would take care of her like a husband should take care of his wife. He didn't want to be like his father, still chasing ass, still alone after all these years, both his children giving up on him. He wasn't going to allow his lad to be a stranger to him, even if Cherri decided she wanted out.

He was just going to have to convince her that she wanted to stay.

He wiped his hands over his face. His damn head was throbbing. His throat was dry. His body ached. It was from lack of sleep. Too many nights in a row lying awake thinking about her. When he took a deep breath, promising himself he would sleep tonight, even if he had to take a pill to do it, he smelled her scent. She walked into the kitchen, her normally shiny mass of waves looking dull and dry, matted to her head. Her face was gaunt. Her skin was gray. His chest tightened. If something didn't change soon he was going to drag her to another doctor.

"Hiya, love," he greeted her.

She looked up at him as if surprised to see him in his own house. "Hi."

At least she had ventured out of her bedroom. Every time he had looked in on her she was staring out of the window, looking at nothing. He was dying to know what was going on in that head of hers.

"Are you hungry?" He stopped himself from ordering her to eat for the baby's sake. He was excited about the baby, but truth be told the baby didn't matter as much as his wife did at the moment. "I could make you something to eat."

She sat down on the stool at the island and nodded. Small as it was, satisfaction filled him. There would be no fight. "Do you want eggs and toast? I've got bacon in here. You want a sandwich, maybe a BLT?"

"Milk." She swallowed then cleared her throat. "Can I have some milk, please?"

"Yes. And to eat, love?"

"Eggs."

He scrambled to the refrigerator and pulled out the eggs, butter, bacon, and cheese to make her a filling breakfast. His hands shook slightly as he placed the plate in front of her. He watched unable to breathe until she put the food in her mouth.

He sighed. She chewed slowly, three, four bites. He watched the food slide down her throat and then she reached for the milk, draining the glass quickly. He couldn't help himself: He reached over, brushed the hair off her face, and kissed her forehead. "I'm glad to see you out of your room, Charlotte. I'm missing my best mate."

# CHAPTER 18

*Keep on keeping on . . .*

Cherri felt a small warm body climb into bed beside her. Her eyelids felt almost too heavy to open, but the smell of dog shampoo made her snap them open. The little thing nuzzled into her chest certainly wasn't her husband. He hadn't tried to crawl into her bed even once.

"Rufus?"

His warm wet doggy tongue came out and lapped at her face, her eyes, her mouth, her cheeks. She was never a fan of wet doggy kisses, but these were nice. These were from her boy.

She couldn't stop the tears from flowing. A sob tore through her throat and she sat up, grabbing him, hugging him close. She missed him. She hadn't realized how much she missed him until this moment. He was a piece of her old life. He was a piece of Baba. He was good memories and love and home all wrapped into one.

"Oh, boy. I missed you."

A rustling by the door pulled her attention away from the dog for a moment.

Her eyes shot to Colin.

"Thank you, Colin. I—I . . ."

He nodded once and walked away. She wasn't sure why, but it physically hurt to watch him go.

Cherri went to find her husband after spending another hour in bed with Rufus. He used to sleep in her bed sometimes. He used to nudge the basement door open and sneak down the stairs. Sometimes she used to wake up and find him there. Baba never let him in her bed, and on cold nights or if it rained he would find her. Why had she let her boy go to somebody else in the first place? Baba would have hated that.

She needed to thank Colin. Rufus made her feel better and made her remember what it felt like to love. Made her remember that she was going to be a mother. Made her realize that her life was only going to be what she made it.

She ran her hands through her wet hair before she stepped outside. She had hopped in the shower a few minutes before and scrubbed off all the yuckiness she was feeling. A week of heaviness had washed down the drain, and when she got out of the nearly scalding shower she felt ready to stop feeling so shitty and get on with her life. Baba was gone. She'd known it was coming. The old woman would have smacked her silly if she saw the way she was behaving.

*Live your own life, dumb-dumb.* And she was going to. The first thing on her list was to talk to Colin. He was in his workshop, his back was to her, but instead of busily working on his latest project he was just sitting on a stool.

"Colin?" She touched his shoulder to find it damp.

He turned, his eyes looking glassy, his face drawn. "You're up."

"You're sick." She placed her hand on his forehead, and then her lips.

"I'm fine." He tried to push her hand away. "It's just a bit of a cold. Don't touch me. You'll get sick."

"No." She tugged him off his seat. "You're burning up. We need to get you in bed right now."

"Stop trying to get out of bed, damn it! You have a hundred-and-three-point-two fever."

He lifted his head to protest but it fell back on the pillow too weak to do anything else. "Don't want you to get sick. Get out."

"No." She crawled in bed beside him with a glass of orange juice and some flu medicine. "I'm going to take care of you, dumb-dumb. It's my job. Now be a good lad and rest your head on my thigh." She put the glass to his lips, holding his head while he swallowed the pills. "Go to sleep now, honey." She ran her fingers through his hair. His skin was so hot, she worried for him.

"Don't leave," he mumbled just when she thought he was falling asleep.

"I'll be here when you wake up."

"No, I meant don't leave me ever. I want to be married to you."

Suddenly the words she'd yelled at him a week ago came crashing back to her. She was scum and she had some making up to do.

Four days after Cherri forced him into bed, Colin emerged. He still felt as if somebody had rubbed three pounds of sand in his eyes, but he didn't feel as weak, or hot, or cold or as miserable as he had the past few days. He was never one to stay in bed unless a warm woman was beside him. He worked with a broken hand, an eye infection, and impacted wisdom teeth, but for the first time since he'd opened his shop he hadn't worked on anything. His projects were backed up. He had deadlines for certain pieces. He couldn't believe he'd let the flu keep him in bed. But all that was over now, and no matter what Cherri said he was returning to his shop.

He stumbled into the kitchen, still groggy from the nighttime medicine she had given him. He needed food before he got ready to work, and after four days of living on just soup and crackers his stomach was finally protesting from the lack of sustenance.

He spotted Cherri standing in front of the pantry, her forehead adorably scrunched in deep concentration. He still had no idea what to say to her. They hadn't gotten the chance to talk much during his confinement. He could barely recall most of his days in bed, only vaguely remembering her wiping his brow with a cool cloth or shoving orange juice in his mouth.

"I need to go grocery shopping," she mumbled. He stood there watching her for a moment. She still wore her nightclothes but she looked better than she had in weeks. Her hair had regained her natural shine. Her skin was dewy. Her eyes didn't look like they were holding on to sadness with a deadly grip. She turned suddenly as if she'd sensed him near her and gave him a shy smile. "Hi."

"Hello."

For a moment neither of them spoke. Neither of them knew what to say.

"Are you feeling better?"

He nodded and opened the refrigerator. She was by him in an instant, her warm hand on his bare shoulder. "I could make you something to eat. We don't have much." She blushed. "I'm planning on behaving like an actual wife and going shopping later today, but we have oatmeal and fruit. Or if you want I could go out and get you something."

"Oat—" He cleared his throat, his voice coming out more like a croak. "Oatmeal is fine."

She sat him down on the stool and began to boil the water for the oatmeal. Her eyes kept wandering to him. He wore no shirt, only a pair of blue flannel pants. He was just getting over the flu. The last thing he needed was to sit around bare-chested in a drafty house, but she couldn't bring herself to order him to re-dress. He was so damn beautiful, and sculpted; his body was something she wanted to run her hands over, just to memorize the feel of it. She realized in that moment how much she missed him. He was her husband . . . Planned or not, this was her life now. She loved him. She had to find a way to be happy with him.

"Do you want coffee?" She set the bowl in front of him.

"No thank you." He shook his head, not looking up at her.

"Oh." Her cheeks burned. "Maybe some milk?"

He grunted no and continued to eat. "Orange juice? Water? Tea? Whiskey? Bathwater?"

He looked at her for a brief moment and then back down at his bowl. "I'll get it myself."

"Okay." She turned away from him, escaping in the sink full of dirty dishes. He was mad at her. She should just accept it. She deserved it.

He came over to deposit his empty bowl in the sink. Yes, she deserved his anger, but she hated when people were mad at her. The need to tease him snuck up on her. She needed to get some of their old relationship back. Things had changed between them; they were going to be bonded together by their baby, by their marriage. They were friends once. They needed to be friends again.

She missed him.

And so she took the hose from the sink and sprayed him directly in the face.

"What the hell!"

Before he could react she sprayed him again, this time all over his hard body. He lunged for her and she took off through the dining room into the living room. He wasn't far behind her, despite her head start. His fingertips brushed her arm. She ran faster, trying to dodge him, but he was too quick for her. He grabbed the back of her nightgown but as soon as his hand came in contact with the fabric he lost his footing and so did she. They tumbled to the floor, the rug breaking their fall. He landed on top of her, his wet body pinning her, both of them laughing so hard they lost their breath. It had been so long since they had been able to do it together, but in a moment it was over. He sobered.

"Are you okay, love?" He moved to roll off her but she looped her arms around his neck, unwilling to let him go. "I don't want to squash you."

"Trust me, I'm fine. Just stay with me like this for a few moments." She ran her fingers through his damp hair, studying every nuance of his face, loving the way his eyes crinkled in the corners. "I hope he looks like you."

He stiffened. "The baby?"

"Yes." She nodded and slowly traced the edge of his jaw with the tips of her fingers. "We could get a hundred thousand dollars for him on the black market and use that money to go to Tahiti."

He scowled at her, but his body relaxed slightly on top of hers. "You can't sell our baby, daft girl."

"No?" She cupped his slightly bearded cheek in her hand. "Oh. Well, I guess we'll have to keep him then. Come with me to my doctor's appointment tomorrow?"

He nodded.

"It may be a bit soon but I think we need to start thinking about the nursery. I want it to be special. I want to paint the furniture. Do you think that would be okay?"

"I don't care," he said quietly. "It's your baby. Remember?"

His words stung but she chose to brush them aside because she knew he didn't mean them. "Yes, but only when he's well behaved and perfect. The rest of the time he can be yours. Do you think we should put the nursery next to our bedroom? I think the room down the hall would be better, but I don't know if I want to be that far from the baby."

"We could—" His face softened a tiny bit, but then hardened again. "I started to make a cradle. You could keep it wherever you sleep for a while."

Was it over between them? No, she couldn't accept that. He was just mad at her.

She lifted her head off the rug to kiss him. It was like their first kiss all over. She was the one doing all the kissing. He was holding back, not even giving an inch of himself to her. She wouldn't accept it. So she kissed him a little longer, letting her tongue sweep deep inside his mouth. His body finally relaxed on hers. The contact heated her insides and made her even hungrier for him, but he still didn't kiss her back.

She broke away and looked up at him to find him staring at her, his face unreadable. "Kiss me back," she breathed. When he said nothing she tried again and for a long time got nothing in return. Just when she was about to give up, when she was about to walk away, he reciprocated and gave her a long hard kiss.

"Will you make love to me tonight, Colin?"

He froze and shook his head.

"Oh." Her cheeks burned. "It's okay. You don't have to."

"Why wait for tonight?" He pulled up her nightgown, not removing it, just pushing it far enough up so that her breasts were bared to him. He stared down at her body, but unlike all the other times they made love there was no warmth in his eyes, just lust. It was almost more than she could handle, and she could feel the tears begin to burn the back of her throat. Part of her wanted to run away. To hide from the world. Half the time she didn't know which way was up. How the hell was she supposed to know how to be married? But she knew she couldn't run away. This didn't just happen to her. She'd made this choice. To be a wife. To be a mother. Plus she loved him. That trumped everything. It had to.

He took her nipple into his mouth with a hard suck. She cried out. It hurt but it felt so damn good at the same time.

His hot wet mouth on her chilled skin. Goose bumps ran up her torso. He noticed and ran his tongue over them, making them worse with each lick. "Colin . . ." She begged him to stop, to keep going, she didn't know. But all too soon her panties were stripped from her body, her legs spread open before him. He touched her there, testing her wetness, preparing her for what was about to come. She moved against his touch, but when she started to get that warm tingly burn, he removed his hand and freed himself from his pants. He pushed inside her with one hard thrust. She saw stars for a moment, shocked by how the invasion felt. It wasn't like the last time. No slow caresses, no sweet touches or pretty words. There were no words at all. Just him pumping in and out of her and because he was her husband and because she loved him, she soon grew accustomed to his size. Her body began to enjoy the sensation of him sliding in and out of her even if her brain wasn't there yet. She grew slicker; an involuntary moan escaped from her lips, and it caused him to pump harder. She wanted to move against him but his heavy body kept her motionless. She could only experience their sex, not participate.

He placed her hand between them and rubbed her enflamed nub, over and over, all while looking at her with that same intense gaze. "Come," he ordered and she did, the shocks of her orgasm causing her entire body to tremble.

He came, too, with a roar and slumped on top of her. It was then she started to cry. She couldn't help it anymore. She had ruined her marriage. Her husband hated her.

# CHAPTER 19

*Breaking up is hard to do . . .*

"Shh, beauty. Please don't cry."

He was shit. A stupid selfish piece of shit.

"I'm so sorry, Colin."

A big stupid, evil bag of shit. He had roughly taken Cherri on the floor. No. He had roughly consummated his marriage to his young, pregnant, grieving wife on the rug in their living room after she had spent the last week nursing him. He hadn't even waited until she was fully ready to accept him.

"I'm a pig." His stomach ached with guilt, not only over what had just taken place but over everything that concerned her. This wasn't the life she wanted. He did this to her. He robbed her of her choices. She should hate him for that.

"I'm pigshit." He had no right to be angry with her. But part of him was.

*I wish I'd never married you.*

The words had played over and over in his head for the

past two weeks and he couldn't get over them, couldn't get over the feeling that he was never good enough to stick around for. The rational part of him knew that that wasn't what was rolling around in her head. She was grieving. She was confused. She'd never had a boyfriend before; how could he expect her to know how to be married? Hell, he didn't even know how to be married. But he wanted to try. He wanted to try with her, not because she was going to have his baby but because she was the only woman he could ever get a chance to glimpse happiness with. With her he could see a chance to create the kind of family he'd always craved as a kid.

"I'm sorry," she wept. "I didn't mean what I said. I—"

"No." His kissed her wet face. "Don't apologize to me. I don't deserve it."

He pulled her up off the floor and hauled her into his lap, trying to search his messed-up mind for an explanation, a way to explain to her what he was feeling. But words, sentences, and coherent thoughts failed him. So he did the only thing he could do. He held her, rocked her, said soft nonsense words, whatever he could think of to soothe her.

Cherri shut her eyes and took a deep breath as the sonographer squirted the cold goopy gel on her belly. She had been taking slow deep breaths since she'd walked into the room. Her heart was racing. Her hands were sweaty. She felt queasy, and jumpy and . . . everything.

"Beauty," Colin whispered as he kissed her forehead. "I feel like jumping out of my damn skin."

Cherri opened her eyes to look at her husband. She could see the anxiety on his face, because it probably mirrored hers. They were going to see their baby for the first time. She thought she would feel different being here today. Happy or overjoyed or something that new mothers should feel, but she felt guilty. When she'd found out she was pregnant, her first thoughts were about her life being over. She was almost angry at her tiny unborn child. And she felt like shit about it. She wasn't sure what had happened, why things had changed, but they had. She was beginning to think of the possibilities. She was going to make the family she never had.

"You're going to jump out of your skin?" she asked her husband, smiling up at him. "I'm surprised my skeleton hasn't made a mad dash for the door."

"There's your baby," the sonographer said to them.

Both of their eyes snapped to the screen and there he was, this little unformed life they had created.

"Do you see where your baby is?" the technician asked as she moved the transducer over her skin.

"He looks like a bean," Colin said in wonder.

Cherri took her eyes off the screen and looked at her husband. His eyes were wide, and they shone with something she had never seen before. It looked like joy. Colin was overjoyed about their child. She hadn't thought about him or his feelings much. She had been stuck in her own world. It was wrong. This was *their* baby. Something they should be experiencing together, and she had said some horrible things to him. She had hurt him. Even if he could forgive her, she wasn't sure she could forgive herself.

"Yes, right now your baby is forming all their organs. If you could really peek inside your womb you would see tiny little fingernails forming and all of their toes."

"It's a bloody miracle," he breathed.

Cherri couldn't take her eyes off Colin. She wanted to see his face, to capture this moment in her mind and keep it there for the rest of her life.

He took his eyes off the screen and looked at her. "That's our baby," she said. His eyes watered, shocking her, and he buried his face in her neck as the tears spilled over.

"Thank you," he whispered. "Thank you."

She didn't know what to say to that, how to accept his

gratitude. She had done nothing but make his life harder and yet he was thanking her.

"I'm so sorry, Charlotte. For yesterday. I'm so sorry."

And now he was apologizing and adding to her guilt. He'd apologized yesterday afternoon, and last night and this morning, but she couldn't forgive him because she had hurt him and she didn't know how to make up for it.

# CHAPTER 20

*I'll get you, my pretty . . .*

Colin tossed and turned for nearly an hour before he threw the covers back and got out of bed.

*You're a fucking idiot.*

He had a beautiful, soft, willing young wife and he was in bed alone. Why the hell had he gotten married if he wasn't going to sleep with his wife?

He knew why. Guilt still rolled around in him for the way he had treated her. He had been an asshole, and what had made it worse was that she didn't seem to think so. She wasn't mad at him. Or upset. Or anything he would have felt if someone had treated him that way. Instead she had gone out of her way to be sweet, trying to make up for something that wasn't her fault. It made him ashamed to call himself a man.

And then there was yesterday, when he saw his baby. Their baby. He lost it. Him. He cried like a bloody woman. The sight of their baby was overwhelming. He was finally going to have his family, the one he'd always wanted as a boy. He had to make things right with Cherri. He had to make her happy. He refused to be like his pop. He had to keep them together. No matter what it took.

He stepped into the dark, chilly hallway ready to scoop her out of bed and bring her back to his. Husbands and wives should sleep together. It was meant to be that way.

He was halfway to her bedroom when he spotted her creeping down the hall. She jumped when she saw him. Suddenly he was second-guessing his plan to reclaim his wife.

"Hi," she said shyly. He cursed silently. He hated that she was so shy around him now. She had never been shy around him before. That's why he'd married her. She was his friend, somebody he could be comfortable around.

"I was just going to get some water," he lied.

"Oh?" She stepped in front of him. "I was just going to crawl in to your bed and do naughty things to you."

"What?"

She grinned at him, that little naughty smile that made him fall in the first place, and unknotted her robe, revealing her soft nude body. He stared at her for a while, mesmerized by it. She was still early into her pregnancy but he could still see the little changes to her body. Her breasts had grown a little larger. Her belly looked different, a little rounder than before. He hardened. The sight of her naked body never failed to produce a reaction from him. Taking his hand in both of hers, she placed it on her breast. It felt different, too. His groin tightened painfully.

His wife. His baby inside her.

She brushed her nipples with his fingertips and then brought them to her mouth, leaving a soft wet kiss behind. Then she took his hands and ran them down her torso, her sides, her hips. Pretty soon she didn't have to do the controlling. His hands had found a mind of their own and stroked the curve of her back, ran over her perfect behind, then cupped it, squeezing it as he brought her closer. She moved against his hardness, rubbing it with her lush body, making it too painful not to be inside her.

"Tell me what you want me to do," she whispered, taking his earlobe between her teeth. "I'm yours."

He opened his mouth over hers. He had no words for her. All he wanted her to do was be who she was and do exactly what she was doing.

He was so lost in their kiss it took a moment for him to realize that she was tugging at his pants.

"What are you doing to me, lass?" He broke away from her panting.

"It's a little hard to have sex with one's pants on, don't you think?"

"It is and trust me, we'll both be naked when it happens in the bedroom."

"I thought you might like to try it here." She traced his tattoo with her fingertips. "Don't men like to have sex in all sorts of places?"

"No." It was true that he had done it in his fair share of bar bathrooms, and parking lots, and even at an amusement park. That had been fun but that was then. Right now he wanted to make love to his wife in their bedroom, not against a wall. "I'm getting old, love." He gave her a lingering kiss. "It's beds for me."

"But I'm not old yet. Maybe I would like to try it." She looked down at his chin. "I don't want you to get bored with me."

"That's impossible, love." He took her hand. "Come to bed with me."

He stripped her of her robe and laid her in his bed. It would be too easy to climb on top of her and drive himself into oblivion but he didn't want to rush it. He removed his pants and lay down beside her. All he did was touch her at first, stroking his hands down her body.

"I'm ready," she said shyly. Her cheeks burned adorably.

"I'm not." He wouldn't last two seconds if he took her now. "I want to touch you."

She blushed again and nodded. "Tell me what you want me to do."

He shook his head. It was the second time she'd asked that. "Nothing. Just relax."

"I—I can't. I want to make you feel good. Show me how to touch you." She reached for his manhood and as soon as her hands cupped it, he let out a hiss. Before he knew it she had him on his back.

"Now I'm king of the castle." She grinned, raising her arms triumphantly.

He grinned back up at her. She was playful in bed. That was one of the things he loved about her. He sat up wrapping his arms around her, kissing her openmouthed. The heat jumped between them, and he throbbed painfully.

*Make it last,* he warned himself. *Make it good for her.*

He rolled them over. He was on top now, smiling into her beaming face. He'd give nearly anything to see her like that all the time.

"I don't think so, lass." He cupped her breast, bent his head to flick his tongue across her nipple. "Have I ever told you how beautiful your breasts are? They are, love." He suckled gently on one breast until she moaned and then the other till she squirmed.

"I know you don't call them breasts in your head. What do you call them?"

"You honestly want to know?" She nodded, her lovely green eyes twinkling. "Tits, but I learned long ago that most ladies don't like them referred to as tits when you're making love to them."

"It does take the romance out of things." She reached between his legs to grip him. "And this? What do you call it?"

"Jerry."

She giggled, and he grew harder in her hand. Once upon a time he had hated gigglers. He probably still did, but a giggle coming from his wife was incredibly sexy.

"You do not."

"I don't, but I feel like I'm teaching my innocent lass dirty words."

She raised a brow at him. "I'm pregnant, naked, and have a penis in my hand. I think my innocence is no longer an issue."

He couldn't argue with that point.

"I call it my pecker most of the time, but when I'm feeling a bit horny it becomes a cock."

"So . . ." She slid her hand down his shaft, mischievousness lighting her face. "So right now I'm stroking your cock."

"Charlotte." He bent to kiss her quiet. "Don't say naughty words."

"Why not?"

"Because I said so." He sat down on the bed pulling her legs over his. She was spread open to him, so pretty and pink, and he marveled that his child was going to be coming out of there in a matter of months. Instead of turning him off, it made him hard enough to burst. "Will you do something for me, love?"

"Anything you want."

"Show me how you touch yourself."

A furious blush covered her body. "I don't do that very often."

She was adorably embarrassed, and a little guilt rose inside him. "You can say no."

He watched her intently for her response. She didn't say a word, just did what he asked, her face a mixture of pleasure and mortification. It was then he realized that she would do nearly anything for him, and it was a hell of a good feeling. He soon replaced her fingers with his own, and she relaxed.

She was so wet, so aroused that being outside her was too much to handle. But first he had to taste her. Her lifted her, touching his mouth to her sweet lower lips, and kissed her deeply. After only two strokes of his tongue she came, and so powerfully that he had to pin her to the bed to keep her from tumbling off it.

"I told you I was ready." She smiled shyly.

"I just wanted to make sure." He fitted his body over hers, kissed her pretty pink mouth, and slid into his heaven.

Hours later they were still awake. He could tell that Cherri was exhausted but for some reason she would not drop off to sleep. Her sleepy eyes were open, taking in his features as she trailed her fingers over his face.

"Why do you keep touching me like that?" It was almost as if she were memorizing his face in case he disappeared.

"I'm sorry." She withdrew her hand.

He brought it back, kissing the backs of her fingers. "I didn't say stop. I rather like being petted like a cat. I just wanted to know why you're doing it."

"I don't know." She curled her fingers into his hair. "I keep waiting for you to yell at me for touching you."

He set his lips to hers. "Now, why would I do that?"

"I don't know. I just never thought we would be here. I never thought we would end up married."

No. He couldn't say he'd pictured them married, either, but he knew the moment he saw Charlotte that she would forever impact his life. "I was damn near obsessed with you for years. If I didn't marry you I was going to go insane."

"You wanted me?" She was surprised.

"From the day I met you. Don't you know how beautiful you are, Charlotte? I could barely keep my hands to myself."

"Why did you? You know I wouldn't have minded."

"I don't know. You're a bit younger than me, love. I know it doesn't matter, but I thought I needed to be with someone my own age. Someone who wanted the same things out of life. But I wanted you so bad that none of that mattered. I needed to have you, and marriage seemed to be the only way I could."

It never left the back of his mind that this wasn't the life she wanted. She never wanted to be his. She had tried to push him away, to put a stop to them the day Baba died. The day he wouldn't take no for an answer. She had always had doubts about them.

And then she got pregnant. She didn't plan on motherhood or being saddled with him. He should have listened to his conscience. He should have stayed away. But he couldn't. Being with her and feeling guilty was a hell of a lot better than being without her and feeling miserable.

"You didn't have to marry me, you know."

"I did. You are having my baby and I'm a selfish lad. I just couldn't have some of you. I needed all of you. I don't want any other man to ever have you."

"Oh." She pressed her hand to her stomach, a sad look crossing her face.

"What is it, beauty?"

"I'm sorry."

"For what?"

"Making you so unhappy."

"That's not true."

"It is." She slid on top of him and pressed a kiss to his throat. "And I would like to make it up to you."

She didn't have to make it up to him. It was the other way around. He needed to find a way to make it up to her. To make her happy. If he only knew how to accomplish that.

They spent the next morning working in the shop. Cherri had tried her best to keep things going while Colin was in bed with the flu but things still got backed up. There were tasks she simply had no skill at. She watched him now as he lovingly polished an old carnival ride that was going into a big New York City museum. He didn't do anything halfway; every piece, no matter who it was for or how much money it brought in, got the same amount of careful attention. He was a master, and to look at him you couldn't tell how successful he was because he never boasted or bragged. He kept his awards tucked away in his drawer, along with the letters from thankful customers.

He was doing what he loved. She wanted that. She wanted to do what made her happy.

"You're staring at me again, lass."

"You're hot."

"Am I?" He grinned at her and sauntered over, his big body seeming to take up the entire room. "You are, too." He wrapped his arms around her and set his lips on her forehead. "Even if you've got paint smeared on your cheek."

They leaned against each other for a long moment, not saying anything. Cherri buried her nose in his shirt so that she could inhale his scent. Linseed oil, shaving cream, skin. Her favorite smell. It soothed her. And today it made her cry.

"What is it now, love? Why are you weeping?"

"I want to tell you something."

He stepped back so he could look down into her eyes. "What is it?" She watched his Adam's apple bob as he swallowed hard. She didn't want to worry him, but this was something she had to do.

"I got offered a job."

He blinked at her then shoved his fingers through his dark hair. "You're going to have to do more talking than that, love."

"It's teaching art at an elementary school in Rhinebeck."

"Oh," was all he said. She was expecting more from him than just an unreadable expression.

"They offered me the job a while ago, but I couldn't take it because I couldn't leave Baba. But they called me again last week and I think I want to take it."

"You couldn't leave your grandmother but you can leave me?" There was a sharpness in his voice that she didn't expect. It surprised her. She'd thought this was the perfect opportunity for him to get his shop back, his space, some of the freedom he had before she shook his life up. He made it clear last night that the only reason he married her was because she was having his baby. He thought he had to take care of her. She wanted him to see that she could take care of herself.

"You're not a seventy-five-year-old woman." She shook her head. "I won't have to worry about leaving you alone all day. The commute was too far. If something had happened to her I would never have been able to reach her."

"You would commute?"

"Yes." She frowned at him. "What's wrong with you? Of course I would commute. I'm not asking you to move to Rhinebeck."

He inhaled deeply and then reached for her, pressing his lips to her forehead. "I should listen," he said quietly. "Talk to me about this job."

"I don't want to be unhappy."

He searched her face. "Are you unhappy, Charlotte?"

"No." She shook her head, unable to make sense of the jumble of thoughts in her mind. "I don't know how to say this. I've had to put off what I wanted for a long time. I had Baba to take care of. I wouldn't give up a minute of the time I had with her, but I always felt like I was missing out on something. And now we are going to have a baby. I'm going to love him but there has never been a time in my life when I could do what I wanted. My life had to get put on hold for Baba. And now that I'm going to be a mother my life will revolve around my child. Before that day comes I want a chance to do some of the things I've dreamed of. I've got to take this job. If I don't, I'm going to feel like I missed out on my only chance."

"I know this isn't the life you wanted."

"It's not—"

"I know, Cherri." He walked completely away from her and back to the piece he was sanding, and she felt like he'd more than just physically left her. "We've got a couple of pieces to finish up. I'll put the word out that you won't be painting any more furniture."

"Whoa." She walked over to him. "Who said I wasn't painting anymore?"

"How are you going to do it, lass?" he said, sounding weary. "You're going to commute two hours, teach all day, and then come home, paint at night, and be my wife. You're carrying my baby. How can you do it all?"

She didn't know. She touched her belly. She was already feeling the effects of her pregnancy. He was right but she didn't want him to be. "This is what I went to school for, Colin. All my life I planned to be an art teacher. I have to try it. I'm not due till September. There's only a few months left in the school year. And I'll be off during the summer. I'm not saying anything is definite. I wanted to speak to you first. I thought the best part of having a husband is having someone to make decisions with."

"Make decisions with?" He shook his head. "I don't think there is any decision to be made. You've already decided what you're going to do."

"Col . . ." She felt near tears again. She felt ridiculous. "I want your blessing."

"You don't need it, love. It seems you don't need anything from me at all." He kissed her head and left the room.

Colin didn't know where he was going until he pulled up in front of Size Me Up. A thousand thoughts were rolling around in his head. He just knew he had to get away from Charlotte, to clear his head, to think about the state of his fragile marriage.

He couldn't lose her. And it had nothing to do with the life they'd created. He just couldn't let her go.

"Colin." Ellis stopped tidying a rack of dresses and walked over to him. She hugged him tightly for a long time. "How is our girl?"

"Better. Bringing Rufus back really helped. Do you have a few minutes? I want to talk to you about something."

She nodded. "We can take a walk. Let me grab my coat."

"No, Ellis." Mike appeared from the back of the shop. "I should talk to him."

Colin stared at Mike for a moment, tempted to refuse his offer. Mike always disapproved of them. He was the last person he wanted to admit to that things were going wrong in his marriage, but Mike was like his brother. He just couldn't turn him away.

"Let's go, mate."

It was April. Spring had just arrived but the air was still chilly, the sky still gray. There were barely any people wandering about the usually busy shops of St. Lucy Street. It was as if the world around him reflected his mood. For a long time he and Mike walked without exchanging a word. They had been friends so long that most of the time they didn't have to say anything to each other, but now the silence felt strained. Colin had barely seen his friend since his wedding day. He had been so preoccupied with Cherri, and being sick, and trying to navigate married life that there wasn't space enough in his head to think about his strained relationship with Mike.

"I know I'm at risk of sounding like a woman," Mike said, "but I miss you, man."

"Oh hell, lad. Next you're going to tell me that you've decided to start wearing female underwear beneath your trousers."

Mike grinned at him, and the tension melted away. "No, but I have started waxing my legs. What's going on with you?"

Colin was silent for a long moment, unable to put all that was going on with him into a few words. "Cherri's not happy."

"Her grandmother died two months ago. Of course she's not happy. She's still mourning."

"It's more than that. She's going to leave me."

"Fuck," Mike said under his breath. "What happened?"

"She wants to take a teaching job an hour away. She says she needs some time for herself. She said she wants the chance to be happy."

"So she told you she's going to move out?"

"Not yet, but it's coming. I can feel it. She didn't want this life. She didn't want to be married or have a baby. I know if she takes this job I'm going to lose her. She's going to walk away just like my mother did."

"You're a huge dumbass." Mike shook his head. "She's not going to leave you. She just wants to have her own thing. Everybody needs to have their own thing. Ellis has her store. You have your shop, and Cherri has her art. I know that alone I'm not enough to make Ellis happy. I wish her world started and ended with me but it wouldn't be right. I probably wouldn't love Ellis if she was that kind of girl. Cherri's not that kind of girl, either. She has to carve out her own niche. She'll never be happy if all she has is you. I know things are tough right now. I know this isn't the way you expected your marriage to turn out, but your only goal in life is to make sure your wife is happy. And if she wants to take a job an hour away, you let her do it. If she wants to take trapeze lessons you offer to pay for them. Trust me, life is better when your wife gets what she wants."

"What about what I want?"

"You want your wife, don't you?"

"Of course I do! Why the hell do you think I married her?"

"Because you love her," Mike said. "You have to. I've

never seen you so miserable before. That's how I knew I was in love. I was miserable as shit and okay with the fact that some woman had me by the balls."

"Bloody hell."

"Damn right. Let's go eat. I've been dying to try those death wings at that new chicken joint. Ellis refuses to come with me."

"That's why you need your mate."

"Yeah. Girls suck sometimes."

Rufus hopped up on the couch and on top of Cherri.

"What the—"

He rested his head on her chest, snuggling into her. She couldn't shoo him off the furniture or away from her. She didn't have the energy to, so she wrapped her arms around Baba's dog and held him close.

"You were in the garbage can, weren't you? You smell like coffee grinds and barbecue chips."

He looked up at her with his soulful doggy eyes and sighed.

"I'm going to go into the kitchen and find a big mess, aren't I? That's why you're here. You're trying to butter me up so I don't try to make doggy stew out of you."

He inched his heavy body forward and licked her chin.

"Gross." She wiped her chin. "But you're right. I'm not going to make doggy stew. We don't have a pot big enough." She scratched behind his ears. "I'm sorry I sent you away. I was a big stupid mess. Baba would have beat me with her cane if she saw how I was acting."

Rufus sighed again.

"I miss her, too. I feel so sorry for Colin. In a matter of months he got stuck with a crazy wife, a garbage-eating dog, and an unborn baby. I royally screwed up his life. If it weren't for this baby he would probably leave me. And if I didn't love him so much I would leave him. He's been gone two hours.

Do you think he's coming back?" She looked down at her dog and kissed his nose. "I've gone freaking crazy. I'm pouring my heart out to a dog. I need to get a grip."

She heard Colin's truck pull into the driveway. She didn't want to admit how worried she was.

She met him at the door. For a moment they just stood there staring at each other. She hated the silence between them. She hated the distance she felt, so she leaned in and kissed him. He looped his arms around her waist and pulled her closer.

"Holy hell, Colin! My mouth is burning."

He grinned at her. "I like kissing you, too, love."

"No." She swiped her hand over her mouth. "My lips are literally burning. Like you've been sucking on chili peppers."

"Sorry, lass. Me and Mike were eating death wings. I only had two. He had six. Ellis is in for a bit of trouble tonight."

"You saw Mike?"

"Yeah. I haven't seen much of him lately."

"Is that because of me? You know you can see him whenever you want. You don't have to stay home with me. I can take care of myself."

"What if I like staying home with you? What if I want to take care of you?" He leaned closer, about to touch his lips to hers. A little spark of anticipation lit inside her. And then she felt the heat of his mouth. She had to pull away.

"Don't kiss me. At least not until you scrub your mouth. I'm eastern European. We don't do spicy."

"Neither do us Irish. But a little spice in your life is okay sometimes." He grinned at her again, seeming to be in a much lighter mood than when he'd left. "We need to go to the car dealership."

"Why, is there something wrong with your truck?"

"No, but if you are taking that job you need a dependable

car. I can't be worrying about you on that long commute every day."

"You're serious?"

"Of course I am. I don't joke about buying people new cars."

"You mean I have your blessing?"

"I mean I want you to be happy here."

It wasn't the same as his blessing. But she was so happy that it didn't matter at the moment. "Bring them hot lips over here."

# CHAPTER 21

*Feels like the first time . . .*

Colin couldn't take his eyes off his wife as she got ready for school. She was nervous. He knew it by the way she buzzed around the room. She had changed her clothes three times. Two pairs of pants lay crumpled on the floor. A sweater lay draped over a chair. She stood looking at herself in the antique mirror he had restored just for her.

"Do I look okay?" Her eyes met his in the mirror. She wore a simple dress the color of jade. It made her eyes stand out.

"Yes, love," he said softly. "You look beautiful, but you looked beautiful two changes ago."

"I couldn't button my pants," she said with a pout. "My belly has popped. But I don't look pregnant. I just look like I've had too many beers. Fat beer-belly Cherri. I wonder if I could get away with wearing my pants below my gut like some guys do. You think I could get away with that? Maybe I could make it a thing. Start a trend. I've always wanted to be a trendsetter."

She was chattering again, just like the old Cherri. He couldn't believe how much he'd missed that sound. "You don't look like you have a beer belly, daft girl." He came up behind her and set his hands on his growing child. "My heart speeds up like a lass on her first date when I see you."

"You're full of shit. You're just saying that because you're my husband."

"Am not." He kissed the side of her face. "Now put your shoes on. You're going to be late."

"I'm scared."

"I know." He stepped away from her. "But I know you're going to be a good teacher. And when you get home tonight I'll take you out to dinner." He picked up the vintage tin lunch box he'd bought for her and presented it to her. "I made you lunch. Turkey and cheese with honey mustard because mayo makes your stomach turn lately. A brownie from the sweets shop. Sweet tea and a bottle of water."

She burst into tears.

"Bloody hell, lass." He gathered her in his arms. "What are you going on about now?"

"Why are you being so nice to me?"

He wasn't being nice. He was being her husband. He wanted to make her happy. He was just doing his job."Because I want to have sex with you later."

"Okay." She sniffed and gave him a wobbly smile. "I can do that for you. What else can I do for you?"

"Nothing. Just get to work."

Fifteen minutes later she was gone. He stood in the driveway for a long time with Rufus staring after the car that had pulled off a long time ago.

*She'll be fine.* He kept telling himself that. It didn't matter that she was pregnant and emotional and got so tired at one o'clock she could barely stand.

*Plenty of pregnant women commute. Plenty of pregnant women work long days.*

*But plenty of those pregnant women aren't my wife.*

"Come on, boy." He slapped his leg. "Let's get to work."

He thought if he buried himself in his work he wouldn't notice Cherri was gone. But that wasn't the case. He looked up at the clock a dozen times an hour and hated himself for it. He was never like this. He felt like somebody's overbearing mother.

But the shop felt empty without her. For months they'd worked side by side. He missed her smell in his shop. The way she hummed quietly to herself when she painted. He even missed the annoying things she did, like leaving half-finished water bottles all over the place. He missed her. He'd gotten used to her in his space. In his home. In his life. And now she was gone. And he was worried that she would be gone forever one day.

Mike was right. If he didn't support her she would resent him forever. She already resented him, even if she didn't show it; he knew he had taken away her freedom to do whatever she wanted with her life when he had gotten her pregnant. He couldn't in good conscience keep her from her dream.

There were twenty-five sets of little eyes on Cherri as she stood in front of the spacious art room.

Kindergartners.

Four- and five-year-olds with little hands, poor fine motor skills, and seriously cute faces. They weren't even her first class of the day. She had taught well-behaved fifth graders perspective and some overly chatty third graders about tessellations. But it was the kindergartners that scared her.

"Mrs. O'Connell?"

"Yes, Elizabeth?" It was her first day and she'd barely had time to memorize any of the kids' name but she knew Elizabeth's.

"You're tall."

"Yes, I know."

"You're taller than my daddy."

"That's nice. Let's talk about the fish we are going to make today."

"Are you older than my daddy? He's thirty-one."

"I'm ninety-seven. I know. I look great for my age." She walked away from the child and addressed the rest of the class. "First we are going to read a story called 'Rainbow Fish' and then I'm going to let you do something that you probably won't get to do in your regular classes. We are going to rip up a whole bunch of paper so we can make our own rainbow fish."

"Are you a giant?"

She looked at Elizabeth for a long moment, her patience slipping. "Yup. I'm a giant and I have a giant dog named Rufus. His favorite thing to eat is children who talk too much in my art classes." She watched Elizabeth's eyes grow wide and felt a tiny bit of satisfaction sneak up inside her. "Now let's get to work."

Forty minutes later Cherri sat at her desk and looked around her empty classroom. She only had two classes left for the day and seemingly nothing to do until they arrived. She was so eager to prove that she could be good at this job that she had already planned ahead for the next two weeks.

It was technically her lunchtime but she didn't feel like eating. Her mind wandered to her friends, to the shop she hadn't worked in for months. She knew they were getting along fine without her, but still she missed them. She hadn't seen much of them lately. She knew they were being polite, trying to give her and Colin some space, but she didn't need space from them. Her marriage wasn't anything like Mike and Ellis's in their early days. Ellis had skewed her idea of what a newlywed was. It wasn't all kissy-face and longing looks. It wasn't sneaking off all hours of the day to make love. Being married, sharing a life with somebody, was hard work. And for the life of her she couldn't figure out if she was doing it right.

"Mrs. O'Connell, please come to the office," she heard over the loudspeaker.

She gulped. Getting called to the principal's office on the first day was not in her plans. Then she remembered what she had said to Elizabeth. It wasn't very teacher-like at all. But it was worth it. The kid didn't make another peep.

"I'm going to get fired before I've made it an entire day."

Her room wasn't far from the front of the building, and as she made her way closer to the office she heard sounds of feminine laughter and a low brogue that never failed to turn her insides to mush.

"Colin?" He wore a black sweater and one of his many leather jackets. His hair was a little wild and he had a hint of shadow on his chin, telling her that he hadn't shaved that morning. He was sexy and looked like the last person you'd find in an elementary school.

But then she touched her belly and remembered. He would be in elementary schools and at soccer games and at concerts. He was her husband. They were going to be parents, and for some reason she had a hard time coming to terms with that.

"Hello, love." He smiled softly at her. It was a shy smile, unlike the one he was giving to the secretary when she walked in. "I've come to do a little sucking up for you. I brought some pastries for the staff. But I've got to tell you, love. You've got the most beautiful-looking women working here. If I had these ladies at my school when I was a lad, I might have gone more." He looked at Janis Millwalker, the sixty-year-old school secretary, and lavished his big sexy smiles on her. "I might have gotten in trouble a little more just so I could spend some extra time in the office."

"Cherri," Linda the school social worker said. "You didn't tell us you had such a charming husband."

That was because she hadn't ever exchanged more than two words with her.

"Or that he was so handsome," said another woman, a teacher whose name she had no idea of. "Where did *you* find *him*?"

Translation: What the hell is he doing with you?

"He found me," she answered, because it was true. He'd gotten to her when she'd least expected it.

There were a total of five women in the normally quiet office. All there to gawk at her husband. She should feel jealous, but she didn't. Colin was a flirt. He had a way with women. She was more curious as to why he was here.

"Is it okay if I take my husband to see my classroom?"

"Just put this on so we know you're a visitor." She handed Colin a large pass before Cherri led him out of the room. He reached for her hand, his large fingers easily sliding between hers. They were quiet as they traveled down the hallway. His hand felt right in hers, but there was something about them that didn't feel right. All that easy comfort that they used to have before they got married had somehow slipped away.

"This is a beautiful school, Charlotte." He looked around her classroom and then sat at her desk.

"What's the matter, Colin?"

He looked up at her and for a second she saw something flash in his eyes. "Nothing."

"Nothing? You drove an hour for nothing? Why are you here?"

He reached for her, wrapping his arms around her waist and settling his lips on her belly.

"How's my boy?"

"He's getting bigger by the moment."

He looked up at her. "And you? How are you feeling? You look tired."

"I'm fine, Colin. I—"

"How was the drive? Was the car okay? I know you were wary about getting an SUV but it's supposed to be good in the snow. I can take it back if you want. We'll get you something you like."

"I love the car, Colin. I know I have the safest, most reliable car on the planet. Especially after you interrogated the salesman for two hours. Why did you come? Are you checking up on me?"

"I just needed to see where you were going to spend your days. And I . . ." He shook his head.

"What? Tell me?"

"Nothing. That's all. I just wanted to see this place. I just wanted to see how you are."

She shut her eyes as he rested his head on her belly again. She ran her fingers though his messy hair, needing to feel closer to him, but somehow she never felt close enough. "You know I was feeling a little miffed at you?"

"Why, *mo chuisle*?"

"What? What was that word?"

"*Mo chuisle*? It's a Gaelic term of endearment. My pa used to say it to my gran. Why were you mad at me?"

"Ellis texted me. Belinda called me. Even Mike sent me an email to ask me how my day was going. I almost thought you didn't care, but I guess I was wrong."

"You were." He stood up and kissed her cheek. "I'll see you at home, love. No painting furniture tonight. Okay? You should rest. I don't want you taxing yourself." He gave her a pointed look.

"Okay, Mr. Bossy Pants."

"You're carrying my child. I think I've got the right to be a bit bossy." He searched her face for a long moment, then leaned in to give her a loud smacking kiss. "Now be a good girl and carry on with your work. I'll be waiting for you when you get home tonight."

* * *

He was pacing, Colin realized after he walked past the front door the fourth time. He was pacing, waiting for his wife to get home. She was late. Again. Last time because she had stayed after for a staff meeting. The time before she said she was getting to know the other teachers in her building. But this time she was really late. He glanced at the clock for the hundredth time. It was a little after seven. She normally left work at four. Even with the long commute he expected her home by five fifteen. Five thirty at the latest. But this week she had been getting home around six. He'd said nothing to her about it. There was nothing he could say.

She had a new job. She needed to get to know her coworkers. She needed to stay for meetings and such. She always let him know when she had one. Even tonight. Even when she was over two hours late, she had called to let him know why. There had been an accident. A tractor-trailer had flipped over, shutting the highway down. She was stuck. And there was nothing anybody could do.

He just said to her, "Okay, love. Get home as soon as you can." But a hard knot settled in his stomach.

A tractor-trailer flipped over. She had seen it happen. She had been that close. It could have happened to her. He didn't like the idea of her commuting so far. He didn't like that she was throwing herself into work even though he had done the drive himself, and seen the school and met the people. He wanted her near him. It was selfish. It was stupid, but ever since he'd found out she was pregnant the need to keep her close by overwhelmed him.

*That's not true, jackass.*

Maybe he wanted to keep her by him for other reasons. They had been married for three months now. Three months. They were newlyweds but most of the time he felt more like her roommate than her husband.

Rufus popped up and flew toward the door as soon as he saw the headlights shine through the window. Colin shot toward the door, too, but forced himself to slow down. To calm down. It was Friday night. They had all weekend. He thought about taking her away for a few days. They hadn't done that yet. They hadn't had a honeymoon. He hadn't even thought about it before. Their life had been so crazy those first few weeks after marriage. He'd thought it would settle down. He was still waiting.

He opened the front door. Rufus bolted out of it. He jumped up on Cherri, trying to lick her face.

"Get down," she said, but her voice had no force behind it.

Colin studied her for a moment, his stomach clenching as he took her in. She was rumpled, her eyes a little glossy, her skin a little pasty. Her face not as full as he was used to seeing it.

"Okay, Rufus. Okay. Hello. I'm happy to see you, too." She scratched behind his ears.

"He's been missing you," he said. *I've been missing you, too.* "How are you feeling, love?" He crossed the driveway and cupped her cheeks in his hands.

She shut her eyes for a moment. He could feel her weariness. It was on the tip of his tongue to order her to stop working, but he couldn't do that. She would hate him for it.

"Despite the horrible accident and the traffic, I'm fine. I had a good day."

"That's good." He led her inside to the couch and bent before her to take off her shoes.

"Don't." She put her hand on his head to stop him. "If you do they'll swell to the size of bowling balls."

He frowned up at her. "You've been on them too much."

"No. No more than usual. It's just one of those days. What do you have all over you?"

He looked down at himself. He was covered in paint and oil and grit. He probably smelled like hell, too. He had been restoring an old gas pump and made a mess of himself. "Just work things, love. I guess you're right. It's been one of those days. I'm going to hop in the shower. Why don't you sit for a little while and relax? We can have dinner together when I get out."

"You haven't eaten yet?" She glanced at the clock above the fireplace. "It's late."

"I was waiting for you, love." He leaned over and kissed her cheek. "I'll be out in a bit."

He was quick about it. His hair still dripping when he returned to where he'd left her. From the window he could see the lights on in the shop. He walked out, not bothering to even put his shoes on.

She was standing in front of an old chest that she had agreed to paint a few weeks ago. One hand on her lower back. One hand resting on her belly. It was as if she was in a trance, but she snapped out of it and took her box of paints off the shelf; in a matter of moments he could see the beginnings of a hummingbird. He stood for a moment, amazed at her skill. Amazed that in a few strokes she could take something plain and turn it into something beautiful. She was meant to paint. He knew that with every ounce of his being.

He walked up behind her, placing his hand on her shoulder. She froze and then turned at him, blinking as if he had broken her trance. He immediately felt sorry for disrupting her. But then again he had been waiting for her to come home all day, and she needed to eat and rest and unwind.

"Charlotte, I was going to take you out for something to eat."

"Oh. Do you mind if we stay in? I want to get some more work done on this chest."

He did mind. He minded a lot. "You worked all day. I thought we could . . . Leave everything behind tonight and just have a nice dinner." He touched her face. "You've had such a long day. Why don't you just leave the chest until tomorrow?"

"I'm fine, Col. I promised this thing would be ready by

Monday. I think I'm going to have to work on it all weekend. Plus I like to do this. It relaxes me."

"I wanted to take you away this weekend. You know, to celebrate your new job. I thought we could spend a couple of days at The Mountain House in New Paltz. They have a spa there. You could get your feet rubbed until you melted."

"Oh. That sounds nice, but I can't. I'm so backed up here."

He nodded, knowing that already. Knowing it was impossible for her to keep up this pace. "You could take a day off from work next week. We both could. We could go for the day."

She grinned at him and then pressed a soft kiss to his mouth. "I just started working, Col. You know I can't take off yet."

"I guess you can't. That's the best thing about working here. You can take off whenever you want." Her eyes widened a bit. His voice was a little harder than he'd intended it to be, but he wouldn't apologize for it. She had only done this to herself. "I'm going to order in. What would you like, love?"

She shook her head. "I'm a little queasy today. I'm not very hungry."

"You have to eat something, Cherri. For the baby's sake."

"Of course." She nodded and placed his hand on her tummy, and he realized it was the closest they had been in a long time. "Is pizza okay?"

"Yes, that's fine."

"Could you bring it to me in here when it comes?" She turned away from him and back to her piece. He wanted to protest, to demand that she sit at the table with him for half an hour. He wanted to share a meal with her. He wanted to talk to her, but he knew there was nothing he could say to change her mind.

*Keep your wife happy.*

His mission in life. But every time he looked at her he wasn't so sure she was.

A week later Cherri lay on Baba's old bed, looking up at the ceiling. She hadn't been back to the house since she had gotten married. It had been too hard to come back and know Baba wouldn't be there. But today she'd decided it was time. Time to clean out the house. Time to donate her things. Time to take whatever pieces of Baba's she wanted to keep forever.

"Look at this stuff!" Belinda pulled a peach chiffon maxi dress out of Baba's closet. "This is fabulous. I would have to take it up a foot, but look at the stitching. You don't see stuff made like this anymore. Look at this, Ellis."

"Oh yeah. We would have to take in the waist a lot. You're the definition of hourglass. It's annoying how flat your stomach is."

"Yeah, but look at my ass." She turned around and wiggled it at Ellis. "I feel like I'm smuggling two balloons under my dress half the time."

"Mike likes big asses. You want to borrow him from time to time to give yours a little squeeze."

"Can I? A girl could use a little boost now and them."

Ellis and Belinda grinned at each other and then as one they turned to look at her.

"Are we being insensitive?" Belinda asked. "Do you want us to shut up? We can totally shut up. We'll be quiet as church mice up in here."

"No. Don't be quiet. I like to hear you two blab on. It makes me laugh."

Ellis stepped closer to her. "But you're not laughing."

"On the inside I am. I'm just exhausted at the moment. This kid is taking it out of me. But don't tell Colin I said that."

"We won't." Ellis sat on the edge of her bed. "Are you

sure you want us going through Baba's stuff? Won't it feel weird to see us wearing some of her things?"

"Absolutely not. I've never seen a majority of the stuff you're pulling out of that closet. The only thing I've ever seen Baba in was housecoats and slippers. I think she would like the idea of you two wearing her things. She loved you. But if you start wearing her housecoats around town I'll lose it. I loved that woman but those were the ugliest damn things on the planet."

"How are you, honey?" Belinda asked. "How are you really? We've been worried."

"I'm fine. I miss her so much, but I'm fine. Colin is taking such good care of me that I'm not sure what to do with myself. It's odd not to have an old lady always on my mind."

"This is your time," Ellis assured her. "You can live the life you want. It's time to enjoy yourself. How's work? Do you love it?"

No. But she couldn't tell them that. She missed spending her days in the shop with Colin. She missed getting lost in painting, missed spending all day transforming drab pieces of furniture into art. She missed Colin's smell and watching him work, and hearing his deep brogue. She missed being with him all day. But she had made such a big deal about taking this job, about being able to stand on her own feet, to do what she thought she always wanted, that she couldn't tell them she wasn't sure if she could spend the rest of her life doing it. "It's only been a few weeks. I'm still getting used it, but it's a good job."

"What about the commute?" Belinda asked. "I used to commute to Manhattan and it nearly killed me. How are you managing? I know you must be so tired after you deal with the kids all day—and to be pregnant on top of it. I don't think I could do it."

She hated the commute. She hated the traffic, but she had

to prove that she could do this. That she could be more than just a mother and a wife. "Colin got me a very nice car. It makes things much easier."

Ellis and Belinda stared at her for a long moment, like they knew she wasn't telling them the whole truth. But they didn't call her out on it. She was glad for the reprieve. Being in Baba's old room, smelling her smell, seeing little reminders of her everywhere was making her emotional. That's why she was glad they were there, to distract her from her sadness.

"Are you all right, love?" Colin walked in, past Ellis and Belinda without a word, and settled on the bed beside her. He stroked the hair out of her face and kissed her forehead. These past three weeks she'd felt the tension in him. He never seemed to be able to relax. He never seemed to be happy.

"I'm fine. I just wanted to lie here for a little while for old times' sake. Are you okay?"

"No. You're wiped out. I can see it on your face."

"I'm fine," she lied.

"You're doing too much," he said a little sharply. It was something he'd said often in the three weeks since she had been working.

She sighed, too tired to argue. "I'm not doing anything, my heart. I'm lying in bed."

His expression softened, and he pressed his lips to her ear. "Is this too hard for you? We can pack up the house anytime. Why don't we go home and just relax this weekend? You've been working like a dog. This house isn't going anywhere."

"If we want it ready to sell by summer then we have to do this." When she'd woken up that morning she had decided it was time to move on. She knew she couldn't, they couldn't, if she hung on to this part of her past. Her life with Baba was over. She woke up knowing that. If she didn't know better she would think the old lady had snuck into her head when she was sleeping and put the thought in her head.

She'd turned to Colin when she'd opened her eyes and told him what she wanted to do. He'd made it happen. He had gathered all their friends and a bunch of boxes and they'd started packing up her old life. She was grateful. To her husband, to all of them.

"We don't need to sell the house," he said to her for the first time. "We can keep it forever. I could turn it into a studio and you can paint here. You don't have to give it up."

"What's the point of keeping it and paying taxes on it and doing the upkeep? We could put the money in a college fund for the baby. I want to give somebody else the chance to grow up here like I did. It seems selfish to keep it to myself."

He nodded and gave her a long, slow, deep kiss. Every nerve ending in her body awakened and she gripped the back of his head, holding him close for as long as she possibly could. They hadn't made love in three weeks, not since her first day at work, and she missed him. She missed them.

There was something wrong but she didn't know how to ask him what it was. She was afraid to. She was afraid it was something they weren't going to be able to fix.

"Okay, *mo chuisle*," he said. She still wasn't sure what it meant, but she liked the way he said it. She liked that he only used it with her.

"We'll finish cleaning it out, but I want you to eat something first. What do you feel like eating?"

"Tuna fish."

"You can't have that. You know what the doctor said. How about a nice chicken sandwich from the deli?"

"With onions and pepper Jack cheese and extra mayo? Oh, and hot sauce. Lots of hot sauce"

He grinned at her. "I see you're back on mayo again?"

"Mustard makes me want to hurl."

"And the hot sauce?"

"You reminded me how much a girl needs a little spice in her life."

He said nothing, just trailed his thumb across her cheek.

"You should bring back some breath mints, too. You'll probably never kiss me again after I eat that."

"I'll get the same thing so we'll be equally stinky." He bent down and pressed a kiss to her belly. "Beware, little one. Your mum is going through her hot stinky phase."

He sat up and turned, seeming to remember that they weren't alone in the room. He was slightly embarrassed to see Ellis and Belinda gawking at them. She could tell by the slight flush that rose up his neck. But no one else would be able to tell. He just flashed Ellis and Belinda his sexy grin.

"Mike and I are going to head out in five minutes. Let us know what you want to eat."

And with that he walked out.

"My goodness," Belinda said softly. "I thought Mike loved Ellis but Colin . . . That man worships you."

"I think he's got a weird fetish for pregnant women," Cherri said, feeling a little sad to see him go. She hadn't seen much of him lately.

"I think he's worried about you," Ellis said. "He seems a little off lately."

She looked at Ellis, surprised that her friend had voiced her fear. "I know," she said, more to herself than to her friends. "He hasn't said what's wrong. I don't think he likes that I work."

Belinda rolled her eyes. "Typical chauvinistic male. He wants you at home, barefoot and pregnant. You work if you want to, Cherri. You do what makes you happy. He's your husband, but don't give yourself up for a man. Trust me, you'll end up hating yourself if you do."

"I agree with that." Ellis nodded. "But I don't think Colin is being a pigheaded man. He didn't grow up in a family like the rest of us did. Now he's got his own family. You and that baby are important to him. He just wants to keep you close because he's doesn't want to lose you."

"I'm not going anywhere."

"You know that and I know that. Colin may seem like this tough guy who doesn't need anybody, but he's really mushy mashed potatoes. All men are. Deep inside they are all little boys just looking to be loved. Talk to him, Cherri. All he needs is a little reassurance."

# CHAPTER 22

*Hello. It's me . . .*

Cherri woke up two days later reaching for her husband, but all she found was an empty bed. A little disappointment crept into her chest. She was going to take Ellis's advice. She was going to talk to Colin. She wanted to do it last night. She had planned to, but cleaning out the old house all weekend had taken a toll on her. It wasn't seeing Baba's things go that bothered her. She knew it was time. She knew Baba was in a better place. She knew she was happy with Papa again. The grief over losing her wasn't suffocating anymore. It was more like a subtle ache and a little sadness. She missed her. She would always miss her. But she knew it was her time to go. It was seeing Natasha's things leave the house that had an unexpected effect on her. She barely thought about her mother, but looking through her belongings, seeing the way Baba had left her room even though she had been gone for so long, made her curious about their relationship.

What had happened to keep mother and daughter apart?

She knew Baba regretted the break in their relationship. She knew that the old woman would have liked to see her only child one last time before she passed away, but things didn't work out that way. Cherri thought about it all night. And she thought about her husband and his parents and their unborn baby. Ellis and Mike had both grown up surrounded by families and siblings, grandparents, aunts, and uncles. Belinda had both her parents and cousins by the dozen. Cherri had always been jealous of them and their loud family gatherings and that they had so many people who were connected to them. She wanted that growing up. It made sense for Colin to want that, too. It made sense for him to want that for their baby. She was starting to understand him.

She wanted to give him as much love as possible. She was just going to have to figure out how to do that.

It was impulse that made her go to her computer and Google her mother. She wasn't expecting much, but her Natasha Rudy came up right away. Tall, bleached blond, beautiful. She was the headliner at a nightclub in Reno. Her website said she was married and a mother to two spoiled bichons frises. For twenty minutes Cherri had studied every picture of her glamorous mother, hungry for knowledge about the woman who'd walked away from her so long ago. There was a contact number and address where she could email her. For a moment she thought about writing. But what would she say?

*How could you walk away from me? Why didn't you come back?*

Looking at the pictures burned her stomach. Natasha appeared to have had a great life. So great, it seemed like she never thought about the child she had left behind. Her dogs were the ones she loved. Her daughter didn't even rate.

She left her bedroom needing to see her husband, her only family. She went down to the shop. Rufus looked up at her when she walked in, but Colin didn't notice her entrance. He was too entranced in his latest project. And while she'd come out just to speak to him she hesitated to make her presence known. Here in his shop he was completely relaxed. Today he was singing. She almost forgot that he did. She was used to seeing him tense and quiet the past few weeks. Now he was truly himself, alone in his element, crooning "Moon River" in his lovely tenor.

She loved him. She should tell him so, but she couldn't bring herself to. She couldn't say the words she said so easily to everybody else.

Why was that?

*Because you're afraid he won't say them back. You're afraid he doesn't feel them.*

He turned as if he'd finally felt her in his space and stopped singing. She opened her eyes to see him looking almost disappointed to see her, as if she'd intruded on his private time.

*Bummer . . .*

"What's the matter? Why aren't you at work? Are you ill? Do you need me to take you to the doctor?"

"There's no school today. Didn't I tell you?"

"No." He shook his head. "You didn't. But you're okay?"

"I'm fine."

He visibly relaxed.

"I wish you wouldn't worry so much."

"I wish I wouldn't, either. It's exhausting."

There was her opening. The perfect opportunity to bring up what she wanted to talk to him about, but she chickened out. "Why don't you sing more often?" she asked him instead.

"I thought about becoming a pop star when I was younger but the lads in my town would have confiscated my balls. So I decided it would be manlier to fix stuff instead."

"Really?"

"No, love." He shook his head.

"Oh."

They were silent for a moment, him standing away from her, halfway across the shop—but it felt like so much farther.

"Why do you sing Andy Williams? I've seen your music collection; you don't have any of him there."

"My pop loved him," he explained. "Used to play him when we worked together in his little shed. I guess it feels right to sing him while I work."

"I was thinking about your father. I was thinking about our family and you and me."

He raised one of his brows slightly. "Were you?"

She nodded, finding it hard to gather her words. She could talk to Ellis and Belinda about anything. She could talk to the damn dog. Why was she finding it so hard to talk to him? "Will you tell me about him? About your father."

He looked disappointed for a moment, but his face quickly went back to unreadable.

"There's not much to say, lass."

She wasn't going to accept that. "Have you spoken to him since we've been married?"

"Just the once."

"Oh." They fell quiet again. And as much as she hated to be the only one attempting conversation, she had to keep trying. "Will you sing to our boy after he comes?"

His face softened at the mention of their unborn child. She wasn't sure why he'd married her but she was sure why he stayed. He wanted to be a father. His love for their child made her love him even more.

"You only refer to the baby as a boy. How can you be so sure he will not be a she?"

She blinked at him. "I don't know." She rested her hand on her unborn baby. "I just know that I'm going to have a little boy that looks like you."

"Aw, lass." He finally crossed the room to get to her, but he didn't hug her like she wanted. He placed his hand on her small belly. "If it's a girl you owe me twenty dollars."

She smiled at him but it was merely a curling of her lips. "Done."

She placed both of her hands on top of his to keep him close to her even if his touch was just on her belly.

"I think you should call him."

"Who?"

"Your father. It would be—"

"No." He shook his head and walked away from her. "I'm done with him. He's a selfish wanker and I don't want him in my life."

"It's not just your life, Colin. It's our life. We are going to have a baby—"

"Our life? Now you're thinking about us? About the baby? I thought that was my job. You've been so busy trying to find yourself that sometimes I wonder how much you really want him."

She recoiled. His words were a slap in the face. "You really think that about me? You think I don't want him?" she asked quietly, her voice sounding foreign to her own ears. "Maybe it's this marriage I don't want."

"Cherri . . ." He came toward her, hands extended, bewilderment on his face. "Don't go saying things like that. You know how much I . . ."

"You what?" she asked calmly. "You love me? Don't even say it. You married me because you pitied me and because I was pregnant. We both know that. Let's not even pretend."

"Cherri." He reached for her again but she stepped away.

"I don't know what to do. I came down here to talk to you. I came down here because I know you're unhappy and I wanted to figure out why. I wanted to fix things between us. But there is no fixing this, is there? So—"

"So what?" he exploded. "Why does it always get to be about you? Your gran died. Your life isn't what you wanted it to be. Whose life fucking is? You think Baba's dying was just hard on you? You think you're the only one who loved her? You think it wasn't hard for me, too? You think it wasn't hard for me to watch you in that much pain? At least you had her. At least you had somebody who loved you that much. You should be grateful. I'm trying to be understanding, Charlotte. I'm trying to give you the best life I can. I'm trying to make you happy but I don't know if I'm coming or going with you."

"You don't ever talk to me! How would you know?"

"I never talk to you because I never see you. You're in the shop painting all night. You took that job an hour away. You work all day. You stay late at school planning your lessons—"

"I have to. I'm new. I have to show them I'm capable."

"We're new! We're married. We're going to have a baby. Damn it, Cherri. Me and you. This was supposed to be our time. Everything else gets in the way of us. I'm sick of feeling guilty. I'm sick of feeling like I ruined your life."

"I never said you did."

"You did. You did say it. Right after we were married, and you tell me every time you put space between us. I didn't expect this from you. I didn't expect my own wife to not want to be around me."

"Colin, that's not true."

"Whatever. I'll save you the trouble of leaving. I'm out of here."

She watched him go. She was frozen to her spot, too bewildered to move. The worst part about it was that he was right. Not about all of it, but he was right. She was so busy focusing on how her life had changed, she hadn't given much thought to how it all affected him. She had been selfish and in the process she had pushed him away.

Colin didn't know where he was going. He just left, so pissed at Cherri, and at himself, that he barely noticed it was raining. He barely noticed that Rufus was at his side until he opened the door to his truck and the dog jumped in the car.

"Get out, Rufus." The dog just sat there staring at him. It was as if he was telling Colin not to walk out on his wife. Not to walk out on his marriage. But he couldn't go back, not right now. "Move!"

Rufus sighed and climbed into the passenger seat. Colin got in, resigned to the fact that he was going to have company. He drove off, tires squealing as he did. He just needed to clear his head. There seemed to be only one thing on his mind these past months. And it wasn't fair. He'd never thought this would happen to him. He'd never thought one woman would sneak into his mind and take over his every thought.

It was foreign to him, to feel this much.

His phone rang. He hit the Bluetooth button on his dashboard, not caring who it was. He just didn't want to think about Cherri.

"Hello."

"It's good to hear your voice, Colin."

*Fuck.*

His body cramped upon hearing her voice.

His ex. Serena.

This was the woman he'd thought he was going to marry. The one he thought was going to be the mother of his children. Instead he had married someone else. Somebody else was going to be the mother of his child. And she was sitting in his shop alone while a ghost from his past made a reappearance.

"Colin, are you there?"

Rufus barked.

"Is that a dog? Do you have one now?"

"What do you want, Serena?" She was last thing he needed right now.

They had met when he restored a piece for the art gallery she worked for. She was a buyer. Dark-haired, hazel-eyed with a body that was tight due to hours of Pilates. They hit it off immediately. She was intelligent and well traveled. She was great in bed. She wasn't clingy. With her living in the city they had only seen each other on weekends and holidays. And so for a year he thought their relationship was perfect. Little did he know that while he was being faithful she was screwing every guy who walked past her in a business suit. He even caught her in bed. Apparently he had arrived for the weekend an hour earlier than she'd expected.

When he'd walked in on her he didn't remember feeling hurt, but disgusted. He was about to sleep with a woman who was sharing her body with everyone else. He also felt stupid. He should have seen the signs. He should have known he wasn't the only man.

"To talk to you. To see how you were. To beg you to forgive me."

Why now? Why after all this time?

"Listen, Serena, I don't have time for this today."

"Will you have time for it tomorrow? I need to know when, Colin. I want to talk to you about it. I know I treated you horribly but you have to know that I did love you. I was just freaked out because I had never felt that way about a man before."

"So you fucked half of Manhattan to make yourself feel better?"

"I don't know why I did it. But I've been thinking about you. There was a write-up about you on a blog I follow. It talked about how much care you take with your work and it made me remember how well you treated me. It made me miss you." She was silent for a moment. "I still love you. I think you should know that."

She loved him? It was ironic when his own wife didn't.

"Please don't call me again. It's over."

"Just meet me for coffee," she said, sounding more composed than she had a few minutes earlier. "It's okay if you don't want to get back together. I wasn't really expecting that. I just want to see you so that I can give you a proper apology. Let me come up there. I promise I won't take much of your time."

"I'm married, Serena. Please . . . Just leave it be."

He disconnected, gripping the wheel so tightly his knuckles turned white. Too many things were crashing down on him. His wife wanted out of their marriage. His ex suddenly wanted him back. It was like a bad joke.

He was so preoccupied with his thoughts that he didn't see the cat dart out into the street until it was too late. He turned sharply to avoid it, and he missed it, but the ground was slick. His truck kept going and it didn't stop until he slammed into a tree.

Cherri was in the shop staring at another one of her unfinished pieces when she heard the door open. She turned around, expecting to see her husband. She had called him twice, asking him to come home, but he never picked up. He never returned her call. He was furious at her and he had every right to be.

But it wasn't him at the shop door. It was Mike and Ellis accompanied by a Durant police officer. "What happened?" They didn't have to speak for her to know that her world was about to come crashing down again.

Their faces were grim. Mike looked as if he was in pain. The police officer came in with his hat in his hands. It couldn't be good news. They wouldn't be here if it was.

Ellis was the first to reach her. She wrapped her arm around Cherri's waist and held her tightly. She held her up. Cherri's knees had started to go slack as soon as they walked in. "Don't tell me he's dead. Don't tell me." She shook her head. It was as if she were suffocating. She had fought with him. She had said some nasty things. He left her. He left her without knowing how much she loved him. "I don't want to know. Don't tell me."

"He's alive," Mike answered. "He's . . . okay. But he was in a car accident with Rufus and they've taken him to the hospital. We've come to take you to him."

"He's alive?"

"Yes. Officer Timms and I used to work together on the force. He was the first to respond to the accident. He knew Colin and I were friends so he called me immediately."

The officer stepped forward. "He's all right, ma'am. He's pretty banged up but he's going to live. The truck is totaled, though. It was by the grace of God he got out alive."

"Where's Rufus? He went with Colin. He loves Colin."

"Yes. He's at the station. He kept trying to get in the ambulance with your husband."

"But he's okay?"

"Not a scratch on him."

Ten minutes later she was at the hospital. Colin was sitting up in bed. His head was bandaged, the side of his face scratched and bruised, and his foot elevated in a soft cast, but he was alive. He was okay.

She took a step toward him, so relieved to see him again that her knees gave out on her. Colin bolted from the bed and hissed in pain as his feet touched the floor. Mike caught her before she slumped.

"I've got her, Colin. Get back in bed."

Ellis walked forward, trying to assist him, but he refused her help. "I'm fine. For fuck's sake get a damn doctor in here for my wife."

# CHAPTER 23

*Nobody does it better . . .*

Cherri hadn't left his side once since she arrived at the hospital. Even after she collapsed. She had refused to be treated by a doctor. She refused to leave the room. Her blood pressure had risen due to the excitement of the day. Nothing to worry about, the nurse assured him, but he was worried. It was a constant state of being for him these past few weeks.

He felt horrible and it wasn't because of the considerable amount of pain he was in. He could barely stand to look at his wife. She sat at his side, her chair as close to his bed as she could get it. Her cheek resting on his palm. Every so often she would stare up at him with her big sad eyes, and he would feel like a bigger piece of shit every time. She felt guilty about the accident, as if their fight had caused it, but it wasn't true. Not totally. He'd walked out on her. He'd chosen to leave. If he had died today, the last person he would have spoken to was Serena. It was not how he wanted his life to end.

"You feeling all right, love?"

"No. I'm feeling miserable and sorry and sick to my stomach and guilty as hell. But I'm happy, too. I'm happy you're not dead. When I saw the police officer at the door I thought they were going to tell me that I'd lost you. I couldn't have taken it, Colin. I wouldn't recover from that. Especially after our fight. I—I . . ."

Her voice cracked and her eyes started to go blurry and he'd had enough. Enough pain and emotion for the day. He squeezed her hand and hushed her. They didn't need words right now. When his car was spinning toward that tree only one thought went through his mind, and it was of her. She was his family. He couldn't leave her.

"I'm so sorry," she whispered as she kissed the back of his hand.

"You have nothing to be sorry for."

"I do. I—"

"My ex called me," he blurted out to stop her unnecessary apology. "I had just hung up with Serena when I crashed. You don't need to be sorry, Cherri. If anybody is to blame for this it's her. Please stop feeling so sorry."

She looked up at him, hurt flashing in her eyes. "Serena called you? Why?"

"She wanted to talk. I hadn't heard from her since we broke up. I—I was surprised."

She was silent for a long time, her face unreadable. "You didn't have to tell me that, you know. You could have kept that from me and had me feeling like a horrible unworthy wife for a very long time."

"What would be the point of that? You're the last person I want to be unhappy."

"You cannot get in the shower!"

"The hell I can't."

Colin only had to stay in the hospital overnight. There

was a gash on his head. He was badly bruised. His ankle was sprained and swollen and he had broken a finger in the accident but he was going to be fine. Cranky as a bear but fine. Cherri thanked God for that. She had seen the truck, which was no more than a huge chunk of twisted metal. She was amazed that anybody could have walked away from the accident alive.

They had been given another chance. She refused to waste it. If the car accident had taught her one thing it was that life was precious. It was too short to spend unhappy. And she was unhappy. They both were. They didn't have to be.

"You can't." She gave her husband a gentle push back onto the bed. "You can't get your bandages wet. And how exactly are you going to stand to shower? You'd better not put any pressure on your foot. It won't heal if you keep trying to stand on it."

"It's fine. It's just a bit sore. Get out of my way and let me bathe."

She stared at him for a long moment.

"You look like your baba when you look at me like that."

"Thank you." She smiled at him, pleased with the comparison. "She used to scare the hell out of me when she gave me her death glare. I'm glad I inherited it. I plan to use it on our children. Now lie down! You're not getting out of that bed."

He threw himself back toward the pillows, wincing as he did. "You're a bossy lass."

She smiled again, and then studied his face, realizing how much she missed him, and their friendship and their easiness. She could fix that, and after yesterday, after almost losing him, she knew she had to fix that. She could make it so she wasn't missing her best friend. It was simple—they needed more time together, and it had just dawned on her how she could make that happen. "I know I'm bossy. I take lessons from Ellis and Belinda on the weekends." She walked toward the bed and bent over him, pressing her lips to his. "I need to leave the house for a little while."

He wrapped his arm around her waist and pulled her on top of him. She tensed, knowing how bruised he was, but he didn't let up so she let herself relax a little and kissed him once more.

"Stay with me," he said softly.

"I need to go to the grocery store," she said into his lips. "I need to buy food so I can take care of you."

"You can take care of me in another way." He slipped his hand under her T-shirt and stroked his long fingers up her spine. "All you have to do is take off your clothes. I promise you, I'll feel a hell of a lot better."

She looked down into his too-handsome face, seeing that look in his eyes. It gave her tingles. "How can you be horny when you're in pain?"

"How can you not know how crazy you drive me? I always want you. Always. There could be a knife in my gut and I would still get randy looking at you. I miss you, love."

"You should hate me," she whispered, the guilt latching on to her. "You should have married someone better than me. Like a model or something." She shook her head. "No, not a model, they're too skinny for you. You like boobies and ass way too much for that. You should have married somebody more altruistic, like a curvy dark-haired nurse who spends her vacations in war-torn third-world countries tending to the needy and looks like Angelina Jolie, but with twenty percent body fat. Or maybe a veterinarian, who does animal rescues on the weekends and likes to hike in the woods and only eats organic things."

"Or an art teacher, who talks way too damn much, with big boobies and a nice round arse and a sweet smile that makes my damn heart flutter."

She frowned at him. "Where the hell are you going to find one of those?"

He laughed at her. A big full chuckle that made his entire face light up. It had been so long since she had seen him laugh, and she knew in that moment that she wanted a life filled with his smiles and laughter. She wanted him to be happy more than she wanted happiness for herself.

Her job would be so easy to give up, but he wouldn't be. She had thought the decision would be hard to make, but it wasn't, and for the first time in a long time, some of the stress floated away from her.

*We're new!*

*We're married.*

*We're going to have a baby.*

*This was supposed to be our time.*

*Everything else gets in the way of us.*

Those words had played over and over in her mind since he had said them. How selfish she was. How stubborn. She was so busy trying to prove to herself that she could do that job *and* take care of herself, she'd forgotten about him. That a marriage was made up of two people. Baba was gone, but he was here and their baby was coming and they were the most important things in her life. She couldn't forget about him, because without him . . . She didn't want to think about a life without him.

"Can I tell you a secret, Col?"

His face grew very serious, and he nodded once.

"Other people's kids annoy me sometimes. That's a lie—they annoy me a lot of the time. There's this one little girl in my class who never stops talking. I know I talk a lot but I wonder how she never runs out of questions—or words, for that matter. Sometimes she's not even talking to anybody, just herself. *I'm going to color this fish purple and this grass should be greener* and it annoys me. Sometimes I wish I had magical powers so I could zap her tongue out. Does that make me a bad person? Do you think our kid will annoy me?"

"Yes." He laughed again and she savored the sound.

"Of course he will. That's what children do. But you're not a bad person, love. I don't know how teachers spend all day in a room full of children. I would go bloody bonkers myself."

"Sometimes I wish I weren't pregnant so I could have a good strong drink when I get home from work. You know I think about writing to some parents and saying thank you for raising a child that makes me want to drink. I think sassy ten-year-old girls were the original reason why wine was invented."

He grinned at her and then gently pulled her face toward his so that he could kiss her. "I know you're saying these things to make me laugh. You love children. Our lives need to be filled with them."

He was right. She could see the future. She could see this house and it wouldn't be an empty place. It needed love. They could fill it with love.

"I have to go to the grocery store." She pulled away from him, but he held on tightly.

"No, you don't. I'll order in."

"No, you won't. Let me do this for you. Let me be your wife and cook for you and clean for you and take care of you." She pressed a quick kiss to his lips. "But only until you get better. I'm not a maid, you know."

He grinned at her again and this time he let her go. "Don't be gone long, lass. Or I might have to look up that Angelina Jolie–looking nurse you were talking about."

"I'll be back in an hour. You can hold on until then. And don't get any ideas about getting in that shower because I'm cutting the water off before I go."

"You're bloodthirsty, lass."

"No I'm not. I just want the pleasure of stripping you naked and giving you a sponge bath myself."

"Oh, love," he said with a twinkle in his eye. "Why didn't you say so in the first place?"

* * *

The next morning Colin hobbled to his shop on his crutches only to find his wife there sitting in front of a cast-iron antique toy horse and buggy. She was staring at it intently. He knew that look in her eyes—it was the same look she had when faced with a blank canvas or dull piece of furniture. It was the same look she had last night when he was lying naked in bed. She was thinking of all the possibilities. He smiled to himself. His girl could be damn creative.

"What are you doing, Charlotte?"

She got up from her place and came toward him, hands on her hips. "What are you doing out of bed? You're not supposed to be up yet."

"I've got a business to run and since you're not in bed with me at the moment I've decided to come down here and give it a go."

"You can't work today. You're in pain. I can take care of things until you get better."

"That's sweet, love. But I've been doing this job all my life. How are you just going to take over?"

She shrugged. "I thought I could do some of the smaller projects. I think I can restore the horse and buggy."

"You think?" He sighed heavily, not wanting to hurt her feelings, especially after yesterday. They had spent the entire day together after she got back from the store, talking and watching TV, making love. It was as if he'd gotten his friend back. He didn't want her to go away again. "I give every customer my best. Every project has to be done right."

"I can do it right." She lifted her chin. "I can do my best. If you'll just tell me what to do I'll do it. I can do a lot, Colin. Let me prove it."

She didn't have to prove anything. He knew there was so much she could do. "You're going to have to remove all that old paint first. There is a medium steel-bristled brush in the third drawer to your left."

Four hours later he was watching her put the final coat of

base paint on the toy. She had done an excellent job. She was meticulous and thoughtful with her work. She asked a million questions along the way, but it didn't bother him. It reminded him of when he was learning how to fix things with his pop. The man never minded when he wanted to know more.

"You've done beautiful work, love. When that dries you can decorate it however you want. You don't need my instruction when it comes to painting."

"No." She looked up at him, her pretty eyes locking with his. "But I like sitting with you. You're a good teacher."

"I like sitting with you, too. I would like to sit with you more." And then it dawned on him. "What about your job? Aren't you supposed to be at work?"

Hurt flashed through her eyes. "Do you think I would leave you after you had a horrible car accident?"

"No. It's just that you just started working. I was wondering how much time you could afford to take off."

"I don't know." She shrugged. "I quit."

"What?" He froze, unable to believe his ears.

"I quit." She got up and took her box of paint off the shelf.

"When did you do that?"

"Yesterday. Before lunch and after the amazing sex we had. You did some good work yesterday and all with a broken finger and a sprained ankle. I didn't know my eyes could actually roll into the back of my head, but now that I do I figured I should stay home and let you try that every day before lunch." She looked away from him, studying her paints as if she hadn't just dropped the biggest of bombs on him.

"But that job was so important to you."

"No." She set her paint down and looked at him for a long moment before she leaned over to kiss his cheek. "It wasn't. It was just a job."

He could still see guilt in her eyes. He knew she still felt bad about his accident, but it wasn't her fault and if she'd quit because of him she would resent him forever. He wanted her around, but not like this. He wanted it to be her choice. He wanted her to be happy with him.

"If you're quitting because of me, don't. I know how much you wanted to work. Being an art teacher was your dream."

"That job wasn't important. I need to be here, Col." She shook her head. "I thought you would be happier about this."

"You know I like you near me, but—"

"I quit, Colin. I quit. And unless you can come up with a damn good reason you don't want me around all day I'm working here." She leaned over and kissed his cheek again. "I'm going to take Rufus for a walk. Why don't you call Mike and Ellis and invite them for dinner? We haven't had anybody over in a long time."

"I'd rather just have dinner with you, love."

"Okay." She smiled shyly at him. "I would like that, too. What can I make for you tonight?"

"Nothing." He shook his head. "We'll have a date. Have I ever taken you out on a date?"

"Nope. You knocked me up first."

He grinned, so glad the easiness between them had returned. It no longer felt like things were crashing down around them. "I'll have to fix that." He reached across the table and grabbed her hand. "Charlotte O'Connell, will you have dinner with me at seven o'clock?"

"Gee, I don't know. I think I might be seeing someone else tonight."

"Cherri," he growled.

She threw her head back and laughed. Her eyes sparkled. Her skin went all glowy. She looked like the old Charlotte, the girl who'd first grabbed hold of his heart and kept it in a choke hold.

"Yes. I would love to have dinner with you."

"Wear that short black dress that makes your legs look three miles long."

She frowned in confusion. "What short black dress?"

"The one you wore the first time I made love to you."

Her smile returned. Her cheeks going a little pink. "Oh, Col, I'm pregnant. I don't think I can get that thing over my belly."

"Wear it anyway and leave your underwear behind, too."

"Perv," she said. She looked at him for a long moment, her smile fading. "I've missed you, Colin."

"I've missed you, too, love."

# CHAPTER 24

*Fooled around and fell in love . . .*

Cherri patted her growing belly as she walked to the shed behind their house. It was time to start thinking about the nursery. She'd never thought she would be here at twenty-two years old. Pregnant. Married. Doing what she loved. It had been a week since she had quit her job. It had been a week since she had stopped her commute and fretting over lesson plans. It had been a week of working with her husband and spending hours getting lost in her painting.

She wanted to paint more. She wanted to paint for the baby that was growing inside her, but she didn't know what. The shed behind their house was where Colin kept all the good stuff. All the pieces he had picked up over the years, the really special things that he didn't have time to work on due to the spike in business. She had come here to look for something she and Colin could put their touch on. She didn't want anything new or cookie-cutter going into her baby's room. She spotted a small toy plane lying beside a large cardboard box on the middle shelf. Maybe that could go into the room. Maybe they could have an aviation theme, but even though she suspected she was carrying a boy she wasn't sure yet. Maybe she should search for more gender-neutral things. She put the plane down and picked up the box. On top was a beautiful silver music box in the shape of a carousel. It would be lovely in a little girl's room. She looked deeper into the dusty box again but instead of pulling out more treasures she pulled out memories of Colin's past.

*Serena.* His ex, making another unexpected appearance.

*Shit.*

An entire box filled with her things. Pictures of her, each more beautiful than the last. Photos of her and Colin together, or him gazing down at her with a dreamy soft smile on his face.

*He kept the box.*

Her chest ached. He loved Serena. Still. Loved her long after their breakup. Seeing the pictures there was no denying it. He wouldn't have kept her things for so long, in the shed, in the place he kept all the special things he wasn't prepared to deal with yet.

Was Serena one of those things he planned to go back to one day? One of those things he would try to fix? Cherri knew he cared about her and sometimes she even felt like he loved her—but did he love Serena more? Did he still think about her? Did he wish that he had the chance to be with her again?

The doubt returned. The guilt. Their marriage was still so new, so fragile. Things were just starting to get easier between them. She was finally feeling hopeful. She was finally feeling the stirrings of happiness. She knew this wasn't the life he'd planned on. Her pregnancy had forced it to change. And now they were married and for her that meant forever.

*But not if he doesn't want it.*

"Cherri? Love, are you in there?"

She heard his voice from outside but couldn't move. She stood there staring at a big blaring sign that their lives together may never be what she hoped.

"What are you doing in here?" He entered, stepping over the pile of unfinished wood in the center of the floor. "It's damn dangerous in here. I don't want you hurting yourself."

She looked up at him, unable to form coherent thoughts.

"What's wrong?" He cupped her face and studied her intensely. "Why are you so pale?"

She shook her head. "I came to look for things to put in the nursery but . . ."

She looked down at the box.

"What do you have?" He took the box from her and glanced down at the contents. "What is all this crap?"

"It's Serena's."

He blinked at her. "What? I got rid of her stuff eons ago."

"You didn't. It's all here. Every picture. Every present. Every memory. I guess she means a hell of a lot more to you than you told me she did." She brushed past him.

He threw the box down on the floor and grabbed her arm, spinning her around to face him. "You're jealous?"

"What if it were the other way around? What if you found my ex's things? What if some man that I loved called to reconnect with me? How the hell would you feel?"

"I'd kill him. I'd find him and kill him and then revive him and kill him again. You're my wife. I don't want anybody sniffing around you."

She shook her head. "You're not understanding me."

"I understand you perfectly well." He took her chin between his fingers and locked his eyes on her. "You have nothing to worry about. I don't love her. We're a family, love. I'm not going to let anything tear us apart. Do you understand me?"

She nodded. He seemed so sure. She wanted to believe

him. But . . . How could she when the man she'd married hadn't married her for love?

The next night Colin opened the bathroom door to find his wife in the tub. Her eyes were closed, in sleep or in such deep thought that she hadn't heard him come in. He simply watched her for a few moments. Her wild hair was plastered to her head, her body stretched out. He could just see the tops of her gorgeous breasts in the bubbly water and the curve of her round belly. He grew aroused looking at her.

"It's kind of rude to walk in on someone while they are in the bathroom and silently stare. Not to mention creepy."

He stepped closer, touching her wet hair. "Is it now? I thought that was one of the perks of being married—getting to watch your wife do things that no other man can."

She opened her eyes and looked at him. "Is it? I didn't get my copy of the marriage handbook."

"I didn't, either. I'm just making this shit up as I go."

She smiled at him. Not a happy smile. Not the shy smiles she had been giving him lately, but a full seductive smile that made him harder than a rock. "Hand me a towel?"

She stood up, all the soapy water running down her body. It was like he didn't know where to look first. Every part of her was appealing. His six-foot-tall wife. Not trim, petite, delicate, or any of the things so many people found desirable. Her uniqueness made her interesting. It made him want her even more. He almost lost control of himself just looking at her. It had only been a couple of days since they'd last made love. She had been so exhausted lately. The baby was growing, healthy, and strong according to the doctor, but he was taking a lot out of Cherri and sometimes she got so tired she barely stayed up past eight PM. He missed her, though. Since he had survived his accident, their lovemaking had been different, more intense almost, and he craved it. He craved her. "Step out."

He didn't hand her the towel, just held it open until she walked into it. He wrapped it around her and then himself. And he held her wet naked body so close to him that air couldn't pass.

"You smell good."

"Thank you," she moaned, placing her lips in the crook of his neck. "You feel good." She leaned back so she could look into his face. "How are you feeling today? Is your ankle okay? I noticed you limping a little this afternoon." She touched the spot on his head where he had smashed it. "You told me you were back to normal."

"I lied. I was never normal, lass. But if you are asking me if I'm well enough to make love to my pretty wife the answer is yes."

"Oh." She wrapped her arms back around him and rested her head on his shoulder.

"Don't you want to?"

"Yes. I miss you."

"Then what's wrong?" A beat of worry entered his chest.

"I don't want things to go wrong again."

She was thinking about Serena. About the phone call they'd shared recently. About the box she'd found yesterday. He couldn't explain it. He had forgotten it there. He didn't keep it around on purpose. Serena meant nothing to him. She had to know that. He had to show her that. He had thrown the box away, taken it directly to the dump, but he wasn't sure it was enough. He wasn't sure he could prove how much she meant to him.

"They won't, love. We won't let them."

"I know things are better but I'm still so mad at myself."

"I'm not mad at you, Charlotte," he told her truthfully. "I know how much you missed your gran. I understand that after you spent your life devoted to her, you wanted a little time for yourself. I want you to be happy. If teaching makes you happy you should do that."

She shook her head. "Painting makes me happy. Being in the shop makes me happy."

He ran his fingers through her wet hair and kissed her forehead. "You can paint in the shop forever if you would like."

"I don't want to be just your wife. I want to be your partner. I want to contribute to this marriage. That's why it was so important for me to work. I didn't want you to think you had to take care of me. I didn't want to be your burden."

"Burden?" He shook his head. "Why the hell would you think that? Cherri, it was me who needed you. Not the other way around."

She looked up at him disbelieving. There was no way he could tell her. He didn't have the right words. He had to show her. He sealed his lips to her until he felt her go slack in his arms. His body heated. His skin tingled. His thoughts melted away. She did that to him.

"It's not like this with anybody else. You're the only woman who makes me feel this way. You're the only woman who makes me go crazy and keeps me running back for more. I don't know how to explain it to you. I was going along just fine in my life until I met you. And you threw me for a curve. You knocked me on my ass. You made it so I can't get enough of you."

She blinked at him, then gave him a soft peck on the lips. "I think I'm going to get those words tattooed on me." She locked her fingers with his and led him to their bedroom, the towel slipping off her damp body as she did.

"Are you? Where?"

"On my ass. I know it's your favorite part of my body."

He chuckled. "I'm partial to you all, love. Your ears turn me on."

"Good." She lay down on the bed and stared expectantly at him. "Come show me how much."

* * *

"Thank you," Mr. Cassum said for the fifteenth time as he vigorously pumped Colin's hand. "My father is going to love this."

Colin felt Cherri's eyes on him as he showed Mr. Cassum the vintage milk machine that they had painstakingly restored. The man had tears in his eyes and a huge smile on his face. It was beautiful, if a milk machine could be so. Shiny, cornflower blue. Cherri had done the lettering by hand in bright yellow. Colin had scraped and scrounged for every original part, and the ones he couldn't find, he made. He had probably restored dozens of old vending machines, but this one he took a little longer with. Mr. Cassum's father was turning ninety-five, and the man wanted to restore a piece of his father's childhood before he passed on. Colin admired the man for doing something for his father. He liked that the two men remained so close. It made him anxious to meet his own son.

"It was my pleasure, sir. It was really nothing at all. Let me show you how it works one more time." He walked over to the machine. "It only takes dimes. So keep plenty of them on hand. Beauty," he called to his hovering wife. "You wouldn't happen to have any dimes on hand, would you?"

"Of course." She gave him a little smile.

She was growing lovelier as she progressed in her pregnancy. He was surprised how much more attracted he was to her now. But her cheeks were rosy and her hair was shiny and there was something about her that kept him staring at her all day. And because he kept staring at her he knew something was off in her world. She had been quiet the past few days. At first he thought it was still about Serena, about the box of things that she'd found, but that couldn't be it. They had talked. Everything was okay. Everything seemed to be okay for a little while.

*Then what is it?*

He pulled his eyes off his beautiful, pensive-looking wife and turned his attention back to his customer.

He spent a few more minutes with Mr. Cassum, helping him load his truck before he returned to Cherri. He stared at her as she worked in the office. She was on the phone with a customer, explaining the process of restoring a bicycle. It was as if she had been working with him for a lifetime. She was so comfortable in the shop. She didn't mind getting dirty. She never got in his way. It made him kick himself for not going after her sooner. He'd never thought he would marry a girl who always had paint staining her fingers, but he was glad she did.

"Mr. Cassum asked me to restore a little red wagon for him next," he said when she hung up the phone. "I told him to bring it by on Friday."

She wrote that down on the calendar before getting up and coming to him.

"Colin." She went to him, wrapping her arms around his middle. "I think you might need to stop taking in new projects for a while."

"What?" He kissed her forehead, letting his lips linger on her skin. "We're a little busy, but we can manage."

"No, baby. I don't think we can. I've got a whole room's worth of furniture to paint. Plus you have fifteen projects lined up. Three of them, I might add, are going to take at least twenty hours of work to complete. We're more than busy. If you want to keep going at this pace you might want to think about hiring somebody."

"Hmm." He kissed the curve of her neck, his attraction to her kicking into overdrive when he felt her belly press into him. "I've got you. I don't need anybody else."

"What about . . ." She lost her train of thought for a moment because his hands grabbed her behind. "After I have the baby? You didn't expect me to keep up the same workload, did you?"

"No, I'd let you rest for a few days and then we'll strap the kid to your chest and get you back in the shop. I don't have to pay you."

"Colin," she laughed, and the slight tightness in his chest loosened. He wanted to wipe the sadness off her face for good.

"I understand what you're saying, love. I might have to consider it in the future, but I like working with you. I don't want anybody else here. I couldn't shag your brains out in this office if I hired somebody, now could I?"

He moved his hands under her baggy T-shirt and rubbed her lower back.

"No, I guess not." She slumped into him, letting all of her weight rest on him for a moment. "I'm glad I married you, Col. I want you to know that."

He was surprised by her words, especially after this past week when she sometimes felt so far away that she might as well have been on another planet.

"I like to hear that. Sometimes I wonder."

"I'm sorry." She blinked at him, her eyes going sad again.

"Don't apologize. I'm shit at being a husband sometimes. I know that." He stroked his hand up her back, under her bra, unhooking it. He needed to make what feeling she was feeling go away. He needed to make her feel good, him feel good. He needed for her to feel the connection. "I know I make a pregnant lady do too much work and sometimes I don't think to ask how you're feeling. But you can always tell me if something is bothering you. I'll try to fix it. You know that."

"I'm fine."

"Then why do I feel like there is something wrong?"

"It's gas."

He frowned at her, studying her for a long moment, trying to piece together the puzzle that was his wife. But he gave up and kissed her cheeks. "You're lying to me, love, and if I wasn't so crazy about you I would spank you."

"You're crazy about me?"

"Totally apeshit crazy mad about you." His hands traveled around to her front to cup her breasts. "I think about you all the time. I want to touch you all the time." He smoothed his hands down her torso to her belly, where he caressed her and his unborn child. "I want to be with you every damn minute of every day."

"Every minute of every day? Why?"

"Why? Because you're as randy as a teenage boy watching his first dirty movie."

She threw her head back and laughed, and more of the heaviness seeped away.

"Am not!"

His hands found their way upward, stroking her nipples until she was humming with pleasure. "Three times last night. I'm getting old, lass. You'll be the death of me. I'm surprised I can stand up straight. I'm surprised all my work hasn't been complete rubbish since I married you."

"Mmm." She kissed his Adam's apple.

"I should get on my knees and thank the Lord that he's given me a woman who never says no."

"You make me sound like a skank."

"No." He gently pushed her down on the couch. "What you are is a very good wife."

For a few minutes all they did was kiss. Scratch that. They were making out. Like oversexed teenagers in the back of a car. Only it was sweeter.

He loved her. This may have not been the life she planned for herself but it was the life they had and he was going to try damn hard to make sure she was happy.

She broke the kiss and looked up at him. "Colin?"

"Yes, darling."

"I—I . . ."

"What, my love?" He gave her belly another rub. "Want me to stop?"

"Don't be dumb."

He grinned. "Want to take this to our bedroom? We'd have more space there."

"Too far." She slid her hand up his shirt to stroke his back. "Listen. I—I—I want to talk to you about something."

"Later." He kissed her throat. "I can't think when you're this close to me."

"Should I dump a bucket o' water on you two or should I just come back later? I know most fathers would be a bit uncomfortable seeing their lad about to shag but it makes me proud. It nearly brings a tear to me eye."

"Pop." Colin looked up, horrified. "What the hell are you doing here? I'd not think you had the nerve to show your face here after our row. What the hell were you thinking?"

"I've come to see yer wife and looking at the lass I can tell you did well." He winked at her. "Hullo, gorgeous, by the way and thank you for inviting me. She ain't no moon pig, son. I can tell you that. A real beauty. I should have known you would have ended up with a soft one. Like father, like son. Big titties and perfect ass." Magnus tipped his hat to her. "Begging your pardon, love. Don't mean to be discussing you like that in front of your face but you are quite enough to get a man's blood going for days."

"Pop!"

"What?" He shrugged. "You know Magnus always tells the truth. Well, get up, lad. I guess you'll be wanting a proper hello. I can't promise you a slow run and embrace like in the movies but would you settle for a *Hiya, lad. You know yer pop is sorry for missing yer wedding.*" He looked around the little office and then back to them. "I've come all the way to this bloody dull place to see you. Now stop being a shit and greet me properly."

Laughter was not the right response in that moment but Cherri couldn't help herself, even though she knew she was about to be in major trouble with her husband. She giggled like an idiot, laughing so hard that her sides hurt. She had been hiding this from him for over a week, but they needed this. Colin needed his father and they needed a family.

Magnus and Colin were like bookends, but where Colin had a calm sort of quiet around him Magnus was bigger than life and crass and gorgeous. Being in the room with two O'Connell men was enough to make her head spin. She tried to pull it together, though. Ever since she had found Serena's things she had been in a funk, and she hated herself for letting a woman who was long gone sneak in and make her doubt herself. She would never be as beautiful as Serena, or as slender or graceful or worldly, but she had something up on the woman. She could give Colin the family he always wanted.

And that's why she'd called his father.

"I can't fucking believe it."

Poor Colin. She could feel the frustration rumble through his body. She could hear it in the thickening of his accent but she would not regret her decision. This reunion should have happened a long time ago.

"Charlotte," Colin barked. "Stop laughing."

"I can't." She wiped a tear from her cheek. "I'm sorry."

"You invited my father here without my permission?"

"Yes," she snorted, still unable to control herself.

"Why?"

"I did what I thought was best. Our baby needs a grandfather. And I want him to have one. If you don't want to talk to your father it's fine. But he's my guest and our baby will know him."

"A granddad!" Magnus let out a loud whoop. "I'm going to be a granddad. I always wanted a wee one to jiggle on my knee."

Before either one of them could say a word Magnus was

upon them giving them kisses and pats, practically squishing them into the sofa.

"For fuck's sake, Pop! We're Irish. You're not supposed to be slobbering on me like a bloody Saint Bernard."

Magnus smiled as he dropped one last kiss on Cherri's cheek. "I can't help it. I'm going to be a granddad."

There was nothing more American than a barbecue, Magnus O'Connell announced. He had been in New York less than twelve hours and he had thrown together a little party. Typical. There were few times in Colin's life where he hadn't seen Magnus with a drink in one hand and a woman's behind in the other. Today was no different.

"We're celebrating life, my lad. And family and happiness."

Colin could barely suppress a snort, listening to his father's bullshit. Since when did family become so important to him? He let a woman take one of his children out of his life; the other he barely had time for. Why the change all of a sudden?

*Charlotte.*

He watched his wife from his spot under the big oak tree in their backyard. She had invited his father to come for a visit. Something he had been trying and failing at for the better part of five years. One phone call from a pretty girl and his father was busting his ass to be here. Maybe Colin should have tried that long ago.

Magnus was on his game today. He told wild stories. He laughed with their guests. He smiled lavishly at Cherri. He kissed her cheeks a dozen times. He patted her growing belly. He stared at her ass. Colin tried to swallow the big ball of jealousy that lodged itself in his throat. His father wouldn't try anything with Cherri. He wouldn't do that to him. Again. Would he? Cherri was more than a girlfriend. She was his wife.

And she looked damn cute in the short red checkered sundress Ellis had made for her. It was very warm for early May. Over eighty degrees and she was walking around the backyard with her long legs and pink-polished toes bare.

"I thought once you married her all the creepy staring would stop."

Colin looked over at Mike and grinned. "Would you rather me stare at your ugly arse?"

Mike took a long swig of his beer. "I thought you would never ask."

Mike could only hold Colin's attention for a moment. Then he looked back to his wife, whom he had barely spoken with since Magnus showed up yesterday. He understood why she'd invited him here. She wanted a family and so did he. But he'd learned long ago that he couldn't count on his father for shit. That any family of his had to be one of his creation. Even now his father's arm was wrapped around Cherri's waist as they studied whatever Magnus was cooking up on the grill. It would never occur to him to touch another man's wife that way. Especially if that man was his son.

"You look like you're about to shit a bag of nails," Mike said, tearing his attention away from his father and his wife.

"Do you see how he's touching her?"

"Yes, I'd swear on my life I saw him with his hand on my wife's ass earlier. But that's Magnus. If they're female, they're fair game. I know what you're thinking, but even your father isn't a big enough asshole to do that to you twice. And you know Cherri would never cheat on you."

He'd never thought Arabella would cheat on him, either, but when he came home one day to find his father shagging her in the kitchen his faith in love diminished. And when he found Serena screwing her co-worker, he stopped trusting altogether. But he would like to think that he knew Cherri, more than he trusted her, knew how her mind worked. He knew that it would never cross her mind to be unfaithful. "No, I don't think so," he finally answered Mike after becoming briefly lost in thought.

She must have felt his gaze because she locked eyes and pulled away from Magnus, crossing the yard to sit on his lap.

"Stop scowling at me." She looped her arms around his neck, resting her head in the crook of her shoulder. "Hi, Mike." She smiled at his friend before returning her attention to him. "You're very ugly when you scowl."

"I'm not scowling." Instinctively he wrapped his arms around her. "That's how my face looks."

"It doesn't. You're quite gorgeous normally. You know that's the only reason I married you. I think you're still mad at me. Are you?"

He didn't answer. Instead he slid his hand under her dress and pinched her bottom.

"Ouch!" She squirmed in his lap. "I didn't actually expect him to show up yesterday. He said he needed to settle some things before he left. I thought he was going to give me some warning before he arrived."

"But that's just the way my Pop is."

She sighed. "I'm sorry for shocking you, but I'm not sorry for what I did. You need to make things better with your father. I refuse to have a totally dysfunctional family. Besides, I honestly thought I would have time to butter you up before he came. And trust me, you would have really enjoyed all the buttering." She glanced at Mike and her cheeks turned red. "Sorry, Mike, but I got half of my ideas from Ellis. Congratulations, you have a very freaky wife."

Colin pinched her butt again.

"Damn it! Stop that." She folded her arms beneath her breasts. How could she still not know how that affected him? "You know what? I don't care if you're mad at me. You can shove it." She pressed a long soft kiss to his mouth, breaking it just as it started to melt his mind. "I lied. I do care. I don't like it when you're mad at me." She sighed dramatically. "My only job in life is to make sure you're happy and I am sucking at it. I'm surprised you haven't divorced me yet."

He forced himself to keep a straight face, even though the corners of his mouth had another idea. He kissed her briefly and patted her bottom. "Go on back to your friends, love, before I start getting ideas."

She kissed both him and Mike on the cheek before she made her way back to Ellis and Belinda.

"She's got your balls in a vise grip."

"Aye," he nodded. There was no denying it.

"You're not really mad at her, are you? Hell, I would have broken the moment she turned those puppy-dog eyes on me."

"I'm not mad, merely irritated. For fuck's sake, I'm not even sure about that anymore."

"That's what happens when you fall in love."

Colin scrubbed his face in frustration. "I'm literally going mad over her. She looks at me sideways and my whole worldview changes. What the hell happened to the man I used to be?"

"You're getting old."

"I must be," he agreed.

"I take back what I said," Mike said quietly.

"What?"

"About you and Cherri. About you taking advantage of her. About you ruining her life. I always thought that you had it out for her, but it was the other way around. You didn't stand a chance against Cherri Rudy, did you?"

"I was bloody doomed from the moment she smiled at me."

"I was worried about her because after Serena you went . . . fucking Looney Tunes on me. I didn't care if you screwed half of New York State, but I didn't want you to hurt her." He sighed. "What happened with Serena anyway? One day I could have sworn you were going to propose, the next you told me it was over."

"You know how I screwed half of New York State? Well, she managed to get the other half."

"Shit. It's no wonder you're so fucked up."

"Yup."

# CHAPTER 25

*A time to heal . . .*

“We should talk about throwing you a baby shower,” Belinda said to Cherri as she, Belinda, and Ellis swayed gently on the porch swing.

“It’s too soon to think about that,” Cherri said, not really wanting to talk about it. She was a bit distracted by Colin, who was being a sulky pain in her ass. He’d barely said two words to anybody besides Mike all day. She was okay with him not speaking to her, but she felt bad for Magnus, who’d come all the way from God knows where to make amends with his son. She’d watched all day as he tried and failed miserably to make some kind of connection with his son.

“How’s business going, lad?” he would ask. “Or how’s that bloody excuse of a football team doing this year?” She knew it wasn’t what Colin needed to hear from the man. He needed to hear that Magnus was truly sorry for a lifetime of letdowns. She knew Colin had a hard time trusting him—or anybody, for that matter. And honestly she didn't know if Magnus was really ready to stop letting his son down. But she hoped so. She hoped this baby would help heal a lot of wounds. They just needed to talk to each other, but they were dumb men. She wasn't sure if they knew how.

"Hello, Cherri? Are you paying attention at all?" Ellis gently smacked the back of her head.

"Nope."

"Care to enlighten us as to what you're thinking about?"

"Colin." She spotted him across the yard with his father and Mike, none of them saying a word, just staring at the grill as if entranced.

"Ah," Belinda sighed. "Young love. How is everything going with you two? It looks like you've finally kissed and made up."

"We have. I think I finally understand him now. He's possessive and overprotective and chauvinistic but I love him so much I could puke."

"Eww." Belinda wrinkled her nose. "But it's strangely sweet at the same time."

"What's going on with you, Belinda?" She turned to her friend. "What's going on in your love life?"

"What love life?" She snorted.

"Men hit on her all the time," Ellis stated. "She's just too damn picky."

"That's not true." She shook her head. "I fell in love when I was in San Francisco. He was all wrong for me but I want a guy to give me the same feeling I felt when I was with him. I want what you two have. I just don't see the point of dating a bunch of losers to get that. If it happens it happens. And if it doesn't—"

"You'll be the spinster who lives alone with her three cats," Ellis said, bumping Belinda with her hip and giving her a sassy grin.

"Such a bitch." Belinda sighed. "Why don't you get together

with my mother? That way the two of you can have a real nagging party."

"What was it about that guy that you can't get over?" Cherri asked.

"Who said I wasn't over him?"

"You did. You haven't had a serious relationship since him. Maybe it's a sign. Maybe you should look him up."

"Maybe it's a sign I should join a convent."

"Food's ready!" Magnus bellowed across the yard.

"Oh great, I'm starving," Belinda said and walked away from them.

Ellis slanted Cherri a look. It seemed they'd hit a nerve when it came to Belinda's love life.

"I'm starving." Cherri came up behind Colin in the shop, resting her hand on his lower back.

He stopped sanding the ottoman he was working on and turned to his young bride, glad for the break. They had been working nonstop for the past few days. New jobs kept coming in, and instead of refusing the work he was running himself ragged. He couldn't make it past nine o'clock most nights, staying awake only long enough to shower, eat, and make love to his very willing wife. "Do you want me to run out and get you something to eat?"

She smiled, shaking her head, and then stood on her tiptoes to kiss his lips. "I'm pregnant, not paralyzed. You don't have to wait on me hand and foot."

He wrapped his arms around her and pulled her closer. "What if I want to?" He knew she had been working hard to help out at the shop between painting her own projects and she never complained. He knew that the pregnancy was starting to catch up with her. Swelling feet, backaches. He ordered her to slow down, to rest, but she ignored him and continued to work just as hard as he did. So he didn't mind rubbing her back, or fetching her meals. His first job was to make sure she was comfortable. "I quite like doing things for you, love."

Her face lit up. "You're already going to get laid tonight. You don't have to try so hard. But the effort is truly appreciated."

He rubbed her belly in slow circles. "I've got to take care of my love."

"You are." She leaned closer to him, her belly preventing them from getting any closer. "But I can take care of you, too, which is why I came to ask what you wanted for lunch."

"Chunky chicken salad on that crusty bread that I like with cheese and bacon and a side of chips."

She rested her head in the crook of his shoulder. "Does that mean you want potato chips or french fries? I always get confused about that."

"Fries. *Crisps* are what we call potato chips, and after you come back I would like you to take a nice long break."

"Okay." For the first time she didn't argue. "When are you going to talk to your father?"

"Charlotte," he warned. Magnus had been there going on two weeks, and while he wasn't disruptive to their lives he was more disruptive to Colin's peace of mind. "Leave me and my pop be. We're fine as we are."

"You think so?" She raised a brow at him.

"Yes." He playfully slapped her behind. "Now run off and get us lunch. Maybe I'll take a break this afternoon and we can sneak off together."

"Oye," Magnus said, sighing, as he walked in. "I know she's a pretty lass, son, but you don't have to hold on to her like a stiff wind will take her away all the time."

"He's right. I'm far too big for any amount of wind to take me away, but you can hold on to me anytime you want." She winked at him. "In fact I prefer it."

*Good lass.*

"I'm going out to get some sandwiches. Would you like one, Magnus?"

"Call me Pop, darlin'. We're family. And yes, if it's not too much trouble, could you pick me up a roast beef with horseradish and some of them cheesy crisp things?"

"No problem. Could you be useful and help Colin out around the shop? He needs help but is being too much of a stubborn ass to admit it." She pulled away from Colin before he had the chance to say anything. "Gotta go. Colin, remember what you promised for when I get back." She kissed both men on their cheeks and left them alone.

He nodded and watched her walk away instead of telling her that under no circumstances did he need his father's help. But he didn't want his father to think that he cared either way. He kept quiet.

"I like your lass." Magnus walked over to Colin's workbench and picked up the old metal pedal car that Colin had yet to touch. "Beautiful girl. She reminds me a bit of your mum sometimes. Lovely. Soft. Dependable. You know, the type a man could really hold on to."

"I don't know what Mum looks like. I don't know anything about her. You never bothered to tell me much."

"That's because there's nothing to tell." Magnus spoke a little more firmly than Colin was used to hearing. "She left us, boy. I didn't chase your mother away. I didn't cheat on her. But she left me anyway. I was never good enough for her." He shook his head as if he was trying to shake his feelings off. "Your lass is different than your mum. She's . . . sweet, she's happy, and she loves the babe she is carrying inside her. Your lass is the type of woman who is made to be a mum."

"Mum didn't want me?" Colin knew that. She'd walked out on him but he had always thought it was because he was difficult. It never occurred to him that she hadn't wanted him from birth.

"I did," Magnus said after a long moment. "I saw you and knew you were my mate for life." He looked at Colin for a long moment before turning back to the toy car. "This can be a beauty again. Paint it baby blue with white trim, bang out those dents, shine it up till it glows. I could do it. The chrome work would take me a pretty amount of time but I could make this as lovely as your lass."

"If you want to," Colin said noncommittally. The truth was he could use the help, and he knew his father's work was as good as his own. The man taught him everything he knew but he'd learned long ago not to depend on his father for anything. The wind would blow in another direction and take him to where pretty women spawned.

"I want to." He picked up a screwdriver and as if it was second nature began to dismantle the car. "I thought you were fucking cracked when you told me you were going to be starting your own business fixing other people's rubbish."

"Why? We used to fix things for people in the county all the time."

"We did, but that was side work, lad. It was never enough to support us. But you proved me wrong, boy. You're making fistfuls of money, aren't you? I thought because you went off to university you would get a job wearing a suit and work in a bank and walk around with a stick up your arse but you're more like me than even I thought. Not comfortable unless your hands are rougher than a cliff's ass and oil comes out of your armpits."

Colin shrugged. This had always been his plan. He'd never wanted to wear a suit or work for another man. He used to watch his father come home after a long day, bitching about what his lousy bosses had forced him to do. He hated to see his father so beaten down. He would only work doing what he loved. His father should have known that, because Colin never kept his goal a secret. He should have known it by the way Colin followed him around when he was a lad, trying to take every piece of knowledge that the man had to give. But maybe Magnus had never noticed. He was too busy falling in love with some woman who would never stick around.

"Do you really think we're alike, Pop?"

"Sometimes I think you're me, only a bit better, but sometimes I wonder who the hell sired you. Because I never know what you're going to do next."

Colin shook his head, disagreeing with his father. "I'm not so unpredictable, Pop. I've lived in the same place for seventeen years. I've had this shop for almost ten."

Magnus disagreed. "You got married, lad. Out of nowhere you got married. You're going to be a bloody father, for fuck's sake. Trust me, that came with no warning. I spoke to you a month before and you didn't say a thing about Cherri. I asked you if you were with anybody and you told me no. And for fuck's sake, Colin, she's young. Barely older than your baby sister." His father pinned him with his gaze. It was uncomfortable. He had never seen Magnus so serious, and for some reason the notion that he'd let his father down made his stomach clench. "A baby and you've gone and knocked her up."

"You think I've made a mistake marrying Cherri? Because—"

"You'll be quiet, lad and you'll listen to me. For once in your fucking life you'll let me be the father. I've been in your shoes. I know the only reason you're married to a twenty-two-year-old girl is because you couldn't control yourself around her."

"Is that how we're alike?"

"I'm not finished!" He slammed his fist down on the workbench. "You never let me finish. You always thought you were so much better than me even as a boy. You thought you knew it all. You treated me like I was the fucking kid and you were the father. So what if I shagged a lot of women.

So what if I couldn't keep your mother around. It doesn't mean I don't know what's best for my own boy. I knew you wouldn't have gone anywhere in Cork. I knew you had to get out. I didn't want you to end up like me and that's the path you were heading down. Why the hell do you think I let you go ten thousand miles away from me to university?"

"You slept with my girlfriend and that's why I left."

Magnus pinned him with a hard stare. "I'm glad that we're finally getting down to it. Because this is what all this shit is about. I slept with your girlfriend. I didn't do it because I wanted her. I did it because I didn't want you taking that carpenter job and getting stuck there."

"What? You're cracked. I was only going to do that till I got enough money to make a go of it with my shop."

"You would have never had enough money, son. I tried to explain it to you. I tried to tell you that it wasn't your path, but you never wanted to listen to me. I had to show you. I had to make you mad enough to take notice."

"So you slept with my girl?"

"She was five years older than you. You fancied yourself in love with her. I knew she was only toying with you. She was going to drag you down. You were meant for more than the life you had. I knew what I did would take you away from me for a time but I never thought I'd not get you back."

"I don't believe this. You spent half the time not giving a shit what I did and now you're acting like father of the century. I'm not buying it."

"Well, don't. But I'm not going anywhere just because you're too much of a wanker to admit that my not showing up to your wedding was not entirely my fault. How the hell did I know you were going to do something as crazy as that? Married? That's the last thing I expected from you."

"It's not about the wedding, Pop. Don't you get it? I kept calling you because I needed you and you never bothered to pick up."

"You needed me, eh?" Magnus raised a single brow at him. "Well, that's a first. You never needed me for nothing your whole life. You never wanted my help. Your whole damn life I felt more like a bothersome roommate than your father. I know I made my mistakes with you, lad, but you never gave me any slack. I was twenty years old raising a baby by myself. Half the time I didn't know my ass from my elbow but I did my best by you." He shook his head, weariness creeping into his features. "I'm tired of fighting with you, boy. Just make sure you keep your young wife happy. I know what it's like to have your love walk out on you. Me and you are more alike than you think."

Magnus picked up the pedal car and walked over to the sandblaster, turning it on and drowning out the possibility of any more conversation. Colin wanted to smash something. He looked at his father, whose face was set in grim determination as he worked. It couldn't be true. None of it could be true. He had slept with Arabella because he didn't care about Colin's feelings. Not to help him. It just wasn't something Magnus would do.

Thinking had become too much for him. Cherri was gone for the moment. He couldn't seek her out to make him forget his troubles and he wouldn't give his father the satisfaction of seeing him walk out in a huff. So he did the only thing he could do. He went back to work.

Cherri sat up in bed waiting for her husband, arms folded beneath her breasts. She glanced at the clock. Twenty minutes had gone by and not a single trace of Colin. Granted it was only nine thirty and a little early for bed, but she had asked him to come up early. She wanted to spend a little time taking care of him. He wasn't himself. She tried to chalk it up to his huge workload or the fact that Magnus was still here, causing him to be cranky. But she knew there was more to it than that.

Magnus hadn't been his usual jovial self, either, the past two days, causing their house to be one big cave of brooding males. They must have had an argument the other day while she was at the store, but neither man had bothered to confide in her and she hadn't bothered to ask. Dumb men. They were too much alike for their own good, neither one of them willing to bend first. Neither one of them saying a word that wasn't absolutely necessary. Cherri was tired of trying to push them together. To make them a family. They were going to have to fix it themselves.

At least they were working well together. Magnus took as much time and care with each project as Colin did. Stone Barley Restorations was producing more quality work than ever before. That alone gave Cherri hope. Colin hadn't asked his father to leave, and Magnus hadn't taken off. They loved each other and Cherri loved Colin. It was past time she told him. Nobody should live without knowing he was loved.

She got out of bed, pulled her bathrobe on, and padded down the stairs to find him in the kitchen bent at the waist, his head stuck in the refrigerator.

"There you are." She walked up behind him and gave his behind a playful pinch.

"Oye!" He stood. She wrapped his arms around his back and pressed her lips into the firm surface.

"I've been waiting for you to come upstairs."

"Oh?"

"Did you forget?" She squeezed him tightly, noting that his body felt slightly softer than before. "You've been working too hard, dear husband, if you can't remember that I made an appointment to show you how much I love you."

"Well, that's nice, lass." The man she thought was Colin turned in her arms. "But I'm afraid that you didn't make that appointment with me."

"Magnus!" Her face was on fire. "I thought you were Colin. I'm so sorry."

"Aww, lass." He wrapped his big arms around her and gave her a fatherly hug. "Don't be sorry. Sometimes I wish I were Colin. He did everything I wanted to do only the bugger did it the right way. I'm guessing I should thank you. You've made my boy happy."

"Did he tell you that?"

Magnus laughed and kissed Cherri's cheek. "My boy? Talk to me about something? Don't be daft, girlie. I can see it in his face when he looks at you."

"I found a box of his ex's things," she blurted out, not sure why she was confiding in her father-in-law. "He got rid of them. But sometimes I wonder if she's the one he wished he could have married."

"No." Magnus shook his head. "Serena was what Colin thought he wanted. He grew up poor in County Cork, with a pop like me who could never get his arse in order. He always went for girls he thought were better. Who he thought were posh, but those girls never did it for him. That's why I'm glad he married you. He may not have wanted to love you but he needed to love you. Don't let some slag from the past make you doubt his commitment to you."

"You really think so?"

"He may treat me like a stranger but I know my boy. Trust me, the lad's done for. Promise me something, lass?"

"What?"

"You've got to be a little understanding when it comes to an O'Connell man. We're not an easy lot. I've messed up when it comes to him. I was a shit father sometimes, and I failed him when he needed me. So don't blame him too much if he doesn't feel like yapping about what's going on in his head. He don't know how, lass. But he's a good man and I'm proud of him. And he's trying his best to do right by you. Old Magnus tried to help you out, though." He nodded. "I told the wanker if he don't treat you right, you'd be out the door."

"I wouldn't!"

He nodded. "If he don't treat you right you should. But I just said that to give him a little scare. When a man really loves a woman, he'll do all sorts to keep her."

"You seem so sure."

"Of course I'm sure! If you weren't married to my boy I'd have you for myself. You're a beauty. I don't usually like them expecting, if you know what I mean, but I'd make an exception for you." He squeezed her, patting her behind. "I'm glad my boy inherited my taste in women."

"He did, now get your hand off my ass."

He removed it quickly. "Sorry, lass. Force of habit."

Colin walked into his kitchen, the plastic bag of frozen custard he had purchased for his wife in his hand. He was supposed to be back sooner but he got stuck in line behind some jackass buying lottery tickets. He wanted to surprise her with a little treat to tell her he was sorry. He'd been stuck in his head for the past couple of days replaying the conversation he'd had with his father. Maybe Colin had been a little hard on him.

"I don't usually like them expecting, if you know what I mean, but I'd make an exception for you. I'm glad my boy inherited my taste in women," he heard his father say. All he saw was Magnus's arm wrapped around Cherri's waist, his hand resting on her bottom.

*Not again. Not with Charlotte.*

Magnus had been right about one thing: Colin had never really loved Arabella. Even after catching his father shagging her, he never felt like he wanted to kill him. But seeing his father coming on to his wife was a different story.

Before he could think he flew at his father, slamming him into the counter and knocking Cherri out of the way. "My wife." He punched his father in the jaw. "She's pregnant, you arsehole. And she belongs to me, you greedy fucking bastard."

"What the hell are you going on about?" Magnus ducked as Colin swung at him again. "I ain't after your wife."

"Don't lie to me, Pop. I heard what you said. I've watched you gawk at her since you've been here. You keep your damn hands off my wife or I'll break them."

"Colin, you dumbass." Cherri grabbed his wrist. "Magnus was not coming on to me. It's not what it looks like."

"No, it wasn't what it looked like the last time, either. Right, Pop? My eyes were lying when I came home to find you fucking my girlfriend in the kitchen. What's your excuse this time? Trying to save me from being happy? If I'd stayed out ten minutes longer I would be walking in on the same scene all over again."

"You asshole!" Cherri flew at him with both fists. "I would never cheat on you. Never! How could you think that of me?" She landed a sharp blow to his chin and then pinched the hell out of his chest. "With your father, you bastard! With anybody? I love you, Colin O'Connell, but sometimes I could smash your brains out."

She went to attack him again but he grabbed her arms and forced her into a chair, kneeling before her. "Stop it, love. You'll hurt the baby." She kicked him, catching him right in the gut. "Oof."

She loved him.

"The baby's fine. Your wife is royally pissed off. I'm the one you should be worrying about. Stupid jerkface asshead. Why are you laughing?"

She loved him.

"Because"—he let out a loud chuckle—"you said you love me." She'd finally said it. He'd known she did or at least had always suspected, but hearing the words come out of her mouth made him feel as if his heart had burst in his chest.

She loved him.

"Did I say that?" She tried to smack him but he was quicker than her and caught both her wrists. "I take it back.

I take back this whole marriage thing, too. I can't spend the rest of my life with a big idiot." Her eyes filled with tears, and that stopped his laughter dead. "I can't believe you don't trust me. I can't believe you think I would sleep with your father."

"Aw, love. Please don't cry. I trust you. I just don't trust my father. He slept with my first real girlfriend. I'm sorry, darlin', but a man has a hard time getting that image out of his mind. And you don't know how afraid I am of losing you sometimes. I'm waiting for the day you say *Enough of this bugger* and walk out on me."

"Well, I won't, you ass, even though I should, but I love you. I've loved you forever and I probably always will. So stop looking for excuses to get rid of me."

"Say it again," he said, wiping the tears from her cheeks.

"What? How much of a stupid jerk you are?"

"No, that you love me."

"I love you. I. Love. You." She poked him in the chest with each word. "Hasn't anyone said that to you before?"

He shook his head. "Nobody who ever meant it. I'm sorry, love." He pulled open her robe and pushed up her nightgown to pepper kisses across her belly. "I'll work on not being such an enormous wanker."

"Your father wasn't trying to sleep with me. He was telling me how lucky you were to be married to a smart, beautiful, talented, far-too-good-for-you woman."

He looked up to see that his father had already gone. "I'll talk to him later." He went back to kissing her heated skin. "We're going to look like an episode of Jerry Springer tomorrow. Me and Pop all black and blue. You barefoot and pregnant."

Cherri ran her fingers through his hair. "Why didn't you ever tell me that your father slept with your girlfriend? No wonder you're so screwed up."

"Why do people keep telling me that?" He looked up at her to find her smiling down at him.

"I love you, Colin. I'll keep telling you that, too."

He stood up, gathering her in his arms and kissing her until she had no air left. "Bed," he managed just before he dragged her upstairs to finish what he'd started.

# CHAPTER 26

*Oh no, not my baby.*

Cherri rubbed her belly as she walked into the shop. She was getting huge. Her feet were no longer visible, and that was a major thing. She always thought her feet were enormous, but it didn't matter to her that her behind was spreading or that sometimes it took her two tries to get out of a chair. She was happy. Quitting her job had been the best decision she had made, not only for her marriage but for herself. She got to paint all day. She got to be in the same room as her husband. It made her giddy. Sometimes she would laugh for no reason, and Colin would just look at her and smile. He told her she was in the giggly phase of her pregnancy and that he loved it. She loved it, too. It beat the hell out of crying.

He was staring at the computer screen when she approached the office. The bookkeeping software was up. She was just about to tell him that she had updated the accounting last night when the phone rang. He absently pressed the SPEAKER button as he scrolled down the screen.

"Stone Barley Restorations. How can I help you?"

"You picked up this time."

*Serena.*

The speaker didn't need to be identified for her to know who it was.

Colin's face changed. Surprise then hurt then anger passed over it. And then an emotion that she couldn't name. She stood there frozen, knowing she shouldn't stand there silently. But she couldn't make herself move. She needed to hear this conversation.

This woman kept popping up in their world, like a cold that wouldn't go away. She was worse than that. She was a threat to their marriage.

"I told you the last time that I'm married now," he said in a furious whisper. "I don't need to hear your apologies. It's done."

"But it's not done for me, I—"

"Charlotte is pregnant."

"Charlotte?"

"Cherri. My wife. We're done, Serena. I don't want to hear from you anymore."

"So you're telling me that you're stuck because your wife is pregnant. You know that doesn't matter to me—"

He gently set the phone back on the receiver, hanging up on her.

Cherri backed out of the doorway quietly. Colin had done the right thing. He had hung up. He had told her not to contact him again, but for some reason she couldn't help but feel lost. Grief almost.

He told Serena they were done because she was pregnant. Not because he loved her. Not because he wasn't in love with Serena anymore. She'd told him she loved him. She told him a hundred times a day but he never said it back. They were friends. They were happy together. They enjoyed each other, but they were not in love. They didn't marry the way most couples did. They didn't have a good start. She kept forgetting that. She had been so happy lately that their earlier problems seemed to have slipped from her mind.

"Cherri, lass." She ran into Magnus on her escape from the shop. "What's wrong with you, girl? You look like you've seen a ghost."

"Nothing." She shook her head. She was dangerously close to tears, but there was no point in crying. It wasn't going to change anything. "I'm not feeling well."

"Does Colin know? I'll fetch him for you. We can't be having you ill when you're carrying me grandlad."

"No." She shook her head. "Don't tell Colin. I think I just need to lie down for a while."

Magnus shook his head. "I'll just see you to your room. Can't have you collapsing."

"You don't have to."

"I do. You're me son's love. I'd do anything for you."

"I think a present might be in order," Colin mumbled as he stared at the books for their business. By some unspoken agreement Cherri had taken them over and done a hell of a job. Not only had she brought in a substantial chunk of business with her painted furniture but she did all the little rubbish things he hated doing, like the books and the supply ordering. That alone was worth marrying her for.

His happy, pretty, giggly wife. It had been so easy to hang up on Serena. She hadn't changed. Still driven. Still unable to take no for an answer. The things he'd originally liked about her were the things he now couldn't stand about her. They'd broken up because she destroyed his trust by cheating on him and now she saw nothing wrong with breaking up his marriage, ripping his tiny family apart. She made him feel stupid all over again. Stupid for thinking he could possibly love her in the first place.

She was so different from his wife, whose simplicity and

kindness made his world brighter. He didn't know if he told her that enough. He wondered if she had any idea how much she meant to him.

"Lad." His father came from the office, a serious frown on his face. "Go see to your wife now. I just saw her outside and she was damn near hyperventilating. I put her to bed but you need to get your arse up there and see to her."

"What?" His heart jumped up and lodged itself in his throat. "What happened? Is she okay?"

"Nothing happened as far as I can tell but you need to put your foot down and order her to stop working. It's not right to make a pregnant lass work so hard."

"I don't make her work at all. I want her to lie around all day and grow my baby but the daft girl doesn't listen."

Magnus shrugged. "You're her husband, son. You need to take care of her."

He nodded and headed for the door, but before he opened it he turned to his father once more. "I'm sorry I tried to kill you the other day."

"Aye?" A smile bloomed on his face. "I'm thinking every lad tries to take his pop once. I just wish you'd tried it when you were sixteen. I really could have kicked your arse then."

"If you're wanting to stay with us, it's okay with me. Charlotte would like that."

"And you?" His raised his brow.

"You're cheap labor. I'd be dumb to turn you out."

Magnus grinned at him. "Go see to your lass."

"I am." As he opened the door, his father called to him. "Yeah, Pop?"

"I love you, lad."

Colin stayed rooted to his spot for a moment, surprised at how he felt hearing that from his father. "Oye, you've become a sentimental bugger in your old age."

"Nah, but I'm about to move in so I figured I'd say it now

so when I do something to tick you off you'll not be so mad at me."

"Smart old man. Oh, and Pop?"

"Yes, lad."

"I love you, too."

He walked out before his father could say anything in return and headed toward his wife. He took the stairs two at a time till he reached their bedroom. She was under the covers, her long body pulled into a tight little ball. He worried about her. The past few weeks he had been seeing the pregnancy take its toll. She was a strong girl but they were due to have a big child. At their last sonogram they could clearly see the baby stretched out taking up as much space as possible. Part of him swelled with pride to see their strong healthy baby, but another part of him felt guilty. Cherri never planned on being a mother so soon. He knew she loved him. He knew that she was going to stay but he sometimes still wondered if she wished things were different.

"Love." He gently pulled the covers away from her face and crawled in beside her. "Pop said you aren't feeling well. You know I get as panicky as a lass on her first date whenever you don't feel well."

He pulled her toward him to see that her eyes were red and watery and her face pale. Something had happened.

"Charlotte?" He cupped her face, stroking her puffy cheeks with his thumb. "What is it, my love? Please."

"I love you."

He wasn't sure what had brought this on, but he leaned down and pressed his mouth to hers. "I know, and I thank my lucky stars for it every day."

"When I married you I planned on it being forever."

"Yes, love. It will be."

"I'm perfect for you."

He couldn't help but smile down at her even though she was clearly distressed.

"You are. Why do you think I married you?"

"Because you knocked me up." She wrapped her arms around him, her belly preventing him from getting as close as he would like. "But you didn't have to marry me. You're not stuck."

He pulled slightly away from her, jarred by what she said. "What're you talking about? What happened?"

"Your . . ." She shook her head. "Nothing."

"What? Tell me."

She stared at him for a long moment, her words seeming stuck. "Why does she keep calling you?"

His stomach dropped. "I don't know. To fuck with my head. I don't need that from her. I've already got you taking up my remaining brain cells. I don't have any space for her."

She just stared up at him. Her sadness seeping into him.

"You know I want nothing to do with her." He didn't know how to reassure her. He didn't know how to prove to her that she was it for him. "I want to show you something." He left the bed and went to his dresser, pulling out a packet of papers. "I've made you a partner."

"What?" She took the papers from him and scanned through them. "You're giving me half your business? Why?"

He shrugged. "I'm not good with words, love. But I wanted you to know that there's no going back. If you own half my business it's like you own half of me. This shop is my life and I want you in it forever. You gave up your job to be here with me. I had to give up something to be here with you."

"Colin . . ." She looked up at him. "You didn't have to do this."

"I did. You're my partner, love. I just wanted to show you that."

She shut her eyes, but the tears still dripped down her face.

"I just have one condition. You have to agree to let my pop stay here with us."

"Excuse me?" She sat up. "You made up with your father?"

"He's good around the shop. It might not be so bad to keep him around. Is that okay with you?"

"Of course, Colin. Of course. He's a good man."

"Good, because I'm going to let him have the run of my shop for a few days. We're going away."

"We are?"

"Yes, there's a little house on the beach in Cape Cod that has our names on it. I would take you someplace tropical, love, but I don't want you flying when you're this pregnant. I promise to get you there someday."

"You know you don't have to take me anywhere. I'm happy right here with you."

"What a lovely thing to say, lass. Now get your stuff. We're leaving in an hour."

They had gone to Cape Cod and come back. Cherri had progressed into her sixth month of pregnancy and then out of it. The summer came. Magnus and Colin along with some contractors began to turn the basement into a lush apartment for Magnus. The two men were getting along the best they had in their entire lives and Cherri . . . She worked on her baby's bedroom. She had a little over a month to go and she was starting to get antsy. She wanted to meet her baby. She wanted to see the thing that had been growing inside her for so long.

Cherri stood back to stare at the mural she has just finished painting on her child's wall. Clouds. Colin had suggested a team of little footballers decked in the colors of Manchester United but she vetoed it. She wanted her baby's room to be happy and peaceful, a place he or she could grow with. It was almost done now, and for some reason Cherri couldn't identify, she felt pulled to this room. Some days she would just sit in the plush rocking chair Colin had made for her and stare at her surroundings. All the furniture was made or restored by her baby's father and grandfather, who had both gone a little overboard as she was nearing the end of her pregnancy. Magnus had bought so many toys they could open a store, and Colin . . . He wouldn't allow her within three feet of the shop, fearing she would give birth the moment she did any work. But that was okay with her for once. Impending motherhood had been taking up all her free brain cells. It was times like this she wished Baba were around. Yesterday had marked five months without her, and Cherri wished that the old woman could have hung around long enough to see her great-grandchild. But there was no use wishing for things that couldn't be. Magnus was going to be a wonderful grandfather. Their baby was going to be a child who was dearly loved. Cherri could ask for nothing more.

Serena hadn't tried to contact Colin again since they had gone away, or at least Cherri didn't think she had. Maybe she had. She trusted Colin. She did. She knew he had too much honor to sneak around behind her back, but there was still a little doubt in her mind, a little curiosity about him and the woman he used to love. It must have been a great love. It had to have been if she was still calling after all this time. If he was still so affected by her calls.

Maybe Cherri couldn't blame the woman. If Colin and her had split she would forever think about him, because love that strong doesn't simply fade away.

Arms wrapped around her as she stared at the wall, and as soon as she felt Colin's hard chest against her back she sagged against him.

*"Mo chuisle,"* Colin whispered in her ear, which she learned from his father meant "my pulse" in Gaelic. It was her all-time favorite endearment. "What're you thinking about?" He kissed her under her ear.

"You. I love you."

"Charlotte." He spun her around and kissed her till she tingled to her toes but he never returned the words. "I'm afraid you've got me by the bollocks, love. I couldn't walk away from you if I tried." He kissed down the side of her neck. "What were you thinking about, my love?"

"Everything," she answered truthfully. "I'm thinking about being a mother. I couldn't walk out on my child. I haven't even met our baby yet and I know I couldn't do it. I'm just wondering how our mothers could walk out on us."

"I've asked myself that question a thousand times."

"I found her, you know."

"Who? Your mother?"

She nodded. "I looked her up on the Internet. She's a singer in Reno. I have her email address. Sometimes I think about writing her."

"What would you say?"

"I would tell her about Baba."

"What else?"

"I'm not sure. What would you say to your mother if she reappeared?"

"Thank you."

"Thank you?" She blinked at him.

"If it weren't for her leaving, my life wouldn't have turned out the way it did. I wouldn't have come to America and met Mike and met you. Her leaving brought me to you. I wouldn't change that. I wouldn't go back."

"You're sweet." She rested her head on his shoulder.

"I'm happy. For me there is no reason to dwell on the past. But if you want to talk to your mum, if you want to see her, we'll make it happen."

"I don't need to. I have all the family I need with you."

# CHAPTER 27

*All's well that ends well . . .*

Colin propped himself up on his elbow and gazed at his wife's nude body. She was heavily pregnant with his child, and no matter how hard he tried he couldn't seem to keep his hands off her. Even now he couldn't stop himself from trailing the tips of his fingers across her chest. Her breasts were so pretty and full, her nipples more sensitive than they had ever been. He ran his palm beneath one breast, then cupped it. Testing its weight.

"You know those aren't going to belong to you anymore once the baby is born."

He looked up at her to find her smiling at him. So damn beautiful, his young wife. And she was happy. Half the time she walked around with a tiny smile on her face, for no reason at all. It made getting up in the morning easy. Looking at her made his chest swell to the point it felt like bursting. A year ago he wouldn't have imagined that his life could be this good. His business was booming. His father was with him. He was going to become a father. It was all because of her.

*You sound like a bloody lass, you wanker.*

*Sod off.*

He didn't care. His wife made him happy.

"I saw them first." He bent to kiss where her heart beat and then brushed a kiss over both her nipples, causing her to shiver with delight. "Besides, we'll use them for entirely different purposes." He ran his hand along her rib cage, over her belly, down her hips, to her thighs, in between her legs.

"I swear there is something wrong with you. I'm as big as a house and you get randy every time you see me."

It was true. It was just after noon, the sun was blazing into their bedroom window. This lovemaking session had not been planned but she'd accidentally rubbed up against him as she was making lunch in the kitchen. He couldn't help himself. He pulled her upstairs and made love to her until she was incoherent.

"You can tell me no, Charlotte. It'll be hard but I can contain myself."

"Why would I say no? I get to spend a couple of hours every day having a beautiful man worship my super-sized body."

He grinned at her. "Forgive me, *mo chuisle,* but I'm afraid you're going to have to put up with me one more time before I go back to work."

"Woe is me." She grinned but opened her arms and welcomed him once more.

Forty-five minutes later they reemerged, lunch still forgotten on the kitchen counter. Colin was supposed to be heading back to the shop but he didn't feel like working much today. They had just a few weeks until their son came, until their lives changed forever, and while he was more excited than he had ever been, he knew they would never be like this again. He wanted to spend as much time with his wife as possible.

He led her outside into the warm August day, stuck his head into the shop, and yelled, "Pop, cover for me here. I'm going to take Charlotte for ice cream."

"Bring me back a triple-thick chocolate milk shake."

"Aye." He slapped his leg as he took the leash off the hook next to the door. "Come, Rufus. We'll get you a cone, too."

"Ice cream." Cherri's face lit up as Rufus happily trotted up to them. "Can I have hot fudge and whipped cream and a cherry?"

"Of course, love."

"On a cone?"

"We'll ask for it on the side." He grinned at her.

"Mmm. Heaven. Let's walk there. I'm going to need to burn off all the ice cream."

He locked his fingers with hers and started down their driveway as a black BMW pulled in. He paused only to tell whoever it was that parking for the shop was around the back. But the person who got out of the car didn't need directions.

Serena emerged from the car, looking nearly the same as the last time he'd seen her. He'd honestly never thought he would see her again. Never thought she would have the nerve to show up at the home he and his wife shared.

"Hello, Colin." She gave him a sunny smile. It was as if all the past had somehow melted away—as if she'd forgotten that she'd betrayed his trust. That he never wanted to see her again. That he was married to his love with a baby on the way.

"Why are you here? No." He shook his head. "I don't care why you are here. Just go. I don't want to see you. I made that perfectly clear the last time." He looked down at Cherri, whose eyes had gone as big as saucers. "I'm so sorry, love." What must she be thinking? He scrambled to find the words, but even he didn't know how to explain the reemergence of his ex. "She's my ex. I . . ."

Serena walked up to Cherri and touched her belly. "Look at you! You're gorgeous and about ready to pop."

Colin yanked Serena away from his wife. He didn't like seeing Serena near her. He didn't want Serena to corrupt his wife with her touch. "Don't go near her."

"Why not? You told me about her. I think it's fair that she knows about me, about us."

"There is no us. And she does know about you and your phone calls. I don't keep anything from my wife. So if you think you're going to show up here and try to shock her with your presence you're wrong." He turned to look at Cherri, who was staring at Serena wide eyes.

*Fuck.*

She looked hurt.

His past was haunting her. And it was time he put a stop to it once and for all. "It's okay, love." He gently cupped her face in his hands and kissed her. "She won't be bothering you anymore." He kissed her again and turned to Serena, giving her a little push toward the shop.

"I can't believe you have the bollocks to show up at my house. You know I'm married. You know I want nothing to do with you. Have you lost your bloody fucking mind?"

"You wouldn't see me," Serena said in that huffy tone of voice he did not miss. "I wanted to talk to you."

"There's nothing to talk about." He yanked open the door, dragging Serena inside. "I'll not have you upsetting Charlotte. Do you understand that? I got married. I don't want you!"

"Lad?" Magnus called. "What the hell's going on . . . Hey, isn't she the slag who slept with half of the city?"

"Pop! Not now."

Magnus frowned. "Does your wife know you're in here with her?"

"Of course she does," Colin snapped. "Please go outside and see to Cherri. Hopefully she hasn't started packing her bags yet."

Magnus scowled at him. "I'll not tolerate you disrespecting your wife, boy. I'll smack you right in the mouth if you do. You get her out of here fast." He walked out, the door slamming behind him.

Before Colin could speak again, Serena reached out and draped her lean arms around him. He went rigid, unable to stand her touch. Two years and she still left a bad taste in his mouth. "Get off me."

"I've missed you, Col." She tightened her hold on him. "I miss your kisses. I miss the way you look when you get up in the morning. I miss the sex. I still love you. Just talk to me."

He pushed her away, folding his arms across his chest. "I'm not having this conversation. It's over. There is nothing left to say."

"Your wife's adorable and she'll give you a busload of kids. She's exactly the kind of woman you need."

"That's why I married her," he said through clenched teeth.

"Yes, but she's not all you need. I know you. I know you need excitement and busy weekends and wild sex. I can provide that for you. Cherri can't satisfy all your needs. That's why I came here—to suggest a little proposition. Actually that's not why I came here at first. I was sure I was going to get you to leave her, but after seeing the girl, I know that's never going to happen. So I'm willing to share if she is. We would only spend every other weekend together. At my place of course. I would never disrespect your wife in her home. And I understand if you can't commit to entire weekends at first. You'll want to spend time with your baby. But we can work out all the details later."

Serena smiled at him as if she had it all figured out. And maybe she did. Maybe in her head this was the only way she could maintain a relationship. She was the most self-centered person in the world. She hadn't changed a bit.

Colin shook his head. He was sad for her. That's all he

felt for her. None of the anger was present. None of the bitterness or the pain was left over. He just felt stupid for wasting any energy on this woman. "You're cracked."

"What?" Serena looked shocked. "You don't want to do this? You'd honestly rather be shacked up with your innocent little wife than me. I can't believe you can't remember how good we were together."

"I remember," Colin answered truthfully. "But Charlotte is . . . She's a hell of a lot better than you are." He turned away from Serena, to spot his wife through the door. She was exactly where he'd left her, only she wasn't alone. His father had one large arm wrapped around her and his hand on his unborn grandchild. It was foolish to think that his father would try to come on to his wife. Magnus had been nothing but fatherly to her. To him, too. He liked having his father around. "I need to get back to my family."

"You have faith in my boy, lass. He'll not do anything to hurt you. I'll beat the bloody shit out of him if he does." He gave Cherri's belly a rub. "That's right, wee one. I'll kick his teeth in."

"Magnus!" Cherri laughed despite the lump in her chest. "Kick his teeth in if you have to, but don't tell my baby that."

"He's a tough one, girlie. I'm sure he'll understand." Magnus grew serious for a moment. "I don't know why she's here, Cherri, but I know my boy. He didn't invite her. I may have screwed up some of this father stuff, but I taught him morals."

"Yes," she said absently. "He's a good man. You did the best you could with him." She watched the shop door, knowing that her husband would be coming out soon. At first when she saw Serena it felt like her world was going to crash in on her. But it was silly to doubt him. He wouldn't leave her. Even if he wanted to. He had too much pride. He wouldn't risk what they had worked so hard to get.

But there was pain in his eyes when he saw Serena. She knew that once he was very much in love with her. But she didn't know how he felt now. It wasn't easy to fall out of love with someone once you'd fallen in love with them. She knew. She would never stop loving Colin. She could be angry at him, frustrated with him, want to kill him, but she would never be able to lose all her love. It was impossible.

It might be that way for Colin. He'd kept her pictures buried in the shed for years after they'd broken up. She shouldn't doubt her husband but it was hard knowing that under different circumstances they may have never gotten married.

"He's coming now," Magnus said into her ear. "I wonder what he did with the slag?"

"Would locking her in a trunk be too much to wish for?"

"Ah, lass," Magnus chuckled. "I thought you would be more bloodthirsty."

Colin walked toward them, his face an unreadable mask. She knew he'd sent Serena away. But she wondered what he really thought about her proposition. Was that what he really wanted? Did hearing it make him wonder if Cherri could keep him satisfied?

"Thank you, Pop. Could you go see about getting her out of my shop?"

"No problem, boy." He squeezed Colin's shoulder before as he went.

"Lass . . ."

"Do you still love her?" She couldn't help but to ask what she had wondered for so long.

Colin blinked at her, bewildered. "Come again?"

"Are you still in love with Serena? You don't have to lie to me, Colin. I won't be mad. I just need to know."

He tilted his head to the side and studied her. "And what would you think if I told you I still was?"

"That you would have a mighty hard time finding a

new place to live because this is the house I am raising your son in."

"Is that all?" he asked softly.

"No. I also think I deserve to be the only woman on your mind. The only one you want to crawl into bed with at night. The only one to satisfy you and make you excited and happy. I won't share you with anybody else, Colin. Even if it's only in your head, because I love myself enough to know I'm worthy of being married to a man who wants only me."

"Anything else, love?"

"No." She shook her head.

He was silent for a long moment and then he began to laugh. He threw his head back until his shoulders shook with mirth.

"What is so funny?"

"You are, you daft girl."

"Why?"

"I don't love Serena."

*Thank you, God.*

"I've told you that a dozen times."

"Yeah, but that was before I saw her in person. She's skinny and she's got kickass arms, and she's graceful and she doesn't trip over her feet and she's got perfect hair and she's beautiful and she's sophisticated. And I can't blame her for wanting you."

"You aren't mad at her for wanting me back?"

"Oh, I could scratch her perfect blue eyes out, but I can't blame her. I know what's it like to be in love with you."

"But you're willing to leave me if I'm in love with somebody else?"

"If you want to be with her it would break my heart but I can't hold on to you and make you unhappy if you think you'll be happier someplace else."

"I won't be happier anyplace else. I married my best friend. Charlotte, I love you."

"Do you?"

"You bloody well know I do!"

She nodded. "I do. Even though you never tell me."

"Bloody women," he mumbled. "Need to hear the damn words all the time. I love you, Charlotte O'Connell. I love your big feet and your big bottom and the way your hair stands on end. I love the way you ramble on about nothing and the way you smile at me and the way you get under my skin. I love you even though you don't know who the Cranberries are. I love you. Hell, I'm obsessed with you. I got you pregnant, Charlotte. Me." He slapped his chest. "The man who has never been careless in his life couldn't keep his hands off you. I couldn't stay away. I can't stay away because I love you so damn much. It may sound like complete rubbish but seeing you pregnant with my boy makes me so damn proud because it marks you as mine. Because just to know it in here"—he pointed to his chest—"was never enough."

"Good God, you're a chauvinist," she said, but she said it smiling. "But I guess I'm stuck with you forever. Come on, Rufus." She grabbed his hand and led him down the driveway. Now that that was settled she could really go for some ice cream.

"Damn right. Even after I die I'll haunt this place just so no other bloke will come sniffing around you."

"That's creepy. I think you should get my name tattooed on your chest."

"That's negotiable. I'll do it if you get my name on your behind."

"I'm giving birth to your child! That should be enough."

He pulled her to a stop and gathered her in his arms. "It is." He set his lips on hers and didn't let them up for a long long time. "How about I get our son's name instead? In fact, I'll get all of our kids."

"All?" She looked up at him.

"Didn't I tell you? I want ten kids."

"Oh fat frickin' chance!"

"Lass, why do you think I married such a young girl?"

"Because you love me?"

"Aye. Because I do."

# EPILOGUE

*8 years later*

Colin held his baby close to his chest as he made his way upstairs. Cherri was home now. He had been so busy tending to the little one that he hadn't heard her come in from the doctor's office. He worried about her. Normally Charlotte was healthy as a horse, but she hadn't been feeling well for the past two weeks. He needed to see what was wrong.

"Daddy!" Cassidy, their four-year-old, came tearing down the hallway as soon as his foot hit the top stair. "Mommy's in there. She says we need to be quiet so she can get some rest."

"I'm sure she did," he said to his yelling child. "Why don't you find Joseph and go play with him? We don't want to bother your mum."

Cass shook her head. "He's painting. He don't want me to bother him when he paints. Can I help Grandpop in the shop? I like the shop. I wish you would let me use the saw."

"I know you do, baby girl, but that ain't going to happen anytime soon." He grinned down at his daughter. She looked exactly like him and had more energy than five boys combined. She loved the shop. She loved to watch him put things back together. Every time he saw her trying to figure out how something worked he swelled with pride.

Joseph Michael, named after her grandfather and his, took more after his mother. He was a quiet boy who loved to draw and paint. He was kind to his little sisters and while most men might have wished for a son who was sports-mad, he was glad Joey was who he was. He couldn't have asked for a nicer boy.

"Is Yuli still fussing?" Cassidy stood on her tiptoes trying to peek at the baby. "Mommy said she was gassy this morning. If she toots she'll feel better."

"I bet she will. Come here and give your father a kiss." He bent down, giving her a loud smacking kiss on the forehead. "Now go find your grandpop. I think I saw him on the deck. I'm going to put your sister down for a nap and check on your mum."

"I want to go check on Mommy, too."

"Later. Go do as I say and I might let you help me sand the rowboat we just got in."

She was off to find her grandfather before he could say another word.

"Ah, silence," he sighed. "Now let's put you down, little one." Yuliana O'Connell was going to be a heartbreaker. At nine months old she was beautiful with big round green eyes and dark brown hair. He was already dreading her teenage years.

Three kids and eight years of marriage later and Colin had never dreamed he could have a life like this. Stone Barley Restorations was busier than ever. So much so that they'd had to hire two other workers just to keep up with demand. Colin's little shop wasn't big enough to do the scale of work they needed to, so they had recently started construction on a bigger building that would be located in the formerly wooded area behind the house.

He and his pop were getting along better than ever. He was amazing with his grandchildren and produced some of the best work that had ever come out of the shop. His pop had seemed to mellow in the past few years. There were no more strings of women. No more broken hearts or tales of woe. He had been seeing a nice lady for the past six months and he had lived with them for over seven years now. It was the longest his father had stayed in one place.

After making sure his daughter was safely in her crib he finally made his way to his wife. She was lying on her side, her arm draped over her forehead, one hand resting on her belly.

"Charlotte, my love." He climbed into bed beside her. "How are you feeling?"

She didn't bother opening her eyes; instead she looped her arms around him and pulled him close. "I'm feeling slightly murderous."

"What?"

He stared at her. She might not be feeling well, but she had only grown more beautiful in the past eight years. She was no longer a girl, but she was still his lass and a successful artist, pulling in more money for one of her hand-painted pieces of furniture than he sometimes made in six months. He was so damn proud of her. Her work had recently been featured on a design show and she now had a three-year waiting list for one of her pieces. She was a wonderful mother, too, giving more to their children than he even thought was possible. He remembered how they had started out, their marriage so shaky in the early days that he'd wondered if they were going to make it. She had been afraid that she would never get to live a life of her own. He sometimes wondered: If she had to do it all over again, would she have chosen this path? But then she would smile at him or kiss one of their kids and those thoughts would vanish.

"Who do you want to kill, love?"

"You. You knocked me up again."

"Again?" His eyes widened. "Already?" He was a little surprised but not shocked. He couldn't keep his hands off her, and after seeing her go through this three times before he should have seen the signs.

"Actually, you knocked me up two months ago. I married a very virile man." She smiled at him and then pulled him into a kiss. "This is the last time I'm going to be pregnant. I get fat as a house every time you knock me up."

"I kind of like it." He ran his hand over her hip and down her backside. "Why do you think I keep getting you pregnant?"

She opened her eyes and finally looked at him. "I have no regrets, you know. Even though our life is sometimes nutty and we can never seem to plan things out, I love this life. I love the way we are. I'm happy. I want you to know that. I wouldn't change a single thing."

"I know, love. You don't have to tell me."

"I do, because we aren't just going to have one baby this time. The doctor thinks there might be more than one. I think we're going to be the parents of twins."

He sat up. "I've got to call the contractor."

"What?" She sat up, reaching for him. "Where are you going?"

"We're going to need a bigger house. Where are we going to put two more babies? Do you think they can manage to put an addition on to the house in seven months?"

"Hey, Irish." She grabbed his arm and pulled him back down on the bed. "Calm down. We have time to figure this out. Can't we just enjoy the peace and quiet for a few minutes before the kids come barging in?"

"Good point." He wrapped his arms around her and pulled her close. "Think we could talk Pop into babysitting for a couple of days so I can take you away? With two more kids, we might never be alone again."

"We shouldn't even ask. Let's just leave and call him from the road."

"Good idea, lass." He grinned down at her for a moment just before he pressed his lips to hers.

"Colin?"

"Hmm?"

"Are you happy about this? We're going to have five kids."

"Of course I'm not happy about this. I won't be happy until we have ten."

She giggled. "Over my dead body, O'Connell."

"I love you, Cherri," he said seriously. "Five kids. No kids. I'm just happy you're my wife."

"That's the reason why I keep getting pregnant." She gave him a mischievous smile. "Lock the door."

"Really?"

He was on his feet and back before she could answer. But instead of climbing into the bed with her he stopped and gazed at her. She had a tiny smile on her face, her hair was loose around her shoulders, and even though they had been together numerous times over the past years he still felt like every time was as good as their first.

"What?" She looked up at him, her eyes going wide.

"Nothing. You're just beautiful."

Her smiled widened. "Okay, Irish. We can have ten kids. You just better make sure you keep the compliments coming when I can no longer fit through the door."

"Deal."

He slid into bed beside his wife wrapping her in his arms, savoring the way her body automatically molded to his. It was times like these, when he was so happy, so at peace with his life, that he felt like kicking himself. Eight years ago he had come up with so many reasons why he couldn't be with her—she was too young, he was too damaged—that he'd almost missed the reason why they should be together. They were just right for each other. They were a perfect fit.